Olivia
Or, It was for her sake

by

Charles Garvice

Olivia
Or, It was for her sake
by Charles Garvice

Copyright © 2024

All Rights reserved.

ISBN: 978-93-64281-01-0

Published by

DOUBLE 9 BOOKS

2/13-B, Ansari Road
Daryaganj, New Delhi – 110002
info@double9books.com
www.double9books.com
Tel. 011-40042856

This book is under public domain

ABOUT THE AUTHOR

Charles Garvice (1850-1920) was a prolific British author known for his romantic novels that achieved widespread popularity in the late 19th and early 20th centuries. Garvice authored over 150 novels, making him one of the most prolific writers of his time. His books were known for their romantic plots, often involving themes of love, sacrifice, and social class. His novels were incredibly popular, especially among the middle and working classes. They were widely read in Britain and America, and many were serialized in newspapers and magazines before being published as books. Some of his notable works include "Just a Girl," "The Outcast of the Family," "Her Heart's Desire," and "The Verdict of the Heart." These novels often featured virtuous heroines and gallant heroes who overcame obstacles to find love and happiness. Garvice's novels typically focused on romantic relationships, often highlighting themes such as love, betrayal, sacrifice, and redemption. He frequently explored issues of social class and the dynamics between wealth and poverty. His stories often carried moral undertones, with characters undergoing personal growth and seeking redemption. Popular Appeal: Despite the lack of critical acclaim, Garvice's novels enjoyed immense popular appeal, reflecting the tastes and sensibilities of his readership.

Cultural Impact: His works offer valuable insights into the social and cultural context of the late Victorian and Edwardian eras, particularly in their portrayal of romance and social issues.

Enduring Readership: While not widely studied in academic circles, Garvice's novels continued to be read and enjoyed by fans of classic romance literature well into the 20th century. Charles Garvice's prolific output and the popularity of his romantic novels have secured his place in the annals of popular literature, particularly as a figure representative of the tastes and literary trends of his time.

CONTENTS

CHAPTER I
SOMETHING OF A MYSTERY

It was in the "merry month" of May, the "beautiful harbinger of summer," as the poets call it; and one of those charming east winds which render England such a delightful place of residence for the delicate and consumptive, and are truly a boon and a blessing to the doctors and undertakers, was blowing gaily through one of the lovely villages of Devonshire, and insidiously stealing through the half opened French windows of the drawing-room of Hawkwood Grange.

Three persons were seated in this drawing-room. An old gentleman, a lady—who would have had a fit on the spot if any one had called her old— and a young girl.

The old gentleman was called Sparrow—Mr. Sparrow, the solicitor, of Wainford, the market town and borough three miles off. The old—the middle-aged and would-be youthful lady—was Miss Amelia Vanley, the maiden sister of the master of Hawkwood Grange; and the young lady was Olivia Vanley, his daughter, and, therefore, Miss Amelia's niece.

Miss Amelia was presiding at the five o'clock teatable; Mr. Sparrow was performing the difficult feat of balancing a teacup in one hand and a bread-and-butter plate in the other; and Olivia was seated at the piano, which she occasionally touched absently as she half listened to the other two. On a chair beside her was a sealskin jacket—there had been snow on this "merry" May morning, if you please—and she still wore her hat.

Above the piano hung one of those old-fashioned circular mirrors which reflect the face and bust of the player, and it presented a face which was beautiful, and something more than beautiful.

We have lost our climate and our trade—so it is said—but thank Heaven, there are still pretty girls left in England. When they disappear, it will be time for us to put up the shutters and vacate the island; but until that happens, it will still be worth living in.

To be consistent with her name, Olivia should have been of a dark and olive complexion; but the only thing dark in the lovely face were the hazel eyes. Her hair was an auburn chestnut, which Joshua Reynolds loved to paint, with eyebrows to match; mouth "rather large," as Miss Amelia declared—she possessed, and was exceedingly proud of, one of the well known speaking doll pattern—but as expressive as the eyes. Face and figure were eloquent of youth and perfect health, and her voice was full of that music which youth and health and womanly refinement and delicacy combine to give.

The Grange was the principal house in Hawkwood, and the room was a very fair specimen of the drawing-rooms in a modern country mansion.

Mr. Sparrow was speaking, and his thin, piping voice chimed in not discordantly with the treble notes which Olivia's hand now and again touched.

"There is—er—something of a mystery about it, and I—er—dislike mysteries, Miss Amelia."

"Do you, really?" responded Miss Amelia, with a girlish simper. "Now, I love a mystery, Mr. Sparrow; but then we poor women are so fond of romance and—and all that. We have the softer, the more poetic nature, I suppose. You men are so hard!" And she stuck her head very much on one side at the tame-looking old lawyer, who straightened himself as well as he was able under the disadvantage of the teacup and plate, and tried to look as if he were, indeed, hard and practical. "And you do think, there is a mystery! How charming! You really must tell us all about it; we are dying to hear the whole—the whole story. Aren't we, Olivia?"

The young girl gave the very faintest inclination of her head by way of response, and silently pressed down a chord.

"There's not much to tell, as a matter of fact," said Mr. Sparrow, with the little cough with which old gentlemen preface a story they are anxious to relate. "Last Friday my clerk came into my room and said that a gentleman wished to see me. He gave the name of Faradeane."

"Faradeane! Dear me, how strange, really!" murmured Miss Amelia, who would have made the same comment if the name had been Smith.

"Yes, Faradeane. It was quite unknown to me," continued Mr. Sparrow, "and the gentleman was quite as unknown. He was a young man and—and a gentleman. There can be no doubt about that. I—er—think I know a gentleman when I see him, Miss Amelia."

"Indeed, yes," murmured Miss Amelia, promptly. "Was he very young?"

"About thirty, I should say," replied Mr. Sparrow, thoughtfully. "Yes, about thirty. A London man; I should say, judging by his clothes. He was very well dressed, very well, indeed. Plainly, but well. I gave him a chair, and he came to the point at once by asking me if I were the owner of The Dell. I said I was, with some surprise, for really I had quite forgotten the little place. It has been shut up so long—it must be just seven years since the last people left it; rather over seven years. He said he had heard that I wanted to sell it, and asked the price. I told him, and—eh—on the spur of the moment, taken so completely by surprise, I stated a price which I cannot help thinking was—er—rather low."

"Then he accepted it?" said the low, sweet voice of Olivia, and Mr. Sparrow started and colored slightly.

"I nearly forgot you were in the room, my dear Miss Olivia," he said, with a smile. "Yes, like the Jew who regretted he hadn't asked more. Yes, yes! He accepted, and at once! 'If you will have the draft deed made out, I'll sign it,' he said, quietly."

"Dear me, how very sudden and prompt!" murmured Miss Amelia.

"Y—es," said the old man; "but we lawyers are not accustomed to such suddenness, and I—er—I felt it my duty to ask him for the name of his legal adviser, to whom I might send the draft, and—er—for references."

"Of course," assented Miss Amelia.

The girl held her hands above the keys, and turned half round, as if absently waiting for the sequel.

"Well, my dear Miss Amelia, I was very much surprised, indeed, by his response to my very natural request. 'Send the draft to me at the George Inn, where I am staying,' he said, quite quietly and indifferently. Oh, quite! His manner was perfect, though—er—rather haughty and reserved, perhaps. 'Send the draft to the George. As to the references, I need not trouble you with them, as I am quite willing to pay any deposit—or the whole amount, if you like, here and now.'"

"Now, really!" exclaimed Miss Amelia, in a subdued murmur.

Olivia struck the chord softly, and smiled.

"Of course, such a proceeding was quite unusual and—er—unbusinesslike," continued Mr. Sparrow; "but it was scarcely one I could object to. I was the vendor, he the purchaser, and—er—in short, I declined to accept any money, and sent the draft to the George the next morning. It came back in an hour, the deeds were engrossed that afternoon, duly signed, and the money paid."

"By check?" murmured Miss Amelia, with some shrewdness.

Mr. Sparrow nodded approvingly.

"No, my dear Miss Amelia, for if it had been a check I should probably, as it no doubt occurred to you, have been able to learn something of Mr. Faradeane through his bankers. The money was paid in gold and notes, which are, to all intents and purposes, untraceable. Thank you; one more cup. Two pieces of sugar. Thank you. In gold and notes. So far, I think you will admit, the proceedings were—er—slightly mysterious."

"Charmingly so," assented Miss Amelia.

"And they are nothing to what follows," said Mr. Sparrow, with a knowing nod. "Having obtained possession of The Dell, Mr. Faradeane has had it put in repair throughout, and is now actually residing there!"

"There was only one thing more mysterious he could have been guilty of," said Olivia, with a smile. "He could have let it!"

"Wait a moment, my dear Miss Olivia," said Mr. Sparrow. "There is nothing mysterious in his living at The Dell, but the manner of his living. In the first place, he is living there with only one servant—a manservant; in the next, no woman is permitted to pass the gate. I must give it as a fact. Old Mrs. Williams, from the farm, was stopped by the manservant as she was entering the gate with some eggs and butter, and informed, quite civilly, but firmly, that no female would be permitted to enter the premises, and that for the future she must leave her basket outside."

"Good gra——" gasped Miss Amelia.

"More than that," continued Mr. Sparrow, in a state of mild excitement; "Mrs. Williams tells me that the place is barricaded as if for a siege, and that a large mastiff is prowling—loose, actually loose!—about the place, day and night."

"Great Heav——" Miss Amelia tried to ejaculate, but Mr. Sparrow, thoroughly warmed to his work, rushed on:

"I've heard, too, from several people, that lights are seen burning in the windows nearly the whole night through. Indeed, the people in the village—of course it's very foolish—declare that Mr. Faradeane never goes to bed. Several persons have seen him walking up and down The Dell lane at the most unearthly hours. Now, Miss Olivia, what do you think of the affair?" and the little man leaned back with an air of satisfaction.

Olivia laughed thoughtfully.

"Yes, it is rather mysterious," she admitted, to his palpable delight. "Do you think that he is a coiner, or simply a gentleman suffering from the pangs of a guilty conscience?"

Mr. Sparrow could not see the twinkle in the dark eyes, and as the sweet voice was perfectly grave, took the question seriously.

"Well, I must confess that the thought did—er—cross my mind; I mean in respect to coining; one reads such—er—extraordinary stories."

"Ah, yes!" breathed Miss Amelia, with a delighted little gasp. "Good gracious! fancy a coiner in Hawkwood! Of course you have hinted your suspicions to Smallbone?"

Smallbone was the village policeman, who, if having nothing to do from one year's end to the other can produce happiness, should have been in a continual state of felicity.

"Well—er—no," said Mr. Sparrow.

"Perhaps it occurred to Mr. Sparrow, aunt, that even coiners are not so utterly imbecile as to set about their work by attracting the attention of all their neighbors," said Olivia.

"Ahem! That is true! That is very true," remarked Mr. Sparrow, with a little cough. "And I confess that the counterfeit coinage theory scarcely holds good. Mr. Faradeane does not give one the idea of—er—that class of criminal."

"Is he more like a burglar?" asked Olivia, with apparent innocence.

Mr. Sparrow shook his head.

"No, no, dear me, no! I think I said he was most distinguished-looking. Quite—er—aristocratic, and—er—patrician. Remarkably good looking, also."

Miss Amelia pushed her chair nearer a book cabinet, and seized "The Peerage."

"Oh, I've looked through that," remarked Mr. Sparrow, with charming simplicity. "There is no mention of the name of Faradeane in that or 'The County Families.'"

Miss Amelia closed the book with a gesture of despair.

"Is there no way of finding out something about him, dear Mr. Sparrow?"

"I know of none," he replied, solemnly.

"And I can only think of one," said Olivia.

Both pairs of eyes were turned upon her with eager impatience.

"Really! Now, what is that, my dear?" demanded Aunt Amelia.

"You might ask him to tell you his history," she said, without moving a muscle.

Aunt Amelia sunk back with a gesture of disgusted disappointment, and Mr. Sparrow coughed.

"I—er—have reason to believe that the manservant was asked a question or two— —"

"By you, Mr. Sparrow?" said Olivia, still with the expression of an innocent child.

The little man blushed.

"Well, not exactly; but my man Walker happened to meet Mr. Faradeane's man, and got into conversation."

"And what did he say?" demanded Miss Amelia, eagerly.

"Well, I regret to say that he told poor Walker to mind his own business."

Olivia had only time to turn to the piano to hide the smile which seemed to flash across her face and dance in her eyes like a ray of sunshine.

"Well, I really never— —Of course, no one will think of calling upon him," said Miss Amelia.

Again Mr. Sparrow colored guiltily.

"I—er—thought it my duty as a neighbor," he said, hesitatingly, "to just call. It was yesterday. The dog"—he shuddered, and screwed up his slender legs, as if at some painful recollection—"the dog is one of the largest and—most awful animals, and I am convinced if the servant hadn't come up at the moment, I— —" He shuddered again. "He said his master was out. I saw Mr. Faradeane walking in the orchard at the side of the cottage quite distinctly."

"Then he was out," said Olivia, gravely.

"My dear Olivia," exclaimed her aunt, "you seem to be quite anxious to make excuses for this extraordinary young man; you do, indeed!"

"Well, it can't be denied that he was out of the house," said Olivia, as gravely as before. "We usually look over the stairs and whisper to the servants to say that we are not at home. For the future I shall imitate Mr.— what-is-his-name's veracity, and go out into the garden."

"The man added that his master never saw visitors," said Mr. Sparrow, solemnly.

There was something so irresistibly ludicrous in the little old man's tone that Olivia's gravity broke down, and she burst into a peal of laughter. While it was ringing through the room, and the other two were staring at her in startled astonishment and indignation, two gentlemen entered. One—an elderly man, tall and thin, with gray hair and eyes that had a look of Olivia's in them—was her father, Mr. Vanley. The other was a young man in flannels—a young man who would have been good looking but for a remarkably faulty mouth and an expression in his eyes which seemed to convey the idea to the spectator that their owner was always on the alert listening and watching, and yet endeavoring to conceal the fact.

As Olivia looked up and met the eyes fixed upon her with a sudden, eager curiosity, then turned aside with as sudden an attempt at indifference, the laughter died away abruptly and a sudden change came over her expressive face. It was as if she had hardened it. A moment ago it had been full of girlish mirth and abandon; now in an instant it was eloquent of reserve and almost hauteur.

"What is the matter, Olivia?" asked Mr. Vanley, not irritably, but with a touch of sober earnestness, almost amounting to anxiety, which was always present with him. "What are you laughing at? Good-afternoon, Mr. Sparrow."

The young man came forward.

"Do tell us, Miss Olivia!" he said, throwing as much eagerness into his voice as possible. "Pray let us share the joke."

"It was no joke," she said, calmly; and turning away, began to arrange some music.

"Miss Olivia was laughing at me," said Mr. Sparrow, almost plaintively.

"My dear Edwin—and you, Mr. Bradstone—you must hear this strange story of Mr. Sparrow's. Now, Mr. Sparrow, I insist!" exclaimed Miss Amelia, clasping her hands in the latest "intensity."

Mr. Sparrow was nothing loth, and Mr. Vanley sank into a chair with so palpable an air of resignation that a smile flitted across Olivia's face. Perhaps that encouraged Bartley Bradstone, for he approached her in a slow, hesitating kind of fashion, and talked to her in a low voice—he was watching her cold, downcast face covertly all the time—while Mr. Sparrow inflicted his story of the mysterious stranger upon Mr. Vanley.

The master of the Grange listened in silence until the narration was complete, and the old gentleman paused to see the effect of his recital; then Mr. Vanley looked up and said, quietly:

"Not a very promising neighbor. One would think he was insane; not that the purchase of The Dell is the act of a lunatic. It is the prettiest little place in the country."

He rose as he spoke, and, walking to the window, looked out pensively at the chimneys of The Dell, which just peeped over the tops of his own elms growing on the slope of the lane, at the bottom of which The Dell nestled.

"Yes, it is," said Miss Amelia; "and I am sure I have always wondered why you didn't buy it yourself, my dear Edwin, seeing that it is almost within your own estate."

Mr. Vanley's face clouded for an instant, and he cast a glance toward Bartley Bradstone; then he said, with a slight shrug:

"I have quite enough to worry about. Besides, I didn't know that Mr. Sparrow wished to part with it."

"I didn't—that is—I had no idea of it," said the old gentleman, nervously. "The—the fact is, this young man—Mr. Faradeane, I mean—took me by surprise."

"At all events, you have got your price for it," said Mr. Vanley, as if rather tired of the subject, "and I"—with a grave smile—"should in all probability have beaten you down."

"I'd rather you had bought it at half the price," murmured Mr. Sparrow, meekly.

"Well, well," said Mr. Vanley, almost impatiently. "It is too late now, and—there's an end of the matter." He turned to the pair at the piano, and regarded them for a moment. "I shall be in the library if you want to see me before you go, Bradstone," he said.

Bartley Bradstone looked over his shoulder carelessly—too carelessly for a young man addressing his senior.

"All right," he said, "I'll look in as I go."

CHAPTER II
"THE CHERUB"

Mr. Vanley was not only Bartley Bradstone's senior, but his superior in looks and status.

The Vanleys had held Hawkwood Grange for centuries, and there was no name better known in Devonshire than that which the squire bore. Twice a baronetage and once a peerage had been offered to the Vanleys; but to a Vanley the old English and old Devonshire title of "Squire" was too dear to be exchanged for any other, though it might be higher rank; and so Squire Vanley, the master of the Grange, refused, and certainly was not the less respected for his refusal of a peerage.

While as to Mr. Bartley Bradstone, as the French wit remarked, "He may have had a grandfather, but no one has yet been found credulous enough to believe it!"

Five years before this notable afternoon, Mr. Bradstone had purchased an estate within three miles of the Grange. Perhaps it would be as well to be exact, and explain that he had loaned money on the place, and, foreclosing, got possession of it.

An old, but rather ramshackle house stood upon it—a house quite large enough for a bachelor, by the way—but Mr. Bradstone pulled it down, and in its place built a huge mansion which, by its highly florid architecture, was far more suitable to South Kensington than North Devon.

It was a tremendous place, all gables and turrets, and being built of red brick, with white stone facings, was terribly conspicuous. Olivia had remarked, the first time she saw it, which happened to be on a blazing hot day, that "no one ought to look upon it, except through green spectacles." And she added that it would be useful in winter—to warm one's hands at!

The interior was decorated and furnished in strict accordance with the very latest canons of the very latest art craze; and, as if to atone for the red glare of the exterior, the inside was cold and repelling.

Mr. Bartley Bradstone, however, considered it perfection; and here he settled down. The country people were shy of him at first. Devonshire is celebrated for apples, cider and—exclusiveness. Nothing was known of the newcomer, excepting that he was rich; there was no doubt about that—immensely rich; and those who had been thrown into his company were not prepossessed by him. There was that look in his eyes, for one thing; and, for another, with all his careful dressing and studiously "correct" manners, Mr. Bartley Bradstone did not seem, to the very particular country people, to be—well, exactly a gentleman.

But after a time the squire, who had met him once or twice in the market town, seen him at church, touched his hat to him at the meet—of course the squire was the master of the hounds—at last the squire made a formal call upon Mr. Bartley Bradstone at The Maples, as he called the red monstrosity.

That which was good enough for Squire Vanley was, of course, good enough for the rest of the county people, and Mr. Bartley Bradstone was not only asked out to dinner, but, greater honor still, had the gratification of seeing the best people of the neighborhood round his own—new—mahogany.

He gave good dinners—too good, it was whispered; too many covers, too many wines, with too much plate, and too many servants.

"It's a pity," remarked Lord Carfield to the squire, as they walked home after one of Mr. Bartley's dinners, "that there is no one to caution these *parvenus* against overdoing it. Give you my word, Vanley, I felt all the evening as if I were dining at one of those new hotels in London, where they give you twelve courses, served in a gaudy room, all gilt and white paint, and play music at you all the time. I suppose you have twice as much plate? I have some"—the Carfield plate was the boast of that part of Devonshire—"but we never think of making a silversmith's counter of our dinner-table every time we ask a neighbor to dinner."

"He means well," said the squire.

"Just so," said the old lord. "That makes it all the worse. It's a hopeless case."

They were near neighbors, and an intimacy sprang up between Mr. Bartley Bradstone, the millionaire, and the Squire of Hawkwood. The young man would ride over—on a long park horse, which he rode abominably!—to the Grange in the morning, and was often easily persuaded to stop to lunch. Sometimes he would remain to dinner, a servant being sent to The Maples for Mr. Bradstone's evening clothes. Miss Amelia quite liked him, and the squire, as has been said, was intimate with him; but he made no way with Olivia. From the first moment she had seen him, when her frank eyes had rested upon his restless, shifting ones, she had kept him at a distance, so to speak.

If her father had brought home the village sweep to dinner, she would have treated him courteously and extended a welcome to him; and that is all she did to Bartley Bradstone. While he— —! He was as much in love with Olivia Vanley as utterly selfish man can be, and he had sworn to himself that he would have her. Now, Bartley Bradstone, though he was not a gentleman, though he overdressed, gave too elaborate dinners, and made occasional mistakes in etiquette, was both rich and clever. The man who had bought him for a fool would have lost his money. Olivia, who despised him, was wrong in doing so. She should have been on her guard and—feared him. All the while Mr. Sparrow was repeating his story to Mr. Vanley, Bartley Bradstone was talking in an undertone to her.

"It's just a simple picnic, a rough affair, but I'll promise you shan't be bored, Miss Vanley," he said. "The squire is coming, and he told me—that is, he said I might ask you. I hope you will come. Lord Carfield is coming, and has promised to bring his son, Viscount Granville. Lord Granville arrives at his father's to-night. You know him—the viscount, I mean?"

"Bertie Granville? Oh, yes. 'The Cherub,' as he is called."

"That's the man," said Bartley Bradstone, with a faint flush. He would not have dared to call him "Bertie" or "The Cherub." "Well, he is coming, and I hope to persuade Miss Amelia, too. But the whole thing will be spoilt if you refuse."

Olivia looked at him from under her lids—the look which makes a man—that is, if he has a sensitive skin—feel as if he had been struck by a whip. "I don't quite see how my absence could spoil your picnic, Mr. Bradstone," she said, coldly.

He lowered his restless eyes, and caught at his upper lip with his teeth. They were whole and even, but rather too large.

"I mean that it would be spoilt for me," he said, and added, nervously, "and—and for the rest, of course. Please say 'Yes,' Miss Vanley."

Olivia looked straight before her, with that expression in her eyes which belongs to the unfettered maiden spirit. "I will see," she said, calmly. "You are not listening to Mr. Sparrow's story, Mr. Bradstone."

He was too wise to press her further, and at once turned away toward the old lawyer, and listened to him for a moment or two; then he turned to the door with a contemptuous laugh.

"You've sold your property to some fellow who is in hiding from his tailor, Mr. Sparrow," he said. "Pity you didn't sell it to me; I'd have given you twice the sum for it this man has given. Shouldn't be surprised if we have the police down here directly looking for him. 'Pon my word, you ought to be more careful, Mr. Sparrow," and with a patronizing nod he left the room, pausing for a minute or two to present his invitation to Miss Amelia.

This last straw broke down Mr. Sparrow's back, and shortly afterward he took himself off, feeling that he had, by selling his property to the mysterious unknown, not only offended his neighbor, but actually lost money!

"How nice of Mr. Bradstone to arrange this picnic, Olivia," said her aunt, when Mr. Sparrow had sorrowfully taken his departure. "He is always so kind and thoughtful in planning these little parties. Of course you will go, dear."

"I don't know," said Olivia, absently.

She was standing by the window, looking down on the chimneys of The Dell, as her father had done, and thinking of the strange character who had become owner of the cottage.

"You don't know! My dear Olivia, what a strange reply. Why shouldn't you go?"

"Why should I?" said Olivia, without turning her head.

Miss Amelia sniffed, and uttered the little cough which always served as a prelude to the lectures which she frequently felt it "her duty" to deliver to her niece.

"Now, my dear Olivia, I do hope that you will not permit yourself to—to—disappoint our excellent young friend. It is evident that he has got up this little affair in your honor, and it would surely be ungracious to disappoint him. Ungraciousness, if I may coin a word, in a lady is, my dear Olivia, unpardonable. Often and often have I, at great inconvenience, accepted an invitation rather than appear ungracious. And I do hope——"

"Is there any tea left, auntie?" broke in Olivia. "You forget me when you are surrounded by your admirers."

Miss Amelia bridled, then smiled, and simpered:

"My dear Olivia, how can you be so ridiculous? My admirers! I'm sure Mr. Sparrow is old enough to be my grandfather"—in which case poor Mr. Sparrow must have been a modern Methuselah—"and as to Mr. Bradstone, it is not me whom he admires——"

"No sugar, thanks," said Olivia, cutting in abruptly.

"No! Any one with half an eye could see who it is that he admires, and whose society he seeks. And I must say, my dear Olivia, while I am on the subject, that for a young girl, scarcely out of her teens, your conduct is too cold— —"

"This tea is cold," said Olivia.

"Far too cold," continued Miss Amelia, disregarding the interruption. "Mr. Bartley Bradstone is a young man worthy of every respect."

"It is a pity his horse doesn't share your opinion, auntie," said Olivia, looking through the window. "It doesn't appear to respect him in the least. Some of these days it will carry its disrespect so far as to throw him off."

"Mr. Bradstone may not be a jockey. I repeat, he may not be a jockey; but, all the same, he is a young man worth due consideration. Olivia, do you forget that he is a millionaire—a millionaire!"

"Neither I nor he forgets it," said Olivia, succinctly.

"Wealth—wealth, my dear Olivia, has its responsibilities and its—its—I may say its claims to our respect."

"Yes, I know," said Olivia. "No one accuses you of forgetting what is due to it, auntie."

"No, my dear. I can lay my hand upon my heart— —"

But Olivia had already stepped through the window, and what Miss Amelia would do or say when she laid her hand upon her heart, must remain a mystery.

Olivia paused a moment, looking out upon the view which stretched over an exquisite panorama of wooded vales, and

"... Meadows all bedight
With buttercups and daisies, elves' delight."

Then she wandered down the broad garden path, and, with the same air of dreamy self-communion, passed out by the lodge gate into the road. Two dogs, which had been lying asleep on the lawn, had sprung up at the sound of her light footstep, and followed her, barking and yapping in frantic delight.

As she stopped to speak to and pet them, there came out from behind the lodge a small pony-cart, in which was seated a young girl. She was about seventeen, with a pretty, innocent face, from which a pair of soft, brown eyes looked out appealingly. It was the lodge-keeper's daughter. She colored with timid pleasure at the sight of Olivia, and pulled up the pony, who resented the operation, and made the courtesy she attempted an impossibility.

"Why, Bessie!" said Olivia, going up to the side of the cart. "Are you going for a drive?"

"Yes, miss," replied the girl, with respectful affection alike in her eyes and in her voice. "I am going to Wainford for father."

"To Wainford?" said Olivia. "I am almost tempted to go with you."

"Oh, Miss Olivia," murmured the girl, with a rapturous delight, "if you would!"

Olivia shook her head laughingly.

"I'm afraid I mustn't, Bessie. Wainford is too far; I should be late for dinner, and the squire would never forgive either of us. Never mind," she added, consolingly, as Bessie's face fell from the dizzy heights of eagerness to the uttermost depths of disappointment; "I will go some other time. I have often wanted to have a ride with you behind that famous pony. What a restless little monkey it is! Take care of him, Bessie! But I suppose you understand each other?"

"Oh, yes, Miss Olivia!" said Bessie. "And you won't come?" with a sigh. "Well! Is there anything I can do for you, miss? Anything I can bring you?"

Olivia was about to shake her head, when, divining that the girl would be somewhat consoled for her disappointment if she had some errand to perform, she said:

"Oh, yes, Bessie! Will you bring me a yard of ribbon to match this on my hat?"

"Yes, miss," said Bessie, brightening up. "To match exactly?"

"Oh, near will do" said Olivia. "Stay!" And, taking off her hat, she clipped a piece of ribbon off a bow. "There, as near as you can get it. I hope you will have a pleasant drive, and remember I am coming with you some day—soon."

"Oh, do, miss!" Bessie exclaimed, or rather jerked out, for the pony, having completely exhausted its patience, declined to wait any longer over such trivialities, and dashed off; and Olivia stood watching Bessie's frantic efforts to reduce the gallop to a trot, until the pony and its pretty, innocent-faced mistress were lost in a bend of the road.

Then, all unconsciously, though she was thinking of Mr. Sparrow's account of the new owner of The Dell, Olivia wandered in that direction, and it was almost with a start that she found herself within a few yards of the gate, through which, according to Mr. Sparrow, no female would be allowed to pass.

The Dell was one of those picturesque cottages which all of us have, at some time or other in our lives, had a hankering after. It stood in a hollow, shaded by some beautiful trees, and in a garden which was literally ablaze with crocuses and hyacinths, and the spring flowers which Wordsworth—and Lord Beaconsfield—so dearly loved. The roof was of thatch, the windows diamond-paned, and the whole place as choice a specimen of a country cottage as ever shone on painter's canvas.

Olivia glanced at it for a moment, then turned aside to follow a lane opposite the gate, when a voice called in accents of delighted greeting:

"Miss Vanley! Olivia!" and a young fellow sprang over a stile and ran toward her.

He was young, not more than twenty, with bright blue eyes, and hair—too short to allow it to curl—of a bright golden yellow. When he smiled—as he was doing now—his whole face, eyes, lips, and even his slight yellow mustache, seemed to smile, and his voice rang out soft and musical almost as a girl's. This was Viscount Granville, the Earl of Carfield's son and heir, though Bertie and the Cherub were his usual appellations, bestowed on him by a vast circle of friends and admirers of both sexes, who did their level best to spoil one of the sweetest natures which Heaven had ever bestowed upon a lad.

Olivia went to meet him with a smile which Mr. Bartley Bradstone would have given a thousand pounds to have called up.

"Why, Bertie!" she exclaimed.

"I'm the luckiest beggar in the world," he said, laughingly, as he wrung her hand in his own ridiculously small one. "Do you know I was going up to the Grange; but I just stepped into the wood to see if I could find an anemone or two—I know you like them—and I saw the dogs. Now, fancy my meeting you, and having you all to myself to walk up to the Grange with! But perhaps you weren't going back? If not, let me come with you, will you?"

"I'm not going anywhere in particular," said Olivia, still smiling at the fair, girlishly boyish face. "I'll go back. Why, what a time it is since I saw you!"

"Isn't it! Isn't it!" he responded, letting go her hand reluctantly, and taking his hat off his forehead, which was the only part of his face untanned. "I am so glad to come back. Yes, two years; seems like twenty. Have I got very gray? Now, be candid, Olivia—I mean Miss Vanley," he corrected himself, with a blush.

"Why Miss Vanley?" said Olivia, blushing too, but looking at him with her frank eyes in a sisterly way that was inexpressibly sweet.

"Well," he said, raising his eyes to her face, "you—you have altered so, you know."

"Is that a polite way of informing me that I am gray?" said Olivia, archly.

"You—you have grown such a woman," he said, his blue eyes all aglow with admiring wonder. "You were quite a girl when I left; at least, I seem to remember. And now"—the pause was as significant as any verbal finale could be—"I suppose I must mind my manners, and call you Miss Vanley?"

"Better keep to the old name," said Olivia. "Why, it seems only the other day we used to play cricket together."

"Yes," he said, wistfully. "I suppose you'd rather die than play now?"

"Much rather," she said, laughing. "And besides, look at my long dress! But tell me all about yourself and where you have been and what you've seen."

"All?" he said, with a smile. "All right; but perhaps we'd better sit down, for it will take some time; say three weeks. Oh, we had an awfully high old time! Been everywhere. And everybody and everything were so jolly, don't you know. But I'm very glad to get back to the governor and"—he glanced up shyly at the lovely face so intent upon and absorbed in him—"and all of you. I wanted to come up last night after dinner, but my father didn't seem to care about my leaving him even for an hour or two. And you are all well? You can't tell how jolly it is to come back to the old place. It's all just the same. No, it isn't, by the way. What on earth is that big red place, like an asylum gone æsthetically mad, on the hill?"

"The Maples, do you mean?" said Olivia, her face crimsoning for one instant, ever so slightly. "That is Mr. Bartley Bradstone's new house. You don't admire it?"

"Good heavens! it is like a blot of red with——" He stopped and colored. "I beg your pardon, Olivia; perhaps he's a friend of yours."

"Oh, we know him," she said, carelessly. "Isn't it ugly; isn't it? But that is the only change, Bertie; you will find us just the same, and very, very glad to see you."

"Isn't that just how you used to speak in the old times?" he exclaimed, enthusiastically. "Now you're the little girl with the long, black legs——"

He stopped and stammered, and Olivia laughed. Suddenly the two dogs set up a violent barking, and the two young people, hurrying to see the cause, saw a huge mastiff with a broken chain attached to his collar traveling down the road toward them.

It is needless to say that neither Olivia nor Bertie was alarmed; but the dogs were very much upset at the terrific apparition, and, yelping, half-indignantly, half-affrightedly, made a noise loud enough to rouse the sleepers in Hawkwood churchyard.

"Is this one of your dogs?" asked Bertie. "(Be quiet, you two! Quiet, Fritz; shut up, Folly!) It has broken loose and followed you, I suppose?"

"It isn't mine," commenced Olivia; but before she—remembering Mr. Sparrow's story—could explain, a tall gentleman opened the gate of The Dell, and came toward them, calling "Leo! Leo!"

The dog stopped instantly, and the owner seemed about to go back with him, when, as if reluctantly, he came forward and raised his hat.

Olivia felt rather than saw his dark eyes fixed on her, and, lifting hers, saw that this distinguished-looking man, with the handsome and strangely grave and reserved face, must be "the mysterious stranger," as she had jestingly called him. He was young, as Mr. Sparrow had said, but the dark hair was touched where it was cut close on the temples with faint streaks of gray, and the eyes, with their singularly impressive expression, were full of a reserved melancholy.

"I am afraid my dog——" he said, in a grave voice. Then he stopped; and Olivia, looking up to see the cause, saw a strange thing.

On Bertie's frank face were two expressions struggling for mastery—astonishment, that might or might not have been recognition, and a desire to crush down all sign of this recognition, if recognition it was.

On the stranger's face was simply a set look of almost grim impassibility. No one, judging by his face, would have guessed that he had ever seen Lord Bertie before.

The pause was only that of a second, a flash of time; and as he continued his sentence, removing the steady gaze of his dark eyes from Bertie to Olivia, his voice remained just the same unfalteringly grave one. "I am sorry that my dog should have annoyed you; he has broken his chain, as you see. I may add that he is particularly quiet, and would not have attacked the dogs. Please forgive me."

He raised his hat again to Olivia, she inclined her head, and, the dog following close upon his heels, he turned and walked back to The Dell.

There was a moment's silence; then Olivia, a little pale—why, she could not have told—said:

"I forgot to tell you of another change. Mr. Sparrow has sold The Dell, and that gentleman, I suppose, is the owner."

"Really?" said Bertie, slowly, and without lifting his eyes to hers. "What is his name?"

"Faradeane," replied Olivia. "Do you know it?"

Bertie shook his head.

Olivia looked at him half-curiously.

"I fancied," she said, "that you looked as if you knew him."

For a second, for so short a time that the pause was imperceptible, Bertie hesitated; then he shook his head.

CHAPTER III
"TO KNOW HER IS TO LOVE HER"

"Faradeane?" replied Bertie. "I never heard the name before."

Nothing more was said on the subject. It was dropped as if by the tacit consent of both; which showed plainly how much they were both affected by the incident; for what would have been more natural than that they should discuss the appearance and manner of this stranger who had come so suddenly and mysteriously into their neighborhood?

Olivia could scarcely have told how much, or explained why, his appearance had affected her. She saw him for a few minutes only, he had spoken about half-a-dozen words, and yet she felt that if she were never to see him again she should never forget the strange expression of the dark, sorrowful eyes, or the peculiar music of the deep, grave voice.

Mesmerism is a recognized fact; and if she had known anything of it Olivia might easily have explained the sensation she felt as that resulting from mesmerization. The dark eyes had seemed to penetrate to her inmost heart, the voice to have set up an echo within her ears which should never fade.

A shadow seemed to have fallen over both her and Bertie, and for a time they actually walked toward the Grange in absolute silence. And for Bertie to be silent was a very remarkable state of things.

It was in the midst of this silence that a voice was heard coming from a walk behind the shrubbery. It was the voice of Mr. Bartley Bradstone, and both Olivia and Bertie heard these words:

"It's a deuce of a mess, a regular tangle; but we'll get out of it. Just trust to me——"

Bertie looked up at Olivia, and saw her start and her dark brows come together.

"Who is that?" he asked, in a slightly lowered voice.

"That is Mr. Bradstone," she said.

The same moment that gentleman and the squire came out upon them.

The squire started slightly, and Bartley Bradstone looked from one to the other with the suspicious, searching look peculiar to him. Then the squire's face cleared, and he gave both hands to Lord Granville.

"Why, Cherub!" he exclaimed, in altogether happier tones than we have hitherto heard him use. "Welcome back! How well you look, my boy!"

"Doesn't he, papa!" exclaimed Olivia, eagerly.

"Why, you've—yes, you've actually grown," said the squire.

"Oh, come now!" remonstrated Bertie, laughing and blushing. "That's rather too thin, even for me, squire."

"But you have. How glad I am to see you! And your father—is he well?" As he turned he caught sight of Mr. Bartley Bradstone, who was standing looking at them with a half-sullen, half-jealous air, and the smile vanished from the squire's face. "I beg your pardon," he said; "let me introduce you to our neighbor and friend, Mr. Bradstone. This is Lord Granville, our old friend Bertie, Bradstone."

The two men exchanged bows; Bertie with a pleasant frankness and cordiality, Bartley Bradstone with hardly suppressed sullenness.

"I was going to call on you to-morrow, Mr. Bradstone," said Bertie. "I am happy to make your acquaintance. My father tells me that you have gone in very heavily for preserving. By George! it was time some one did, for, begging the squire's pardon, pheasants and partridges in Hawkwood were getting very rare birds, indeed!" and he nodded with much gravity at Mr. Vanley.

"Oh, yes," said Bartley Bradstone, with an affected drawl. "I'm going to preserve; it's the duty of every country gentleman, I take it."

Bertie looked at him quickly, and a shade of disapproval swept over his handsome, girlish face. Bartley Bradstone's voice was that of the cad, and of course Bertie detected it.

"The squire hasn't preserved as closely as he might have done," he said, rather gravely for him, "because he is too tender-hearted to the village people."

"The village people will find me a very different kind of customer if they come poaching on my land, my lord," retorted Bartley Bradstone.

Now, a gentleman, though he be a commoner, does not address a nobleman, to whom he has been introduced on equal terms, as "my lord," and this time Bertie glanced coldly at the new neighbor, and, apparently now quite satisfied, turned from him to the squire and talked with him.

They made their way to the house, Olivia and her father chatting over old times and Bertie's travels with Bertie, and thus Bartley Bradstone was left out in the cold, or thought that he was. He stopped at the bottom of the flight of steps and looked at his watch.

"It's time I was going," he said, sullenly.

The squire started.

"I hope you'll stay to dinner, Bradstone," he said, and the preoccupied, almost anxious look which had been absent while he had been talking to Bertie, came over his face again.

"No, thanks; I've got an engagement," replied Mr. Bradstone. "Good-day; don't trouble, I can get my horse," for the squire made a movement to accompany him; and raising his hat a couple of inches to Olivia, who bowed in silence, he strode off.

An awkward silence fell upon the three.

"That's—that's a very clever young man," said the squire, with a little cough; "very clever. I think you'll find him quite an acquisition to the neighborhood, Bertie."

"Oh, yes," said Bertie; "rather a—er—rough kind of fellow, isn't he? Not very good tempered, is he?" and he looked with a smile from the squire, whose brows contracted, to Olivia, whose face seemed like a mask in its cold reserve. "Not quite a—a gentleman?"

The squire bit his lips.

"Well—he is a very good-natured young fellow, and"—he paused again—"very rich."

"That's more his misfortune than his fault, perhaps," said Bertie, with a laugh.

"Misfortune!" echoed the squire, in a strange tone; then he laughed. "I don't think he would so describe it. I rather think it is his fault."

"I see," said Bertie, easily. "Made his money himself, and all that. Well, that's in his favor, anyhow. I dare say he is a good fellow, and it's a capital idea of his, this preserving. Oh, yes! I like a man who has made his own fortune, don't you, Olivia?"

"It all depends," replied Olivia, dryly.

The squire glanced at her, not impatiently, but anxiously, questioningly, doubtfully.

"I've never heard a word against Mr. Bradstone," he remarked, with a querulousness which was so new to him that Bertie almost stared at him. "He is the essence of good-nature, and has exerted it on—on several occasions. I hope you'll like him, Bertie."

"Of course I shall—if you wish it," said Bertie, promptly and heartily.

"I wish it?" repeated the squire, almost frowning; "why should I——" Then he stopped short, and rather inconsistently said, with something like irritation: "My dear Bertie, the man has settled here in our midst, and—and is our neighbor. But don't let us talk any more about him. Come in. Of course you will dine with us?"

But, strange to say, Bertie, with a faint accession of color, pulled out his watch and shook his head.

"I can't, I'm sorry to say. I'll come over to dinner to-morrow, if I may."

The squire looked disappointed.

"I thought your father would have spared you to-night, my boy," he said. "But come over to us to-morrow, then," he added, as he shook his hand.

Bertie lingered a moment or two beside Olivia, after the squire had gone up the steps.

"What do you think of Mr. Bradstone, Olivia?" he said, in a low voice.

Olivia smiled faintly; then her brows contracted.

"Exactly as you do," she replied, and held out her hand.

Bertie took it and held it.

"Yes? Then why on earth does the squire have him here, and—and—praise him, and all that?" he asked. "I never knew him make excuses for a cad before."

Olivia looked straight before her.

"I give it up," she said; "ask me another."

Bertie looked at her averted face with a half-troubled questioning, then his brow cleared.

"I tell you what it is, Olivia," he said, as if he had found the solution, "the squire is too good-natured by half, that's what it is!"

"I dare say!" she said, quietly. "Mind, we expect you to-morrow!" and covering him with one of her rare smiles as with a flash of sunlight, she drew her hand from his clasp and ran up the steps.

Bertie watched her till she had disappeared through the French window; watched her with an expression on his handsome, girlish face that made it very sweet and tender with its reverent admiration; then, with a little sigh of wistful longing, turned and walked quickly across the lawn.

He passed out into the lane that led to The Dell, and stopping at the rustic gate, pushed it open.

As he did so, a man dressed something between a butler and a gamekeeper, came toward him.

"Can I see— —" commenced Bertie; then he stopped, for the "mysterious stranger" himself appeared in the doorway and walked down the path.

"Hallo! why, my dear— —"

"Mr. Faradeane," interrupted the owner of The Dell. "Come in, Lord Granville," and he opened the door.

Bertie, coloring with a look of mystification and bewilderment, passed in and followed his host into the sitting-room of the cottage. The latter shut the door, and placing his hands—they were long and white as a woman's, but as strong as a blacksmith's—on Bertie's shoulders, gently forced him into a chair.

"Well?" said Mr. Faradeane, standing over him and looking at him with a strange smile, which was as sad as the shadow that dwelt in his eyes. "Well?"

"Well!" repeated Bertie, almost glaring at him. "My dear— —"

"Faradeane," interposed the other.

"What on earth does this mean?" continued Bertie.

Instead of replying, his companion took a cigar case from the mantelshelf and tossed it to him, then slowly and deliberately lit a pipe.

Bertie took a cigar, but instead of lighting it, stared round the room at the old oak chairs and table, at the gun and pistol rack over the fireplace, at the books in the bookcase, at the grave and singularly handsome face of his host.

"A light?" said Mr. Faradeane, with a smile which was almost an amused one. "Better smoke, my dear Bertie; there is nothing like tobacco on these occasions."

Bertie pliantly and helplessly lit his cigar, and, still staring at the dark, thoughtful face, said:

"Well, this beats— —"

"Cock fighting," filled in Mr. Faradeane. "Fire off all your battery of astonishment, my dear Bertie. Don't mind me."

"Yes; but I say!" exclaimed Bertie. "This is—don't you know—extraordinary! What on earth! My dear— —"

"Faradeane," put in the other, quietly.

Bertie sprang to his feet, but the strong, white hands fell softly on his shoulders and forced him into his chair again.

"Take time, Bertie," he said, grimly, "take half an hour, if you like. But don't forget that my name is Faradeane."

Bertie leaned forward and stared at him for a moment in densest perplexity; then he laughed.

"Confound it!" he said, "this is the strangest business; Why, my dear— —"

"Faradeane," put in the other, with a faint smile. "I'm sorry to interrupt you, Bertie; but if walls have ears, as they say they have, I have the strongest objection to their hearing the name you will persist in trying to shout. I know what you want to say, what you want to ask. You want to ask me why I am living in this out-of-the-way place, and why I decline—absolutely decline—to be addressed by any other name than that which I have, I am afraid, rather obtrusively given you."

"By George!" said Bertie, puffing at his cigar, "that's just what I do want to know! I parted from you rather more than two years ago in London, and left you as jolly and chirpy as a cricket; well, not exactly that, for you never were one of the mad ones; but you were all right, at any rate, and now— — It's the strangest business! Why, I scarcely knew you just now, when you came up with the dog; you've—you've— —"

"Aged so much!" finished Faradeane, with a grim smile, as he leaned against the mantelshelf and looked down at Bertie's bewildered face. "Yes, I have aged, Bertie. But not so much as some people have done. Didn't Marie Antoinette's hair turn white in two days? Whereas mine, you see, has only got speckled in a couple of years. Still, I'll admit I am, as you say, changed."

"What—what has happened, old fellow?" asked Bertie, in a lowered voice. "I'm afraid you have had some big trouble— —"

The other looked down at him and then at the floor, and appeared to be considering some question. Presently he looked up again and shook his head.

"I've been wondering whether I could bring myself to tell you my story—the story of the last two years, Bertie; and I'm sorry to say that I have come to the conclusion that I can't. For two reasons: First, because the recital would shock you, and cause me a rather unpleasant half hour; and secondly, because the secret is not all my own. I'm only a partner."

"Secret! There is a secret! And you—you——"

The other held up his hand.

"Take care!" he said, warningly. "My man is just outside. I beg of you not to speak my name."

"No, no, I won't. I will be careful," said Bertie, flushing. "But you have a secret—Faradeane! You who were always so—so——"

"Too 'high and proud' for that kind of thing, you were going to say? Thanks for the compliment, my dear Bertie; but, alas! it is quite unmerited. I have a secret, and I cannot tell it to you."

"And it is of such a character," said Bertie, slowly, and regarding him with pained surprise, "that you feel compelled to—to——"

"Hide myself here like a poisoned rat in a hole," put in the other, calmly. "Yes, it is. It is so bad that it has put me out of the world as completely as if I had turned hermit. The shady side of Pall Mall and I have seen the last of each other, Bertie; I have bidden good-by to the world you and I found so pleasant. Scarcely that, however, for I left it so suddenly as to leave no time for good-bys."

"Great Heaven!" murmured Bertie, still staring up at the handsome face with its sombre, quietly resigned smile. "But—but why did you come here? Why didn't you go abroad?"

Faradeane smiled.

"For the best of all reasons. Because my pursuers, when I disappeared, at once jumped to the conclusion that I had sought refuge on foreign shores, and are now, I humbly trust, spending their time and energy in scouring the Continent after me."

Bertie almost groaned.

"Your pursuers!"

Such a word in connection with the noble form and face seemed, indeed, incongruous and absurd.

"Yes, my pursuers," said the other, gravely and quietly, "and now you wonder what it is that I have done. I wish I could tell you, Cherub, but I can't. There are some things a man cannot bring himself to confess, even to his dearest friend; this is one of them. And now what will you do?" he asked, fixing his eyes intently upon Bertie's eloquent face. "I've told you enough to show you that my society is not desirable, and that you will do wisely to get up and go. You see, after all, it is a mistake on your part. The man you are listening to is not the old friend you mistook him for, but only a certain Mr. Faradeane, a perfect stranger who somewhat resembles that old friend. Take my advice—I don't offer it often—take my advice, Lord Granville; make a polite bow, excusing yourself for intruding, and leave me."

Bertie's face grew crimson, and he sprang to his feet and laid his small hand upon the broad, straight shoulder.

"Is thy servant a dog that he should do this thing?" he said, in a voice that trembled with indignation. "What do you take me for, old fellow?"

Faradeane put up his hand, and clasping the tiny one, pressed it in silence for a moment.

"I might have known what you would say, Cherub," he said, his voice softening for the first time. "I might have known——Well, so be it! But remember, remember"—impressively—"that it is, indeed, and in truth a mistake, and that I am not the man you mistook me for. I am Harold Faradeane, and you make my acquaintance for the first time to-day."

Bertie nodded, and dropped back into his chair.

"I—I consent," he said, in a low voice. "Of course I consent. But is there nothing I can do——"

"Nothing," was the calm and instant response. "My case is beyond the help of man. Neither you nor any one else can help me, Bertie. I have got to 'dree my weird,' as the Scotch say, and—alone!" He looked round the room slowly, then went on: "You asked me why I chose this place. It was an accident. Knowing that the people who were hunting me"—Bertie winced—"would jump to the conclusion that I had gone on the Continent, I determined to remain in England. In the course of my wanderings I happened to come upon this place. Its utter seclusion struck me; its beauty— it's pretty, isn't it?"—Bertie nodded—"its beauty completed the conquest. You remember, I was always inclined to the artistic in the old days when I was not an outcast and a fugitive," and he smiled.

Bertie sighed.

"You don't know how it pains me to hear you talk like this, Faradeane!" he said, in a low voice.

"And it costs me a great deal to talk like it, though I try to hide it," said the other, gravely. "I don't think there is much more to tell you. It isn't much, is it, that I have told you?"

Bertie shook his head.

"And—and you mean to remain here? What will you do with yourself? Do you intend to live in complete seclusion—to make no friends?"

Faradeane was silent for a moment.

"I shall remain here until chance puts my pursuers on my track," he replied. "What am I going to do?" He shrugged his shoulders. "That's rather a difficult question to answer, Cherub. I find time hangs rather heavily on my hands; but I read a great deal, and I write. You know I always had a knack of scribbling. And I have indulged myself in a horse; he and I—it is a new one—are very good friends already. As to friends of the human kind, barring yourself, Cherub, I must do without them. If you like to take pity on the recluse, and run in now and again, well and good; but no one else."

"Great Heaven!" muttered Bertie; "and you—you who were so popular, such a favorite with us all! I——Forgive me, Faradeane; but while I have been listening, a possible idea has struck me."

The other laughed.

"Yes, I know what you mean. You have almost doubted my sanity; have felt inclined to set me down as mad." He put his hands on Bertie's shoulders, and looked down at him with an expression which haunted the light-hearted Cherub for many a day. "Bertie, I wish I were mad!" There was a moment's pause. "Yes, I wish I could persuade myself that it was a horrible dream, and wake up——"

He stretched out his arms, and drew a long breath, then let them fall to his side and turned away.

Bertie rose and went to the window. It is not "the thing" to exhibit emotion, even on behalf of one's dearest friend; but there was a suspicious moisture in Bertie's blue eyes.

He turned to him after a moment or two.

"One question more, Faradeane, about your affairs. They must give you a great deal of trouble, anxiety. Can I do nothing to help you respecting them?"

Faradeane shook his head.

"No, thanks, Cherub. Just before I fled I placed all of my business affairs in the hands of Elsmere, my solicitor. He does everything; acts as my other self, in fact, under a power of attorney, as they call it. He is the only man who knows my whereabouts, or my present name, excepting yourself, and I can trust you both, thank Heaven. I have given out that I am a woman-hater—there is more truth in that, by the way," he put in grimly, "than you think; and my man has instructions to allow no petticoat to enter the premises. I dare say the simple folks down here will be rather curious; but they will get over it in time. At present I rather think they imagine that I am a little mad, and give me a wide berth. The dog, too, is supposed to be dangerous—he is as quiet and gentle as a lamb, poor old fellow!—and so I fancy I shall be left alone. And now that's enough, and more than enough about myself. Let us talk about a far more interesting subject—you; where are you staying—what are you doing?"

"I am staying with my father," said Bertie. "You have never met him?"

"No, I am glad to say," said Faradeane, grimly. "I should not like him to know me as I was—and as I am! Was that your sister with whom I saw you this morning?" he asked, rather abruptly.

A beautiful rose tint suffused Bertie's face.

"No, no!" he replied. "That was Miss Vanley."

Faradeane nodded.

"The daughter of the squire here? I have heard of him through my man."

"Yes," said Bertie; "Olivia. Didn't—didn't you think she was very beautiful, Faradeane?"

Faradeane turned to the fireplace to knock his pipe out, and nodded.

"Yes," he said, slowly.

"I think she is lovely!" said Bertie, in a low voice. "Olivia was always beautiful; but now—I hadn't seen her for two years," he went on, "and—and she startled me. She has grown into a woman. I wish you knew her, old fellow. She is as good as she is beautiful. She is just the girl you would approve of, I know. You always said that women were stupid; you wouldn't say it of Olivia. Not that I mean that she's clever in the way of knowing all the things women go in for now; no, not clever in that way; but—but— — Oh, I can't describe her! You must know her to understand what she is like."

The other man watched, with a smile, the handsome face, as it grew rapt and enthusiastic.

"You have described her very well, Cherub," he said, quietly. "'To know her is to love her, and to love her is a liberal education,'" he quoted.

Bertie's face flushed.

"That's just it!" he exclaimed. "You always put things so well, Cly— — I—I beg your pardon, I mean Faradeane!" he stammered.

"Be careful, Bertie," said the other, gravely. "Try and get used to my name. A slip at an unwary moment and I am"—he shrugged his shoulders— "ruined. Yes, Miss Vanley is something more than lovely. It is a face 'that carries goodness in its eyes.' You ought to be very happy, Cherub."

Bertie grew scarlet as a poppy.

"No, no," he said, hurriedly. "You—you have quite misunderstood. I—I——There is nothing between us—no engagement, I mean. I—I don't think, I've no reason to think, that she cares——Why, don't you see, dear old fellow, that I'm not worthy to—to——Oh, no!"

"No?" said Faradeane. "I thought——Well, you are still happy in loving her," he added. "Yes, though you never have an iota of hope, though you may never dare to tell her of your love, though your lips may never touch her hands, you are still happy in loving so sweet, so good a woman."

His voice had grown very earnest, and there was a subtle ring of pain in it that found an echo in Bertie's heart. He hung his head.

"I know what you mean," he said, in a low voice.

"'Tis better to have loved and lost than never to have loved at all,'" said Faradeane. "Better to have loved an angel from afar than——" He stopped short suddenly. "But there's every hope for you, Cherub," he said, with a smile.

Bertie shook his head.

"I did think once—that is, I have thought of her always, and while I was away I sometimes plucked up heart, don't you know, to fancy that I might have a chance. But now I've seen how beautiful and queenly and altogether too good for me——" He stopped with a sigh. "Besides, there is some one else in the field," he added, ruefully.

"Yes?" Faradeane looked at him inquiringly.

"Yes," said Bertie. "There is a fellow there—confound him! I fancy he is always at the Grange—a man named Bradstone. He has built that huge furnace, The Maples."

Faradeane nodded.

"I know. He is a financier, or something of that kind. I have heard of him. But surely Miss Vanley——"

"No," said Bertie, promptly, but with a troubled look. "No, I don't think that Olivia cares for him, or is even very friendly; but"—he paused—"but the fellow is very much at home there, and the squire seems to have taken to him."

"I see," said Faradeane; "but keep your heart up. From the glimpse I got of Miss Vanley's face I don't think she is the girl to be smitten by Mr. Bradstone. No!" and a grave smile flickered across his face as he looked dreamily through the window. "No, I don't think you need be apprehensive in that quarter, Cherub. If there is any truth in a woman's eyes, Miss Vanley has a soul above the reach of such a man as this Bradstone."

Bertie laid his hand upon his arm and pressed it gratefully.

"This is just like you, old fellow!" he said. "You understand at once, and—and always know how to sympathize and encourage a man. Thank you! Thank you! Ah, I wish you would know her," he added, wistfully.

For a moment Faradeane stood silent and dreamy, then he roused himself and almost sternly said:

"No, no! by no means! And now, Cherub, you had better go. This is long enough for a first visit to a man you have never met before," he smiled. "Some one has certainly seen you come in and will see you go out, and will be—confound them!—curious. If you are asked—you see I am obliged to coach you in falsehood," he put in bitterly, "you can say that you called to remonstrate with me for allowing that savage dog of mine to be loose; and that, finding me rather a decent kind of a man, you stopped to make my acquaintance."

"Very well," assented Bertie, sadly.

"And now, good-by," said Faradeane, gently pushing him to the door.

Bertie held his hand for a moment or two in a firm grasp, and then went down the path. At the gate he looked back. The tall, graceful figure was leaning against the door-post, and there was something in the attitude, something in the expression of the handsome Van Dyck face, a suggestion of such terrible loneliness and hopelessness and despair, combined with a noble kind of resignation and calmness, that the Cherub's tender heart throbbed with a sympathetic pain.

Harold Faradeane remained there lost in thought for a moment; then, followed closely by the huge dog, he went back to the room, and, as if with an effort to discard something from his mind, sat down to the table and began to write.

He wrote for a few moments with that rapidity which indicates a stern determination; then gradually the pen slowed off, and presently he was absently sketching something on the blotting-pad.

Suddenly he started, and he gazed at what he had drawn, and a strange expression—of fear, almost—leaped into his eyes. He had drawn an outline, striking in its truth, of Olivia's face.

With a kind of groan he sprang to his feet, tore the sketch into fragments, and, striding to the door, scattered them to the winds.

"Great Heaven!" he murmured, with a bitter smile. "Bertie must be right. I must be going mad! Stark, staring, raving mad!" and he thrust his hands into his pockets, and leaned against the door with his head drooping despondently upon his breast.

Suddenly in the silence of the gloaming—it was almost dark in the tree-shaded Dell—a sound smote upon his ears, and caused him to look up quickly.

It was the sound of a runaway horse, and no man who has heard it once can ever mistake it. It was coming down the road in the direction of the cottage. He ran down the narrow, flower-lined path, and vaulted over the gate just as a small pony, with a light cart behind it, came tearing up. Faradeane made a spring for the pony's head, and caught the reins. Even small ponies, when they are on the bolt, are tough customers to tackle; and Faradeane was thrown to the ground. When he got to his feet again after a sharp tussle, and still holding to the reins with a grip of iron, he was shocked and horrified to see a slim, girlish figure lying half in and half out of the cart.

CHAPTER IV
A WOMAN-HATER

Dinner was over at the Grange, and Miss Amelia and Olivia were in the drawing-room waiting for the appearance of the squire, who, for form's sake, lingered behind for a quarter of an hour in the dining-room to sip a glass of the famous Vanley port.

It was Miss Amelia's custom every evening during this quarter of an hour to enjoy a peaceful snooze in an armchair carefully placed by the footman out of the light of the lamps, from which she awoke on the appearance of her brother to declare with a start that really in another moment she should have been asleep.

Olivia was sitting as usual with a book in her hand; but this evening the volume remained open at the same page, and instead of reading she was thinking of her strange meeting with the "mysterious stranger" of The Dell.

It need scarcely be said that Olivia was not sentimental. She was the last girl in the world to invest any one with a romantic halo or to "get up a sentiment" over any man; but try as she would she could not dismiss the remembrance of the handsome face with its sad eyes, and the grave voice with its almost tragic tones, from her mind, and it was with a feeling of actual relief from her own too persistent dwelling upon him that she heard the door open, and, looking up, saw her father enter.

Miss Amelia heard it too, and jerked herself upright with the usual "Is that you, Edwin? Another moment," etc.

Olivia, looking at her father, saw that instead of the smile of amused incredulity with which he usually received Miss Amelia's assertion, his face wore an anxious and thoughtful expression, and as he came up to her to get his cup of coffee, she said in a low voice:

"Is anything the matter, papa?"

"Anything the matter?" he repeated, with a little start. "No. What should be that matter?"

"I don't know," said Olivia, "but I thought you looked rather worried, dear."

"No, no," he said, with a forced kind of cheerfulness. "I am a little tired, I think, that is all. I am sorry Bertie did not stay to dinner."

"So am I," said Olivia, promptly. "How well he looked! Dear Bertie!"

The squire glanced at her.

"Or Mr. Bradstone," he said. "I thought he meant staying."

"Yes?" said Olivia in a colder voice.

"A good fellow, Bradstone!" said the squire, stirring his coffee. "I don't think Bertie did him justice this afternoon. If he knew him as well as I do——"

"But you do not know him very well, papa," said Olivia, gently.

The squire frowned slightly.

"I don't know why you should say that, Olivia," he said. "I—you—have seen a great deal of him——"

"That is true," responded Olivia, dryly, "and all we have seen is to his credit. Don't let us discuss Mr. Bradstone, papa," she was saying almost pleadingly, when the butler entered, and, approaching the squire, said something in a low and guarded voice, and the squire's face changed.

But Olivia's ears were quick, and she caught the word "accident."

"Oh, papa! what is it? Tell me, Fleming." Fleming, the butler, glanced from her to the squire. "Something has happened," she said, growing pale, but speaking calmly and composedly, for Olivia was not hysterical by any means. "What is it? Why do you not tell me, papa?"

"Don't be alarmed," said the squire, putting his hand upon her arm. "There has been an accident. Tell us again, Fleming; you need not be afraid of your mistress."

"It's Bessie Alford, Miss Olivia," began the butler.

"Ah!" breathed Olivia, with a little, piteous catch in her voice. "Poor Bessie! the pony!"

"Yes, miss," said Fleming, gravely. "The pony—she was driving him home—has run away with her. I always told Alford that it wasn't safe for her to drive. He's run away and Bessie is hurt."

Olivia's face grew pale.

"Bessie hurt!" she murmured, piteously.

"What's that? Who's killed?" exclaimed Aunt Amelia, springing to her feet like a jack-in-the-box. "Don't attempt to keep it from me. I will know who is killed! Oh, dear! I feel—I feel as if I was going to faint. Fleming, a glass of water. Oh, Edwin, I know something dreadful is going to happen!" she wound up with a groan and a wail.

Fleming stolidly got her a glass of water; no one else took any notice of her.

Olivia stood for a moment pale and thoughtful; then she moved to the door.

"I must go to her, papa," she said. "Where is she, Fleming?"

"At the lodge, miss," he replied, gravely. "The pony fell down or was stopped not far from there—I have not got the rights of it quite, miss—and they carried Bessie home."

Olivia opened the door, and, disregarding her aunt's shriek of "Where are you going, Olivia?" ran into the hall and caught up a shawl. The squire, without a word, put on his hat, and they went out together.

"Poor Bessie!" murmured Olivia, as they ran down the drive. "I warned her against the pony this afternoon."

They saw lights moving behind the windows of the lodge, and in response to the squire's knock a boy opened the door.

"I will wait here; send for me if you want me," said the squire.

Olivia passed in, and ran noiselessly up the stairs, and pushed open the half-closed door of Bessie's room.

For a moment she saw only the pretty, innocent face lying white and pale upon the pillow; then as she entered she saw, in the flickering of the solitary candle, a tall figure bending over the bed.

It moved as she entered, and, turning, presented the face of Mr. Faradeane.

For a moment the two, girl and man, looked at each other, and she saw in that moment that the face was paler even than when she had seen it in the afternoon, and that there was a blood-red mark across the left temple. Alford stood by—stupefied and useless.

She drew near the bed, and went down on her knees beside the unconscious girl, and was about to murmur her name when she felt a hand upon her arm, and a voice said in low accents of command.

"Don't speak to her, please."

Olivia looked into the grave, handsome face with a meekness utterly novel and strange to her.

"Can I—can I do anything?" she whispered. "Poor Bessie!"

"Yes," he said in the same low, calm tone. "Get me some cold water."

She glided to the water-jug, and poured some out for him, and watched him in a frenzy of anxiety as he bathed the girl's white forehead.

But, great as was her anxiety and excitement, she noticed—and remembered long afterward—how gently and pityingly he did his work. He, the woman-hater!

"Is—is she much hurt?" she whispered, after a time.

"No," he whispered, in reply. "She is stunned. Do not be alarmed. She will recover consciousness presently."

"Are you—are you a doctor?" asked Olivia, a few minutes later; and the question was caused by the calm, deliberate way in which he did what was best to be done.

He smiled.

"No; but it is not the first accident I have seen. She will come to presently. I have sent to Wainford for the doctor. Do not be alarmed; there is no danger."

Almost as soon as he spoke, Bessie opened her eyes, and, after a wild glance or two, fixed them upon the pale, handsome face bending over her.

"Is—is he hurt?" she faltered.

"Do you mean me?" said Mr. Faradeane. "No, I am not hurt in the least."

Bessie heaved a sigh, then she caught sight of the cut on his temple.

"What's that? You are hurt!" she exclaimed.

"That is nothing," he said, with a smile; "I think you had better not talk."

But Bessie did not agree with him, evidently.

"He saved my life—this gentleman, Miss Olivia!" she panted. "I was just falling under the wheel when he stopped Toby, and I saw him go down." She shuddered. "Yes, Miss Olivia, he saved my life, he did!" and her large, innocent eyes fixed themselves on Mr. Faradeane, and filled with tears.

He smiled.

"You will be quite ashamed of talking such nonsense when you have recovered, Miss Bessie," he said. "Now drink this, will you, please?" and he held a flask of brandy to her lips.

She sipped it obediently, her brown eyes fixed upon his with the gratitude, the devotion which one sees in a dumb animal often enough, but in a human, alas! only too seldom. Then, with a sigh, she turned her face away, and closed her eyes.

Mr. Faradeane stood upright.

"She will be all right now," he said. "No bones are broken, thank Heaven! It was the shock as much as the blow on the forehead that stunned her."

There was a step on the stair, and the local doctor entered.

Mr. Faradeane drew him aside, and gave a short and succinct account of the accident.

"Yes, yes," murmured the doctor, "and you, sir? you seem to have been hurt!"

"Not in the least," said Mr. Faradeane, "not in the very least, thanks," and, with a bow to Olivia, he passed out of the room.

Obeying an impulse she could not resist, Olivia followed him, and, darting at the squire, who was standing outside the lodge door, said:

"He—this gentleman—saved Bessie's life!"

The squire started, as well he might, and approached the tall figure.

"My daughter tells me, sir," he said, "that this poor girl owes her life to your courage and presence of mind. I hope you will allow me to express my sense of your bravery. My name is Vanley——"

For a moment Mr. Faradeane stood and regarded him with a frank smile; then his face changed suddenly.

"No thanks are due, sir; good-night," he said, gravely, almost sternly; and before another word could be said he raised his hat and passed them.

CHAPTER V
THE KEY TO THE RIDDLE

The squire looked after the retreating figure in astonishment, and then at Olivia. She was trembling slightly, and the red and white were chasing each other on her downcast face.

"What is the matter? Who was he? Why did he go off like that?" he said.

Olivia was silent for a moment.

"That is the gentleman who has bought The Dell, papa. Mr. Faradeane."

The squire started.

"It was he, was it? And he saved Bessie's life?"

"She says so, papa. He was hurt. Did you see the marks on his forehead?"

"No," said the squire. "I scarcely saw his face, and yet from what I saw of it I should say, emphatically, that he was a gentleman."

"Oh, yes!" murmured Olivia, drawing her shawl round her.

"Most certainly a gentleman. It was a striking face. What nonsense was it that Sparrow was talking of a coiner or something of that kind? He could not have seen the man."

"It was not Mr. Sparrow, but Mr. Bradstone, who suggested that Mr. Faradeane was a coiner," she said in a low voice.

"Nonsense!" said the squire, almost impatiently. "That is not the face of a man in hiding from the consequences of some vulgar crime. There was not a trace of vice in it. Sad and melancholy it was, without doubt, but——Why did he go off like that?"

Olivia was silent a moment.

"You heard what Mr. Sparrow said, papa. He is a woman-hater."

"What, Sparrow!" exclaimed the squire, staring at her.

"No, no; this—this Mr. Faradeane."

"And he takes the trouble—and gets knocked about—in saving a girl's life. What rubbish!" he said. "That is a poor kind of woman-hater. Sparrow has got hold of some cock-and-bull story. I scarcely listened to him this afternoon, and don't remember what it was he said; but it is nonsense, utter nonsense. This man is a gentleman. I never saw a finer face." He paused and knit his brows. "Now I recall it, I seem to think that I remember having seen it before."

Olivia drew nearer to him with an eager expression in her beautiful eyes.

"Papa!"

"Yes," he said, "I have a vague kind of impression, but I can't fix it. Are you coming now?"

Olivia breathed a short sigh of disappointment.

"I thought you might have remembered," she said. "I will come in one moment, papa. I must just see Bessie again."

"All right, I am in no hurry," said the squire, and he sat down on the settle outside the door, and instantly, as it would seem, was absorbed by his own thoughts.

Olivia ran upstairs on tiptoe, and entered Bessie's room.

The girl turned her large, innocent eyes upon the lovely face of her young mistress with eager gratitude.

"Not gone yet, miss?" she said in a low voice.

"Not yet, Bessie. Are you better?"

"I am all right now, Miss Olivia; only weak and trembling like. Has—has the gentleman gone?"

"Mr. Faradeane? Yes," said Olivia, and she leaned down and smoothed the white coverlid.

Bessie drew a long breath.

"And I scarcely thanked him!" she said.

"Oh, but I think you did, Bessie," said Olivia.

The girl shook her head, and the color came into her pale, childlike face.

"I couldn't thank him long enough, miss. He did save my life, though he made light of it, and put it off as nothing at all. Toby had bolted, and was racing like the wind, and the gentleman—tell me his name again, miss; it is a hard one to remember, and yet it sounds nice——"

"Faradeane," said Olivia.

"Ah, yes, Faradeane! I shan't forget it. Well, miss, he came out of the cottage, straight like a lion, and he leaped onto Toby. I could just see him before I fainted, and Toby knocked him down, and I thought he was killed, and then—I don't recollect any more till he carried me in here. He said he wasn't hurt, miss; but I saw the blood running from his forehead." She shuddered. "Ah, miss, if I were a lady like you I could thank him as he deserves; but I'm only a poor girl that doesn't know how to speak what she feels."

"I think you thanked him very prettily, Bessie," said Olivia. "But I don't think he wanted or liked being thanked. He would not stop to speak to papa, outside, just now."

A swift look of apprehension rose to Bessie's eyes.

"Ah, miss, he was hurt, and was trying to hide it; he didn't want the squire to see. Oh, Miss Olivia, what shall I do? There is no one there to see after him."

Olivia soothed her, and returned to the squire.

"Bessie thinks Mr. Faradeane was hurt, badly perhaps—and that was the reason he did not stay, papa," she said, with a little catch in her voice.

"Eh?" said the squire. "Well, that may be so." And, instead of turning up the drive, he went down the lane toward The Dell. Olivia walked in silence by his side, and the squire stopped at the gate, and put his hand upon it. It was fastened securely. "The gate is locked," he said, looking puzzled and baffled.

Olivia touched his arm, and pointed to the window, upon the white blind of which was the shadow of a tall figure pacing up and down.

"Look, papa," she whispered.

The squire stared at the shadow with a thoughtful frown.

"That is an unhappy man," he remarked to her, also in a whisper. "At any rate, he is not so much hurt as Bessie imagined."

"No," said Olivia, with a little sigh of relief. Then she touched her father's hand. "Come away, papa," she said, almost inaudibly. "I—I feel as if we were watching him."

"Well, so we are," retorted the squire, with a suppressed laugh. Then he looked at her uneasily. "Yes; let us go home," he said. "You look tired and upset. This has been too much for you. I will walk down in the morning and inquire how he is. I suppose he will not refuse me admittance. I am not a woman."

And he laughed.

But Olivia did not echo the laugh as he had expected; and she remained silent all the way along the drive.

Meanwhile Mr. Bartley Bradstone had ridden back to his splendid and gorgeous house in anything but a good humor. Your parvenu, while he would give half his newly gotten wealth to be a gentleman, invariably hates every gentleman he meets. Bartley Bradstone had taken a dislike to Lord Bertie, first because he was a gentleman, and secondly because he was, evidently, an old friend of Olivia's, and possibly a lover. As he contrasted her manner to Bertie with the cold reserve with which she treated him, he clinched his teeth and jerked at the reins, making the horse start and shy.

"She treats me as if I were the dirt under her feet," he muttered, sullenly, "just the dirt under her feet! And I like her all the better for it, confound her! But it's a dangerous game to play with Bartley Bradstone, Miss Olivia, if you only knew it! Perhaps the day will come when you will lower your pride a little. It will be my turn then. By Heaven! I'd give—I don't know what I wouldn't give, to see you at my feet! And it shall come to that, too, or I'm not the clever fellow people think me. It is very hard if Bartley Bradstone isn't a match for a dozen Lord Granvilles, though he is the son of an earl."

He rode up the long, newly planted avenue to The Maples, and a couple of grooms came out to take his horse; but, as they had kept him waiting half a moment, he snarled at them as he flung himself from the saddle and mounted the stone steps—painfully white and new—which led to the front entrance. A footman was waiting to take his hat and stick, and his valet stood at the top of the stairs.

The squire and Lord Carfield were capable of hanging up their hats for themselves; but that would not have been "good enough" for Mr. Bartley Bradstone, who liked to see his gorgeous footmen whenever he could, and insisted upon being waited upon, literally, hand and foot.

He passed through the hall—which, notwithstanding its painted windows, and men in armor, and brown oak, looked as new as the rest of the place—and, going into the dining-room, rang for a glass of sherry; the squire would have got it for himself from the sideboard, but Mr. Bradstone flung himself into a chair while the butler and footman "served" the glass of wine on a heavy silver salver. The master of The Maples drank it, and looked round with a restless sigh.

"I was a fool not to stay, after all," he muttered. "It was cutting off my nose to spite my face. It's deuced dreary here by one's self, but it shan't be for long. Before long she'll be begging me to stay at the Grange—yes, begging me."

Then he got up, and, with his hands thrust in his pockets, wandered about the room. Presently he cast a glance at the many pictures, all in heavy gilt frames, and stood before one representing a girl reading a book. It was a recent purchase, and he had bought it because he fancied that it somewhat resembled Olivia; and twenty times a day he would stand before it and gaze at it.

"I'll have her own portrait here presently," he murmured, moodily. "I'll give Millais the commission to paint it the day we're engaged."

This resolution seemed to afford some satisfaction, for with something less of his recent sullenness, he rang the bell for his valet to dress him for dinner.

As he did so the footman entered with a note on the salver.

Bartley Bradstone opened and eyed it with an expression of displeased surprise.

"Where is he?" he asked.

"The person is in the hall, sir," replied the footman.

"Show him into the library," said Bradstone; then he stood looking at the sheet of paper, which contained only two words—"Ezekiel Mowle"—with a thoughtful frown, and a few minutes afterward went into the library.

In the brand-new room with its brand-new furniture and rows of newly bound books sat, on the edge of one of the morocco chairs, a thin, hatchet-faced man, dressed like a clerk. He would have served very well as a model for Uriah Heep; but instead of that "'umble" personage's red hair he wore a palpable wig, whose hyacinthine curls, clustering in pious falsehood upon the cadaverous forehead, made the face look like a skull; indeed, being close shaven and without a single eyebrow or eyelash, it would have closely resembled one under any conditions.

Bartley Bradstone shut the door close.

"Well, Mowle," he said, with marked coldness, "this is an unexpected pleasure. What has brought you down here?"

Mr. Mowle stretched his thin, colorless lips by way of a smile, and coughed apologetically behind a huge, bony hand.

"I thought it best to run down, sir," he said, and his voice matched his person, being hollow and strained, as if his throat were totally devoid of moisture. "I considered the question most anxiously, Mr. Bartley, and I thought it best to run down," and he glanced upward with a peculiar expression of servile obsequiousness.

"What's wrong?" demanded Bartley Bradstone, eyeing him with suppressed irritation. "Why didn't you telegraph, whatever it is?"

Mr. Mowle fingered his chin and blinked his lashless lids.

"The wire's useful, but not always to be trusted, especially in country places like this. The young lady at the office is generally so curious, having so little to do, Mr. Bartley. I might have written, but I thought from what you said that time was important; so I ran down."

"Yes, yes, I see you have," said Bartley Bradstone, with ill-concealed impatience; "and now you're here you had better stop to dinner— —"

Mr. Mowle shook his head.

"No, no, thank you, sir. There is a train in an hour and a half's time, and I've kept the fly— —"

Bartley Bradstone frowned.

"There is no occasion for that," he said, with bombastic pride. "I dare say I can find something to take you back to the station." He rang the bell. "Pay the flyman and discharge him," he said to the footman, "and order the dogcart."

Mr. Mowle, pawing at his lank chin, watched the pompously attired footman with a vapid air, and then allowed his eyes to roam round the extravagant decorations and furniture of the room.

"You'll have some wine?" said Bartley Bradstone.

"Thank you, sir; thank you, Mr. Bartley; but I'm a teetotaler, if you remember."

Bartley Bradstone nodded.

"Oh, yes, I remember. But what is it?"

Mr. Mowle produced a pocketbook from the interior of his shiny frock coat, and, taking out a paper, handed it to Bartley Bradstone.

"You can rely upon that information, sir," he said in his hollow voice.

Bartley Bradstone looked at the paper.

"When did you get this?" he asked in a constrained voice.

"At a quarter past ten this morning. I considered it, and caught the eleven fast train, Mr. Bartley," he replied, meekly.

"And—and you think it is right?" said Bartley Bradstone in a low voice.

"I'm sure of it, sir," replied Mowle. "I got it from a source which has never yet sold me. I'd stake my oath upon it, sir."

Bartley Bradstone went to the window and looked out, probably to hide the light of satisfaction which gleamed in his eyes. Then, after a moment or two, he turned to Mowle again.

"You were quite right to come down with this, Mowle," he said; "it is too important to be trusted to a wire."

"Thank you for your approbation, Mr. Bartley," said Mowle, servilely.

"According to this," said Bradstone, touching the paper with his forefinger, "the person named—we will mention no names, Mowle, just, take the initial V.—according to this information V. is liable for something like forty thousand pounds. That's so?"

"That is so," assented Mowle, blinking, and rubbing his chin. "Rather more than less, Mr. Bartley. Nearer fifty. Of course it's a secret."

"How do you account for it?" asked Bartley Bradstone, thoughtfully, and watching his companion covertly and closely.

Mr. Mowle stretched his lips into the undertaker-like smile, and coughed.

"Seems singular and improbable, doesn't it, sir? Here's a gentleman, a tip-top swell, as we may say, one of the old county families, looked up to and respected as a sound man, and yet——" He rubbed his chin, and smiled again. "This is the key to the riddle, Mr. Bartley: Wild oats!"

Bartley Bradstone sank into a chair and nodded.

"Wild oats, sir! Mr. V. began it early, and kept it up as long as he could. Went to the Jews—and the Christians. I don't know which is worse," and he coughed again. Bartley Bradstone's eyes dropped with a faint shadow of consciousness.

"Borrowed right and left on *post obits* and I O U's and reversions, and on anything or nothing. Quite the old story, Mr. Bartley. Sixty per cent. interest, any interest they liked to put on, so that he had some money to play ducks and drakes with."

"That was before he came into the property," said Bartley. "Why didn't he pay it off then?"

"He did; some of it," replied Mr. Mowle. "He has been trying to clear it for years past; but this kind of thing's not easily got rid of, and these have been bad times for landlords. There are a good many in the same fix as Mr. V., but not so badly, perhaps."

"And he cannot pay it off now?" asked Bartley Bradstone.

Mr. Mowle shook his head.

"If my information is correct—and I'll answer for it—he certainly cannot."

"How is it that his condition has been kept so secret? No one suspects it here—in his neighborhood."

"The gentlemen who hold the bills are only too pleased to keep quiet while he pays the interest, of course; sixty per cent."

"Of course," assented Bartley, "and have you got a list of the names of these people?"

"Yes, sir," said Mowle, and he handed him a paper from his pocketbook.

Bartley Bradstone examined it, and whistled.

"Tough customers!" he said. "Sharks, all of them. Are you sure this is all?"

"I am quite sure," said Mowle. "I may as well tell you, sir, that my informant is the confidential clerk to Mr. V.'s solicitors." He paused a moment. "He owes us a hundred or two——"

"Us?" said Bartley Bradstone, with a frown.

Mr. Mowle coughed and glanced up nervously.

"I beg your pardon, Mr. Bartley; I should have said me! He owes me; just so."

Bartley Bradstone eyed him with suspicious displeasure.

"Look here, Mowle," he said. "That's rather an awkward slip of yours. I hope it doesn't occur with other people. They'll be asking who the 'us' is."

"No, sir; no, Mr. Bartley, I'm careful. I'm cautious in the extreme. Why, Mr. Bartley, if you think of the years I've kept the business dark——"

"I know, I know. I only warned you," interrupted Bartley Bradstone. "Once let a hint of our connection get abroad, and—well, I think you know the consequences. I've still got that interesting little check you so kindly signed with my name."

Mr. Mowle's colorless face grew livid, his cadaverous lips twitched, and his bony hands closed convulsively.

"You've no reason to fear, Mr. Bartley," he said, almost inaudibly, his hands shaking.

"No, it is you who have reason to fear," retorted Mr. Bradstone. "I'm a man of my word, as you know, and I mean that if the slightest suspicion is aroused that you are working for me, I hand that check over to the police and send you to penal servitude."

Mr. Mowle nodded.

"I know you will, sir," he said, moistening his lips, "and I am cautious accordingly. I think you'll admit that, Mr. Bartley? For nearly twelve years I've worked for you, and thousands upon thousands have passed through these hands"—he extended them—"and every penny has been accounted for. And no one—no one, Mr. Bartley—has ever heard me mention your name, or suspected that you were my master."

Mr. Bradstone nodded.

"It's well for you they haven't," he said, coldly. "It is more important than ever that our connection should be kept dark. I don't like the risk of your coming here even."

"I've been very careful," said Mowle, meekly; "I didn't give the servant my name. I said I'd brought a note from your London tailor."

Mr. Bradstone nodded.

"Yes, and you're right in going back to-night. Now take my instructions."

Mr. Mowle took out his pencil, and looked up at his master with a dogged intentness.

"Buy Mr. V.'s debts," said Bartley Bradstone, coolly, but with his eyes downcast.

Mr. Mowle did not start, but his eyes blinked, and he turned them upon Bartley Bradstone.

"You quite understand—I made myself clear, I hope, sir—that Mr. V. couldn't possibly pay if he were pressed?"

"Yes, I understood," said Bartley Bradstone. "I don't suppose he could. All the same I want these bills and I O U's. All of them, mind! Don't let one escape."

Mr. Mowle nodded.

"I shall have to pay, sir," he said, succinctly.

Bartley Bradstone sighed.

"Yes, I expect so, confound them! Do the best you can; but buy them, and as soon as you can. When you have got them all, let me know. That's all."

Mr. Mowle closed his book.

"Very good, sir," he said, shutting his lips. "I won't detain you longer, sir. Everything is going on all right, as you saw by the last statement."

Mr. Bradstone nodded, and opened the door.

"You've got a little time to spare. You may as well see the house," he said, carelessly.

"Thank you, sir; thank you, Mr. Bartley, if it's not giving you too much trouble," croaked Mr. Mowle obsequiously, as he followed him.

"This is the hall," said Bartley Bradstone, waving his hand. "Notice this window, Mowle. It cost me fifteen hundred pounds."

Mowle blinked at the window, and cast a fishy eye round the oaken panels and the men in armor.

"The drawing-room," said Mr. Bradstone. "Decorated by Marks. I paid him four hundred pounds. Had the furniture designed by Fox."

"Beautiful! beautiful!" murmured Mowle.

"And this is the dining-room. Sorry you can't stay to dinner, I'd have shown you the plate."

"Superb apartment," croaked Mowle, peering in with his shoulders bent meekly.

"Library you've seen. Here's the billiard-room. Electric light, you see."

"I see, sir. Delightful."

"Come upstairs. First corridor. My rooms," and he signed to a footman to open the door.

Mr. Mowle peered into the luxurious bedchamber and dressing-room, and his gaunt eyes took note of the silver toilet set and Brussels lace draperies.

"Fit for a prince!" he croaked.

"Guest chambers No. 1 and Nos. 2 and 3. There are fourteen of them, all like this," said Mr. Bradstone.

"Delightful! quite delightful!" murmured Mowle. "Fourteen, Mr. Bradstone?"

"Fourteen," assented the owner. "Reading-room and ladies' boudoir, gray and yellow satin. Piano, Collard & Collard grand. Pictures by Long and Leighton."

"Splendid! Fit for a queen, Mr. Bartley!" exclaimed Mowle, staring about him.

"Statuary gallery," said. Mr. Bradstone. "'Sleeping Nymph,' two thousand pounds. 'Hercules,' by Boehm, a thousand pounds. Group, by

Gleichen. Down there is the palm-garden—fountain of scented water. My own room." He passed into a small room, luxuriously furnished, with cabinet pictures on the walls, and a large iron safe in the corner. "Books, guns, and all that kind of thing," he said, waving his hand. "Safe by Milner." He looked round, and, seeing the footman was out of hearing, added, with a smile, "That's where your little check is, Mowle."

Mr. Mowle's face went livid, and he passed his hands over each other as if to warm them. "Don't, Mr. Bartley, don't!" he murmured, hoarsely.

Bartley Bradstone laughed.

"Oh, it is as well to remind you," he said, coolly. "That door leads to the stables. This way," and he led him across a courtyard covered by a glass roof. "Here you are; twenty-four stalls. I hunt, you know."

"Yes, sir."

"Yes. That's my best horse. Gave two hundred and fifty for him."

"Beautiful creature, sir."

"Yes. Carriage horses—six of them. And here's your dogcart. Sure you won't have anything before you go?"

"Nothing, thank you, sir," replied Mr. Mowle. "Thank you for showing me over, Mr. Bradstone. It is a truly beautiful place, and fit for a king. Beautiful! I'll see that your kind orders are properly executed, sir. Good-day."

Mr. Bartley Bradstone nodded. "Good-day," he replied, and, his hands thrust into his pockets, he returned to the house to dress for dinner.

Mr. Mowle climbed into the dogcart, and was driven rapidly away. At the end of the avenue he laid his hand upon the arm of the groom.

"One moment, young man," he said.

The groom pulled up the impatient horse, and Mr. Mowle turned and looked back at the house.

"And to think that I made it all!" he muttered. "You—you *beast!*" Then he said aloud, "Thank you; drive on now, please."

CHAPTER VI
THE FORTUNE-TELLER'S WARNING

As a rule it is only necessary to arrange a picnic to insure a wet day; but the day of Mr. Bradstone's picnic proved an exception, and the morning was as clear and bright, and almost as warm, as a spring day in the sunny south.

Mr. Bradstone had bestowed a great deal of thought on this little outing which he had planned for Olivia's amusement—and his own advantage, of course—and when, but only the day before, she consented, in response to the squire's pressure, to join the party, Mr. Bradstone redoubled his exertions.

Lord Carfield had been asked; but, while accepting for Bertie, he had declined for himself. "My picnic days are over, Mr. Bradstone," he said; "I have arrived at the period when cold pie and salad, when eaten in the posture absolutely unavoidable on these occasions, settle somewhere in the small of my back. But my son Bertie will be delighted, I am sure."

And he had spoken the truth. Bertie would have eaten cold pie or poison, if, by so doing, he could insure a few hours of Olivia's society.

The only other persons besides the Vanleys who had been asked were Mary and Annie Penstone, the two daughters of Sir William Penstone, whose estates lay about five miles from Hawkwood Grange.

They were going to ride over to Glenmaire, the spot Mr. Bradstone had fixed upon for the luncheon, and Mr. Bradstone had arranged to drive the squire and Olivia to the rendezvous in a brand-new mail phæton, of which he was, not altogether without reason, exceedingly proud. Imagine his disappointment, then, when, having dashed up to the Grange door, he saw Olivia standing on the steps in her riding-habit, and Bertie just below her with his arm hooked in the bridles of his own and her horse.

"I—I thought you were going to drive with me and your father, Miss Olivia?" he said, as she gave him her hand; and he muttered some almost inaudible response to Bertie's cheery "Good-morning!"

"Did I promise?" said Olivia. "I don't think it was a distinct promise. I had to ride into Wainford this morning for some medicine for Bessie, and I kept my habit on."

"I am afraid I am the culprit, really, Mr. Bradstone," said Bertie, pleasantly. "I rode over to ask after Bessie at the Lodge, and, being lucky enough to find Miss Vanley just starting for Wainford, I persuaded her to ride to Glenmaire. Her horse really wants a little more work."

Bartley Bradstone bit his lip. After all his carefully laid plans, this young lordling had managed not only to balk him, but to snatch a *tête-à-tête* gallop with Olivia.

"I'm afraid you'll be tired," he said, ignoring Bertie's explanation. "I should have thought you would have sent for the medicine."

Bertie's eyes opened widely, and he looked at Olivia to see how she would take this piece of impertinence; but her clear, calm gaze did not change in the slightest.

"Yes, I might have done so," she said, quietly. "However, if you wish me to drive, I can change my habit in ten minutes."

"Oh, no, it isn't worth while," he said; "don't trouble."

"Very well," said Olivia, at once.

With an effort Bartley Bradstone cleared the sullen cloud from his brow, and forced himself to look more amiable.

"And how is the girl?" he asked. "I heard some cock-and-bull story of this accident. I always knew she'd have an accident with that brute of a pony. One of my men said that that fellow who has taken The Dell had a hand in it—startled the pony or something."

Olivia did not offer to correct this amiable representation of the affair, and stood flicking her habit with her whip in silence; but the ready flush rose to Bertie's face in a moment, and he said:

"You have heard an extraordinarily wrong version of the story. Instead of being in any way the cause of the accident, Mr. Faradeane, at some peril to his own limbs and life, stopped the pony, and saved Bessie from a serious fall."

"Oh! quite a hero," said Bartley Bradstone, with as much of a sneer as he dared display to a viscount.

"As you say, quite a hero," assented the Cherub, simply.

At that moment the squire appeared at the door, and came down the steps.

"Sorry to keep you waiting, young people," he said, in a brighter tone than usual; but his face fell as he saw that Olivia was in her habit. "I thought you were going to drive with Mr. Bradstone and me, Olivia," he said.

"And so I shall, if you will wait ten minutes," she said.

But Bartley Bradstone had got his temper under mastery by this time, and he said, quickly:

"Indeed you shall not take the trouble to change, Miss Olivia. I won't wait a minute."

And with a nod and a smile he sprang up to the box-seat and took the reins.

Olivia watched them drive off in her calm, reflective way, and then allowed Bertie to lift her to her saddle.

He was in the seventh heaven of delight which followed the dread of the loss of her society, and the two rode side by side, as they had ridden scores of times when they were schoolboy and schoolgirl, chatting with frank freedom on Olivia's part, and with that half-shy timidity which the timorous lover always feels.

By the time they had reached Glenmaire the Cherub's light-heartedness had awakened a responsive sentiment in Olivia's breast, and she was laughing and forgetting the sudden and mysterious repulse which Mr. Faradeane had inflicted upon her on the preceding day, when Bertie pulled up, and uttered an exclamation.

"Good heavens! Just look at that!"

Before them, in a space which had been cleared for the occasion by Mr. Bartley Bradstone's woodman—Glenmaire was a part of the property he had purchased—were four huge footmen in the Bradstone livery setting out an elaborate collation, adorned by a complete service of plate, and flanked by several magnums of Pommery.

A luggage *fourgon*, with a pair of horses in silver-plated harness, which had conveyed the feast from The Maples, stood at a little distance, and presiding over the whole of the preparations was The Maples' butler in regulation white tie and suit of solemn black.

"Good heavens!" exclaimed Bertie, "fancy a picnic with plate, four footmen, and a butler!" And he laughed; then, with his usual good-nature, he added, quickly, "But it is awfully good of Mr. Bradstone to have taken so much trouble."

"Yes," said Olivia, dreamily. "But he might have had a brass band."

This so tickled the Cherub that he burst into a loud laugh, which brought two bright-eyed, fresh young girls to their side. They were the two Penstone girls, who were in nowise remarkable, excepting for their position as Sir William's daughters—the baronetage was one of the oldest in the county—and their perfectly frank and unenvying delight in, and admiration for, Olivia.

To these two simple country girls there had never been, since the world was created, so beautiful and clever and altogether fascinating a creature as Olivia Vanley.

They pounced upon her, one on each side of the horse, and clung to her with loving eagerness.

"Why, dear, we thought you were never coming!" exclaimed Mary, drawing the supple neck downward that she might kiss the fresh, red lips. "How well you are looking!"

"And how beautiful!" murmured Annie, drawing her gauntlet from her hand.

"You flatterers!" said Olivia, kissing them both and slipping from her horse.

"We were so afraid you wouldn't come," said Mary, "and we are so glad to see you, you can't tell. And isn't this delightful? So kind of Mr. Bradstone! And you rode over with dear Bertie. No wonder he looks so bright and happy!" and she shot a half-playful, half-jealous glance from her boyish eyes at the Cherub, who, having got rid of one of the giants in plush, was mixing a salad.

"He will look ever so much brighter and happier when he has had some lunch," said Olivia.

"For Heaven's sake persuade him to send some of those fellows away, sir," said Bertie in a low voice to the squire, as they seated themselves; "it isn't a bit like a picnic with them hovering like huge birds-of-paradise over us!"

The squire shrugged his shoulders.

"Let him alone—he means well," he said, good-naturedly.

Bartley Bradstone came up to them at this moment. He was looking flushed and excited and—fussy.

"Have you got all you want? Miss Olivia, let them give you some of this *pâté*. Squire, I think you will find this champagne correct—Pommery '73."

The butler swooped solemnly down with the bottle, just as he would have done in the dining-room at The Maples.

It was fearfully and dreadfully unlike a picnic; but the high spirits of the two Penstone girls rose even above the overwhelming presence of the footmen and butler, and they were soon laughing and romping, and Olivia was smiling at them in sympathy, when suddenly, in the very middle of the informally formal repast, and just as Mr. Bartley Bradstone was mentally congratulating himself upon its complete success, a man and a woman, with a couple of children clinging to them, came through the opening of the trees. The woman stopped short, and, with the true gypsy whine, said, as she hungrily eyed the costly spread:

"Will the pretty ladies cross the poor gypsy's hand with silver, and let her tell them their fortunes?"

Mr. Bradstone looked up, almost choking with rage. That gypsies should dare at any time to trespass upon his property was bad enough to bear, but that they should inflict their odious presence upon his special picnic party was simply unendurable.

"What do you mean?" he demanded, angrily. "Here! Go away! Go away at once!"

The woman shrank back a little; but the man, at the sound of his voice, gave a little start, and came a step nearer.

"We means no harm, gentleman," he said, whiningly, his dark eyes fixed upon Bartley Bradstone's angry face. "Let the wise woman tell the pretty ladies' fortunes."

Bartley Bradstone was about to send them about their business with the nearest approach to an oath he dared to utter in the presence of the ladies, when Mary Penstone, with a laugh, said:

"Oh, don't send them away, Mr. Bradstone. I should like to have my fortune told, I should indeed."

"It's all nonsense," he said, with ill-concealed impatience.

"But is it?" demanded Annie, eying the dark-hued gypsy woman, wistfully. "Oh, yes, of course it is, I know; but let her stay, Mr. Bradstone, just for a minute. Mary, lend me a shilling. I'll be the first."

Mary did not possess the coin; but Olivia found one, and Mary, with manifold gigglings, gave it to the gypsy.

The woman crossed the soft palm with it.

"Your fortune is easy to tell, miss," she said. "You'll marry the man of your choice and live happy."

Annie snatched her hand away with a disappointed pout of her full lips.

"I don't think that's worth a shilling," she said. "It's a swindle. I ought to have fallen in love with the wrong man and died of consumption. Now, Mary."

But Mary declined, positively.

"Well, you, then, squire," said Annie, tugging at his arm.

"My fortune's made or marred long ago," he said, shaking his head as he tossed half a crown to the woman.

"Well, then, it's Olivia's turn," said Annie. "Now, Olivia, you must, you must have your fortune told."

Olivia smiled, and held out her hand promptly.

"Don't prophesy anything very dreadful, please," she said.

The woman crossed her long, shapely hand and peered at it; then she slowly let the hand drop.

"Is there any other gentleman or lady would like their fortune told?" she said.

"Oh, but that isn't fair!" exclaimed Annie Penstone. "You must tell this lady's, you know."

The woman glanced at her, then at Olivia.

"Am I to tell it, miss?" she said.

Olivia smiled. "Of course," she said. "Why not?"

The woman took her hand, and looked into her eyes, just as a short-sighted person might have done; then she glanced behind her at the spot where the man stood in an attitude of perfect repose and self-possession, his dark eyes fixed upon Bartley Bradstone.

"Shall I tell this pretty lady her fortune, Seth——"

The man nodded, and the woman in a low voice said:

"There are lines of much sorrow, miss, and much doubt. You will mate with a man you do not love, and love a man you do not mate. But in the end——"

She stopped short, and, dropping Olivia's hand, bent over one of the children.

Olivia smiled her calm, sweet smile.

"It is your turn now," she said to Bertie; but Bertie, with affected horror and awe, shook his head.

"Your experience is enough for me," he said.

"That will do," said Bartley Bradstone, and he flung a coin toward the group. "Clear off now."

The woman darted at the coin, but as her hand closed over it she said:

"Let me tell this gentleman his fortune."

"Oh, do! oh, come, Mr. Bradstone!" exclaimed the two Penstone girls in chorus. "In common fairness— —"

"Oh, I'm quite ready," said Bartley Bradstone, but with anything but alacrity; and, leaning on his elbow, he extended his right hand reluctantly.

"The left, if you please, gentleman," said the woman.

"You are mighty particular," he said, with an uneasy laugh, and he shifted his position, and gave her the left hand.

As he did so the man took a step forward, and whispered something in the woman's ear.

Her face did not change from its impassibility, but she bent lower over Bartley Bradstone's hand, and amidst the almost solemn silence she said in the dreamy voice she had adopted in the former cases:

"It is a fair hand, a clever hand; but there are lines that trouble the poor gypsy. Lines of the past, and the coming future. Beware of the woman with the black eyes and the cut lip."

Bartley Bradstone changed color, and snatched his hand away.

"That will do," he said. "Don't bother us with anymore, but take yourselves off. And look here; I don't allow gypsies to settle or squat, or whatever you call it, upon my land."

The woman tied the coins she had received in the corner of her apron with deliberate composure, then, dropping a curtsey, followed the man, who had already struck into the thick undergrowth.

"How delightful!" exclaimed Annie Penstone. "Mr. Bradstone, I believe you had them brought here on purpose, just to make your picnic complete."

"No, I didn't," he said, abruptly. "I hate them. They are the worst thieves— —" He stopped. "Bring some more wine," he called to the butler.

"Beware of the woman with the cut lip and the black eyes, Mr. Bradstone!" exclaimed Annie, laughingly.

The butler filled their glasses, and in the midst of the general laughing and talking Bartley Bradstone was recovering his composure, and feeling pretty comfortable again, when he heard the sound of horse's hoofs, and looking up, saw a man on horseback riding into the glade.

The horse was a hunter of good character, and his rider was evidently so lost in thought that he had thrown the reins almost on the animal's neck, and was perfectly indifferent to the course it was taking.

All the picnic party stared at him, and Mary Penstone had just time to whisper to Olivia "What a handsome man!" when Bartley Bradstone sprang to his feet, and seized the horse's loose rein.

It was bad enough to have his grand picnic interrupted by ill-conditioned gypsies, but that an unknown rider should dare to intrude was simply intolerable.

"Here, you, sir!" he exclaimed, angrily, "do you know you are trespassing?"

The gentleman pulled up, and looked from the angry face below him to the rest of the party with a half-awakened expression.

Then he drew the rein from Bartley Bradstone's grasp, and, looking at him calmly, said:

"I beg your pardon. I did not know I was trespassing."

"But you are!" insisted the giver of the feast. "This is private land, and you ought to know it! Confound it, sir, you've no right to ride over private property like this!"

The stranger's face flushed; but before he could speak Bertie sprang to his feet, and approached the two men.

"Mr. Bradstone," he said, "this gentleman is a friend of mine, and I can assure you that he had no desire to trespass— —"

Bartley Bradstone looked from one to the other with his characteristic expression of moody suspicion.

"A friend of yours! Of course that makes a difference. I suppose it's all right."

Olivia had risen, and came slowly toward them. The rest kept their seats.

"Yes, this is a friend of mine—Mr. Faradeane," said Bertie; and he laid his hand upon the bridle of the stranger's horse.

He looked from Bertie to Bartley Bradstone, and then at Olivia, and on her face his eyes seemed fixed.

"Although a friend of Lord Granville, I am still a trespasser," he said, "and I beg your pardon;" and he turned and rode off.

Both Bartley Bradstone and Olivia turned upon Bertie.

"Is he a friend of yours, Lord Granville?" demanded Bartley.

Olivia said nothing, though her eyes were eloquent enough. The color rose to poor Bertie's face.

"It—it is Mr. Faradeane, of The Dell," he stammered—fancy the Cherub stammering!—"I made his acquaintance the day his dog ran loose, Olivia. That's all."

CHAPTER VII
A SIMPLE BIT OF CHARITY

It was the morning after Mr. Bradstone's elaborate picnic, and the clock was striking twelve as Olivia, with her hat and jacket on, knocked at the door of the squire's den, as the room in which he kept his guns and fishing-rods, and in which he transacted his business as justice of the peace, was called.

She knocked twice, then, having received no answer, opened the door and entered.

To her surprise she saw her father seated in his well-worn leather chair, bending over the table, his head leaning on his hand. Before him was a goodly—or evil—array of papers, and his face, as he raised it, wore that anxious and troubled expression which Olivia had seen upon it so often of late.

"I beg your pardon, papa," she said. "I did not want to disturb you, but I knocked twice, and, thinking you were out, ventured in. I want a book for Bessie."

The squire was an inveterate novel reader, and there was always a goodly stock of popular fiction lying about the den.

"A novel. Yes, my dear," and he made an attempt at rising; but Olivia went to him quickly and put her hand upon his shoulder.

"No, you shan't trouble, dear. I can find it. You are busy, I can see."

"Busy?" he said, in a dull way. "Oh, yes, I am, rather," and he sighed.

"Is it anything very troublesome, anything I can help you with?" she inquired, as she turned over the pile of yellow-covered volumes. "I can sometimes, you know."

He shook his head with a mirthless smile.

"I am afraid not, my dear," he said, cheerlessly. "This is a matter which——" He stopped and gazed at her with a sad, vacant expression. "Have you found a book for Bessie? By the way, speaking of her reminds me. I called upon that strange Mr. Faradeane this morning."

Olivia bent over the heap of dusty books, and, after a moment's silence, said:

"Yes, papa; I am glad of that."

"Are you? Why? Well, there's not much to be glad of, for he was not at home."

"He was out riding, perhaps," she said, with the faintest tinge of disappointment in her voice.

"No, he was in," said the squire, dryly. "He was in the house, for I saw him at the window as I went up the path."

Olivia looked round thoughtfully.

"You saw him——"

"At the window. Yes; and he told his servant to say that he was not at home. I must say I was much annoyed. I am not used to rebuffs of that kind, especially from strangers. I was so irritated that I felt inclined to tell the man that I had seen his master, but I thought better of it, and left a card. I think this young fellow is acting in a very extraordinary fashion."

Olivia seemed to ponder for a moment. "Why, dear?" she asked, in a low voice.

"Why?" repeated the squire, with the nearest approach to impatience he ever permitted himself toward his darling. "Well, first by buying The Dell in the strange way he did, and then shunning all intercourse with his neighbors in the mysterious fashion he adopts. I hate mysteries! In my opinion, there is always something shady and shameful at the bottom of them."

"Mr. Faradeane does not look as if he had anything to be ashamed of," she said, in the same low, thoughtful voice.

"No," assented the squire, impatiently; "that is what puzzles me. I never saw a more gentleman-like man, or one with a more prepossessing face. But his manners and conduct——" He pulled up. "However," he continued, "if he prefers to live a secluded and isolated life, why that is his business, not mine. I shall not call again, of course."

"No," said Olivia; "yet Bertie likes him."

"Likes him? How do you know that? Oh, because he spoke up for him yesterday. I don't know why you should say that he 'likes' him."

"I watched Bertie's face," said Olivia, quietly.

The squire knitted his brows.

"It was very unfortunate, his turning up as he did yesterday. And those gypsies, too. It was very annoying for Mr. Bradstone. Did you enjoy the picnic, Olivia?"

"Yes," she replied, indifferently, and turned to the books again.

"It was an admirable luncheon." he said, watching her, with the deep lines graving themselves in his forehead; "admirable. Mr. Bradstone must have spared no expense or trouble. He did his very best to make it a success."

"Oh, yes," she assented, coldly; "I think it was a success. Annie and Mary enjoyed themselves."

"Yes," he said, leaning his head on his hand, and watching her with the same troubled, anxious, wistful gaze. "Yes. Was he very attentive to them? I didn't notice. It would be a very good match for one of them. He is a very rich man, Olivia."

"Is he?" she said, with supreme indifference. "I think this will do for Bessie; I remember reading it. It is full of incident, and yet the characters talk naturally — — "

"Bartley Bradstone is very rich," said the squire, ignoring her criticism of the novel. "He would be a good match for most girls. If he were in London he would be snapped up at once."

"I dare say," said Olivia, turning the leaves of the book carelessly.

"Yes," said the squire, thoughtfully, "money is everything nowadays. It is all that any one thinks of, and Bartley Bradstone has it in abundance."

"Is it all any one thinks of?" said Olivia. "We don't think of it much, dear; but I suppose that's because we have enough of it," and she smiled with blissful serenity.

The squire shifted in his seat and smiled, but, oh, how uneasily!

"Yes, yes, I dare say," he said, "and Bradstone is a good fellow in spite of his money."

"Yes?" said Olivia. "I think I will go now, papa; Bessie will be waiting for me," and, with a nod and a loving smile, she left the room.

The squire looked after her with the same troubled, wistful gaze, then with a deep sigh returned to the heap of papers upon the table.

Olivia, with the book she had selected, and a basket of hothouse flowers, walked down to the lodge.

At the little wicket gate stood Alford, Bessie's father, smoking a pipe, which he instantly caused to disappear as he touched his hat to Olivia.

"Good-morning, Alford!" she said. "How is Bessie this morning? Better, I hope."

"Yes, Miss Olivia, much better. She be more like her old self again this morning—thanks to you, miss, and Mr. Faradeane. She says to me last night that it was worth while being knocked out of the cart to get all the kindness she have had from you and him, miss. Of course, we know how good-hearted you be, miss, as we're used to it; but we didn't expect it from a perfect stranger, so to speak. If Bessie had been his own kith and kin he couldn't have been more kind; and I says, I do, miss, that to set all these here stories again such a thorough, kind-hearted gentleman—ah, and true, brave-handed man, miss—is a crying shame."

"They speak ill of him! Who?" asked Olivia.

Alford looked rather embarrassed, as if he had said more than he had intended.

"Oh, miss, you know what Hawkwood folks be! They give every stranger a bad name if they don't know his mother and his father, and all he's been and what he is. And as they don't know nothing about Mr. Faradeane, why, they just blackguard him, that's all. I was in the George last night—I just looked in for a drop o' brandy for Bessie, in case she wanted it," he put in hurriedly and with a little cough, "and I heard some of 'em a-talkin' nonsense about him; but I set 'em down, I did, miss, and pretty smartly. Harry Tucker says I cracked his skull; but don't you believe that, miss, it's impossible—it's too thick."

Olivia could scarcely repress a smile at this naïve statement.

"I'm afraid you will get into trouble, Alford," she said, with her gentle gravity.

"Oh, no, miss," he responded, cheerfully, "don't you be afraid of me. But if it meant six months in jail I'd stand for the gentleman as saved my Bessie."

"And I think you're right," said Olivia, with a sudden warmth which astonished Alford, and made her blush a moment afterward. "I—I mean that of course it is absurd to suppose that because Mr. Faradeane is a stranger he must necessarily be disreputable—and—and—unworthy. Why, Alford, a wicked man would never have risked his limbs for Bessie, as Mr. Faradeane did."

"Do not be too sure of that, Miss Vanley," said a voice, and Olivia, starting, turned and saw the man she had been defending. He had come round the bend by the thick garden hedge, unperceived by either Alford or herself.

Olivia stood with her hands on the gate, white and red by turns, and Alford coughed and shuffled in awkward confusion.

Mr. Faradeane regarded them with a faint smile that was more sad than mirthful.

"As a rule, listeners hear anything but good of themselves, Miss Vanley," he said, raising his hat. "This is the exception. Thank you for your defense, but I fear that it is not, as the lawyers would say, a sound one."

Olivia fought down her strange shyness—strange because it had never until now attacked her in the presence of any man.

"Was it not?" she said, in a low voice. "I thought it was a very reasonable proposition."

He shook his head, still with the same grave smile.

"Some of the worst men have been conspicuous by their courage as well as their crimes. There was a convict the other day who stood up on behalf of a warder who had been attacked by the rest of the gang, some fifteen in number. When they came to inquire into the man's antecedents they found that he, who had defended his keeper at the risk of his own life, had been sentenced to penal servitude for a particularly bad case of manslaughter. That's a modern instance. Ancient history is full of examples of bad men who have exhibited, not once, but many times, extraordinary courage— have even done braver things than stopping a small pony," and he smiled.

"Ah!" grunted Alford, "I thought it was coming to that. Mr. Faradeane always tries to make out as it was nothing at all; and look at his forehead," and he pointed to the scar.

Olivia raised her eyes to it, and met his grave, sad, half-smiling gaze, beneath which her own drooped instantly.

"I am afraid you won't succeed in persuading me that I am even a second-rate hero, Alford," he said. "How is Bessie this morning?"

Alford told him that she was much better, and Mr. Faradeane turned as if to go, when a sudden impulse seized Olivia, and, falteringly, she said:

"I—I am so sorry for what occurred yesterday at the picnic, Mr. Faradeane."

He stopped and looked at her absently for a moment, as if the incident had escaped his memory; then he said:

"Pray don't give it a moment's thought or regret. Mr. Bradstone's indignation was very natural. Trespassers are a nuisance at any time; but at a picnic they are intolerable. I have written to Mr. Bradstone apologizing for my intrusion, and assuring him that 'it shan't occur again.' I hope you had a pleasant day."

"Very," said Olivia; and he turned to go again, when she said: "My father called on you this morning. He was sorry to find you were out."

He looked down at the path in grave silence for a moment; then he said, as he raised his eyes to hers:

"Will you please thank Mr. Vanley for his courtesy. I live a very solitary and secluded life, Miss Vanley."

"Does that mean that you decline his acquaintance?" asked Olivia, in her straightforward way.

His brow furrowed with a wistful, troubled frown.

"I am afraid it does," he said. "I am what is called a recluse, a misanthrope——"

"What is called," said Olivia, quietly; "a misanthrope who stops runaway ponies, and takes the trouble to inquire daily after a sick girl! Isn't that a little inconsistent?"

He smiled.

"You are rather hard upon me," he said, in a low voice. He paused. "I am sorry I did not see Mr. Vanley this morning; but consider—what sympathy, what friendship could exist between Harold Faradeane of The Dell and the Squire of Hawkwood?"

Olivia flushed.

"Do you think my father values a man by the size of the house he inhabits, Mr. Faradeane?"

"I think him a high-minded English gentleman," he responded, with grave earnestness, "but between a man in his position and a man in mine there is a vast difference."

Olivia bit her lip, and turned aside with a slight bow.

"Will you give these to Bessie, Alford?" she said, as if she had finished with Mr. Faradeane.

He stood with his dark, sad eyes fixed on the ground; then he approached her.

"I have offended you," in a low, almost an appealing voice.

Olivia turned to him with lowered lids.

"Oh, no."

"Your words say 'No,' but your tone says 'Yes,'" he said.

Olivia tried to laugh.

"Well, you must admit that one may be rather displeased at having one's overtures of friendship declined, however politely," she said.

He dug a stone out of the path with his stick; then he looked up at her.

"You have put the case candidly; but think, Miss Vanley—your father knows nothing of me. He has paid me the attention of a call, because I was so fortunate as to be of slight service to one of his servants. Am I to take advantage of such an accident? He knows nothing of me, remember."

"My father is perfectly free to choose his friends," she retorted. "He would have called on you, even if this accident of Bessie's had not occurred."

He struck the pebble he had dug out, and sighed.

"Do not tempt me," he murmured, in so low a voice that Olivia did not hear him.

"What did you say?" she asked.

He fixed his dark eyes on hers.

"Miss Vanley," he said, the lines of his forehead deepening, as if he were going through a mental struggle, "I came to this place resolved to isolate myself, separate myself, from the society of my fellowmen. My reasons are of no consequence in the argument. I came here to bury myself. Chance, accident, Providence, as some would call it, has thrown me into intercourse with my neighbors."

"Providence," murmured Olivia.

He inclined his head.

"Your father has come to me and extended the right hand of fellowship— —"

"He was not the first; there was Bertie—I mean Lord Granville," put in Olivia, softly. "You consented to know him."

"The Cherub?" he said. Then, as Olivia looked up with a start, he colored. "He is called the Cherub, is he not?"

"Yes," she said, perplexedly. "I did not know you knew that."

He nodded.

"Yes, I have made the acquaintance of Lord Granville. His *sobriquet* is pretty well known, I think."

"Every one likes Bertie," she said.

He glanced at her inquiringly, as he assented:

"Yes, and there must be a great deal of good in the man or woman whom everybody likes. Speaking of the Cherub, here comes the flutter of his wings," he added, as Bertie's voice was heard in the lane.

"There is some one with him. It is my aunt," said Olivia, as Miss Amelia's falsetto was heard joining with Bertie's. The next moment they came around the corner.

"Oh, here is Olivia!" said Miss Amelia. Then she pulled up short, with a little, affected start at sight of the tall, handsome man.

Bertie came forward with his usual eagerness.

"We have been looking for you, Olivia," he said, his eyes dwelling on her with the light that always shone in them. "And I told Miss Amelia this would turn out a sure find. Good-morning, Faradeane!"

Miss Amelia gave another start, and coughed nervously.

"This is my aunt—Miss Vanley!" said Olivia. "This is Mr. Faradeane, aunt."

Miss Amelia bent her head.

"Delighted, I'm sure!" she simpered in the conciliatory voice which old ladies use to dogs and dangerous characters. "Quite a—a—pleasant surprise."

Mr. Faradeane bowed, with the suspicion of a smile flickering under his mustache.

"I'm sure we are all very much indebted to Mr. Faradeane for his heroic rescue of Bessie Alford, very much so—ahem!" and she coughed again. "I hope it will prove a lesson to her. All these things, if properly viewed, are sent for our good."

"Mr. Faradeane was certainly sent for Bessie's, on this occasion," said Olivia, strangely irritated by her aunt's half-suspicious, half-irritating manner.

Bertie, with his usual promptitude, cut in to set matters on an easier footing.

"I'm glad to hear Bessie's better. I called as I was going up to the house. And now, Olivia, I'll bet you two to one in Dent's best that you don't guess what Miss Amelia wants me to do."

"May I have three tries?" said Olivia, with a smile.

"Something good and laudable, I am sure," said Faradeane.

Miss Amelia's gaze softened, and she bridled and smiled.

"Oh, thank you, Mr. Faradeane," she simpered.

"Is it to subscribe to the Mothers' Sewing Club?" said Olivia.

"No," said Bertie.

"To teach in the Sunday-school. No?" as Bertie shook his head. "To give the pug or the canary a dose of medicine?"

"No!" he cried, triumphantly. "You've lost. I take large nines," and he held out his tiny fist. "Miss Amelia's modest request is that I should give a reading at the forthcoming village entertainment."

Olivia laughed.

"I'd forgotten the entertainment," she said.

"My dear Olivia," murmured Miss Amelia, solemnly, "you should never be weary of doing good."

"I do too little to be anything like weary," said Olivia. "Of course you have consented, Bertie?"

He made a gesture of mock horror.

"I!" he exclaimed. "Great goodness! Fancy me attempting to recite! Why, I should have stage fright, and fall in a fit off the platform!" and he laughed. "Now, Faradeane here is a first-class amateur actor, and used to all this kind of thing——" He pulled up short, warned by Faradeane's grave, steady gaze, and Olivia's look of astonishment. "That is, I should think so," said poor Bertie. "He looks like it, while I——Oh! the mere thought of facing a room full of people sends cold shivers through me."

He had not got out of it so badly after all, and, quite unwittingly, Miss Amelia helped.

"Really," she simpered, surveying the handsome face, with its grave smile, "really, I think Bertie is right, and that Mr. Faradeane has—er—that kind of face, and I am sure he will not refuse to help us in our effort to amuse our humbler neighbors."

"And air our own accomplishments," added Olivia, with a smile.

"My dear Olivia——" began Miss Amelia, with her severest air; but Bertie cut in again.

"I think you'd better, Faradeane," he said; "that is, if you can, and I think you have got the reciter's face. Something awfully tragic, you know."

"Such as 'The Little Vulgar Boy,' or 'The Jackdaw of Rheims,'" murmured Miss Amelia, coaxingly. "Some people insist that they are too frivolous; but I maintain, and always shall maintain, that we may draw a lesson from even the most trivial stories."

"'The Little Vulgar Boy,' for instance, aunt. What is the lesson?"

"Not to put any trust in strangers," said Mr. Faradeane, quietly, and with the same flickering smile.

Olivia colored, Bertie looked embarrassed, and Miss Amelia laughed awkwardly.

"Oh, come," said Bertie; "I'm sure you will give them something with a moral tagged to it. Better say yes, Faradeane."

There was silence for a moment or two.

"Perhaps I'd better state that the proceeds of the entertainment will be devoted to the funds of the Muffin and Crumpet Society," said Miss Amelia, with due solemnity.

Mr. Faradeane looked up gravely.

"That decides it," he said. "I shall be very pleased to place my poor services at the disposal of so worthy a cause."

"You see, Olivia!" exclaimed Miss Amelia. "You are always laughing at the society. Now, Mr. Faradeane, whose opinion is, I am sure, of the greatest value, testifies to its great usefulness."

"Any cause advocated by Miss Vanley," he said, with a bow, "must necessarily be a laudable and deserving one."

Miss Amelia simpered and bridled with pleasure, and Olivia turned to hide a smile.

"I am going up to see Bessie," she said. "Will you come with me, aunt?" and she bowed to Faradeane and nodded smilingly at Bertie.

"Good-morning, Mr. Faradeane," said Miss Amelia, giving him her hand graciously. "You will not forget. The twenty-ninth, at the schoolroom. I will send you a programme. Let me see; I think I shall put you between the vicar's concertina and Miss Browne's 'Three Little Pigs.'"

"Good gracious!" exclaimed Bertie, aghast.

"I understand, Miss Vanley," said Mr. Faradeane, with perfect gravity; and, linking his arm in Bertie's, he raised his hat and walked away.

For some few moments the two men did not speak; then Faradeane said:

"You are thinking that I am a weak-minded kind of idiot, eh, Cherub?"

Bertie gave a little start.

"I——No, I wasn't thinking about you, old fellow," he replied. "I was thinking of Olivia. How beautiful she looked this morning!"

"Yes," assented Faradeane, succinctly.

"I think her lovelier and sweeter every time I see her," continued Bertie, with a sigh. Then he pulled himself together. "But I say, fancy finding her and you chatting together like old friends!"

"Yes, and after my solemn declaration the other day that nothing should induce me to know her or any one else," retorted Faradeane. "But men propose and the gods dispose. Only this morning I refused to see her father, and now——"

"I'm glad, awfully glad," said Bertie, eagerly. "I can't tell you how delighted I was to see you with her. And I tell you what, old fellow: you may consider yourself highly honored. It isn't every one Miss Olivia is free and—and pleasant with at starting. As a rule, people think her stiff and—and—cold, don't you know, till they know more of her."

Faradeane nodded, with his dark eyes bent on the ground.

"Yes, she could be stiff and reserved," he said, more to himself than to Bertie.

"Rather! They all call her proud, and so she is, in a right way. God bless her! She is everything that is right to me. And you have promised to spout for them, old fellow! I'm awfully glad of that, too."

"Yes," said Faradeane, grimly. "The man who falls into the river may just as well take a bath; he couldn't be wetter. So go all my resolutions to the winds!" he added, with a kind of desperation. "But mind, Bertie, our compact remains in full force. I am still the Harold Faradeane whose acquaintance you made the other day for the first time! Remember, you do not know, cannot guess, how much depends on your caution."

"I know. I'm awfully sorry I made that slip," said Bertie, penitently. "But it is so hard to talk as if you and I were strangers until the other day."

"Hard as it is, you will have to do it, Cherub," responded Faradeane, gravely.

"And I—I cannot help you—you will tell me nothing?" said Bertie, gently.

"You cannot help me; and I can tell you nothing," replied Faradeane.

As he spoke they reached the gate of The Dell, and saw a woman coming down the path from the cottage. She held something closely wrapped in her thin shawl, from which proceeded the unmistakable wail of a sick child.

Faradeane smiled grimly.

"The first time the gate has been unlocked, and the great disturber of man's peace finds entrance instantly," he said.

"Why, it's the gypsy who told our fortunes yesterday at the picnic, you know," said Bertie.

The anxious, black eyes flashed from face to face, and she dropped a curtsey.

"Will you help a poor woman in distress, kind gentlemen?" she said.

"Oh, come, my good woman," said Bertie, "your memory is a short one. Why, you made enough yesterday to keep the wolf from the door for some days."

The woman looked at him keenly, but not angrily.

"I didn't ask for money for myself," she said; "it's my child—my little girl," and she drew the shawl a few inches from the child's face.

"What's the matter with her?" asked Bertie, in quite a different voice.

Faradeane leaned against the gate, and looked on with an absent air of preoccupation.

"She's ill, sir," replied the gypsy. "She was took ill yesterday. I don't know what ails her. It's my only one, kind gentlemen, and——" She stopped and looked at Faradeane. "Ah! it's hard to understand a mother's feelings."

"I dare say," said Bertie, gently. "But why do you keep her out in the open air? The day is chilly, and you earned plenty of money yesterday to find shelter for her."

The gypsy shook her head slowly.

"That's gone, sir," she said, with that quiet resignation which women acquire, Heaven help them!

"I see," said Bertie. "Your husband—the man who was with you——"

She nodded, and raised her hand to her lips with the action of drinking.

"Yes, gentlemen, he's my husband, and the money's gone where it always goes. If he'd only left me enough to buy a blanket or a thick shawl for her; but——"

She stopped and rocked the child, crooning to it soothingly.

Bertie put his hand in his pocket, then uttered an exclamation of disappointment.

"By Jove! I've left my purse in my other coat. Faradeane, lend me——"

Faradeane straightened himself and came forward.

"Let me look at the child," he said, in his low, musical voice.

The woman looked up at him for an instant with the mother's searching glance; then, reading something in his eyes that reassured her, threw the shawl off the child's face and turned it toward him.

It was a poor, thin little mite, whose face should have been white, but was flushed and burning.

Faradeane took it from her.

"Don't be afraid," he said, gently, as she clung to it a little.

"Are you a doctor, gentleman?" she asked, looking up at Faradeane, eagerly.

"No, no," said Bertie. "But you can rely on what he says. What is it, Faradeane?" he asked, in a lower voice.

Faradeane looked at the child attentively.

"Fever," he said. "The child has been exposed to this charming English spring of ours. Poor mite!"

The woman's dark eyes grew moist, and her hands clasped together with a spasmodic action.

"Is—is it going to die, gentleman?" she asked, huskily. "It's—it's the only one I've got left, and—and, bein' a girl, I've got fond of it like," she added, apologetically.

"I hope it won't die," he said, gently, "but it is very bad. This thin shawl—wait a moment," and he handed the child back to her.

She pressed it to her bosom with a choking sob, and bent over it speechlessly.

Faradeane came out of the cottage again presently with a traveling wrap of gray fox and sable; a rare and costly fur even for a man of wealth—a wrap which many a lady would have coveted with the fiercest longing.

As he was wrapping this round the child, touching it as gently as he had done poor Bessie, Bertie laid his hand upon his arm.

"Isn't that rather extravagant, old fellow?" he said, in a voice too low for the woman to hear. "A blanket would have served the purpose, besides, the father will requisition that the moment he sees it."

Faradeane shrugged his shoulders.

"It will keep the little one warm till it gets to the hospital. That's where you're to send it." He took out his pocketbook, and, tearing out a sheet, wrote a few lines on it. "Take the child on to the doctor's at Wainford, and do as he tells you. He knows me; he is the doctor who is attending Bessie Alford," he looked round, to explain to Bertie. "Tell him that I will pay what the hospital people demand, and here is some money to go on with. Keep it from your husband—if you can," he added, grimly.

The woman took the paper and the money, and looked from the child, whose wailing seemed already less despairing, to the costly rug, and, lastly, up at the handsome face and the sad eyes regarding her with a grave pity.

Her black eyes filled, her lips twitched, but for a moment she seemed speechless; then she looked at Bertie appealingly.

"I—I can't tell him," she said, piteously. "If it was for myself, I could thank him; but it is for the child, and—and I don't know; but in my heart," and she pressed the child to her with a fierce energy, "but I feel it in my heart."

"That's all right," said Faradeane, nodding to her, soothingly. "Oh, wait; I must give the doctor your name. What is it?" and he took the paper from her.

"Liz Lee," she said, with a little catch in her breath.

He filled it in instantly, and returned the paper to her.

She looked at Bertie.

"Ask him if he'll tell me his," she said, addressing Bertie again instead of Faradeane, as if she could not trust herself to speak to him directly.

"Faradeane," said Bertie; "go and do as my friend tells you."

The woman nodded, and, with a long, steady look at Faradeane, turned down the path and out of the gate.

Bertie turned to Faradeane.

"That was kind of you, old fellow," he said. "Just like you, too—so thoughtful and—and considerate."

Faradeane seemed to wake up, as if from a reverie.

"My dear Cherub," he said, banteringly, "why will you try and throw a glamour over a simple bit of charity which really costs me nothing?"

"Yes," said Bertie, "that's true; it costs you nothing to speak and look so that the woman was too moved to speak and look at you. And you tell me that you have committed a wrong which ought to shut you out of society," he burst out.

Faradeane's head drooped, and, with a half-suppressed sigh, he laid his hand on Bertie's shoulder.

"Hush!" he said. "Let us go in now and get some lunch."

The woman moved rapidly, and yet carefully, so as not to disturb the now sleeping child, down the lane in the direction of Wainford.

She had gone about a couple of hundred yards when the man who had been with her at the picnic came along the road.

His face was flushed, and his gait distinguished by that unsteadiness which is displayed by the individual who is just on the brink of the drunkard's seventh heaven.

She shrank back and looked round, as if with the idea of avoiding him, but his sharp, black eyes—sharp even when dim with drink—saw her, and he came across the road.

"Hallo, Liz," he said, thickly, "whadger done? Wher'yer been? Is that the kid? Why——" He stopped short, and laid a hot hand upon the fur. "Where'd yer lift this?"

"I didn't lift it, Seth," she replied. "It was lent to me by a gentleman. Have you got any money left, Seth? I want it for Lizzie; she's that ill," she added, with the cunning of her kind, knowing well that if she didn't ask money of him he would of her.

"Money! no," he replied, with an oath. "It's gone, every copper of it. Why didn't you get some from the solt as gave you this? It's a stunner!" he went on, stroking the fur lovingly, his eyes growing sharp and covetous. "This 'ere's worth a mint o' money—two or three pound, most like. Give it to me, Liz, and I'll sell it to the landlord o' the George."

"No, no, not this, Seth. It was given for Lizzie. Look how warm she is——"

"Hang the kid!" he retorted, harshly; "wrap it in a sack—anything. What! Do you mean as you'd waste a valuable thing like this on a brat?"

"Leave it alone," she said, her voice changing from the pleading to the fierce. "Let go of it, Seth. You shan't have it!" and her spare hand closed on it with the clutch—well, the clutch of a mother defending her child.

The man snarled and snatched at the fur, and in doing so turned up a corner and showed the lining of crimson silk. There was something embroidered on it in gold thread, and he bent down to look at it.

The design, whatever it was, had been partly picked out or cut away; but a portion of a crest and an initial still remained, and Seth's eyes were glued to it for a moment.

Then, in a changed voice, he said:

"Who gave you this, Liz?"

"I don't know," she panted. "Let it go, Seth. You shan't have it, if I die for it. Let me go with the child."

"Hold your noise," he said, between his teeth, and glancing round. "Who wants it? You may go to the devil, and the kid with you, for what I care. Just let me know where you got this skin, that's all."

"I got it from the gent as lives in the cottage in the hollow, Seth," she said, drawing the fur from his hand. "He was good to me, he was——"

"He gave you money!" he said, sharply.

"No, no money," she replied, with ready falsehood; "nothing but the rug. But it wasn't that; it was the way he spoke and handled poor Lizzie. And he says she's bad, Seth! And I'll lose her—yes, I'll lose her like the rest." Her voice broke. "Let me go!"

"Stop your sniveling!" he snarled, and as he spoke he tore out the corner of the lining which bore the partly-erased coat-of-arms.

"There you are," he said. "That's all I want. Be off with you."

CHAPTER VIII
"TOO LATE!"

Two days after that of the incident with Liz Lee, Harold Faradeane walked with his slow, firm step up to the Grange, and inquired for Mr. Vanley, and as he stood in the drawing-room, to which the footman had conducted him, his handsome face wore a look of half-bitter, half-cynical self-contempt. Only a few days ago he had assured Bertie that nothing would induce him to emerge from his seclusion, and here he was returning the squire's visit.

"No man is so great a fool as he who knows himself to be one!" he muttered; then, as the door opened, he turned to greet the squire.

He was received by the squire as if the latter had quite forgotten that he had been refused admittance to The Dell; and Mr. Faradeane was too cultivated a gentleman to offer any apologies for the denial.

The two men got into conversation at once, and the squire, who had been much prejudiced against the newcomer, almost unconsciously began to be "taken" with him. The grave and self-restrained manner and the handsome face, which had fascinated Olivia, prepossessed her father.

Whatever mystery hung like a dark cloud about Mr. Faradeane, it was patent that he was a gentleman, and anything but one of the common or garden kind. No matter what topic the squire started, his visitor could converse upon it, and, what was more, evidently knew something about it.

And he talked in that most pleasing of fashions, as if he were talking for the sake of hearing what his host had to say, and with the easy deference which marks the man of good birth and breeding and high refinement.

Nearly three-quarters of an hour passed before Mr. Faradeane, glancing at the clock on the mantelshelf, rose, and said:

"I have detained you an unconscionable time, Mr. Vanley; but, indeed, that is more your fault than mine."

"You have not detained me at all," responded the squire, in his quiet, direct way. "I am an old man, and am delighted to meet with one so well informed, and, permit me to add, so good a talker as yourself. You must have seen a great deal of life, Mr. Faradeane."

A grave look seemed to settle for a moment on the handsome face, and the dark eyes grew momentarily sadder, and the squire instantly saw that he had touched a tender spot; but almost immediately the younger man replied, with a smile:

"Yes, more than most men of my years, sir."

"I am afraid you will find Hawkwood rather dull, and the inhabitants very old fogies; but we must do our best to amuse you. I don't know whether you care for fishing; if you do, I hope you will flog the river as often as you please. I am afraid to say how long it is since I threw a fly."

"Thank you," said Mr. Faradeane. "Yes, I am an angler."

"And in the autumn I can promise you some fair shooting. The keepers tell me that the birds are looking well. I hope you intend staying with us. We've a very good pack of foxhounds, and I know that you ride, for I have heard one of my grooms expatiating on the fine qualities of your horse."

"Thank you again, sir," said Mr. Faradeane. "He is a fairish hunter, and a very good companion. Yes, I intend remaining for some time, I hope, in Hawkwood. I have purchased The Dell, as you may have heard."

"Yes," assented the squire, almost reddening angrily as he thought of the unwarranted suspicions Mr. Sparrow had given expression to about the newcomer.

"I came to The Dell for rest," said Mr. Faradeane, "and had intended playing the hermit, but"—and the rare smile shone in his eyes for a moment—"but your kindness has rendered that impossible."

"I should think so," returned the squire, with unusual heartiness. "You are not the stuff of which hermits are made, Mr. Faradeane, and I am only afraid we shall trespass on your good nature. Hawkwood does not get a novelty very often, and will, very properly, regard you as an acquisition. I understand my sister Amelia has already cajoled you into assisting at one of her local enterprises. Take care! If you give an inch to one of these charitable ladies, they will take an ell!"

"It is a very small inch," said Harold Faradeane, simply. "I am only going to recite at some penny readings."

"And the next thing she will want you to do will be to take a tray at a tea-meeting," said the squire, with a laugh.

"Would that be very difficult?" inquired the younger man, with such quaint gravity that the squire burst into a laugh of keen appreciation.

It happened that Olivia was passing through the hall at the moment, and the sound of her father's laughter, which had become so rare of late, almost startled her.

"Who is in the drawing-room?" she asked of the butler.

"The squire, miss, and Mr. Faradeane of The Dell," he replied.

Olivia stopped short with a sudden throb of her heart that sent the blood to her face, and she bent down and gathered the skirt of her habit—she had just come in from a gallop—to hide it.

"Mr. Faradeane, the new gentleman, miss," said the butler, and he moved toward the door as if to open it for her, but Olivia shook her head.

"No, I am not going in," she said, and went quickly upstairs. As she did so, the drawing-room opened, and she heard the squire say, in his most genial tone—the tone which indicated that he was peculiarly well pleased, "You must let me show you round the old place, Mr. Faradeane," and she paused and listened for the grave, musical voice replying in the affirmative; then, leaning over the old oak balustrade, looked down at them as they passed out, with a strange expression on her lovely face—an expression which it had never yet worn for any man she had seen!

The squire and Mr. Faradeane made their way round the grounds, and presently, as if unconsciously, the elder man linked his arm within that of the younger, an action very unusual with the squire, and one which indicated the favorable impression his visitor had made upon him.

"It is a very beautiful place," said Mr. Faradeane, when they had made the round of the flower gardens and lawns, and looked in at the great, walled garden, with its hundreds of peach and nectarine trees, and at the long length of green-houses in which the gardener grew the choice flowers which would, if he had entered them, have taken the first prize at all the local shows, "a very beautiful place; I think it would be sinful not to be proud of it, Mr. Vanley."

The squire looked at him with a nod of appreciation, then suddenly his face clouded, and he stifled a sigh.

"There is plenty of room for improvement," he said, as if to account for the sigh.

"There always is," said Faradeane. "Fortunately, no place is perfect—we should tire of it very soon if it were. Don't you think a plantation on that rise to the left of the lawn would be a good thing?"

The squire nodded.

"Yes," he said, moodily. "Yes; but it would cost——" He stopped and glanced at the handsome face quickly. "I'm afraid you think I must be very niggardly to grudge a few hundreds for so evident an improvement; but——"

He paused; and Faradeane, with the tact which seemed so easy when he chose to display it, said:

"In these days no man has too much money."

"That is true," assented the squire, as if glad of the excuse so pleasantly offered. "Quite true; these are hard times for us landlords everywhere."

"Indeed they are," acquiesced Faradeane.

The squire looked at him.

"Are you one of the unfortunate army of landowners?" he inquired.

Faradeane paused for half a second, then he laughed.

"You forget that I am the landlord of The Dell, and quite half an acre of garden land! And that reminds me that I must be going. Thank you very much, Mr. Vanley."

The squire shook the strong, shapely hand warmly, and stood for a moment looking after the tall, patrician figure as it made its way with strong, easy stride across the grass; then he went back to the house with a grave, wistful face. Perhaps he was wishing that Heaven had given him such a son as a brother to his precious Olivia; or, perhaps he was thinking of the plantation and the hard times which made the expenditure of the "few hundreds" not only difficult, but impossible.

Olivia was standing at the door, waiting for him.

"You have had a visitor, papa?" she said, quietly, and in the tone one uses when one has rehearsed a speech—almost too careless and indifferent.

"Yes, yes," he said, "Mr. Faradeane. He has just gone. I am sorry you were not in to see him."

"Was he worth seeing, then?" said Olivia, still too carelessly.

"He is one of the most cultivated men I have ever met," replied the squire, warmly and emphatically, "and when I think of the absurd nonsense old Sparrow talked the other day, I am inclined to call him an idiot. Mr. Faradeane is a gentleman every inch of him, and one of the most charming young men possible."

"I am very glad you like him, as he is so near a neighbor," she said.

"Yes, liking is the word. He has quite taken a hold on me. The reason for his coming and burying himself at The Dell may be a mystery, but it is no unworthy one; I am quite convinced of that. He talks admirably; not with the straining after-effect which is the great vice of the present day, but with the pleasant manner of a man who wants to hear you as well as himself. By the way, your aunt has caught him for that entertainment of hers on the twenty-ninth. Do you think he would dine with us?"

"Do I think?" replied Olivia, raising her dark brows with a smile. "You know more of Mr. Faradeane than I do, papa? What do you think?"

"I don't know," said the squire, thoughtfully. "I've an idea that he forced himself to call, and that he might decline. It isn't pride; no, that man couldn't foster so vulgar a sentiment; not pride, but a strange kind of reserve that crops up now and again in his manner and conversation. Strange! Perhaps it is some past trouble. Well, we can but ask him."

Olivia turned her head aside, and toyed with a branch of Virginia creeper.

"Very well, papa; any one else?"

"Eh? Oh, yes, if you like. Bartley Bradstone and Bertie. Bertie likes him, I'm sure; and Annie and Mary Penstone. As many as you like—no, don't make it a large party. I fancy he would prefer a very small one."

"You are more considerate of Mr. Faradeane's whims and fancies than you usually are of other people's, papa," she said, with a smile.

He looked at her as if the same idea had struck him.

"Am I? Well, I've taken a fancy to him, I suppose; at any rate, I should like to know more of him. Ask him, and see what he says."

Faradeane was sitting at his desk writing, when, the next morning, a groom rode over with the invitation, and he took it and looked at the address, in Olivia's handwriting, for a good minute before opening the envelope. Then he read the short, formal note, and reread it; got up and lit a pipe, and paced up and down with the letter in his hand, a troubled, wistful expression on his face, an expression of hesitation, over which longing predominated.

"Too late!" he muttered; "too late to draw back now. I have passed the Rubicon, and yet—oh, fool! fool!"

Then he sat down and wrote a formal acceptation.

People did not refuse an invitation to dine at the Grange unless they were positively compelled, for the squire's dinners were as nearly perfect as they could be; and those who did not set their hearts on the dinner found the prospect of a couple of hours spent in the Grange drawing-room, with Olivia to talk to and perhaps to sing for them, equally irresistible; and all the guests the squire had named to Olivia came up to time on the twenty-ninth.

It was an early dinner, for the entertainment commenced at eight, and all but the squire, whom wild horses would not have drawn out of his house after dinner to an entertainment, were going to Aunt Amelia's concert.

Annie and Mary Penstone had driven over in the afternoon to snatch a very precious quiet hour with Olivia, and they were both on the tiptoe of feverish curiosity and excitement about the mysterious Mr. Faradeane.

"Is he so very strange, Olly dear?" asked Mary, eagerly, and in a hushed voice. "We hear such extraordinary stories—all invented, of course—but do tell us! What is he like? Of course, we know he is handsome. Annie says that he is the handsomest man she has ever seen; but that's nonsense while Lord Granville is here. What does he seem like? What does he talk about?"

"Papa could tell you better than I can," replied Olivia, smiling. "I have only spoken to him once or twice. He has a very pleasant voice and—but you heard him speak at the picnic."

"Oh, yes, wasn't that awful! I shall never forget the look of his eyes! If he had looked at me like that, so—so, not contemptuously quite, but so calmly and indifferently—I can't express it—as he looked at Mr. Bradstone, I should have gone through the ground!"

"Like one of the patent tube wells," said Olivia.

"Don't laugh at me. I mean what I say, dear," said Mary, pouting. "I'm sure I shall be afraid to speak to him, in case he should snub me. He looks as if he could be awfully severe."

"He is not, I assure you; a child could play with him," said Olivia.

"There you are, laughing again. It's all very well for you; of course, he'd be nice to you, everybody always is; nobody could be otherwise to such a dear, beautiful girl; but poor Annie and me— —"

"Poor Annie and me will be quite safe," laughed Olivia. "Mr. Faradeane does not even bark, least of all bite."

This was a few minutes before dinner, and the entrance of Bertie and Bartley Bradstone stopped the interesting conversation.

"We are only waiting for Mr. Faradeane," said the squire, glancing at his watch, after the usual greetings had been got through.

"Faradeane?" said Bartley Bradstone as he stood in an easy—too easy—attitude, his evening suit cut in the very last fashion, and a costly diamond blazing in the center of his white shirt-front. "Faradeane? Is he coming?" and his brows came down with the half-sullen, half-suspicious frown.

"Yes," said the squire, "and I am glad to say we have struck up a friendship. He is one of the pleasantest men— —"

"He might be polite as well as pleasant," said Bartley Bradstone, looking at his watch. "It isn't quite the thing for a newcomer to keep us all waiting."

Bertie cut in quickly.

"It wants two minutes to six," he said; "your watch is fast, Mr. Bradstone."

"It's one of Dent & Frodsham's chronometers," he retorted.

"It's fast all the same," said Bertie, firmly, but pleasantly. "I timed mine at the station an hour or two ago."

Before Bartley Bradstone could meet this argument, the door opened, and the footman announced Mr. Faradeane, and the great hall clock chimed the hour.

Every eye was, not unnaturally, turned upon the latest guest, and Olivia thought that Annie was right as she glanced at the tall figure and handsome face. Unlike Mr. Bartley Bradstone, his dress-suit was not in the latest cut, and instead of a blazing diamond was a plain black pearl.

An expression of approval shone in the squire's eyes, for Faradeane's appearance in evening dress confirmed the squire in his good opinion of him.

"You have just come in time to prevent a duel of time-pieces," he said.

Aunt Amelia simpered.

"I, at any rate, was sure Mr. Faradeane was not late," said she, graciously.

"Then, as a reward, you shall be taken in by him," said the squire, offering his arm to Mary. Bertie, the highest in rank, escorted Annie; and, Faradeane having Aunt Amelia, Olivia was left to Bartley Bradstone.

"This is a rough-and-scramble meal," said the squire, as the butler lifted the cover from the fish, "but if you will perpetrate such follies as penny readings, you must pay the penalty."

"My brother ridicules our humble efforts to amuse and instruct our brethren, Mr. Faradeane; but he is always doing good himself, which he never mentions."

"Nor permits any one else to mention," said the squire.

"'Do not let your right hand know what your left hand doeth,' as the man said who put a bad shilling in the collecting-box," said Faradeane.

Annie and Mary almost started. Was this the mysterious stranger whose dark, contemptuous eyes had smitten them with awe? And could it be possible that his first words should be a frivolous jest? They began by being astonished, and continued so during the whole of the meal, for Mr. Faradeane, if he did not quite "set the table in a roar," kept them all perpetually amused.

If it had not been so perfectly natural and free from the appearance of effort, it would almost have seemed as if he were playing the part of the wit with a purpose; but the musical voice was quite easy and unstrained, and the dark eyes were cloudless and unreserved. The squire glowed with sympathetic delight as epigram after epigram fell quite naturally from his guest, and Bertie's eyes sparkled with fun as he laughed at the dry humor and happy repartee.

Only two persons seemed unmoved. One was Bartley Bradstone, who sat in half-sullen, half-envious silence, taking no part in the conversation beyond a monosyllabic response, and inwardly and palpably chafing at the success the newcomer was obviously making.

The other was Olivia. At first she had smiled with the rest, but presently she happened to glance round the *épergne* which stood between her and Mr. Faradeane, and at that instant she caught his face off its guard, as it were, and saw a strange sadness falling like a shadow on his eyes and hovering about his lips. It was gone in a moment, but its remembrance haunted her, and she knew that the wit and the humor and the light-heartedness were assumed, and magnificently assumed, to hide some secret sorrow.

And as she listened as he told a story which convulsed Bertie and Annie and Mary, and made the squire laugh the hearty laugh which was so rare with him, there flashed upon her the well-known anecdote of the comedian who succeeded in convulsing a theatre with laughter while his thoughts were fixed upon his favorite child, who lay dying while he played.

"A most delightful man!" exclaimed Aunt Amelia, as the ladies filed into the drawing-room. "I never laughed so much in my life."

"Nor I!" exclaimed Mary and Annie. "And he scarcely smiled himself. Did you see the squire laugh, Olly, dear? Why, he isn't at all what I fancied he would be! I'm not a bit afraid of him. But you didn't seem so amused, dear; you didn't laugh scarcely at all. Why was that?" and she wound her arm round Olivia's waist.

"It's because I'm so stupid," replied Olivia. "You must make allowances, Annie."

Meanwhile the butler—who had only succeeded in maintaining his solemn gravity through the dinner by going out into the hall and getting rid of his laughter—had placed the Hawkwood port on the table, and left the gentlemen to discuss it.

"You have a wonderful memory, Faradeane——No, that's unfair, a wonderful vein of humor, I ought to say," said the squire.

Faradeane, who had sunk into his chair after the ladies' exodus, looked up with a slight start. "Your first remark is the right one," he said; "I have a good memory."

"Yes," said Bartley Bradstone. "It reminds me of Russell, who said once in the House that 'a man was indebted to his memory for his wit, and to his imagination for his facts.'"

There was a moment of ghostly silence; then Faradeane said, with perfect ease and amiability:

"Quite right, Mr. Bradstone, your quotation hits me to a nicety. I have a good memory."

"I've heard most of the stories a score of times," said Bartley Bradstone, filling his glass.

"And I haven't heard one," said the squire; "but I have been out of the world so long."

"You couldn't have heard them, squire," said Bertie, warmly, "seeing that Faradeane invented them on the spot."

"Not all, Cherub," put in Faradeane, with a faint smile.

"Well, nearly all. I remember you telling that one about Limerick races——" He stopped and caught at his wine glass as Faradeane's eyes grew grave and warning. "I mean I remember that story years ago."

"I never heard it before," said the squire, "and am just as grateful as if Mr. Faradeane had invented it," and he laughed. "Well, now, take some wine, for we must have a cup of tea with the ladies before you start."

Bartley Bradstone filled his glass, but Faradeane and Bertie left theirs empty, and a few minutes afterward they went into the drawing-room.

CHAPTER IX
"THE BIRD IS NETTED"

The ladies had got their outdoor things on; but Olivia stood at the teatable with her gloves off to give the gentlemen their tea. As Faradeane went up to her for his cup, she raised her eyes to his face curiously, and felt no surprise at seeing it wear its usual grave and half-sad expression. She had instinctively known that he had been acting during the dinner, and the light-heartedness which had so enchanted the rest, was but seeming.

He met her gaze and smiled faintly, and her eyes fell.

"Were you going to ask me something?" he inquired, in a low voice.

"No, no," she said, confusedly. "Will you have some sugar?"

"You see," he said, "you were going to ask me something."

Feeling as if his dark eyes had read her innermost thoughts, she flushed, and turned away to put on her gloves.

"We really mustn't be late, Mr. Faradeane!" exclaimed Aunt Amelia, who was "got up" in a hat and jacket rather more youthful than Olivia's. "The dear people will be so anxious, you know."

"I am ready," he said, and he went toward Olivia to offer her his arm to the carriage, then stopped suddenly, as if he had remembered something, and looked round for Bertie, who sprang forward to her side instantly.

Olivia saw the sudden change of partners, and for a moment she hesitated; then, with lowered eyes, she put her hand on Bertie's arm.

The rest followed, and Faradeane got into the carriage with Annie and Mary, much to their delight, and somewhat to their awe.

"Well," said Bertie, eagerly, in a low voice to Olivia, "what do you think of him?"

"Of him?" asked Olivia, with an affectation of doubt.

"Of Faradeane," said Bertie. "Isn't he splendid? By Jove! he was at his best to-night—I mean I should think so," he stammered, with a mental banning of his carelessness. "That's what I call humor, Olivia, don't you? Anybody can make you laugh—I mean any low comedian, but not as he does. He makes you think at the same time, don't you know. You know what I mean."

"Yes, I think I do," she said, in a low tone. "Is Mr. Faradeane always in such good spirits?"

"No, by Jove! poor old fellow!" said Bertie, regretfully. "He is generally awfully sad and quiet. I think he came out strong to-night to please the squire and amuse Annie and Mary. They were delighted, weren't they?"

"Yes. And you think Mr. Faradeane had no thought of our amusement and applause—yours and Mr. Bradstone's and mine?" she asked, with her rare smile.

"No; I think he exerted himself for the squire and the girls. It's just like his good nature."

"You appear to have become very intimate with him in a short time," said Olivia.

Poor Bertie colored a deep red, which the darkness luckily concealed.

"Well, you see, he's the sort of man you do learn to know quickly; so—so frank."

"Frank!" with a smile.

"Well," he stammered, "not exactly frank, but——"

Olivia laughed.

"Never mind," she said. "What you mean to say is that you admire him very much, and that, like papa, you have 'taken to him.'"

"That's it," said Bertie, with a sigh of relief. "So the squire likes him, does he? Well, I'm not surprised. I hope they'll be great friends. He'll cheer the squire up, and he wants it, dear old squire."

Olivia turned to him with anxious eagerness.

"Then you have noticed that papa has been dull and low-spirited lately?" she said.

"Yes; I—I don't think he has been quite up to his usual form. He looks bothered and worried about something," said Bertie. "But don't be uneasy, Olivia; it can't be anything serious. What could trouble him?"

Olivia looked vacantly at the feathers nodding on Aunt Amelia's hat.

"I don't know of anything," she said, thoughtfully. "No, there can be nothing. What is Mr. Faradeane going to recite to-night?" she asked, after a pause.

"I haven't the least idea," replied Bertie. "He has said nothing to me about it. Whatever it is will sure to be well done, you may depend. Here we are."

The entertainment had evidently been regarded as an event of some importance, for there was a tolerably long string of carriages at the door, and Olivia, as she entered the schoolroom on Bertie's arm, saw that the place was crammed. Their appearance was the signal for a burst of clapping and stamping, and passing up a narrow lane between the chairs, they made their way to the platform amid a hearty welcome.

Aunt Amelia, "all becks and nods and wreathed smiles," ushered them into chairs—all except Faradeane, who took his seat in a corner among the audience—and the performance was proceeded with.

It was like the usual village entertainment. There was the church choir with a part song—sung by half-a-dozen girls and young men, the former all giggles, the latter all hands and feet. Then the vicar, with a vacuous smile, obliged with a solo on the concertina—by no means badly played; and Faradeane would have enjoyed it if the worthy man had not opened his mouth at all the high notes, and frowned terribly at all the low ones. Then a pale young lady sang a sentimental ballad in a voice which only reached the first two rows of chairs; and, following her, a pale young gentleman, with narrow shoulders, growled out "The Village Blacksmith."

The audience, gentle and simple, applauded everything vociferously, and when the pale young lady forgot her words, applauded louder than ever. A lady and gentleman sang the "Glou Glou" duet, which, though they had practiced it, say, two hundred times, was not quite in time even then; and then the vicar, adjusting his eyeglasses, announced that Mr. Faradeane had kindly consented to give them a recitation.

Every eye turned upon the handsome, grave-faced man in the corner, and Olivia's among them.

He rose, amid the stamping and clapping which welcomed every announcement, and slowly and unobtrusively mounted the platform.

For a moment he looked round, as if to ascertain the size of the room. Then, in a low, but clear tone, said, "The Dream of Eugene Aram."

Everybody knows the poem. It is the best of Tom Hood's, far and away, and he was a poet of no mean order. It is the confession of a murder made to a schoolboy by the usher, who pretends that he is only telling a dream, whereas he is really giving every detail of his crime, and the remorse that haunts him.

Faradeane began, in a light tone that reached the remotest corner of the room, to describe the school and the boys, and then gradually, and yet as it seemed suddenly, to assume the character of the murderer, upon whose conscience the crime rides so terribly that he feels constrained to confess it.

Gradually the voice grew deeper, graver, more intense; and as he approached the verse which tells of the crime, the silence in the crowded room was intense. Step by step the confession proceeded, until it reached the point where the murderer in vain endeavors to conceal the body of the man he has slain, and at this point the voice, the gesture, the very face of the reciter were so awful that a shudder ran through the audience, and from the center of the room a woman's sobs rose audibly.

Olivia sat, her eyes fixed on Faradeane's face, her heart almost motionless. She had seen good actors in their strongest characters, but she had seen nothing more terrible than this "Dream of Eugene Aram" as recited in the village schoolroom.

Every now and then a thrill of horror shot through her; then, as the guilty man told of the remorse that haunted him as he stood among the school children, all so pure and innocent, and tried, unavailingly, to join in their evening prayers and hymns, she felt the tears rise to her eyes, and a big lump grow in her throat.

The effect was awful, and when, in his ordinary tone, the reciter wound up with the lines which record the arrest of the guilty usher, she sank back with a sigh of pity and relief. For a moment or two the audience stared at the reciter, at this stranger with the handsome face and sad, dark eyes, in awful silence; then Lord Carfield broke the spell by a vigorous clapping of hands, and amid a storm of applause, Mr. Faradeane, with a faint smile, stepped quietly and slowly from the platform.

As he did so he glanced—was it by accident?—toward Olivia.

She met his glance for a moment, then lowered her eyes, and turned to speak to the vicar, who, worthy man, was sitting with his hands clasped on his knees, and his eyes and mouth wide open.

"My dear Miss Vanley," he gasped, "what an exciting recitation! I—I don't think I ever heard anything more—more terrible. Mr. Haraden——"

"Faradeane," said Olivia.

"I beg your pardon—Faradeane—is a most accomplished actor, most accomplished."

"Oh, thank you so much, so very much," murmured Aunt Amelia, jerking her feathers at Faradeane. "It was wonderful, perfectly wonderful. I was never so horrified in my life! Why, it has made our poor little entertainment quite distinguished! How could you do it?"

"It is not very difficult," said Mr. Faradeane, with a smile. "You are all too good-natured, Miss Vanley," and he sank into his corner and was hidden from the curious and awestruck gaze of the audience.

The entertainment proceeded; but after the event of the evening, the part songs and duets fell flat, and the big audience dispersed, thinking and talking of nothing but "The Dream of Eugene Aram" and the strange gentleman who had made them shudder and turn pale.

As the Grange party left the room, Lord Carfield came up.

"Where is your friend, Mr. Faradeane, Bertie?" he asked. "I wish you would introduce me. I never heard Hood's poem better done."

Bertie, who had Olivia on his arm, looked round and beckoned to Faradeane.

"My father," he said, "wants to know you, Faradeane."

Mr. Faradeane came forward and bowed.

The old earl looked at him with a rather puzzled expression.

"Haven't I seen you before, Mr. Faradeane?" he said.

Mr. Faradeane looked him steadily in the face.

"I think not, Lord Carfield," he said.

"No! That's strange. I had a fancy that we had met before this. Allow me to thank you for an intellectual treat. Your recital of 'Eugene Aram' was remarkably good; remarkably good. I never heard it better done, never."

Mr. Faradeane smiled.

"There are hundreds of people who could do it better, Lord Carfield."

"I dare say," said his lordship, "but I have never heard them. It made me shudder; but that is the effect you wanted to produce, no doubt. What amazes me, though, is how a man who hasn't committed a murder—I don't suppose that you have, Mr. Faradeane?" Faradeane smiled strangely. "What astonishes me is how a man who hasn't slain a fellow creature could portray the feelings of the criminal so closely as you have done."

"It is all trickery, Lord Carfield," said Faradeane.

"Oh, of course," said Bartley Bradstone, who was standing near, and listening with a moody bitterness. He had been watching Olivia during the whole of the recital, and had remarked, with furious jealousy, the effect produced on her. "It's just a knack," he said.

Lord Carfield turned to him with that slow, calm regard which always drove Bartley Bradstone half mad.

"Mr. Bradstone is quite right," said Faradeane, and the pleasant assent chafed Bradstone still more than Lord Carfield's cold glance.

"We'd better be going, hadn't we?" he said, and almost pushing past Bertie, he offered Olivia his arm.

As she put her hand upon it, he felt that she was trembling, and looked at her with an ugly red glowing in his face.

"This confounded business has frightened you!" he said, almost loud enough for Faradeane to hear. "In my opinion, that kind of thing isn't fit for a mixed audience."

"I am not frightened, thanks," said Olivia, coldly.

"You are trembling, then," he said, with barely suppressed fury.

Olivia looked at him very much as Lord Carfield had looked, and taking her hand from his arm, turned to Miss Amelia. "Are you ready, aunt?" she said, and waited until she came up to her.

Bartley Bradstone bit his lip at this distinct rebuke, and was forced to walk down the room alone.

As he approached the door, chafing with envy and mortification, a lad entered, and, looking round, came up to him with a telegram.

"What's this?" demanded Bartley Bradstone, roughly.

"A telegram, sir," the lad said. "The postmaster said I was to bring it here, as it might be important——"

"He is a fool," said Bartley Bradstone. "Besides, a telegram at this time!"

"I had to ride over with it from Wainford, sir," said the lad, shyly, "and I didn't like to come in till the entertainment was over."

Bartley Bradstone opened the envelope, scowling, and read the telegram. It ran thus:

Have got all you want. The bird is netted.

Mowle.

He crushed it in his hand, and looked furtively round as if he almost suspected that the rest of the party knew its purport; then his face cleared, and he glanced at Olivia with an ugly smile of sinister significance.

"You snub me, do you, my lady?" he said, under his breath. "You'll change your tone presently, I fancy."

And he went into the open air mumbling the words of the telegram.

"Mowle's a fool to send such a wire," he said, wiping the perspiration from his forehead. "But he's right. The bird is netted!"

CHAPTER X
IN THE MOONLIGHT

When they came out of the schoolroom into the open air, the moonlight was streaming over the pastoral scene, lighting up the crowd of people still talking of the wonderful "Dream of Eugene Aram," as they made their way through the string of carriages.

Faradeane paused to say good-night; but Aunt Amelia would not offer her hand.

"My dear Mr. Faradeane!" she exclaimed, "surely you would not leave us! Bertie, the squire quite expects you back to smoke a cigar with him; do, do persuade him to come with you. Really, I feel that I cannot lose you, Mr. Faradeane."

Faradeane hesitated; but Bertie, eager to snatch a few more minutes of his idol's society, pressed his arm.

"Come on," he said. "The squire will be pleased, I know."

Olivia stood silent, her eyes fixed dreamily on the moonlit scene.

"Must we go back in those stuffy carriages," she said, in a low voice. "Can we not walk, aunt?"

"Certainly you may," replied Miss Amelia. "But I think I will ride; these night dews are rather treacherous, I'm sure," and she dropped her head on her shoulder, and simpered, "Mr. Bradstone will be kind enough to take care of me."

Bartley Bradstone's face would have supplied a fine study for a painter of character, but he was helpless; and with a stifled oath, gave her his arm.

The two Penstone girls, of course, drew back, and declined, with distinct emphasis, the mere idea of riding.

"All right, then," said Bertie. "Come on!" and the young people set out.

Annie and Mary, in their eagerness to vent their amazement and pent-up enthusiasm, caught him timidly, but effectually, by either arm, and began at once:

"Oh, Lord Granville, did you—now, did you ever hear anything like it? Wasn't it simply wonderful?" etc., and poor Bertie, closely arrested, saw his goddess walk on with Faradeane.

He did not offer his arm, and they went on in silence for some minutes.

Any attempt to describe the varied emotions which swept through Olivia's sensitive heart would be impossible.

The spell of his voice was on her still; the fascination of his dark, handsome face still held her in thrall.

Women admire men for many qualities; their strength, their good looks, their courage, their art, sometimes—but not often, alas!—their wisdom. And to-night, under the moonlight, Olivia was full of admiration for this man whom the gods had dowered with so many gifts. He had proved his courage in risking his life for Bessie, his face was handsome enough to haunt the dreams of a sculptor, and to-night he had exercised a power of imagination and voice and influence that had moved a crowded audience.

Think of it! An impressionable girl, full of poetry, and ready as wax to receive an impression, and wonder not that as she walked beside him she felt magnetized, attracted, fascinated.

She was pale still, still slightly tremulous, and her breath came slowly and heavily. Lines of the exquisite poem into which he had breathed life and reality still rang in her ears. She could find nothing to say that would not have sounded to her ears hideously commonplace.

And it was he who first spoke.

"Miss Vanley," he said, "I have an uncomfortable feeling of guilt."

She looked up at him instantly, with that look which a woman turns upon the man on whom her mind is fixed.

"Guilt!" she echoed.

He smiled at the almost tragic tones of her voice.

"Yes, I have an uneasy feeling that I have made you uncomfortable with my uncanny performance."

"No," she said, slowly, "not uncomfortable."

"It was a stupid thing to do," he went on. "Stupid and unsuitable to the bulk of the audience; but my excuse—well, my only excuse is that I knew no other piece, and was too—well, too lazy to learn any other. I will never recite it again."

"No?" she breathed. "Don't say that. It would be a waste. It was beautiful—beautiful—and yet so sad. I——" She paused. "I have read the poem—everybody has; but I did not know it was so dreadful until to-night."

"Because I give it with all the usual tricks," he said, half-contemptuously. "That is why. But it is a great piece of verse—and dreadful."

"My sympathies are all with Eugene Aram," she said, dreamily. "It is wrong, I know."

He looked at her for a moment in silence.

"Yes, it is wrong," he said. "One should not sympathize with the man who commits a crime; but I understand. His sufferings were almost an expiation."

She shuddered slightly.

"Yes, and he was sorely tempted. But do you think that it is—natural? That an educated man should commit such a crime——"

"Education!" he said, slowly; and in the aftertime which cast such an awful shadow over her life, she recalled his words: "Has that anything to do with it? Education teaches us to conceal our passions; it does not, cannot destroy them! No, under the thin veneer which civilization plasters over us, lie the old savage instincts, and if you scratch your man of refinement deep enough, you will find the passions of the barbarian still existing. Given a temptation fiery enough, and your man of rank, position, education will fall."

"That is terrible," she breathed; "and you think that any one—any one—could be tempted to commit—murder?"

His dark eyes rested on her.

"It depends on the temptation," he said, as if rather communing with himself than answering her. "Some men could not be induced to commit even an indiscretion for the sake of all the mines in Peru, but for another motive—the one motive—lust of power, ambition, revenge, love——" he paused, and the word rang in her brain—"he would descend to any crime—aye, even murder."

The faint shudder ran through her again, and he seemed to know it, for he said, in a lighter tone:

"But this kind of morbid talk is shamed by such a night. What a lovely moon! It reminds me of those lines of Heine:

"'Goddess of our sleeping hours
When silver tints the drooping flowers.'"

and he repeated in a low, musical voice, that seemed to sing the words, the whole of the short poem; surely one of the sweetest in the German tongue.

Olivia unconsciously drew nearer to him, and the words, the voice, dispelled the faint terror that had throbbed through her.

"I don't know it," she said, almost piteously. "I seem to know nothing. All my life has been spent half asleep——"

"Ah, don't regret it!" he said, gravely, with a touch of sadness in his voice. "Your life has been a beautiful dream! May the awakening never come! Don't speak of it remorsefully! To me it seems so precious——" He paused. "It is a perfect life for one like yourself. Do you see that star?" He stopped, and pointed upward. "Would you drag it from its place and its calm serenity to flicker in an oily lamp? Keep your pure and beautiful life as long as you can! Some day——"

He stopped.

"Some day?" she murmured, gently.

"Some day," he continued, "the temptation will come to you, the star of my thoughts, to descend and become a part of the hard and cruel world. Stay in the heaven of your present serenity, Miss Vanley!"

It was strange talk in this prosaic, practical nineteenth century; but it did not seem strange or forced to Olivia. She drank in every word, and, if she did not at once feel its meaning, mentally stretched out her hands and sought for it.

Just to keep him talking, to hear the deep, musical voice again, she said:

"Is the world so wicked, then?"

"Wicked and foolish," he said; "and its folly is worse than its wickedness. I have made one discovery as I passed through it. Do you know what it is?"

"No," she murmured, drawing nearer to him.

He laughed softly, and pushed his hat from his brow with a half weary gesture. "It is this: That though wickedness may go unpunished, folly never does. A man may commit a crime—many—and pass through the world undetected and unpunished, but if he commit a folly, Nemesis follows and closes upon him at once. And the moral of this is——"

He stopped.

"That it is wiser to be wicked than foolish," she said.

"Exactly!" he assented, with a strange smile.

Bertie and the two Penstones had passed them, and reached the turning to The Dell, and here Olivia and Faradeane overtook them.

"I don't think I ought to go any farther," he said, half-stopping; "your father has had enough of us to-night."

"No?" she said. "Why?" She paused, half timidly. "Why should you go; it must be lonely at home."

"It is lonely," he said, with a smile half sad. "No one but I can tell how lonely."

"Why do you — —" she began, and then stopped again.

"Why do I live like a hermit and a recluse?" he said, gently. "We have some of us ceased to be masters of our own actions, Miss Vanley; I am so unlucky as to be one of those unfortunates."

She looked up at him with the timid, shrinking glance of a woman whose heart aches with sympathy, and yet who has not power to give it.

"If I—if my father—could do anything," she murmured.

He held out his hand and took hers, and he held it, not pressing it, but enfolding it in his strong, shapely one.

"You have done much already," he said, in a low voice, "more than you can guess; yes, much more. Good-night, Miss Vanley."

Obeying an impulse, one of those impulses which were rare with her, she raised her beautiful eyes to his.

"That is my aunt's title," she said, with a faint, flickering smile. "My name is Olivia."

He looked at her for a moment gravely, and yet with a sort of troubled wistfulness; then he said, in as low tone as hers:

"Olivia! Good-night, Miss Olivia!"

Then he called to Bertie, waving his hand toward Olivia, and turning aside, strode into the dark lane that led to The Dell.

"Oh! isn't he coming to the Grange?" exclaimed Annie Penstone, as Bertie brought Olivia to them. "Isn't he really coming? It's too bad! I wanted to talk to him, to ask him all sorts of things! And you have had him all the way to yourself! Now that isn't fair, is it, Mary? What did he talk about, Olivia?"

"I don't know," said Olivia, dreamily.

They found Aunt Amelia and Bartley Bradstone waiting for them in the hall, the former still simmering with excitement over the success of her concert, and the latter glaring sullenly, with suppressed rage and jealousy.

All through the meal, which was a kind of "scratch" supper, while Annie and Mary and Bertie, all speaking very fast and at the same time, were giving the squire an account of the sensation Mr. Faradeane had created, Bartley Bradstone and Olivia sat in silence. Now and again he glanced at her thoughtful, dreamy face in a half watchful, half suspicious manner, but she seemed to be quite unconscious of his presence, and presently got up and went to the piano in the adjoining room and began to play softly.

"That's a sign that we can take ourselves off to the smoking-room; come and have a cigar," said the squire, and as he passed Olivia, he gently patted her cheek. She put up her hand and took his and laid her face against it, but said nothing, and the two men left the room.

"I shan't smoke," said Bertie, as he reached the door. "I shall stay and talk to these children," nodding at Annie and Mary, but he glanced at Olivia as he spoke.

Bartley Bradstone dropped into the chair the squire motioned him to, but he seemed uneasy and restless, and after a moment or two, he got up, and, clearing his throat, nervously, said:

"I am glad we are alone, squire, for I wanted to speak to you on a—a private matter."

The squire glanced at him with a return of the apprehensive, hunted look in his eyes.

"Yes! What is it? Wait a moment, till I have lit my cigar. Now," and he seemed to pull himself together like a man prepared to receive bad news, or an unwelcome shock.

Bartley Bradstone grew pale; he was evidently as ill at ease as the squire.

"I—I want to speak to you about Miss Vanley—Miss Olivia," he said.

A tremor passed over the squire's face, and he lowered his eyes.

"About Olivia?" and his voice sounded dry and husky.

"Yes," said Bartley Bradstone. "I don't suppose you have been blind to the—the fact that I sincerely admire, and—and, indeed, that I—well"—he stammered—"I love her, and I want you to give her to me for my—wife."

As he spoke the last word, his voice suddenly dropped and grew hoarse and indistinct. So much so that the squire, who had not expected such deep emotion, started and looked up at him. Bartley Bradstone's face was perfectly white, and his eyes were fixed on the ground.

"I have been devoted to—to Miss Olivia for months past," he continued. "I'm not good at this kind of thing, and I don't express myself very well; but what I've said is true. I do love her, and I'll do all in my power to make her happy."

He cleared his throat, and took up a match to relight his cigar, which had gone out.

The squire stared at the carpet with grave, troubled eyes for a moment. He had expected this; in his heart of hearts he had desired it, and yet—yet now it had come, it seemed to chill him with an indefinable repugnance.

"Have you spoken to Olivia, Bradstone?" he asked, and his voice was rather that of a man speaking of a funeral than a contemplated marriage.

Bartley Bradstone colored.

"No," he replied. "I have said nothing to Miss Olivia. I thought it my duty to come to you, her father, first; it's the proper thing, isn't it?"

"Yes," assented the squire. "Yes—usually, thank you—yes, of course it is the proper thing. But——" He paused. "But I ought to tell you at once that in this matter my daughter will be quite uninfluenced by me—I mean that she will be left to decide for herself completely."

"Then, if she says 'Yes,' I'm to understand that you will not object?" said Bartley Bradstone.

The squire looked up at him with a half sad, half reluctant expression in his eyes.

"Why should I object?" he said, as if to himself. "We have known you for some time, you are a near neighbor, and—I speak frankly, Bradstone—you possess the wealth without which, alas! few marriages can be happy."

"Yes," said Bartley Bradstone, and for the first time he drew himself up. "I think I can satisfy you on that point. I think I may say that Olivia will, as my wife, be able to live as comfortably as she has done as your daughter."

The squire winced at the vulgarity and familiarity of the speech, as he nodded assentingly.

"It is a consideration that has weight with me," he said. "But I ought to tell you, though you do not need telling, I am sure, that it will not have a feather's weight with Olivia."

"Most women like money," said Bartley Bradstone.

The squire winced.

"Yes, most. But not Olivia. She cares nothing for it. She would be as contented in one of the keeper's cots as here at the Grange or at The Maples—that is, so far as money is concerned. But all this is premature and useless talk. You have not spoken to her yet, you say. It will be time to—to talk of the financial part of the subject after——"

He paused and suppressed a sigh.

"No, I don't agree with you, sir," said Bartley Bradstone, with an air of great respect, but eyeing the grave, sad-faced old man out of the corner of his restless, suspicious eyes. "I like everything to be fair and aboveboard——"

"Fair and aboveboard!" echoed the squire, almost angrily.

"I—I mean straightforward and plain," stammered Bartley Bradstone. "I must tell you what I intend to do if Olivia accepts me and becomes my wife——"

The squire rose and leaned his elbow on the mantelshelf and his head on his hand, and seemed engaged in some mental struggle for a moment; then he raised his head, and looking every inch the true-hearted English gentleman, he said:

"Wait a moment, if you please, Bradstone. Before you say any more, I think—I am sure—it is my duty to be as plain and straightforward—aye, to use your own words, as 'fair and aboveboard' as you are. I have to tell you this: You may suppose, and very naturally, that as the daughter of the lord of the manor, of a man with a large estate and occupying a prominent place in the county, Olivia will have a dowry suitable to her position."

Bartley Bradstone opened his mouth; but the squire, with a gesture of gentle dignity, motioned him to silence.

"Hear me out. I find it difficult to tell you what I have to tell you. I say that it is only reasonable that you should suppose my daughter would come to you with a marriage portion suited to her rank in life. I am sorry, bitterly sorry, to tell you that Olivia will go to the man she marries with empty hands!"

If the squire had expected his auditor to express astonishment or chagrin, he was agreeably relieved, for Bartley Bradstone merely nodded his head.

"It is a matter of perfect indifference to me, sir," he said, with a shrug of the shoulders. "It is Olivia I want, not money; thank Heaven I have enough—too much, perhaps—of that already. If you give me your consent——"

"One moment more," said the squire, interrupting him in a low voice. "It is my duty to tell you something more, Bradstone. If you are utterly indifferent to the fact that she will have no dowry, you may consider that, as my only child, she will and should inherit this," and he waved his hand. "What if I tell you that she will not even do that?"

Again Bartley Bradstone expressed neither surprise nor disappointment.

"No?" he said. "Well, that is of no consequence to me, sir. As I said, it is Olivia I want, not money nor the Grange; though, mind you, I think it a pity that a fine old property that has been in the family so long— —"

"Should depart from it forever," said the squire, in a low, sorrow-stricken voice. "A pity! Yes! But so it must be! Bradstone, having told you this much, I may—indeed, it is my duty to—tell you all. You see before you a man who is a living lie"—his voice broke—"a sham and a counterfeit, the Squire of Hawkwood who cannot give his daughter a poor thousand pounds as a wedding present, the lord of the manor every acre of which he is in hourly danger of losing. Bradstone, I am weighed down, sunk to my neck in debt, and the Grange may at any moment be in the bailiff's hands."

He did not drop into a chair or burst into tears, did not even utter a groan, but stood with pale, set face and steady, unflinching eyes—the aristocrat even in this moment of his deepest humiliation, the humiliation of having to confess his ruin to this parvenu, would-be son-in-law.

Bartley Bradstone looked at him with the grudging admiration of a vulgar mind for that higher type which it can never hope even to imitate; how he would have sighed and groaned and groveled if he had had to make such a confession!

"There is my case," said the squire, after a moment's pause. "And I shall not deem you selfish or unreasonable if, after having heard it, you withdraw your proposal, Bradstone."

"But I do not do anything of the sort," said Bartley Bradstone. "I repeat it. It makes no difference to me, sir—not a bit. As to the estate going, I'm not so sure that that can't be prevented."

The squire shook his head sadly.

"Oh, I don't know," said Bartley Bradstone, thrusting his hands into his pockets. "I'm not so sure of that. And now, sir, let me imitate your candor. You've told me how you stand; I'll tell you my position. I believe—it's difficult to calculate exactly—that I'm worth three-quarters of a million, more or less, and I should think— —"

The squire raised his brows.

"Yes, that's about the figure. Now, if Olivia says 'Yes,' if she accepts me, I'm prepared to settle fifty thousand pounds upon her for her life, for her own, you know, and I'll give her The Maples, too. If that isn't enough, if you think that it ought to be more— —"

The squire's pale face went crimson, and he made a gesture of repudiation.

"No, no! It is most liberal, most generous," he said, and for the first time his voice quivered. "It is too large a settlement for a portionless girl——"

"Not for my wife," said Bartley Bradstone, with a charming self consequence which made the poor old squire shudder inwardly. "A man who is worth three-quarters of a million doesn't miss fifty thou. In fact, I expect that your lawyer fellows will want a great deal more than that——"

The squire reddened.

"My lawyers will express my sentiments, Bradstone," he said, quietly.

Bartley Bradstone bit his lip.

"I mean they'll consider that it ought to be more, and if they do, I'll make it just what they want. In fact, I'll do anything to get—to—prove my love for Olivia; and I'll undertake to make her happy, if a man could do it."

The squire did not hold out his hand, as a father usually does under such circumstances, as he would have done, for instance, if Bertie or some one like him had made the speech, but he bowed his head in acknowledgement.

"It is a liberal, generous proposal," he said. "You have my consent, Bradstone, and—and my best wishes. But remember that Olivia will be left perfectly free; by no word or look would I endeavor to influence her. If she accepts you, it will be of her own accord, and if she should refuse——"

Bartley Bradstone bit his lip again.

"You will understand that the—the matter is at an end."

"I understand, sir," he said. "And now we have settled, perhaps I'd better speak to Olivia," and he flung his cigar in the fireplace.

The squire gave a slight start.

"To-night?" he said. "Well—yes—I suppose a lover's impatience——"

"Oh, I don't like it," said Bartley Bradstone, with a faint laugh. "But it's been my motto all through life that if a disagreeable—I mean a hard job has got to be done, it's better to set about it at once and get it over. I shall speak to Olivia to-night—the sooner the better. If I waited"—he hesitated, then blurted it out—"if I waited, I might wait too long; some other fellow might step in. I'll go now, I think, sir."

"You will find her in the drawing-room, and alone, I think," said the squire, with a faint sigh. "I heard the Penstone carriage go a quarter of an hour since."

"So did I," said Bartley Bradstone, with a knowing look. "I was only waiting for their departure," and he went out.

He had not told the squire that he held all his bonds in his hands, and that at any moment he could crush him, ruin him, turn him out of the Grange. Bartley Bradstone was clever enough to know that if he had done so, and had also intimated that his price for sparing her father was the daughter's hand, the squire would have turned him out of the house, and probably kicked him into the bargain. No, Bartley Bradstone, though a vulgar *parvenu*, was too clever to make such a false move. He reserved it. That was all.

CHAPTER XI
A BID FOR LOVE

For all his outward show of composure, he was feeling anything but comfortable, and as he stood with his hand upon the drawing-room door, there was a strange look upon his face, a look that expressed something more than the usual lover's despondent timidity, something more than the ordinary nervousness; it was rather that of a man who was playing a dangerous and a desperate game, and who stands upon the brink of a precipice, which, lined as it may be with flowers, means, if he should fall, death and destruction.

"The old man was easy," he muttered, "but it's different with her. By Heaven, if she knew!"

The thought, whatever it was, seemed to increase his uneasiness, and he wiped the perspiration from his face, which had suddenly grown white under the reflection.

Then he opened the door. Olivia was alone, and seated at the piano, but not playing. Her hands were lying clasped loosely in her lap, her face and her whole attitude expressive of complete abstraction—so complete that she did not hear him open the door, and it was not until he was close beside her and had spoken her name, that she knew he had entered.

"Mr. Bradstone!" she said, with a slight start. "I thought you had gone," she added, coldly.

The sullen look came into his eyes for a moment.

"No, I ought to have gone; but I have been talking with the squire," he said.

"Yes?" she said. "Is my father in the library?" and she half arose, a plain intimation that she should, if Mr. Bradstone would leave her free to, join him.

"Yes, he is in the library; but will you wait a minute, Miss Olivia——"

She sank back, and began putting the music together.

"You can't guess what we have been talking about, I'll be bound," he said, with a feeble attempt at a laugh.

Olivia just frowned at him.

"I haven't any intention of trying," she said, not insolently, but with an indifference which was sublime. It made Bartley Bradstone wince—simply wince.

"You'd be surprised if I told you it was—you," he said.

She looked at him now, a look of calm displeasure and incredulity.

"I should, indeed!" she said.

"But we were," he continued, trying to smile, and leaning on the piano; "we were talking about you, and have been for some time. I—in fact—don't be startled, don't be angry—I went to ask him to—to let me—in fact—I've told the squire that I love you, Olivia."

Her face did not change, not a muscle moved. She simply regarded him with cold incredulity, and the amazement which one expresses at the impertinence of an inferior.

"You don't believe me; but I did. You must know—you must have seen," he went on, huskily, his hands clasping and unclasping each other, "that—that I loved you. I do love you; I've loved you ever since—Olivia, won't you say a word? Don't, for Heaven's sake, don't stare at me like that! Your father did not treat me like this——"

"My father?" she said, after a pause. "You told my father what you have told me?"

"Yes, I did. I know what's proper, and I went and told him before I spoke to you. And now, Olivia, now you know, what do you say? Wait a moment. I—I'm afraid I haven't done the best for myself. I'm—I'm not a lady's man, and I've sprung it upon you too sharply. But it was dangerous, this hanging about and waiting, and—and I got anxious. But you know it now. I'm not a bad sort of fellow, I fancy, and I can offer you——"

She rose from the seat and moved toward the door. He stood in front of her, desperate—imploring.

"Let me pass, please," she said, quietly.

"Wait, wait!" he exclaimed, huskily. "You're treating me badly, like the dirt under your feet, by Heaven! This isn't the way I was treated by your father."

Olivia stopped and looked at him.

"You are right and I am wrong," she said. "I beg your pardon, Mr. Bradstone! This is not the way my father would treat you. Whatever he may have felt, he would have behaved with courtesy. Yes, I beg your pardon! You tell me that"—she paused, as if the words cost her an effort—"that you love me, and ask me to be your wife?"

"I do, I do!" he broke in. "I love you to distraction! I haven't a thought in the world but you! You are just life to me; I swear it! I've told the squire what I will do—I'd spend my last penny in making you happy! I'd lay down my life——"

She stopped him with a cold, but queenly gesture.

"Please," she said, in a low voice, "I am sorry, very sorry, Mr. Bradstone, but it cannot be; I mean that I cannot be your wife."

"You can't? You refuse?" he stammered, his small eyes growing red, and an ugly stiffness coming over his mouth.

"I do refuse, as gently, as—as considerately as I can," said Olivia. "I am grateful to you for the honor——" She stopped. "Oh, let me pass, please, and never, never"—and her dark brows came down straight and majestic as Diana's—"never speak like this to me again!"

He did not move; but stood regarding her with feverish and sullen resentment.

"That's not what your father says," he said.

Olivia looked at him with imperious questioning.

"What do you say?" she said.

"I say that it wasn't in this way your father heard me," he answered, sullenly. "He didn't treat me like this—he consented."

Her eyes flashed back the retort, and as eloquently as eyes could speak, said: "You lie!"

His face grew red; it had been white a moment ago.

"You don't believe me?" he said.

"I do not! Let me pass, if you please, Mr. Bradstone."

"But I say it's true!" he exclaimed; "I say he consented! He's ready to accept me for a son-in-law if you'll say 'Yes,' and——" He paused. "I think you will say 'Yes,' with all your cursed pride!"

The word slipped from him, and he would have recalled it the moment after he had uttered it.

But its effect upon Olivia was not what he expected.

"You are right, Mr. Bradstone," she said, quietly; "I am proud, and apt to forget that others have as much pride as I have. I beg your pardon again. You have misunderstood my father; I am sure of that— —"

"No, I haven't," he put in.

"I know my father," she said, as quietly as before, "and it is impossible that he should have—have spoken as you say he did. Let there be an end of this. I thank you for the honor—it is an honor for any woman to receive an offer from a man—I thank you, and beg you to believe that it is impossible that I should accept it."

"Why?" he persisted.

Her lovely eyes rested on him for a moment, then looked aside.

His face went white.

"I understand," he said, hoarsely, "you—you think I am no more than the dirt under your feet. You think, because I made my own way in the world, and haven't got an old name or a title, that it's an insult for me to ask you to be my wife! You wouldn't treat Lord Bertie or—or that fellow Faradeane like this— —"

At Bertie's name a smile flickered about her lips, but at Faradeane's a wave of color swept over her face and neck.

"Ah!" he said, with passionate anger. "That's true, I can see. But let me tell you that I think myself as good as either of them. Stop"—for she had made another attempt to pass him—"as good, and better. Could either of them offer what I do? I've just told your father that I'd settle fifty thousand pounds upon you. I tell you now that that's nothing to me; I didn't make it more for fear of hurting his feelings; but I tell you I'll settle a hundred, two hundred thousand— —"

She put out her hand.

"Oh, hush!" she said, as if his words covered her with shame. "If it were a million— —"

"Oh, I know," he broke in, huskily; "it's as he said. You don't care for money. It's all the same to you whether a man's poor or rich; but money's something. Olivia— —"

"I am usually addressed as Miss Olivia Vanley," said Olivia, flashing down upon him.

He bit his lip.

"I say it's all the same to you; but it isn't to him. No! And I'll bet that before we part to-night you'll consent, as he did."

She looked at him, calmly—questioningly. For a moment there arose in her mind the suspicion that he had been drinking, and he read it in her eyes.

"No, I'm not drunk!" he said, bitterly; "I'm only half mad, driven so by your words and looks! And I mean what I say—you will consent, as he did!"

"Consent to marry you!" said Olivia, stung into retort.

"Yes," he said, sullenly; "for his sake, if not for mine or yours."

"For his sake—for my father's?" she said.

He nodded.

"Yes. Look here, Olivia, we've been beating about the bush long enough. You've treated me like a dog—yes, you have; or like the dirt under your feet. And I don't deserve it. No, by God! for I spared the old man——"

"You spared——"

"Yes, I did. I could have told him what a cleft stick I'd got him in, but I didn't; I knew you wouldn't like it. I knew you'd rather he remained in ignorance till the affair was over."

"I'm afraid you are wasting your breath, Mr. Bradstone," said Olivia. "I do not in the least comprehend you——"

"But you will presently," he said, with a half-cunning, half-furious smile. "Look here; your father, the squire, is, as he put it, a fraud——"

She drew herself up, and sent a lightning shot from her eyes that made him quail.

"Leave the room!" she exclaimed, pointing to the door.

"Stop!" he said. "Wait!" for she had swept, with the dignity of an insulted goddess toward the bell. "So help me Heaven, it is true! He will tell you so himself, if you are foolish enough to ask him. He is a fraud—well, well, he's a ruined man, then. Up to his neck in debts, the Grange is sunk, the very furniture under a bill of sale; nothing can save him—nothing. He will have to turn out, neck and crop. Turn out! You don't know what that means. But he does! The day he leaves here a ruined, broken man, dates his death-warrant! It does, by Heaven! and out he goes, unless you accept me, Olivia!"

"Unless—unless——Oh, you are mad!" she panted.

"Am I? No, I'm not. It's you who are mad—with pride. Do you think I'm an idiot and don't know what I'm talking about? What I tell you is true; and what is more, I hold your father's bonds——"

"You— —"

"Yes," and he nodded, with a smile. "I've got 'em, one and all. At a word from me, he can be sold up and turned out. A word, a sign, and"—with a sudden, sullen light in his suspicious, restless eyes—"and, by God! I'll do it if— —Look here, it will rest with you! Say you'll be my wife—by Heaven! I'll do my best to make you happy—and the day we're married I'll put the whole of these bonds and mortgages into your hands—you can light a fire with them. And I'll do more; I'll give you twenty thousand pounds—fifty— what do I care! I tell you I'm a millionaire! Money is dirt, stones, dross—you can fling it broadcast, roll in it— —"

She stopped him with a gesture, entreating, piteous, desperate.

"Does—does he—my father—know this?" she panted.

He smiled cunningly.

"No," he said. "No; I knew better than to tell him. I leave it to you to decide whether he goes out of the Grange to die of a broken heart. He doesn't know it."

"Thank God!" she cried. "Oh, father, father!" and she sank into a chair and covered her face with her hands.

He stole up to her and ventured—actually dared—to lay his hot hand upon her white arm.

"Hush! hush!" he stammered, "I can hear him coming. Don't—don't cry. You can't help yourself. I'll—I'll leave you to think of it. Remember, it's life or death for him, just that—life or death," and with a thirsty, wistful look, as if he would have liked to catch her up in his arms, he stole from the room.

As he paused outside the door to gain his breath, a smile of triumph shone on his face, wet with perspiration; then suddenly it changed, and his features were momentarily distorted by an expression of abject fear.

Then he seemed to shake off the emotion, and with a husky laugh, he muttered:

"I've got her, and by Heaven, I'll do it! She's worth it!"

CHAPTER XII
BY PROXY

Little dreaming of the scene that was being enacted by Olivia and Bartley Bradstone, Bertie started on his way home. He meant to walk to Carfield, and to think of Olivia every inch of the way. He had always loved her as a boy, and when they were playmates; but now he found his love of that absorbing kind which masters a man's whole being and dominates his life.

Carfield was no great distance for a young man in first-rate condition, and he set out at a steady pace, thinking of Olivia at every step. Dearly as he loved her—perhaps because he loved her so dearly—he could not summon up courage to tell her so. They had been playmates together; it had been "Olly" and "Bertie" for as long back as he could remember, and yet—yet he had not the courage to go to her and say, "Olivia, be my wife!"

"I am a coward, that's what it is!" he murmured, ruefully. "Now, if it was Faradeane, instead of me——"

He pulled up short. Strangely enough, the comparison had occurred to him at the very moment he was passing the top of the lane in which The Dell stood.

After a moment's hesitation he turned into it, and opened the gate. As he did so, he saw, or fancied he saw, the figure of a man cross the path and disappear in the shrubs that grew on each side.

"Is that you, Faradeane?" he said. "Who's there?"

No response came, and deciding that it was a trick of his imagination, aided by lights and shadows, he went up to the door.

It was ajar, which seemed strange to Bertie, and pushing it open, he entered, and opened the door of the sitting-room.

Faradeane was sitting beside the table; he had thrown off his dress coat and waistcoat, and was leaning on the table with his head resting upon his arms.

"Faradeane, old fellow!" said Bertie, softly.

He started, and sprang to his feet, with a look, not of apprehension, but as if he had been suddenly awakened from some painful reverie, and Bertie felt a pang shoot through him at the pallor and the wanness of the handsome face.

"Well, Cherub," he said. "Is it you?"

"Yes. I startled you. I'm awfully sorry. Were you asleep, old man?"

Faradeane smiled.

"No, only thinking. Well, have you come from the Grange? Sit down."

Bertie sank into the chair with a sigh.

"Yes. I've just come from the Grange. I'm sorry you didn't join us. I left them all talking of your wonderful performance——"

Faradeane made a little gesture of deprecation, as much as to say that he had already received more than his due in that way, and, placing a cigar box on the table, lit his pipe.

"It was kind of you to look in, Cherub," he said; "and I am very glad to see you. Make yourself comfortable, and accept my gratitude—and some whisky-and-water."

"As to gratitude—well, to tell you the truth—but I say, old fellow, I thought I saw you in the garden in the front as I came in just now."

Faradeane shook his head as he held the match to his pipe.

"No, of course not, because you were sitting here; but I could have declared that I saw the figure of a man cross in front of the window——"

Faradeane dropped the match, and strode to the door, then stopped short.

"My man, my gardener, groom, valet, factotum," he said. "He was looking round for the night, I dare say." And he sank down into a chair opposite Bertie's. "And now what was this truth you were going to tell me, Cherub?"

Bertie colored, and shifted in his seat nervously.

"Well, it wasn't altogether an unselfish deed, this dropping in upon you at this time of night. By the way, it is awfully late!"

Faradeane waved his pipe.

"It is never too date to receive a friend, Cherub. Day and night are all one to a man who takes no interest in either. You have come to talk to me—to ask me something. Isn't it so?"

Bertie nodded.

"You always seem to know," he said, with quiet admiration. "I did come to talk to you, to ask you to do me a great favor."

"Consider it granted, even to the half of my kingdom," responded Faradeane. "What is it?"

Bertie was silent for a moment; then, blushing like the rose, and with downcast eyes, he said:

"What—what do you think of her now—of Olivia, Faradeane?"

Faradeane was sitting with his arms folded at the back of his head, his eyes fixed in dreamy patience and kindliness upon the fair, girlish face; but at this abrupt question his expression changed and his arms dropped.

"What do I think of Miss Vanley?" he said, in a slow, constrained voice.

"Yes, old fellow. You can't tell how anxious I am to get your opinion. You see, you are the dearest friend I've got, you always were my friend and all that, and I—I naturally——"

Faradeane nodded, and seemingly intent upon his pipe, which had suddenly got stopped up apparently, said:

"I think she is a very beautiful girl. Cherub, and something a very great deal better than beautiful."

"I knew you'd say so, but I wanted to hear you say it!" exclaimed Bertie, with suppressed fervor. "I knew you admired her——"

Faradeane raised his head sharply.

"You know that I admired her! How should you know that? Have I shown it in any word or look?"

_ "No, no; don't be angry, my dear fellow," responded Bertie, quickly. "No, no; but I felt somehow that you did."

"Oh!"

"And I'm certain she admires you. I'm sure, if you'd seen her face as she sat to-night while you were reciting, and at dinner time, too, with her eyes fixed upon you——"

Faradeane's pipe seemed to trouble him again.

"Oh, I could see that she was immensely taken with you; and who wouldn't be? Don't smile like that, old man; I mean all I say; and it was because I am so sure that—that—she likes you and looks up to you, that I came in here to you to-night. The idea only struck me as I was passing the top of the lane."

"Oh," said Faradeane, quietly; "and what was the idea, Cherub?"

Bertie fidgeted in his chair, and sighed.

"Look here, Cly——"

Faradeane raised his head with a warning glance, and Bertie, coloring crimson, stumbled on:

"I—I beg your pardon; Faradeane, I mean. It's just this: I'm half beside myself to-night. Being with her all this evening has set me all a-quiver, and—and the sight of that fellow Bradstone has upset me so terribly that— that I must—I must know my fate. I can't go on any longer! I've got a dread upon me that if I don't speak out now, at once, and tell her how I love her, and—and ask her to be my wife, that I—that this fellow will get before me, and——"

He stopped and wiped his brow with a hand that quivered.

Faradeane looked at him with his dark, sad eyes.

"And you came to ask my advice? You shall have it. Obey the impulse, Bertie; go and tell her you love her, as you suggest——"

He paused, stopped by a look in Bertie's eyes.

"Well?"

"I—I—that isn't what I wanted," said the Cherub.

"No? What do you want, then?"

"I—I want you to do it for me," said Bertie, in a low voice.

For a moment Faradeane sat motionless and speechless; then he laughed. It was a strange laugh, fuller of pain than of mirth, almost a laugh of bitterness.

"You—want—me to tell her?" he said, slowly.

"Yes," said Bertie, in his eagerness leaning forward with clasped hands. "That's what I want. Try as I will, I can't find the pluck. You'll think I'm a coward, I know. I can't help it. If you only felt as I do! I tell you, old fellow, that when I think of going to her, and saying—what I should have to say— I—I—my voice leaves me. You don't know what she is. She might laugh at me, or she might turn on me with one of those cold, far-away looks in her eyes; and—and both ways of taking it would—would settle me."

He paused for want of breath.

"Now, you—you could tell her how I feel; you could say just the right thing, and—and convince her that I love her so dearly that I'd rather die than live without her."

Faradeane laughed again; the same sad, half-bitter laugh.

"Don't laugh at me, for Heaven's sake," implored Bertie. "It's fun to you, but it's death to me, Faradeane. And don't refuse me. I know what I'm about. I know what she thinks of you—yes, already, though she has only known you for a few days. A man who loves a girl as I do Olivia—well, he gets sharp, and notices every little thing about her, every look and word, and I know that she would listen to you, that you could persuade——"

"Stop! Are you mad?" exclaimed Faradeane, sternly.

Bertie looked up, and saw that the handsome face had grown white, almost pallid.

"What have I said?" he exclaimed, penitently. "Have I offended you? I didn't mean to do so. What I said is true. You have an influence over her——"

Faradeane rose abruptly and leaned his elbow upon the mantelshelf, and his head upon his hand, and there was silence for a moment; then he raised his head. "You are talking arrant nonsense," he said, not sternly, but coldly. "Miss Vanley thinks no more, cares no more, is no more influenced by me than—than she is by her footman. Put such an absurd idea out of your foolish head. She does not give a thought to me, whom she has not seen for more than a few minutes, on as many days. Talk sense, Cherub, or—or go home to bed."

Bertie looked up at him with a firmness which was almost obstinacy.

"You may bully me as much as you like, Faradeane," he said, and not without a certain quiet dignity, the dignity of conviction. "But you won't succeed in convincing me that you have not a great deal of influence over her. Why, I watched her—do I ever take my eyes off her?—every time you spoke; and whatever she was doing or whoever she was listening to, she turned to you at once. Besides, don't you influence everybody? Haven't you always been able to do anything you liked with anybody? And Olivia—oh, I could see to-night that she thought more of you than any one else."

The pale face seemed to grow hard and set as if with some hidden struggle, some suppressed pain.

"That is enough of this nonsense," he said. "Love works madness in some men's brains. It has worked madness in yours. I am no more to Olivia"—he stopped, and swept his hand across his brow, with a gesture of annoyance—"I mean Miss Vanley, than the beggar at her gates."

Bertie rose, pale, too, and with an expression of disappointment.

"Then—then you won't do this for me, Faradeane?"

"If you mean, will I go and ask Miss Vanley to accept you, go to her and propose for you, I certainly will not," was the swift, almost stern response. "Go to her yourself! Why, do you think I am made of wood, clay, iron, that I can bear any better than you the mockery of her laugh, the scorn of those eyes——"

Bertie stared at him.

"Why, what will it matter to you?" he said, innocently. "You won't be telling her that you love her—won't be asking her to be your wife."

For the first time Faradeane's face grew crimson, and his dark, sad eyes drooped.

"Sit down," he said, pointing to the chair. "Your madness is affecting me. It is catching. Sit down." Bertie dropped meekly into the chair, and Faradeane paced up and down the room for a moment or two; then he stopped suddenly and looked down at the handsome, the girlish face, with its trusting patience. "You—you still persist in this insane idea of yours?" he asked, almost harshly.

Bertie nodded.

"Yes, I do. Faradeane, if you knew how much I rely on you——"

Faradeane uttered an impatient exclamation.

"But I do. See here; I have a kind of faith that if you—if you would tell her to—to accept me, that she'd do it. Laugh at the idea as much as you like, but you can't destroy it. It's there, and I can't get rid of it. Cly—I mean Faradeane, for Heaven's sake say 'Yes!'"

Faradeane looked down at him with steady, yet dreamy gaze; then he seemed to straighten himself, to brace himself, as it were, and said, slowly:

"Well, I will do it."

Bertie sprang to his feet, his face flushed with relief and gratification; but Faradeane held up his hand.

"Stop! No gratitude! No thanks! If you knew how I hated"—he stopped and bit his lip—"how I disliked it, you would not say a word."

Bertie seized his hand.

"But I must thank you, old fellow! The best, the dearest——"

"When am I to do this?" interrupted Faradeane in a strained, harsh voice.

"Soon! As soon as you can to-morrow!" replied Bertie, all in a fervor. "I can't wait any longer—I can't, indeed! Ah, if you knew how I love her!"

"Perhaps I can guess," caustically.

"But you can't. You see, she is nothing to you; just a pretty, lady-like girl——"

"Just a pretty, lady-like girl," echoed Faradeane in a strange voice; "exactly."

"But to me she is a goddess, an—an angel. Oh, dear old man, do the best you can for me. I leave it all to you. Tell her that I love her better than life itself; that I—but you will know what to say better than I can tell you. You won't be all of a tremble as I should be. You, not caring for her, will be cool and collected, and—and will persuade her. I should break down and stumble and stammer; but you—you see, it's a matter of perfect indifference to you!"

"Exactly," said Faradeane, and his voice sounded almost harsh and hoarse; "and now——"

"Yes, I'm going," said Bertie, seizing his hat. "I won't thank you——"

"Don't."

"I can't. I shall never be able to pay you——"

"I don't think you will," slowly, almost inaudibly, came the retort.

"But it's just like you. I knew you wouldn't refuse me, though you might not like it at first."

"I don't like it at last. But go now, Cherub," and he laid his hand half protectingly, half pityingly, upon Bertie's shoulder and gently led him to the door.

"Good-night, old fellow; and thank you a thousand—thousand—— Look!" and he sprang into the bush. "Faradeane, there is some one—some man here in the garden!" he exclaimed in a hushed and startled whisper.

Faradeane was at his side in a moment.

"Where?" he asked in a low, calm voice.

"There—there in the shrubs in the shadow. I saw him!"

Faradeane sprang to the spot indicated by Bertie's pointed finger, and searched among the bushes.

"There is no one there," he said, quietly and calmly. "Your nerves are overstrained."

"Where is that dog of yours?" said Bertie.

Faradeane nodded toward the back of the house.

"In the kennel," he said.

"Let him loose—do now! I am sure——Come and let us get him."

They went round to the back and loosened the dog. Both of them went, which was a mistake, for if one of them had remained behind he would have seen Seth, the gypsy, glide out from among the shrubs and vault over the low palings.

The dog bounded across the garden, destroying the flowers, and growling angrily; but after sniffing about for a minute or two, he came back and licked Faradeane's hand.

"There was no one," he said. "Good-night."

"Good-night," said Bertie. "I trust you with my future happiness, old fellow."

"I shall not betray you," was the low-voiced response.

Then he sent the dog back to his kennel, and returned to the parlor.

For a minute or two he stood leaning against the table with his hand before his eyes; then he drew himself upright, and, filling his pipe, smoked furiously.

"I must do it!" he murmured. "But—how hard! How hard! Oh, fool! fool!"

CHAPTER XIII
THE PLEADER

The dawn crept through the window and found Harold Faradeane still pacing to and fro. Later the morning grew rosy and bright and soft with the breath of early summer, and, as he rode up the lane, the rays of sunlight pierced the intervals of the pines, and fell slantwise upon his handsome face and short, wavy hair. It was a morning when one is tempted to join in the concert of the birds; but there was no sign of lightness of heart in the pale face, and a shadow as of coming pain was on the dark eyes.

He rode up to the Grange gates, and was passing through when he saw a slim, girlish form, closely wrapped in a Shetland shawl, half sitting, half lying on the rustic seat beside the lodge porch. It was Bessie. At sight of him a delicate rose tint suffused her face, and a swift change, as if one of the rays of sunlight had touched them, flew into her eyes.

Harold Faradeane pulled up the high-bred horse and slipped from the saddle.

"I'm glad to see you out, Miss Bessie," he said. "You are looking your old self again; but you must take care."

"I—I am all right, quite well now, sir," said Bessie, with the slight, little pant in her voice which always came there when she spoke to him. "Quite well."

"But you are not to be reckless, all the same," he said. "For instance, keep that nice shawl more closely round you," and he drew it together.

Bessie's face grew red, and she stifled a little sigh that was like the quiver of a leaf stirred by the wind, as his hands touched her.

"You are very good to me, sir," she said, in a very low voice. "Yes, it is a nice shawl, isn't it? It is one of dear Miss Olivia's. She brought it down to me this morning, and put it round me with her own, dear hands."

His own hands fell from the shawl, and his eyes dropped.

"That was kind of her," he said, almost coldly.

"Kind! Why, she is all kindness, she and you, Mr. Faradeane."

He smiled absently.

"I'm afraid I'm made of something more than that, Bessie. And Miss Vanley has been here, has she? Has she gone back to the house?"

"No," said Bessie, gravely. "She said she was going into the Spinney — the wood, you know, sir."

She paused a moment, looking wistfully at him, and with the quick intuition which was a never-ceasing subject of Bertie's admiration, he said:

"Well, Bessie?"

She colored, and plucked at the fringe of the shawl.

"I don't think she was quite happy this morning, Mr. Faradeane."

"Not happy!" he said, slowly. "Why?"

"Well, I think, I am sure she had been crying. She was so pale and — and sad. And, besides," naïvely, "I know for certain she had been crying, because she smiled and tried to laugh; and I could — could — —"

"Hear the tears in her voice," he said, more to himself than the girl.

Bessie nodded quickly:

"Yes, that's the words, sir; and it seems so — so dreadful to me that Miss Olivia should have any trouble; it's just as if an angel were to cry," and her own eyes grew dim.

"I understand" he said. He stood for a moment looking down at the path, and flicking his leg with his riding whip; then he said: "And Miss Vanley went to the wood, Bessie?"

"Yes, sir," she replied; "and, oh, Mr. Faradeane, if you — —"

She stopped, abashed.

"Well?" he asked, with a faint smile.

"I was going to say, only I'm afraid, if you'd only go and find her and talk to her. She thinks so much of you — —"

She stopped again, for the smile had suddenly vanished from his face.

"That's nonsense, Bessie," he said. "But, as it happens, I want to see Miss Vanley, and I'll go and find her."

"Yes, sir," said the girl, humbly. "Are — are you angry with me?" and her lips quivered piteously.

"Angry with you, my dear child!" he exclaimed, reassuringly, and he patted her arm under the thick shawl. "Why should I be angry? But"—he paused almost imperceptibly—"but you must not talk such nonsense as that Miss Vanley thinks much or at all of me——"

"But she does!" interrupted Bessie, eagerly. "If you only heard her——"

"I mustn't hear you any longer, you foolish child, or I shall miss Miss Vanley."

And with another gentle and—to Bessie—forgiving touch, he turned and rode toward the wood.

All through the night Olivia had lain awake, tossing to and fro, like a soul struggling in chains. The scene with Bartley Bradstone seemed like a hideous dream, from which, try as she would, she could not awake.

That he should have dared to tell her that he loved her, have asked her to be his wife, was torture enough to her proud, maiden spirit; but that her father should be in his toils, and his happiness and even life—for she knew that Bartley Bradstone spoke only the truth when he said that to leave the Grange would mean death to the squire—was an agony almost insupportable.

At any time in the past the idea of accepting him would have been repugnant; but now, since the last few days, she shrank from the prospect with an absolute loathing. She rose, pale and weakened, bewildered; she felt she could not meet her father that morning. She dreaded to hear even Bartley Bradstone's name. And yet what escape was there for her? If what he had said were true, he held her in an iron thrall. For her father she would sacrifice anything—life itself. But she must have time to think, time to realize the awful ordeal through which she must pass; time to learn how to school her voice and conceal the agony that racked her.

Taking up her hat, and telling the footman that her father was not to wait breakfast for her, she went out, caring nothing about the direction she should take, and, after leaving Bessie, she wandered aimlessly on to the woods and threw herself down on the thick undergrowth in an abandon of misery and dread.

She—she Bartley Bradstone's wife; she who could not endure the sight of his face, she upon whose ear his very voice and laugh jarred! It was terrible; and yet—and yet there was no other way of saving her father, whom she loved with a passionate devotion. Her hot hands clasped each other fiercely, her cheek burned as if she could almost feel the outrage of the man's kiss; then the paroxysm passed, and left her pale and wan and weary, and she lay with her head against a tree and her hands lying loosely in her lap, lovelier in her exhaustion than in her passionate indignation.

And it was at this moment that Harold Faradeane, leading his horse up the narrow footpath, came upon her. For a moment she did not hear the sound of the horse's feet upon the thick undergrowth of moss and bracken; then it seemed as if she felt the dark, sad eyes fixed upon her, for she turned her head and, her pale, lovely face growing warmer, rose to her feet, putting her hand to her brow with a half-startled gesture.

He tossed the bridle over the horse's neck, and came toward her; and as he did so Olivia knew why the idea of being Bartley Bradstone's wife seemed more terrible now than it had done a few weeks ago: knew by the sudden leap of her heart, the swift rush of her young blood through all her veins at the sight of this other man!

"I'm afraid I've startled you," he said, as he took her hand; it burnt and throbbed like an imprisoned bird in his firm grasp. "Miss Bessie told me I should find you here, and I was lucky enough to hit upon the right path. What a delightful spot you have chosen! A Dryads' perfect nook," he added, talking to give her time to recover from her surprise, and looking round slowly.

She put her hands to her face and smoothed her hair, with one of those delicate, little touches peculiar to her, and stooped for her hat, which she had tossed aside, but he was quicker, and got it for her.

"Thank you," she said, and her voice, sweet at all times, smote upon his ears like a melody too subtle for description. "Yes, it is pretty; I—I often come here. Were you going to the house? My father is in, I know. I will come, too."

"I was going to the house," he said, and he spoke slowly, as if he were keeping a strict guard upon his words, his very tone. "But it was not to see Mr. Vanley; I wanted to see you."

"To see me!" she echoed, and, his gaze fixed on the ground, he did not see the sudden expansion of her eyes or the swift rush of blood to her face. "To see me!" and her hand stole shyly to her heart for an instant.

"Yes," he said. "You are surprised that I, who am almost a stranger, should wish to speak to you alone; but one is not always the master of his own actions, not always a free agent. Miss Vanley, will you promise to listen patiently to me, however much I shall try your patience, your sweet gentleness? Will you not sit down?"

She sank on to the grass, and looked up, and yet not at him, for her eyes were heavy with a strange shyness, and it seemed to her that he must hear her heart beat, it echoed with such full joy every word of his musical voice.

"I shall try your patience," he said, with a suppressed sigh, still looking on the ground. "I came this morning to stand here before you as a suitor" — her face grew pale and her lips quivered, and a wild thrill of joy ran through her — "as a humble suitor, as a man pleading for something dearer even than life!" His voice broke for a moment. "Yes, dearer than life. You see I find my task difficult; even now, now that I have ventured to begin, I would draw back if I could — —" She glanced up at him, half-amazedly, half-sorrowfully. "For I realize how great, how precious a treasure it is that I am striving for. But I am not free — a stronger will than mine impels me. Miss Vanley forget if you can — I know it will be hard — that I am almost a stranger, that you know nothing of me, and — listen to me. Do not send me away till I have told you what I came to tell you, what I would have kept from you, even now, if I had not given my word."

Again the look swept over her face.

"You will not wonder that a man should love you. I don't think it is possible for any one to see you, to hear you, to be in your presence for one short day without loving you."

No words can describe the infinite tenderness and reverence, and yet the infinite sadness of his voice. At that moment, even so soon, she could have stretched out her arms to him.

"No!" he continued. "No one could help loving you, and no one loves you more dearly, more truly, more passionately. That I can say with perfect truth; and I beg, I implore you to believe it! There are better, wiser men, but none in all the world who will more greatly prize the treasure of your love, if you will give it him."

She sat, her hands clasped, her eyes hidden under their long lashes. All thought, all remembrance of Bartley Bradstone, of her father's impending ruin, had passed from her. She was living, absorbed, in this, the one, the great moment, of her existence.

"If a life's devotion can insure your happiness, I can pledge it. I do so. Of all else I say nothing. You know something of him already; I think, I know you can trust him. What will you say to me, Olivia?" The name slipped from him unawares. "What answer shall I get? Will you trust yourself to the man who loves you with all his heart and soul? Will you make him the happiest or the most wretched man in all the world?"

Olivia Or, It was for her sake | 127

He had grown earnest, for all his guard upon his words and voice, and as he made his final appeal he bent over her.

She lifted her eyes to his, then raised her hand.

He took it, and his own closed round it with a quick, almost painful grasp.

"You say 'yes!'" he said, then he dropped her hand as if some hidden pain had overmastered him, and sprang, like a wild animal breaking his bonds, to his feet. "Bertie is a happy man!" he said, almost hoarsely, turning away his head.

Her hand fell into her lap, her face grew white, her eyes expanded with a look of doubt, dread, horror.

"Bertie!" she breathed.

He turned slowly, and she saw that his face was as white as her own, and reflected something of her own horror. "Yes, Bertie," he said, almost sternly, as if struggling against some terrible impulse. "It is of Bertie—Lord Granville—I have been speaking. It is for him I have been pleading."

"For—him!" she panted, her bosom heaving, her hands clinching spasmodically.

"Yes," he went on, more hurriedly. "He has loved you since you were playmates, loved you with all his heart and soul, so passionately that he feared, dreaded even to tell you, lest you should make light of it! Why do you look at me so? Are you angry? God knows it was unwillingly enough that I did it! I would sooner—but he won me over! I was mad to promise him, but I did so, and——Miss Vanley!—Olivia!"—and he drew nearer—"did you think"—his breath came fast, a light, almost fierce, flashed in his eyes—"did you think——Heavens! I can't speak it!"

She had found nerve and strength—the strength which is born of shame. All her soul seemed burning with the shame of the mistake she had made; every nerve throbbed.

"I—I"—she panted—"I don't understand. Of course it was—Bertie."

He drew back and looked at her fixedly, grimly.

"Of course it was—Bertie. I—knew. Yes, I knew," and she almost stamped her foot, "and I meant to tell you, if you had given me time that—that it was—'No!'"

"No!" he echoed.

"No!" she repeated, almost fiercely. "No—a hundred times! Go and tell him so—and tell him that if I loved him as he says he—he loves me, I would not stoop to marry a man who sends another to—to—plead for him."

He still looked at her with a grim, fixed gaze.

"Is that your answer?" he asked, in so low a tone that it was almost inaudible.

"It is!" she responded, with a pant. "Why do you not go? You can tell him," with a cruel smile, "that you did your best, that you are not to be blamed; that if he had had any chance you would have succeeded in your—mission. Yes," with a strange thrill, "you—you did your best!"

He stood with his hands behind his back, his head lowered under the storm of her fierce, maiden passion.

"Why do you not go?" she repeated, impatiently, "or do you wish me to?"

He held up his hands as if to stay her; then, not even lifting his hat, turned and left her.

Out in the park, out of her sight, he stood and looked round him like a man who has received an overwhelming shock, which, for the time, has bereft him of his senses; then he went toward his horse, which was quietly nibbling at the boughs.

As he did so he heard a sound behind him, a sob such as one hears from the woman whose heart is breaking.

He dropped the bridle, and a shudder ran through him as he stood for a moment awestruck; then he sprang back. She was lying full length on the ground, her arms extended, her face lying upon the grass, her hands clinching the bracken; a picture of a living soul writhing in an agony of shame and wounded love.

He was beside her in an instant, his strong arms around her, his voice, full of passionate love and self-reproach, calling on her name.

"Olivia! Olivia! my love! my love! Olivia!"

Weakened, exhausted, she was powerless to resist him, and he held her in his arms, her supple form pressed against his breast, his eyes looking down into hers with a mad, wild hunger, an infinite sadness.

A moment—ah, but it was a lifetime!—passed, then suddenly a cold wave seemed to sweep over him, and, still holding her, he rose to his feet.

She felt the change, be it what it may, and drew back from him, leaning against a tree, panting and quivering.

And he stood and looked at her in silence—a terrible silence.

At last his voice came hoarsely, as if with difficulty.

"Olivia—Miss Vanley! Forgive me! Forgive me! I—I was mad! I forgot—I—I forgot! Forgive me and forget every mad word——"

He hung his head.

She looked at him, a look of terrible questioning. He had called her his love, had held her in his arms, and now he asked her to forget.

She drew herself up, white and trembling, but strong in her woman's pride.

"Forget! Yes!" she said. "But not forgive! You—you should have waited until—until I told you that I have promised to be Bartley Bradstone's wife, Mr. Faradeane!"

Then, drawing her skirts close, as if to avoid touching him, she swept by him, and left him standing with bowed head and heaving chest.

CHAPTER XIV
THE FUTURE SON-IN-LAW

It was the first great agony in Olivia's life. White to the lips, quivering with the shame which only a pure-hearted girl whose love has been repulsed can feel, she made her way homeward.

It was easy enough to carry her head erect, and to assume a proud and haughty mien while she was within Faradeane's sight; but as she neared the Grange she felt herself drooping, and she was quivering and trembling in every limb as she entered the hall.

She was ascending the great staircase on her way to her room, to give vent to her pent-up feelings in secure solitude, when a footman came up to her.

"Mr. Bradstone, miss," he said, handing her a card on a salver. "He is in the drawing-room with Mr. Vanley."

Olivia hesitated, but only for a moment; then, in a voice that sounded strained and unnatural, she said:

"Very well, I will see him in a minute or two."

Then she went upstairs to her room, and flung herself on the bed, and for a few minutes lay motionless, struggling for calm and self-possession.

She had passed the Rubicon; she had declared herself engaged to marry Bartley Bradstone, and she would carry out her resolution; but how gladly would she have died rather than go down and tell him so!

She rose after a few minutes and bathed her face, then went slowly downstairs.

The squire had left the room, and Bartley Bradstone was walking to and fro over the thick Persian carpet, biting his nails, and looking like a man waiting for the verdict of a court trying him for a capital offense, and as the door opened he turned with a start that was very much like that of a culprit.

Olivia did not offer him her hand, but stood before him with pale face and downcast eyes.

"You wished to see me," she said, and the words sounded like those spoken by a cleverly-constructed automaton.

"Yes," he said, nervously, raising his restless eyes to her beautiful face. "Yes, I—I could not wait any longer. I—I was anxious and—and upset. I meant to give you more time, but—I haven't slept a wink since last night. Miss Vanley—Olivia—you can't guess how I love you," and he moistened his dry lips.

"You love me?" said Olivia, as if to herself.

"Yes," he responded. "Is there anything strange in that? Why shouldn't I love you? All—all the men I know, all the men who know you, do, and why shouldn't I? I'm not made of wood or stone. I do love you!"

"And you want me to be your wife?" calmly, coldly, almost like a statue.

He winced at the matter-of-fact words.

"Of course. Yes, Miss Vanley—Olivia——"

"It is so strange," she murmured, again as if to herself.

"Strange! how strange?" he echoed, fidgeting with his handkerchief.

"Strange that you should want me, while I——"

She stopped and eyed him with a look in her dreamy, tear-dimmed eyes, that ought to have stricken him to stone.

"You—you mean that you don't lo—care for me?" he said, eagerly. "Miss Vanley—Olivia—I don't ask you to, I don't expect it. Why should I? I know I'm not fit, that I'm not worthy, that there are many men better fitted—I mean—I don't want you—that is, I don't count on that. Not at present. I'm content to wait."

"To wait until I care for you?" she said, in the tone of a person who is making a bargain, a hard bargain.

"That's it," he assented, with feverish eagerness. "I'm content if you'll only promise to—to try and think of me as your husband. I know you won't go from your word."

"No, I shall not go from my word," she said, slowly.

"No, I know that, I know I can trust you, and that is the reason I am so anxious to get you to say that you will be my wife."

"I see," she said, her lovely eyes looking beyond him into vacancy. "You are easily satisfied, Mr. Bradstone."

"Am I?" he retorted, nervously. "I don't think I am."

"Yes," she said, dreamily, pushing the hair from her forehead as if it were a heavy burden; "there are so many girls who would be so glad to hear what—what you have said to me; so many! Better, prettier girls than I am."

"I don't know any better or prettier," he said, curtly. "There is no one in all the world that I have ever thought of speaking to— —"

"You are very rich," she said, breaking in upon his protestations with calm self-possession.

"Rich? Yes, I'm rich. I told you so—I didn't exaggerate. If it is money you want— —"

"I do want money!" she said, calmly. "You promised, offered me, how much?"

"You shall have all you want," he replied, promptly. "I'm not a mean man; no one has ever called me that. I'll settle forty, fifty thousand pounds— —"

"Settle," she said; "what does that mean?"

"It means for your own use; tied to you— —"

She thought a moment.

"How much is it that—that my father owes?" she asked.

Her lips twitched.

"Forty thousand, or thereabouts."

"You know, of course you know?" she asked, and her eyes dwelt upon his with a dull questioning.

His face reddened.

"I—I happen to know," he answered. "Fifty thousand would clear him."

"It is a large sum of money," she said; and she murmured, "Poor papa!"

"It is," he assented. "It's a big sum, look at it as you will; but I'm ready— —"

"You will give it to me—give it to me unconditionally," she interrupted in a low, clear voice.

"Yes, I'll give it to you the day we are married, and unconditionally. You can do what you like with it. Fling it in the gutter or—or—hand it over to the squire. It's a large sum of money,"—slowly, reluctantly—"but it's nothing to me. You don't know—nobody knows—how rich I am. I've made money by the hatful; I'm making it now. You shall have everything you want; every wish, however extravagant, shall be gratified. I'll make a settlement on you in addition to that— —"

She shook her head.

"I want that sum, and no other," she said, slowly. "I want that money to do what I like with."

"You shall have it!" he responded, eagerly.

"And you are content?" she asked, her eyes resting on his face with a calm wonder that was more terrible than contempt. "You are satisfied with your bargain, content to buy me——"

"Oh, Miss Olivia!" he cried, deprecatingly.

"But you have bought me," she said, in a low voice, "and you know it. You do not expect me to love you. You only wish me to be your wife, and you ask no questions——"

He reddened; then turned pale.

"I—I ask no questions," he said, and his voice came huskily and heavily. "No, I am content. I—I don't suppose I am the first man who's made love to you. You're too beautiful"—Olivia glanced at the glass curiously, as if at some other face—"too—too good a match for me to hope for that. But—I'll chance all that."

"You will take the risk?" she said, in a low voice.

Her words seemed to affect him strangely. He changed color, and darted a look of distrust and suspicion at her from his restless eyes.

"What do you mean? What risk?" he said, nervously.

She shook her head.

"Risk of the future," she said. "Does anything but unhappiness and misery spring from such a marriage as this would be?"

He drew a breath—it almost seemed of relief.

"Oh, as to that," he said, "I am not uneasy. Why should we be unhappy with everything we want, everything that money can buy? It's the people who are poor who are miserable and discontented. They have to pinch and screw and stick in one place; while we—you shall do as you like, go as you like. I'm fond of The Maples—because it's near the Grange, and—and you; but if you don't like it, I'll buy another place for you anywhere. I think I told you that the other night; I know if I didn't, I meant it. I spend all my time thinking how I can please you, and I will do it! What do you say? Let me have an answer. It—it isn't fair, it isn't like you, who are so kind and thoughtful always to—to other people, to keep me in suspense."

"No," she said, as if to herself, "it is not fair. And I have made up my mind. I had made it up before I came into the room."

"You had?" he breathed, evidently in an agony of conflicting hope and fear.

"Yes, Mr. Bradstone, I mean to accept your proposal if—if you would promise me the money."

He came forward with a half-fearful promptitude, and an inarticulate cry of satisfaction.

"You say 'Yes,' Olivia! If I will promise you! Why, I'd lay every penny I possess at your feet this moment, if you wished it." And he really quite believed his capacity for such a sacrifice. "Every penny. Oh, how happy you have made me!"

He drew nearer, and timidly took her hand in both his, and fondled it with humble eagerness.

And as she let her hand remain, there flashed through her mind, her heart, the passionate face of Harold Faradeane; there had been no timidity, no servility in his fierce caresses for the few short moments they lasted.

She allowed him to hold her hand in his for a minute or so, then slowly withdrew it, and walked to the window. He followed her hesitatingly.

"May I stay?" he asked.

"No!" she said, not coldly, but with a terrible calmness. "I want to think—I would rather——"

"I understand; of course you'd like to be alone—after all this. I'll go and tell the squire——" he said, smothering a sigh of disappointment.

She turned on him quickly.

"You will not tell him——"

"About our bargain? No, trust me," he said, with a sharp smile and a gleam of cunning in his small eyes. "Good-by, then, till——"

He waited for her to fix a time, but she merely murmured "Good-by," and with a wistful glance at her, he left the room.

She stood looking out at the bright flowers, her face pale, and wearing the rapt, preoccupied expression it had borne all through the interview. Then, as she heard the door open, she forced a smile to her lips, and turned with her back to the window to receive her father.

"Olivia!" he said, coming to her quietly. "Is this true?"

"That I am engaged to Mr. Bradstone, papa?" she said, with an unnatural cheerfulness. "Quite true. Has he told you?"

"Yes; the poor fellow is half mad with joy; I never saw him so—but let me look at you!"

And he took her in his arms and looked at her searchingly.

She bore it for a moment or two, then hid her face on his shoulder.

"Are you pleased, papa?" she said, in a low voice.

"Pleased?" he echoed, and there was a strange ring in his grave voice, a vague anxiety. "Yes, yes—that is, if you are pleased. It is for you to decide, my child. I have said all along, I have told him repeatedly, that not by word or look would I seek to influence you. If I have, it has been unconsciously."

"No, dear," she murmured. "And you have not. It is of my own free will—and you are pleased? Tell me, papa."

She seemed to crave a word of approval or satisfaction from him.

"Of course I am pleased," he said, gravely. "Bartley—by the way, you must not call him Mr. Bradstone any more—Bartley is a good fellow. I have always said so, and though you might have done better, as the cant of the world goes, he is a wealthy man, a very wealthy man, I think, and that means so much now, Olivia."

And he stifled a sigh.

"Yes," she said, softly. "I know that, and Mr. Brad—Bartley"—the name seemed to leave her lips awkwardly—"is generous."

"I think so, I think so, I have always said so," he assented, as if he were eager to emphasize the good points of his future son-in-law. "Did he speak to you of money?" he said, after a moment's pause.

"Yes," she replied. "He told me that I could have as much as I wanted. That was generous, papa!"

"Very. It bears out my estimate of his character," he said, his brow knitting itself. "He—he told you that?"

"Yes," she said, in a low voice.

He drew a breath of relief.

"Heaven grant you have done wisely!" he said. "Of one thing there can be no doubt; he loves you very deeply, Olivia."

"Yes," she assented.

"And you?"

She kept the brave smile on her face.

"I shall make him as good a wife as I can, dear," she said. "I—I think he will be very happy."

He drew her to him and kissed her.

"It is of your happiness I am thinking," he said, in a low, nervous voice. "But I think you have done right. Heaven send you every joy, my child. You have been, and will still be, all the world to me—all the world——" He broke off abruptly, as if unable to continue, and, gently releasing her, walked aside for a moment. Then he came back to her. "You will live at The Maples, Olivia? I could not lose you—I could not! There must be an understanding—a bargain."

A faint shudder ran through her at the sound of the hateful word.

"There shall be a bargain, dear," she said, smiling. "Mr. Brad—Bartley has just told me that we should live where I please, and the nearer I am to you—ah, if we could only live here!"

"Why should you not?" he responded, eagerly; then he checked himself with a laugh. "No, that would be asking too much, even of Bartley, generous as he is. But The Maples is not very far, is it? Not very far. I shall see you every day. You will still be the sunlight of my life, the comfort of my old age. See how selfish I am!"

She flung her arms around him with a sudden *abandon*, and he felt her quiver and tremble as she sobbed.

"Yes, I shall still be your child, papa. You will never let me go far from you. Promise—promise!"

"Hush, hush, Olivia!" he said, soothingly, his own voice trembling. "This is my fault. Come, come; this is not very complimentary to Bartley. Why, dear, you must remember that you don't lose your father because you gain a husband! Bartley and I are quite close friends, and we shall be closer now. Run up to your room, my dear, or he will see you have been crying, and feel hurt. He loves you, thank God! No man could love you more devotedly."

CHAPTER XV
A WOMAN'S WAY

Faradeane rode home slowly through the wood. It was well for him that his horse was sure-footed, and picked its way safely through the undergrowth, for its master rode like a man who has suddenly lost his sense of sight and hearing. Unguided, the animal bore him to the gate, and then Faradeane, with an effort, raised his head and threw off the kind of lethargy which had held him.

He threw the bridle to his man and entered the cottage. As he did so, Bertie sprang out of a chair to meet him, with an eager, anxious expression; then he stopped short and uttered an exclamation of dismay.

"Great Heavens! are you ill?"

Faradeane closed the door carefully, and dropped his hat on the table.

"No—that is, yes; it's of no consequence." He went to the sideboard and drank some wine. "I—I beg your pardon; help yourself. You'll want it," he added, not unfeelingly, but with a sad, decisive air.

"Then—then you've seen her?" faltered Bertie. "I thought you would go to her this morning. You have seen her— —"

"Yes, I have seen her," assented Faradeane, dryly.

"And—but there is no need to ask you the result," breathed Bertie, like a man resolved not to show the agony that is devouring him.

"My face is that of an unsuccessful ambassador, is it? Yes, my mission has failed, Cherub. I am sorry."

Bertie turned his back to him and was silent for a moment; then he said, hoarsely:

"What did she say? Tell me."

"What did she say?" repeated Faradeane, dropping into a chair and passing his hand over his brow with a weary gesture, as a smile of bitter self-mockery shone for a moment in his eyes. "I don't know. What does it matter?"

"You don't know?" echoed Bertie, turning to him. "For Heaven's sake, try and remember! I—I can bear it, whatever it was. Did she laugh?" and his lips quivered.

"Laugh! No, she didn't laugh much," replied Faradeane, grimly, as the vision of the slim, graceful form lying full length in its *abandon* of misery rose before him.

"Then she took it seriously? What did you say to her, Faradeane?"

"I said all I could. I did my best. Believe that, Bertie. I can't tell you what I said, but I pleaded as if"—he paused, and his lips came together tightly—"as if I were pleading for myself. I could do no more. Would to Heaven I had not done so much!" bitterly.

"And what did she reply? Did she say 'No' straight out?"

"No, she didn't."

"Then there is—there may be some hope! You took her by surprise; she was frightened, perhaps. She'll think it over," said Bertie, excitedly.

Faradeane rose and laid his hand on his shoulder, firmly, yet, pityingly.

"Cherub, there is no hope," he said, in a low, grave voice. "I should be your bitterest enemy, instead of your best friend, if I allowed you to think that there was. There is none. Accept it, Bertie, once and for all. Be a man; there is no hope—there never has been. If you had pleaded for yourself, if an angel had pleaded for you, instead of me, it would have been the same."

"She—she never cared for me?"

"Yes, she cares for you as a sister cares for a brother. Be content with that——"

"Content!" Bertie burst out. "Content! You are mad, Faradeane!"

"I dare say," was the calm, sad assent. "We are all more or less mad, Cherub; but I would rather be loved as a brother by Olivia—Miss Vanley—than as a husband by any other woman——"

He stopped abruptly, and Bertie stared at him.

"You can't know what love—such love as mine—is!" he said.

Faradeane smiled.

"Perhaps not," he said, grimly.

"I tell you—but what is the use of talking? Faradeane, my life is ruined. I don't care what becomes of me. I staked everything upon her; I loved her as no man ever loved a woman before. I—oh, old fellow, tell me the truth! Is there no hope for me?"

Faradeane shook his head.

"Not a fragment," he said, solemnly.

"If I—if I went to her myself——"

"As you should have done at first," said Faradeane, grimly. "Would to Heaven you had. No, Bertie, none. Don't go to her. Accept my report. Why should you harass her? I tell you that there is no more chance of her marrying you than there is of her marrying—the Sultan of Mocha. Be a man, Cherub. There are other women——"

Bertie put up his hand.

"Don't," he said, wincing. "I can't bear that anyhow. I'm—I'm very grateful to you, old fellow. You did what few men would have done, what I would have asked no other man to do, and—and I'm grateful. Even now, crushed and knocked out of time as I am, I can scarcely realize it. I thought she might not consent right away, that she might say she'd think it over——"

"There was no occasion for her to do that," said Faradeane, grimly.

Bertie looked up sharply.

"You mean that there was—some one else?" he said, with the acuteness of a man whose nerves are on the rack.

Faradeane nodded.

"There is! Who—who is it?"

"Mr. Bartley Bradstone."

Bertie groaned.

"That fellow! Merciful Heaven! Bradstone! Oh, Faradeane!"

"You are surprised?"

"Yes; surprised is not the word. Why—why, I never thought that she would accept him. I knew he was pursuing her, but I never thought—if I had any fear at all, and it only came to me while I was waiting here, it was that it was you she might care for."

Faradeane's face went white.

"It is you who are mad," he said, sternly.

"Forgive me," pleaded Bertie, wiping the perspiration from his forehead. "But I've seen her with both you and him; and I've heard her speak to him, seen her look at him as if she disliked him, while to you she was all smiles."

Faradeane sprang to his feet.

"That will do!" he said, in a low, harsh voice. "You are scarcely accountable for your words to-day, Bertie; but don't you see, great heavens, man, how you are giving her away? Is Miss Vanley the kind of woman to engage herself to one man while she is in love— —Bah! pull yourself together, and face the inevitable like a man," and he paced to and fro impatiently.

Bertie hid his face in his hands, then he looked up.

"Faradeane, I'm sorry I should have said what I did, and yet I could have borne it better if—if it had been you, instead of him. You are—well, you are yourself, and are worthy of her."

Faradeane stopped and put up his hand with a bitter laugh.

"Worthy! I!" he said, in an undertone.

"Yes," said Bertie, stubbornly. "In all this—this mystery that hangs about you, I know how worthy you are; I could have borne it, I could have looked forward to the time when I could have cared for her as a sister, and— but this man! Why, Faradeane, has she ever looked at him or spoken to him at all pleasantly? Hasn't she snubbed him and treated him in such a way as would have made you and me go and cut our throats?"

"That's a woman's way," said Faradeane, grimly; "to treat a man like a dog and then—marry him."

"But not hers!" responded Bertie, with earnest conviction. "You don't know Olivia as well as I do." Faradeane smiled sadly. "She has none of the unwomanly meannesses. No, there is some other reason."

Faradeane stopped short and looked at him.

"Do you mean to say that it is because the man is rich?"

Bertie shook his head.

"Heaven knows that can't be the reason. The squire is a rich man; the estate— —"

"Besides," said Faradeane, more to himself than Bertie, "that would be a reason for accepting you!"

Bertie colored and shook his head.

"No it wouldn't. Everybody knows how poor we Carfields are. My father has been retrenching for years."

Faradeane shrugged his shoulders.

"We might talk till the moon turned black," he said, "and still be far enough away from her motives. The question is, what will you do?"

"What can I do?" replied Bertie. "There is only one thing left for me to do; to get away from here as soon as possible, and to fight out the battle as best I can. I shall start at once."

"Where to?"

"To—to the devil!" responded Bertie, desperately.

Faradeane laid a strong hand on each of his shoulders, and looked him full in the face with a steadfast gaze.

"No, not in that direction, Cherub," he said. "There is no forgetfulness to be found in that gentleman's company. That way, indeed, madness lies. Be a man, dear boy. Other men have suffered——" He paused. "Well, yes, some of us have suffered worse pangs than are torturing you just this minute, and we have gone whither you said. Some of us have come back with much difficulty; others have remained, and gone down to the unfathomable pit. Take the word of a man who was lucky enough to draw back in time; there is no comfort to be found in that direction. If you must go, take my advice and go out into the wilds. There is nothing like Nature. She is the one universal mother of consolation. Go and seek her in her wildest aspect; go and have a shot at some big game—Africa—the Rockies—anywhere you can find room to fight your battle in. And then—when you have won—come back and learn that there is no sorrow that time cannot teach you to forget, no wound it cannot heal."

"My life is over," said Bertie. "The best thing I can do is to try and get rid of it."

"Well, yes, so it is," said Faradeane, with a sad smile. "And you'll find that the very first moment that is likely to occur you will cling to that same life pretty tightly. Ah, Cherub, don't think I am unfeeling. I know—I tell you I know, how you feel!" and his hands pressed his shoulders soothingly. "Good-by, dear lad. You've one thing on your side—youth. You'll still be young when you come back and tell me that you have found your heart again, and—lost it to some one else."

Bertie bit his lip, and forced the tears back from his eyes, for there was something inexpressively touching in Faradeane's words and tone.

"Good-by, old fellow," he said, taking his hat, "I can't tell you how grateful I am to you. When I look back and remember how constantly you have been my friend; how, many and many a time, you have lifted me out of a scrape, it seems hard to part from you. But I'll go as you advise me. Africa's the best place, I think," ruefully. "And you'll stop here?"

Faradeane nodded.

"For the present, yes."

Bertie sighed.

"I envy you. You will be near to her, at any rate. Faradeane," suddenly, "will you do one thing for me?"

"I don't know; my last promise got me into a scrape that makes me cautious. What is it?"

"It isn't much. It's only to—to remember how—how dearly I loved her, and to promise, if anything should happen to her, any trouble, anything wrong, that you will stand her friend, as you have stood mine. You see, I've learned to rely on you so much——"

"What is likely to happen to the wife of the wealthy Mr. Bradstone?" said Faradeane, pacing to and fro again, with knit brows. "Well, well, I promise. Is that all?"

"That's enough!" said Bertie, simply. "Now, good-by."

"Good-by; be a man, Cherub!"

His white hand closed round the lad's soft, girlish ones and wrung them; then the two men parted, without another word.

CHAPTER XVI
BARTLEY BRADSTONE'S VICTORY

The news of the engagement spread like wildfire, and caused almost as much excitement in the county as a general conflagration would have done. The consternation and disappointment among the eligible men, who had each one cherished a secret hope that the prize might be his, was fearful.

"Confound these city beggars!" said one young baronet, who had laid constant siege to Olivia's heart for three hunting seasons. "They carry everything off nowadays. Seems to me that a man's thought nothing of—by the women, at any rate—unless he has made a pile of money out of cotton or stocks and shares. Here's the fellow without a grandfather, or an ounce of blood in his veins, carries off the loveliest and sweetest girl we've got. Hang me if I don't go and get a stool in a confounded counting-house, and make a pile myself. I don't know what's come to things nowadays; it's all money, money, money."

Aunt Amelia was delighted, and almost went into hysterics, when Olivia quietly told her, the morning after Bartley Bradstone had been accepted.

"I am so glad you have taken my advice, my dear," she said, pressing a spasmodic kiss upon Olivia's white forehead. "Ah, if I had only had some one to advise me when I was your age; but I was a giddy girl, and would have my own way. I was always too particular, too fastidious, my dear; that has been my great fault. But you are different, thank Heaven, and know how to take advantage of your opportunity; which I never did, alas! And it is a splendid opportunity. Birth and all that kind of thing are all very well, but money is the thing nowadays, and dear Bartley—you don't mind my calling him Bartley, I hope, dear? Say so at once if you do, I'm sure I am the last to presume——"

"Call him anything you please, aunt," said Olivia, wearily.

"Very well, dear; what was I saying? Oh, dear Bartley is so—so nice, so really nice with all his wealth, that I am sure you will be happy. And when is the wedding to be? Now, don't blush."

It was a very pale blush, if any, that rose to Olivia's face; it went paler, indeed.

"There has been nothing said of—a wedding," she replied.

Aunt Amelia nodded.

"Just so; quite right. But remember, my dear, that nothing is so—so unwise as a long engagement. You never can tell, men are so—so fickle nowadays, and there are so many girls. By the way, how mad those poor Penstone girls will be. I am sure they were both setting their caps at him."

Olivia rose with a laugh that was almost hysterical, and left Miss Amelia to gloat over Annie's and Mary's supposed disappointment in solitude.

The people flocked to the Grange to offer the usual congratulations, and presents poured in to an extent that caused the hall porter some embarrassment, and Olivia received both congratulations and presents with a manner which, though all her dear friends agreed in declaring it perfect, rather puzzled them.

"If she had been married for a year, instead of only going to be, she could not take it more coolly," said Mary to her sister, as they drove from the Grange after their visit. "I can't make the darling out quite. Did you notice how pale she was, and how—I don't know how to describe it—how *distraite*? I hope I shan't look like that a few days after my engagement. Do you think she really loves him, Annie? It is so unexpected, isn't it? I wouldn't breathe a word of doubt about our darling Olivia, but there was Bertie Granville, for instance—so handsome and nice, and he loved her to distraction, any one could see that. Oh, I wish she were going to marry him, now."

"Don't be silly," retorted Annie. "Why should she marry Mr. Bradstone if she doesn't want to? You don't suppose that it was for his money—she, the squire's only daughter and heiress!"

And this argument of Annie's was put forward throughout the county whenever any one expressed astonishment that Mr. Bartley Bradstone should have carried off the prize which so many had coveted, or ventured to suggest that his money had something to do with his success. Why should she, the daughter of the wealthy Squire of Hawkwood, want to marry money? And this argument was always found unanswerable.

Mr. Bartley Bradstone bore himself very modestly, considering the greatness of his victory. He was a little louder in his speech, perhaps, and there was a look of elation in his small eyes which was pardonable in a man who had snatched the Rose of Hawkwood before the envious eyes of far better men than himself; but his speech toned down and his look of elation diminished when he was in the presence of his betrothed.

He went to the Grange every day, and nearly every day he and Olivia rode or drove out together, accompanied by Aunt Amelia or one or sometimes both of the Penstone girls, and though Olivia was always cheerful and pleasant with him, it was a cold kind of cheerfulness, a forced sort of pleasantness. The paleness which Mary had remarked had not disappeared, and there had come into the dark eyes a far-away look, which might represent the quiet joy of an engaged girl, but was rather sad and unsatisfactory for the man who loved her. And he did love her, more deeply and intensely each day, with an absorption which only the truly selfish man who has set his heart upon gaining an object is capable of.

Three or four times a week he dined at the Grange, his place, as was his right, beside Olivia, and all through the dinner she sat and listened when he spoke, and answered, when a reply was necessary, with the same far-away look in her eyes, the same pallor on her cheeks.

One evening after dinner, when the squire and Bradstone had come into the drawing-room for their tea, which Miss Amelia was dispensing with nods and becks and wreathed smiles, that lady said, suddenly:

"Oh, Edwin! what is this I hear about dear Bertie? Is it true—it can't be true—that he has gone off suddenly to Australia to shoot lions?"

Olivia was sitting on a low chair beside the open window, a book lying on her lap, page downward, her eyes fixed on the tall elms that lined the drive. For a second a warm flush rose to her face, but for a second only, and her gaze did not falter.

"I shouldn't think it could be true," replied the squire, dryly, "seeing that it is impossible."

"There are no lions in Australia, unfortunately, Miss Vanley," explained Bartley Bradstone, as he carried the cup of tea to Olivia.

"No? Really? How interesting! You are always so well informed, Bartley. But is it true that he has gone off to some other dreadful place among wild beasts and savages?" she persisted—for to Miss Amelia the whole earth beyond, say, Italy and France, was a ravening wilderness.

"He has gone out on a hunting and shooting expedition, yes," said the squire, absently.

"Now I do call that so stupid!" exclaimed Miss Amelia. "Why on earth couldn't he be satisfied to remain at home? Why did he go, do you know? Some love disappointment, I suppose!" and she laid her head on one shoulder and sighed.

"I don't know," replied the squire. "He did not come to bid us good-by; the vessel left suddenly, Lord Carfield says. I only heard of the boy's departure from Mr. Faradeane——"

Olivia was holding her teacup for some milk, which Bartley Bradstone had brought her, and it slipped suddenly from her fingers, spilling the tea over her pure white frock.

Bartley Bradstone had his handkerchief out, and was on his knees at her side in a moment, but she drew back out of his reach. "It is of no consequence," she said, calmly.

"I'll get you another cup. That pretty dress! Won't you let me wipe it for you?" he pleaded, tenderly.

"No, no, thanks," she returned in a voice of suppressed irritation. "I will go and change it," and she moved to the door; but as she did so, Aunt Amelia exclaimed:

"That delightful Mr. Faradeane, now really!" and Olivia paused to gather up some fancy-work from the piano. "He was such a great friend of Bertie's, was he not? And I don't wonder. Such a charming man! I really do wish he were a little more—more sociable. You might ask him to dinner again, Edwin."

The squire rose and shook his head.

"It is no use," he said, "Mr. Faradeane has plainly indicated his desire to be left alone. I asked him yesterday, and several days before, when I met him out riding. I am afraid he has been, and is, ill."

Olivia put her hand upon the door, but still waited.

"Oh, I am so sorry! Fancy how dreadful to be ill and all alone in that solitary spot!" said Miss Amelia. "Poor man! I really think you ought to call, Edwin, and you, too, Bartley. I wonder"—with an air of maiden timidity—"if he would think it intrusive or—or pushing, if I sent him some beef tea."

The squire laughed quietly.

"Better not, you think, Edwin? Well, perhaps so; one can't be too careful. But I really think you ought to call, Bartley."

"I will, if you like," he said, but not very readily. "Shall I, Olivia?"

She turned her pale face slightly toward him.

"I do not care," she said, and opening the door, went out, and up the stairs to her own room. She stood by the white bed looking dreamily before her for a moment or two, her father's words echoing dully in her ears; then she remembered why she had come upstairs, and was about to ring for her maid, when a great wave of heat seemed to sweep over her.

"I can't go back and listen to them talking of him—not just yet, not just yet!" she murmured, putting her hand to her throat. "He has been ill—but what is he to me?" with a dry sob. Her hat and a fur cloak were lying on a chair, and she took them up absently, and putting them on, went down the stairs on to the terrace.

"Just five minutes alone!" she murmured. "Five minutes to think—no, to forget! Oh, if I could forget!" And she beat her hand upon the balustrade. "It would all be so easy if I could forget."

She stood for a moment or two looking wistfully down into the dusky avenue; then a sudden desire to lose herself in its shade possessed her.

"I'll go and see Bessie," she murmured. She had not been near the girl since the engagement, fearing the scrutiny of the simple, loving eyes more than she had dreaded aught else. "Yes, I'll go and see Bessie!" and she passed down the steps.

As she did so, Bartley Bradstone's commonplace figure came out by the drawing-room window and stood clearly defined against the light.

"Olivia! Olivia!" he called.

She drew back into the shadow and set her teeth; then, as he went in again, evidently to look for her in the house, she glided rapidly into the avenue, and went toward the lodge. She had almost reached it, was within touch of the big gates, when the figure of a woman passed through the open one and stood before her.

Olivia's nerves were strained to their utmost tension, and she shrank back with a low cry of alarm.

The woman stretched out her hand pleadingly.

"Don't, don't, miss!" she said, in a suppressed whisper, "I've not come to hurt you!"

"Who are you? What do you want?" asked Olivia, trembling a little, but recovering her presence of mind, for it seemed to her that she had heard the voice before.

The woman came nearer, and the light of the lodge window falling on her face, Olivia saw that it was the gipsy who had told their fortunes at the picnic.

"You know me, you remember me, miss," she said, still in a whisper, and with a kind of hurried earnestness.

"Yes," said Olivia, breathing more freely, for there was a sad and weary expression in the woman's face, which called for compassion rather than fear. "Yes, you are the gipsy. What do you want?"

"I want to see you, miss, to speak a few words," replied Liz. "I've been watching for you, waiting for a chance to see you alone; but he's always with you."

"He?" said Olivia.

"Yes—Mr. Bradstone," continued the woman, hurriedly. "To-night I was thinking of sending a message to you by the girl who lives here——"

"Bessie?" said Olivia, wonderingly.

"Yes, miss, that's her name. I know she loves you, and that she'd be secret. Miss, I'm doing it at the risk of my life——"

Olivia flushed.

"What is it you want? What is it you are doing?" she asked, with a little pant.

The woman's terrible earnestness was telling upon her.

"I've come to warn you, miss," replied Liz, drawing a little closer.

"To warn me!" repeated Olivia, shrinking back, suspiciously.

"Yes, miss, a solemn warning! Don't treat it lightly; give heed to it, for Heaven's sake. I wouldn't do it for everybody. I wouldn't risk what I'm risking to-night for any other's sake. I'm a fool to do it for yours, but you spoke to me kindly, and—and——What's that?"

She broke off with a glance of terror toward the road.

"I hear nothing," said Olivia, half convinced the woman was mad. "Be quick, please, I—I cannot wait. Of what do you warn me?"

"Is it true that you are to marry Mr. Bradstone, miss?" she asked, earnestly.

Olivia inclined her head.

"Yes."

"Then, for the love of Heaven, and while there's time, draw back. You don't know——"

"Stop," said Olivia. "I cannot listen to you. Say what you have to say against him—for you have something to say—before him. I will not listen," and she moved aside.

The woman caught her arm with a gesture of despairing imploration.

"Wait! wait! For your own sake, lady! For God's sake, listen to me! There's danger——" Olivia paused, and the gipsy, with a little catch in her voice, as if she were struggling for breath, hurried on: "If you don't believe what I am going to tell you, if you think I'm lying, ask him, ask this Mr. Bradstone, if he knows——"

Her voice dropped, and Olivia, more moved than she knew, bent lower; but at that moment, before the woman could utter another word, a man's voice, thick with drink, and threatening, rose from the other side of the gate:

"Liz! Liz! Where the devil are you?"

The woman shrank, as if she had been struck; then, drawing her shawl over her head, whispered, reproachfully, "Too late!" and crying, "Here I am, Seth!" hurried through the gate into the road.

CHAPTER XVII
BLINDED BY SELF-CONCEIT

Olivia waited for a moment or two, until her heart beat less wildly, then went to the lodge door, which was usually unlocked, but to-night she found it fastened, and knocked. Bessie opened the door, and uttered an exclamation of surprise and welcome.

"Miss Olivia! Is it really you? Come in," and Bessie led the way into the sitting-room, which her natural good taste had converted into a pretty little parlor. "I thought it was father, miss. Were you surprised to find the door locked? Father bade me keep it fastened, as there were some gypsies and suspicious characters about, he said—but, oh, miss, what is the matter? Are you ill?"

She broke off as Olivia sank into the chair, and with a deep sigh put back her shawl.

"No, I'm not ill, Bessie," replied Olivia; "only a little—worried."

And she tried to smile, but her eyes filled with tears.

Bessie, with womanly tact, gently took off her mistress' hat and shawl, and silently resumed her seat and went on with her work.

Olivia leaned back with her eyes closed and her hands clasped listlessly on her lap. What was the meaning and extent of the gipsy woman's warning? What was it she was going to tell Olivia to ask Bartley Bradstone? Was it some trick of the woman's with the object of extorting money? These and similar questions flashed through Olivia's harassed mind, and she could find no answer. That there should be any secret in common between a gypsy tramp and Bartley Bradstone, the wealthy owner of The Maples, seemed impossible and absurd; and yet the woman's words and accents bore a terrible earnestness, a tone of solemn entreaty and truth which haunted Olivia.

What should she do? To this question the answer came readily enough. One knows what to do with an anonymous letter; throw it in the fire and forget it; and how, than with scorn, could she treat a vague accusation or insinuation made by a vagabond gipsy against a man of Bartley Bradstone's respectability—her future husband?

Her future husband! The sting lay in those significant words. Was it not her duty as his affianced bride, to tell him of the incident, and leave the matter in his hands? Yet how could she bring herself to do it? The woman's interrupted communication might have referred to some past incident in Bartley Bradstone's life with which she—Olivia—could have no concern, and she could scarcely go to him and demand his confidence, perhaps his confession of a past wrong—she who had, even since their betrothal, treated him with cold civility, and kept him at arm's length.

No, she could take no notice of the woman's warning; after all, it was probably a prelude to a request for money; these gypsies, she had always heard, were accomplished and daring beggars; an attempt to coax or extort money from her or Bartley was probably the woman's only motive.

She sighed again, as she arrived at this decision, and put the matter from her mind.

"Are you rested now, miss?" said Bessie, gently.

"Yes, Bessie," replied Olivia; "I am all right now. I am tired and—and I was frightened by meeting a gipsy outside the lodge."

Bessie looked up quickly.

"Father was right, then, miss—there are some of them about. Father's in the woodshed; shall I call him and tell him to look after them?"

"No, no," said Olivia, quickly, with a slight flush; "they are far away by this time, I dare say. I haven't been to see you for some time, Bessie," she went on, hurriedly, changing the subject.

"No, miss," said Bessie, softly. "But I didn't expect—I knew you would have a great deal to do." She faltered and colored. "I've heard the news, miss, and"—she dropped her work and clasped her hands, her eyes fixed with affectionate earnestness on Olivia's pale face—"I do pray you may be happy!"

"Thank you, Bessie," said Olivia, a slight flush passing across her face. "Yes, I am going to marry Mr. Bartley Bradstone; so you see you will not lose me altogether."

"No," said Bessie, with a quiet sigh; "that thought comforts me a little. The Maples isn't far, and—and you'll let me see you sometimes, Miss Olivia?"

"As often as you like, Bessie," said Olivia. "But you speak as if I had been ordered to execution," and she smiled.

Bessie colored, and took up her work again.

"Did I, miss? I didn't mean to; I only meant that it—it was a surprise."

Olivia's eyes dropped.

"Such things are always a surprise, Bessie," she said. "I came to ask how you were, but I see there is no need to do so. It's just the Bessie of old, sitting there so quietly and happily at her needle— —"

A strange look flashed across the girl's face, and she bent still lower over her work.

"Yes, miss, I'm all right now," she said, quietly. "Father was afraid that the fright would upset me for a long time; but Mr. Faradeane says such care was taken of me that I shall come to no harm. I'm quite right now."

At the mention of Faradeane's name, Olivia started slightly, and reached for her shawl.

"Have you seen—Mr. Faradeane lately?" she said, coldly.

Bessie looked up quickly; no tone or accent of her mistress' beloved voice could escape her.

"No, miss; not here at the lodge—that is, I've seen him at a distance riding and walking. He's been ill, miss—very ill, I'm afraid."

"What has been the matter with him?" asked Olivia, in a constrained voice, as she drew the shawl round her.

Bessie got up and knelt beside her, and fastened it.

"I don't know—nobody seems to know. He didn't leave the cottage for some days, and nobody saw him. Father called, but the servant wouldn't let him see him, and simply said his master was ill and he had instructions to let no one in. Father would have taken upon himself to send for the doctor, but he knew it would be no use. Mr. Faradeane is like iron, miss, when he says a thing."

"Well?" said Olivia, with suppressed anxiety.

"Well, then he came out and I saw him riding. He wasn't like the same man, miss, so pale and worn-like he looked. Father says he has had some great trouble, he's sure; but I can't think what it can be, can you?"

"No; how should I know, Bessie?" responded Olivia, almost sternly.

Bessie sighed.

"No, miss," she assented, meekly. "I suppose nothing can be done—I mean to help him, if he is ill or in trouble. I'd"—her pretty face flushed, and her voice quivered—"I'd walk a hundred miles barefoot to serve him——" She stopped and restrained herself. "But I'm only a poor, ignorant girl, miss, and can't do anything. What seems so dreadful is his loneliness. From week's end to week's end no one goes near him, now that Lord Bertie has gone away. He was the only friend he had, father says."

Olivia rose and put on her hat.

"Mr. Faradeane does not wish for any friends, Bessie," she said, speaking with an air of indifference. "I am sorry he has been ill, and glad that he is better. As for any trouble, I don't know——" She stopped. "I must go now, Bessie. You must come up to the Grange; there are some dresses I want you to look over."

"Yes, miss," said Bessie, obediently, and, taking up her hat, followed her to the gate.

"Where are you going, Bessie?" asked Olivia.

"With you to the Grange, miss," replied Bessie, firmly.

"Indeed you shall not," said Olivia.

"But I mean to, miss," retorted Bessie, steadily. "You've been frightened already to-night, and that's quite enough. I am coming to take care of you."

Olivia regarded the slim, girlish figure with a laugh.

"Why, you silly child, and who is to take care of you coming back alone?"

"I can take care of myself, miss," said Bessie, firmly.

"Go in at once," commanded Olivia. "Do you think I am afraid to run up our own drive? Why, what a coward you must think me."

"I mean to go——" began Bessie, more firmly than before, when both girls were startled into silence by the sound of a third voice.

"I will go with Miss Olivia, if she will let me, Bessie," it said.

"Mr. Faradeane!" said Bessie, with a little catch in her voice. "Yes, sir, you shall go."

Olivia's heart seemed to stand still at the sound of the voice which had been the first and only one to thrill it to its secret depths, and her face went pale. With a great effort she forced a slight laugh. "Bessie disposes of me as if I were her exclusive property," she said, and the effort she made to control her voice caused it to sound hard and cold. She moved on, and Faradeane, taking her remark as permission, walked by her side. Olivia's heart was beating wildly. Scarcely for a moment since her scene with him in the wood had he been absent from her thoughts. At night in her dreams she could hear his voice calling her name, calling her his darling! Shame and love— alas! yes, love—battled for mastery within her as she felt the influence of the near presence of the man who had absorbed her whole life, who had become to her, as the old Persian poem says,

"The sun and the moon and the stars and the light thereof."

this man who, while he had dared to take her in his arms, had stopped short of asking her to be his wife.

She felt now, as her face burned as if with fire, that she ought to send him from her with a cold word of dismissal; but she could not, for there was a miserable conviction within her heart that he was her soul's master, and that she was his slave.

For some minutes they walked on in silence, Olivia with her shawl drawn round her, almost concealing her face, Faradeane with his head erect, his hand thrust in his pocket, a set look of earnest thought upon his pale, haggard face. At last he said:

"Miss Vanley, I find it difficult to speak to you to-night, almost impossible to say what I feel it is my duty to myself, and to you, should be said." His voice was very low and grave, and his eyes, as they turned to her, were full of sad earnestness. "I know what it costs you to talk with me thus—how much you wish to rid yourself of me."

"Why should I?" she said, though she knew.

"Because you feel that I have forfeited your esteem, that I have acted dishonorably. You will think still worse of me when I tell you that I cannot, that I dare not explain my conduct to you the other day—that I am compelled to suffer the continuance of your contempt and scorn because I am unable to tell you all, to lay my heart bare to you. But it is so," he sighed. "I asked you to forgive me when we parted in the wood. Is it possible that you may learn to do so? Yours is a sweet and pitying nature; extend your mercy to a man who needs it very badly."

The words, the tone, went straight to her heart.

"I—I forgive you," she said, almost in a whisper.

He made no response for a moment, and the silence was more eloquent than words.

"Let me speak one more word," he said.

She made a slight gesture of assent.

"Lord Granville has gone—left England, you know. Will you believe that I broke as well as I could the sorrow your refusal cost him?"

"You—you did the best for him, your friend," she said, faintly. "Yes, I can believe that."

"Yes, I did the best," he said, gravely, "and he has gone, I think, wisely. Before he went he exacted a promise from me. May I tell you what it was?"

"Yes," she said, simply, her eyes fixed on the ground, her heart beating in sad harmony with every word of his grave, musical voice.

"It was this: Bertie's—Lord Granville's love for you was of that order which loves still though it can never profit by its love. Though you are lost to him, you are still the one being in the world for him, and it is not saying too much to say that he would lay down his life for you." Her eyes filled with tears. "If he could have trusted himself he would have stayed near you to be ready at any moment, at any cost, to do you service; but he was not strong enough, his love made him weak. Miss Vanley, Bertie asked me to promise that I would, as it were, take his place—that I would be ready, should the occasion present itself, to lay my services at your feet. You smile."

"Smile!"

"It sounds absurd that I should presume to tell you of such a promise, that it should be thought probable by either of us men that you, who are so fully protected—you, the daughter of the lord of the manor, should ever need any assistance. Yes, it is absurd, but I have given my promise, and now I ask you, for Bertie's sake, to humor this farewell wish of his and permit me to remain your—friend."

She was silent.

"Do not imagine that I shall think you hard or unforgiving if you refuse. I shall understand; I do understand. But if you can do so, let me consider that you permit me to keep my promise to Bertie. He would give his life for you, and I——" He stopped abruptly. "I shall never be required to prove how gladly I would do anything for you; but will you let me think that if at any time you needed me, improbable as it sounds, you would remember Bertie's compact with me?"

They had reached the terrace by this time, and the light fell full upon his face, eloquent with an expression which made its sad resignation almost noble. She turned her eyes to his, and held out her hand.

"For Bertie's sake," she said, in a low voice.

He held her hand in his firmly, not pressing it.

"It is a compact," he said, gravely. "Believe me, I will keep it. If ever the time should come——"

He stopped abruptly, for the window was flung open, and Bartley Bradstone came out hurriedly.

"It's—it's thoughtless and—and cruel of her," they heard him say, angrily. "Out at this time of night and alone——"

"My dear Bartley," said the squire's quiet voice, "Olivia has been so accustomed to wandering about the place since she was a child."

"Oh, ah, yes, that's all very well; but it's different now," retorted Bartley Bradstone; "things are altered. She ought to remember that she's going to be my wife, and——"

By this time Olivia and Faradeane had partly ascended the steps, and he had seen them. He stopped suddenly and glared down at them with an expression of angry suspicion and jealousy which rendered his rather good-looking face positively ugly, and a passionate oath leaped from his lips.

"This—this is pretty!" he exclaimed, looking between them—for even in his passion he could not face Olivia's clear, cold eyes, or Faradeane's calm gaze.

"Where have you been, Olivia?" asked the squire, gently.

She went up to him and laid her hand on his arm.

"I ran down to the lodge to see Bessie, and Mr. Faradeane kindly offered to come back to the house with me, dear," she said.

"Oh, Faradeane, is that you?" he said, coming forward. "How do you do? Thanks for taking care of my little girl; she is rather a runagate," and he smiled as he held out his hand.

Faradeane shook hands with him and then held out his hand to Bartley Bradstone. Bradstone looked for a moment as if he were going to refuse it, and his face went from white to red, but he took the proffered hand at last.

"Rather a—a strange coincidence, isn't it?" he said, breathing hard. "Were you spending the evening at the lodge, Faradeane?"

Harold Faradeane looked at him calmly, without the faintest sign of resentment of the insinuation.

"No," he said, "I happened to be passing, and heard Bessie propose to escort Miss Vanley up the avenue, and offered myself as a substitute."

"Oh," said Bartley Bradstone, with as much of a sneer as he dared display, "which she accepted readily enough, of course?"

The crimson flooded Olivia's face and neck; but Faradeane met his covertly furious face with calm self-possession.

"Which Miss Vanley was kind enough to accept, as you say," he said. "We met with no adventures on the road, and I return her to you safe and unharmed," and he smiled.

"Thanks, thanks; come in, come in, all of you," said the squire, hurriedly, with a spasm of pain at Bartley Bradstone's exhibition of temper.

Faradeane looked at his watch.

"Too late, thanks," he said, lightly. "Good-night, good-night, Miss Vanley," and he raised his hat. Then he turned to Bartley Bradstone. "Splendid night for an astronomer, Bradstone."

The other man glanced up at the sky, and then at Faradeane's calm face.

"Eh!" he said. "What do you mean?"

Faradeane looked around to see if the squire and Olivia had got indoors and out of hearing, then said:

"One word with you, Bradstone."

"Well, what is it?" sullenly.

"Walk with me to the lane," said Faradeane, quietly.

Bartley Bradstone hesitated for a second, and his face began to grow pale.

"I—I—it's late, and beastly chilly," he stammered.

Faradeane moved on, and the other man followed as if he had been dragged. When they had gone a couple of hundred yards, Faradeane stopped.

"You wish to quarrel with me, Bradstone," he said, regarding the other with calm intentness.

Bartley Bradstone's face went ashen, and he shrank back and put up his arm as if to ward off an expected blow.

A bitter smile crossed Faradeane's lips.

"Do not be a coward as well as a fool," he said, with quiet contempt.

Bartley Bradstone flushed—anything above a cur would have been spurred into at least the semblance of courage at the terrible scorn of the tone.

"You—you dare— —" he began, blusteringly.

Faradeane's hand dropped upon his arm, and grasped it in a grip of iron.

"Speak more quietly, please," he said, "and don't threaten. Why, man"—and he smiled grimly—"if I were as helpless in your hands as you are in mine you would not dare to strike me." He dropped the arm, which felt as if it had been seized in a vise. "Listen to me. You wish to quarrel; I do not, for a reason which you would not understand if I gave it to you. You have insulted me, which is—nothing. You have insulted the lady who has stooped to be your promised wife."

"Stooped!" blustered Bradstone, but very quietly.

"Yes; how low, you alone know," said Faradeane, his eyes fixed on Bradstone's face, which went white. "Do not venture to do so again. Why, man"—and for the first time his voice showed signs of the emotion which racked him—"have you so little sense as not to appreciate the treasure you have secured? Are you such a hopeless fool, so utterly blinded by self-conceit, as to undervalue the prize you have snatched?"

"I am not so blind as not to see your game— —" began Bartley Bradstone.

Faradeane held up his hand.

"Silence," he said, sternly. "Do not connect her name with mine, even in your thoughts. You know as little of my heart and my motives as you know—Heaven help you!—of hers. Be content with your success; try, in Heaven's name, try with all the strength you possess, to be more worthy of her. You think you love her—be sure you reverence her! I use no empty threats, Bradstone, when I say—I who am separated from her by a gulf that can never be bridged—that I demand her happiness at your hands. Dare to insult her again as you have done to-night— —" He stopped, his face set, his eyes flashing. Then he laid his hand upon the other man's now trembling arm. "That's enough; we understand each other, I think."

"I want to know— —" stammered Bartley, looking him up and down, but carefully avoiding meeting the steadfast regard of the now calm eyes.

"You want to know by what authority I dare bid you to be careful of her happiness as you would of your wealth. By the authority which goes with the title of—friend. Yes"—his voice changed—"I am Miss Vanley's friend in more than mere name. I know you, Bradstone; I read you through and through the first time we met, and I warn you against—yourself. It is because I am her friend that I will not quarrel with you. More: I am willing to regard you as"—the words came with some difficulty—"a friend, so long, and no longer, as you guard and protect her happiness. The moment you cease to do that——" He stopped, and looked the craven steadily in the eyes. "Go in now, and if you have a spark of manliness and gratitude in you, beg her pardon. Stop!" for Bradstone, not daring to utter the oath which trembled on his lips, made a movement as if to avail himself of the permission to retreat. "Think over what I have said, and for the future do not regard me as—your rival. If you and Miss Vanley had never met, there could have been no closer tie between her and me. Let that satisfy you. Good-night. As her future husband, Bradstone, I offer you my hand."

Bradstone took it with lowered face, and Faradeane, with another steady look at him, turned and walked away.

Bartley Bradstone stood staring at the ground for a moment or two; then he raised his head, and, shaking his fist in the direction Faradeane had taken, relieved himself with a series of oaths.

If, as the Spaniards, say, bad men's curses come home to roost, Mr. Bartley Bradstone's future hencoop would have been full of them.

"Friend! Yes, I know the sort of friend. I'm not taken in by your fine talk! I'm not such a fool as you take me for! Friend! I've got a treasure, have I? Yes, a treasure you'd like to rob me of; but you won't, I think, my fine Mr. Faradeane! No, I think not! You threaten me, do you? I'll show you! Yes, and I'll have her soon, too!" he breathed passionately. "There's no time to lose if I understand your game, Mr. Faradeane." He tugged at his cuffs, and endeavored to calm himself as he walked toward the house. "Yes, I'll do it; the iron's hot, and I'll strike, and then——"

CHAPTER XVIII
"I'VE FOUND HIM!"

Two nights after this resolution of Mr. Bartley Bradstone's, Seth, the gypsy, might have been seen making his way along the crowded Strand. There is never too much room either in the road or on the pavement of that famous thoroughfare at any time; but just before eleven, and from that hour to midnight, it is, perhaps, the most densely thronged of any of the London streets, and Seth had to shoulder his way through the usual streams of humanity which emerge from the various theatres, on their way home or to the supper-rooms and restaurants.

It would have been rather difficult for the casual observer to have recognized Seth the prowler of country lanes, for, in place of his rough and well-worn cords and gaiters—torn by many a midnight poaching expedition, and stained by mud and rain—he wore a dark-colored suit, and a stylishly-cut covert coat, which gave him the appearance of a decent young farmer up in London for a meek-and-mild spree; but though he had changed his attire, he could not change his swarthy complexion and his small black eyes; and the wary, alert look which the gypsy acquires, say a month after he is weaned, was enough to distinguish him from the crowd of commonplace countenances by which he was surrounded.

Making his way as much by slipping in and out like a lurcher as by force, he threaded the Strand throng, and, crossing Leicester Square, went up to the Palace of Amusement, which stands, glaring with light and gilding, at the northern end.

For a moment or two Seth looked up and down, then approached one of the boards which hung outside with a glowing list of the attractions which awaited the person who should be fortunate enough to possess the shilling necessary for admission.

He stood looking on for a minute, with the dense, vacant expression of a man who cannot read; then, beckoning to a matchboy who was hovering about him, said:

"I don't want no lights, but I'll give you a penny if you'll read this 'ere."

The boy grinned, and, with an air of suppressed pride and pity nicely commingled, read down the list of celebrities which made up the night's programme.

"But what's the use, guvnor," he said. "They've all done their turn and gone 'cept one or two. There's only Bella-Bella and the ballet left."

Seth's eyes flashed with a momentary satisfaction.

"What's her name?" he inquired.

"Bella-Bella," replied the urchin. "She's got to go on; she's prime, she is! If you ain't seen her you ought to. She's put on near the last, because the swells drop in late, don't you know. Look at 'em going in now," and he jerked his matchbox toward several men in evening dress who were then ascending the steps. "She's the great draw, and no wonder! You should just see her! She's stunning, that's what she is! Plank down yer shillin', guvnor, you won't be sorry; there ain't a trapeze artist in London to beat her."

"All right, I will," said Seth, with an air of indifference, and, tossing the boy a penny, he went in and paid his shilling. But the shilling seats were too far from the stage to please him, and he changed into the stalls, took a cigar and a glass of whiskey-and-water, and cast his keen, cunning eyes round him.

The Palace of Amusement, as every one knows, is perhaps the most magnificently decorated place in London, and its appointments are palatial enough to startle and bewilder the countryman who sees them for the first time; but Seth's carefully guarded countenance displayed no surprise or bewilderment, whatever he may have felt; and he sat and smoked and listened to the band of forty first-class performers, and watched the mixed audience of "swells," counter-jumpers, and frivolous women with half-closed eyes.

Several of the gentlemen who had entered just before him had taken seats near his, or were lounging against the elaborately-gilded and painted walls with that air of long-suffering boredom which distinguishes their class, and Seth, while he gave one sharp ear to the band, kept the other open to the conversation around him.

"Just in time," yawned one gentleman. "I suppose her ladyship's going to perform to-night?" he said, addressing the chairman, a fat man in evening dress, with a large diamond—or something fairly resembling it—in his vast expanse of shirt front, and stones of great value—or none—in his wristbands.

"Oh, yes, my lord," he replied, with an oily smile. "Bella's on the spot to-night."

"In a good humor, eh?" remarked another, with a laugh. "The last time we were here she cut up rough and wouldn't go on."

"That was because there wasn't quite large enough audience for her, Sir 'Arry," said the chairman, who appeared to know them all. "She'll be all right to-night; the house is nearly full. Won't you take a seat, gentlemen? Plenty of room, my lord," and he waved a be-ringed hand toward the table.

The young lord—he was little more than a boy—glanced up at the ropes and the net above his head, and laughed.

"No, thanks," he said. "That net doesn't look overstrong, and much as I adore Bella-Bella, I don't care to have her dropping on my head."

Seth, who also was not lacking in wisdom which prompts a man toward self-preservation, got up and leaned against the wall out of reach of the net.

"Oh, she won't fall, my lord," said the chairman, with a satisfied smile. "Bella knows a trick worth two of that; trust her for taking care of herself. Here she is!" and, striking the table in front of him with an ivory hammer, he shouted, "Order, gentlemen!" in stentorian tones.

The band grew louder, and then, amid a general silence, a woman sprang onto the stage.

She was tall, but so exquisitely made, and every limb so perfectly proportioned, that she did not look more than a medium height. She was, of course, dressed in silk tights, which displayed her handsome figure, and that small portion of her attire which was not composed of silk tights was of ruby plush, flecked here and there by diamonds, which in this case were real; but few would have given a second glance at the diamonds after seeing her face. It was a singular one. She was dark, and her hair, tightly coiled at the crown of her shapely head, was black, and the face was striking in its mixture of audacity and simplicity. She came to the footlights with a smile that was at once defiant and self-assertive, but at the same time there was a look of almost gentle depreciation, of childlike gayety, in her dark eyes.

It was as much her beauty as her marvelous skill on the trapeze that drew the crowds to the Palace during her engagement.

As she came forward into the glare of the footlights, Seth raised his eyes and looked at her with piercing scrutiny, then softly and slowly drew back, slid back, into the shadow of the balcony.

Her appearance was the signal for a loud outburst of applause, and a buzz of excitement ran through the audience, "the swells" drew a few inches nearer, as if fascinated, and the band, which had paused during her reception, broke into a gay and exhilarating air.

She acknowledged the enthusiastic welcome with a smile and a nod, while a couple of stage attendants in gorgeous liveries seized a rope that hung from the lofty ceiling, and with every sign of respect brought it within her reach. She sprang at it as a cat springs at a bird, and, with a grace and ease almost incredible, drew herself up to the trapeze, which hung at a giddy height above the stalls.

Trapeze performances are very much alike, but Bella-Bella's was distinguished by its audacity, and the grace with which it was executed. She and the trapeze seemed to be part and parcel of the same machine. One moment she was swinging by one hand, her lithe body at right angles; the next she was suspended by her feet and nothing else, her face smiling down at the audience beneath her, as if to hang head downwards forty yards above the earth were the commonest of feats. There was a ladder suspended lengthways just below the ceiling, and, with an effort which seemed effortless, she reached it, and traveled along it, first by one hand and then by one foot. Then she dropped like a feather to the trapeze again, and knelt on one knee. Suddenly, while the applause was almost deafening, she uttered a cry of feigned terror, and dropped like a stone into the net beneath. Broken as her fall was by the net, it would have shaken the life out of an ordinary man, to say nothing of woman, but almost instantly she was on her feet again, and, seizing the guide-rope, was slowly swung onto the stage.

A roar like that of the wild beasts of Ephesus rose from the excited audience, and she stood looking round with slightly flushed face and parted lips, scarcely bowing, but receiving the general applause as if it were her due—as, doubtless, it was—then turned to go. As she did so she glanced down at the group of gentlemen, and gave them an almost imperceptible nod.

"All right," said the young peer with a smile; "she'll come. Did you see her nod? By George! she was better than ever to-night; what do you think, Harry?"

"Yes," drawled the man addressed. "Some night she'll be 'best,' and that will finish her! Come on; she won't take long, and there'll be the devil to pay if we keep her waiting."

They moved languidly toward the gorgeous corridor, with its electric light and mosaic walls, its costly hangings and tropical ferns, and Seth, whose sharp ears had heard every word, softly and cautiously followed them. The men passed out, and made their way round to a dimly-lit street at the back of the vast building, and Seth, keeping well in the shadow and having anything but the appearance of a man who was following them, lurked at their heels. They stopped at a door over which was a lamp bearing the words "Stage Entrance," and one and all took out cigarettes, and smoked them with an affected sort of patience.

"Confound her, what a time she is!" said his lordship. "I suppose if we went on without her and left a brougham she'd cut up rough?"

"For a certainty," said Sir Harry, "and we don't want the evening spoiled."

As he spoke the door opened, a woman's voice said in clear, bold accents, "Good-night," to the door-keeper, and Bella-Bella came out.

"Here you are, then!" she said, nodding to the group. "What are you waiting for?"

"You said you'd come to supper," said his lordship.

"I didn't," she retorted.

"You nodded your head," said Sir Harry.

"Well, there was nothing in it," was her swift response.

His lordship laughed, languidly.

"Oh, come on!" he said; "the brougham's in front."

"Then bring it round," she commanded. "The pavement's damp, and I hate wet like a cat."

As she spoke she glanced round. Seth had kept in the shadow—out of sight; as he thought—but her eyes, not unlike his in their keenness, saw him instantly, and she leaned forward with a quick, and, indeed, catlike movement.

"Who's that?" she inquired.

The men turned and stared at Seth, and, after a moment's hesitation, he came forward. As he did so she shrank slightly, very slightly, and her face paled for a second; then she laughed, and held out her hand.

"Well, I never!" she exclaimed. "It's you, is it? How are you?" The group of aristocrats stared with the languid surprise which fashion permits. "How long have you been in London? Have you been inside? What did you think of me?" Then before Seth could reply she turned her flashing eyes on the group. "Well!" she said, defiantly, "what are you staring at? This is a friend of mine—a relation—my cousin Seth. He's just up from the country. Aren't you, Seth? Sorry I can't join you at supper; he and I want a talk," and she held out her arm for him to take.

"Oh, nonsense!" said his lordship, with a disappointed drawl. "You can talk after supper as much as you like. Bring your cousin with you."

She laughed strangely.

"So I will!" she said. "Come on, Seth. Let me introduce you: Lord Wardlaw, or the Baby; Sir Harry Roke, and so on and so on," and she nodded to one and the other. "Now, then, where's that brougham? My cousin's going to ride with me and you, Baby; the rest of you can go as you like. Come on!" and, linking her arm in Seth's, she led the way to the carriage.

They drove to one of the restaurants, and ascended to a private room, in which a brilliantly lit supper-table was laid out. Bella-Bella flung her hat and plush jacket to a waiter, and sat herself at the head of the table, and motioned Seth to the seat beside her. She took no further notice of him—an example which the rest politely followed.

The waiters brought an elaborate supper; champagne of the first brands flowed like water; and while the laughter and the chatter grew louder and louder, Seth worked his way through the long menu, and swallowed glass after glass of the costly wine with the keen enjoyment and the impassiveness of an Indian, a Turk, and a gypsy!

As the meal proceeded, Bella-Bella's spirits rose. Her clear, bell-like voice rang out above the rest, her laughter set the glasses tingling, and presently his lordship, encouraged by her good-humor, said:

"What about a song, Bella?"

"All right!" she exclaimed. "What will you have?" and, tossing down a glass of champagne, she sang, with a "go" and a spirit which would have won her as much applause at the Palace as her trapeze business, one of the popular songs of the day.

Her audience clapped and knocked the table—very much, dear reader, for all their aristocratic refinement, as the audience at a "friendly lead" in one of the slums would have done; but Seth remained silent, his eyes fixed on the tablecloth.

"My cousin don't like that kind of thing," she said, without glancing at him. "This is more in his style," and in lower tones she sang a song in some gibberish which was unknown to all but Seth, whose eyes flashed though his face did not move a muscle.

"What language is that, Bella?" asked Sir Harry, with a laugh, as the applause subsided. "Italian? Spanish? It sounded like the last, I fancy?"

"Never you mind," she retorted. "It's a lingo my cousin understands, so he's cleverer than you."

Then she broke out into the last comic ditty, and had them worked up to a pitch of languid delight, when suddenly—so suddenly that her words came into the middle of the chorus (in which they all joined) and could be heard above it—she said, sharply:

"That's enough. I'm tired. You can go."

"Oh, but, by Jove! it's early yet, Bella!" remonstrated the young lord.

"Early or late, I'm tired," she retorted, with a smoldering savageness. "You haven't been hanging by your heels or doing the big drop, or you'd be tired. Anyway, I'm tired of you. Baby, it's time you were in bed. Good-night, all of you!"

"Come on, she'll be in one of her tantrums in another moment," said Sir Harry in an undertone.

They laughed, got their hats, and, wishing her good-night, sauntered out, his lordship lingering a moment to pay the bill—Seth eying the pile of gold, as the waiter deftly swept it up, with a keen hunger—and the two were left alone.

"Shut the door," said Bella to the waiter; then, when it was closed behind him, she sank into the chair, and leaned her head on her hand.

Seth waited with the same impassive silence, and it almost seemed that she had forgotten him, when suddenly she raised her head and looked at him. Her face had grown pale and haggard, and there was a weary, worn look in her expressive eyes.

"Well?" she said. "What have you followed me for? How did you find me?"

He looked at her with an expression half-sullen, half-threatening.

"Find you! Yes, I'd trouble enough. I've been looking for you for months. I might have known you'd come to London."

"You might," she said, with a tired kind of contempt. "But London's a big place."

"Yes. I shouldn't have found you even now, if I hadn't seen a likeness of you in one of the shop windows."

"Ah, yes! I see!" she said, shutting her lips tight. "And now you've found me you want money, I suppose?"

"Of course," he assented, roughly.

"And suppose I don't choose to give it to you?" she demanded.

"Then," he began, but he stopped as she sprang to her feet and looked down at him with her black eyes flashing angrily.

"Look you here, Seth!" she said, slowly, and between her white, even teeth. "You know me by this time, and you know whether you can frighten or bully me. You tried it once, and you know the result! I'd rather die"—she caught up one of the knives and flung it down again with a gesture of defiance—"than be the slave of any man, least of all of you!"

He took a bunch of hothouse grapes from the plate, and picked them off one by one, keeping his small, dark eyes fixed on her watchfully.

"I'd rather die!" she repeated. "If you think because I'm up in the world you're going to live on the money I risk my life for, you're mistaken. I'm not afraid of you, Seth; I'm not afraid of any man living——"

"'Cept one," he remarked, quietly, watching her keenly.

"It's a lie!" she retorted. "I wasn't afraid of him, and you know it! Afraid! No, it's him that has cause to fear, and to fear me!" She shook herself with a catlike motion. "But I don't want to speak of him. The time'll come when I'll show you, and him too—but that's neither here nor there. You've come after me for money, and I've told you that you won't get any. I've done with you and yours——"

"No gypsy can get clear of her people," he said, as if he were stating an established fact beyond question.

She laughed defiantly.

"That's rubbish," she said, promptly. "All that nonsense is dead and gone. What, do you think I'd own a set of dirty tramps?"

He sprang to his feet, his face flushed for the first time.

"You'd better keep that between your teeth, my girl," he said, threateningly.

"Then don't you drive me to it," she retorted in a more subdued tone. "How much do you want—five pounds?"

He sank back in his chair, and resumed the grapes with a laugh.

"I want twenty times as much."

Her eyes flashed down on him.

"Then you may go!" she said, resolutely. "A hundred pounds!" scornfully, "why should I give it to you—what harm can you do me?"

"Perhaps I can do you some good. Oh, I don't want you to give it me for nothing. I'll sell you something fair and square."

"You'll sell me something?" she repeated, frowning. "What do you mean? Speak out."

"All right," he said, tossing the grape-stems on the cloth. "I'll sell you some news, my girl."

"News?" she echoed, leaning forward, her eyes fixed on his face.

"Yes," he said, with a confident nod. "News you'll be glad to pay me more for than I've asked. *I've found him.*"

She sprang upright, and, clutching his arm, bent down till her face, deadly white, was close to his, her black eyes flaming with intense excitement.

"You've—you've found him!" she breathed.

"I have," he said, coolly, shaking his arm free of her steel-like clasp.

"Come outside"—he glanced at the door—"come out of this, and I'll tell you!"

CHAPTER XIX
"LOVE CAME TOO LATE"

Mr. Bartley Bradstone, as he left the garden after his remarkably unpleasant interview with Harold Faradeane, decided to strike while the iron was hot. He had got the net round Olivia; he resolved to draw it tight. From that evening he kept a close guard on himself, and his manner changed—for the better. In fact, to the casual observer he would have passed as a remarkably good-tempered man. He was polite to the servants, deferential to the squire, attentive to Miss Amelia, and to Olivia was devoted and reverential.

Not only the Grange people but outsiders noticed the change.

"Bradstone has improved since his engagement," said Lord Carfield. "But daily intercourse with Olivia Vanley would tame a savage and educate a bear!"

He watched Olivia as a cat does a mouse, and she was quite afraid of expressing a desire for anything, lest he should rush off and procure it for her.

To Harold Faradeane, too, his manner was quite friendly; and he had plenty of opportunity for showing it, for Faradeane came often to the Grange now.

Sometimes he would walk in after breakfast, sometimes before they had finished. In the latter case, he would sit and talk with the squire until the meal was over; then go round the stables with him, or ride over to some farm on the estate. And Olivia noticed that whenever Harold Faradeane came her father's face brightened, and lost something of its anxious look. In fact, the old man had conceived a great liking for the handsome, grave-voiced owner of The Dell, a liking that grew day by day into a warm friendship.

To Olivia, Faradeane's bearing was one of quiet, respectful courtesy. At first the color had risen to her face, and her heart had leaped at his approval; but though his appearance always sent a thrill through her, she learned to master her emotion, and greeted him as calmly as he greeted her.

Sometimes he would be persuaded to walk over and dine with them, and on those occasions she put on one of her best frocks, and was more than usually careful with the thick coils of hair which nestled like a crown of silk on her shapely head. Often she stood before the glass when her maid had left her, and looked at herself with a strange, absent air, seeing not the reflection of her own face, but his, as she recalled it on the day he had bent over her and taken her in his arms.

Then she would sigh heavily—and ah! so wistfully and wearily—and go down to the drawing-room to see his tall, patrician figure and handsome face beside the plebeian one of Bartley Bradstone, her future husband.

All through the dinner Bartley Bradstone would covertly watch the two, even while he was apparently engaged with his plate or in talk with the squire; but his sharp, suspicious eyes never detected the slightest hint of any understanding between her and Faradeane. Always pleasant and courteous, sometimes witty and amusing, Faradeane never singled her out for any special attention of any kind; and Bartley Bradstone guessed nothing of the scene in the woods, had no idea of the effect upon Olivia which every word of Faradeane's, every smile of his, produced.

The days sped on without anything of consequence occurring, until Bartley Bradstone struck.

One evening, just after the post had come in, Olivia went into the study to get a fresh supply of notepaper, and found the squire pacing up and down, with an ashen face and tightly-drawn lips. In his trembling hand was an open letter, which, at her entrance, he crushed up and thrust into his pocket.

"Papa!" she said in a low, anxious voice, and, going up to him instantly, "what is the matter?"

"Nothing, nothing, dear!" he said, and his voice sounded harsh and strained. "That is, I have had a troublesome letter."

"Let me see it, dear," she said, putting her arms round his neck.

"No, no!" he replied, hurriedly. "It—it is nothing you would understand; only a business matter."

"But let me see it, dear," she pleaded. "I may be able to help you; at any rate, I can share the trouble with you," she added, sweetly.

But he shook his head.

"No, no; you could not help me. It—it is an old affair, that has cropped up; it will be all right, but it has taken me by surprise. Leave me now, dear. Bartley is waiting for you."

"Shall I tell him to come to you? He understands business, at least," she added, with a touch of bitterness he did not notice.

"No," he said, with a faint tinge of color coming into his white face. "Why should we worry him? Go now, dear; I would show you this letter if it could do any good, but it could not."

She stole out, and the harassed man flung himself into a chair, and, flattening out the note, read it again and again, with the persistence of a man completely overwhelmed and bewildered.

It ran, in a hard, angular hand:

> Sir—I beg to give you notice that I hold your notes of hand for various sums amounting in the whole to the total of five thousand eight hundred pounds, and that, being in want of money, I shall be obliged if you will take up the notes at my office on or before the twenty-sixth instant. I also beg to inform you that the mortgages on the Home Farm and Swivelscote have come into my possession, and that I have lodged formal notice of foreclosure with your solicitors. Trusting you will not be inconvenienced, and regretting that the tightness of the money market compels me to trouble you, I remain, your obedient servant,
>
> Ezekiel Mowle.

The squire sat and pondered—if his confusion of mind could be termed pondering—over the letter. He had never heard this name of Mowle before, but at once understood that it must be that of some money-lender; some man who had, for reasons best known to himself, bought these debts, and, as he had a perfect right to do, required them paid.

He knew that the Home Farm and Swivelscote were both mortgaged above their value, and that any attempt to re-borrow the money would be futile. They would have to be sold. The Home Farm, that had been part and parcel of the Grange estate for centuries, and Swivelscote, which had been granted to the Vanleys by King Charles II.—they would have to be sold, and with them would go the pride and repute of the good, old name!

"Thank God, I have no son to reproach me!" murmured the squire, with quivering lips. "Thank God, my child will marry a rich man!" and he hid his face in his hands as he bowed over the letter of Ezekiel Mowle.

Olivia went into the drawing-room, and found Harold Faradeane alone. He was standing by the window, his clear-cut face and stalwart figure silhouetted against the red light of the setting sun, and he turned as her footsteps fell upon his ear; light as her tread was, he knew it.

They had never been alone together since the night he had brought her home from Bessie's, and at another time Olivia's heart would have beaten wildly, and her color would have come at finding herself alone with him; but to-night she was too anxious about the squire to remark it.

His quick eye, which always seemed to dwell upon her face with a grave, guardian kind of watchfulness, noticed that something was amiss instantly.

"Is anything the matter?" he asked, in a low, earnest voice which never failed to find an echo in her heart. "Forgive me, but I thought you looked — worried."

For a moment she hesitated, and a strong impulse to tell him seized her; but she put it from her, alas!

"Did I?" she said, forcing a smile. "Perhaps I am anxious about the dinner. We have a new cook, you know."

His eyes rested upon hers — smiling so bravely! — for a moment, then he smiled.

"I cannot fancy you anxious about the dinner," he said. "Is that all?" and his hand held hers, or, rather, let hers go, slowly and reluctantly. "If there is any other trouble I shall ask you to remember our compact, and tell me."

She was moving away, but turned her face toward him with a doubting, wistful expression in her lovely eyes. Even then she might have spoken and all her future changed, but her evil genius sent Bartley Bradstone into the room at that moment, and with a bitter smile she turned, thinking:

"If I tell any one it should be — my future husband."

He came across the room, looking in more than his usual spirits, with a light in his eyes which seemed like that of coming triumph, of confident victory, and began talking in a light and laughing tone.

"How well you look to-night, dearest!" he murmured as he passed Olivia, and she smiled again as she thought how blind he was, and how keen-sighted was the other man. "Ah, Faradeane!" and he shook his hand vigorously. "Jolly evening; we shall have plenty of birds if this goes on. Of course you'll consider yourself free of all my shooting. Glad to see you at any time, don't you know."

"Thank you," said Faradeane, in the quiet manner in which he always addressed him; "that's very kind of you."

"Oh, I like treating a neighbor as a neighbor; that's my form—always was. Where's the squire, Olivia? Miss Amelia, you'll lose your character for punctuality," and he pulled out his watch, and nodded and laughed at that lady, who, in an elaborate dinner-dress, which would have been juvenile for a girl of twenty-one, was casting side-glances of approval at her figure in the pier-glass.

"I'm sure you gentlemen would destroy any one's good habits," she simpered, slapping him with her fan. "Often and often I hurry and scurry my maid so that she sends me down a perfect fright lest I should be late, then you come in a quarter of an hour after the bell has rung. Oh, you men, you men!" and she reached out and made a dab at Faradeane, who smiled gravely down upon her as a huge mastiff looks down in kindly pity on a spaniel.

At that moment the squire entered, and Faradeane saw at once how pale and harassed he looked. Bartley Bradstone, however, appeared to take no notice, and he greeted him in the same half-boisterous way he had done the others.

All through the dinner the squire seemed depressed, though he made a valiant attempt to be cheerful, and all through the dinner Bartley Bradstone's spirits seemed to rise. He took more wine than usual, too, and seemed disposed to linger over the Château Lafitte after Olivia and Aunt Amelia had gone.

Faradeane, who rarely drank more than one glass with his dessert, arose.

"I'll smoke my cigarette on the terrace," he said, and the squire nodded with the gentle smile which the father might bestow on a favorite son.

Bartley Bradstone looked after the tall, thin figure with an evil, envious glance.

"Faradeane isn't much in the way of company, is he?" he said, disparagingly.

The squire looked surprised.

"I think he is the most entertaining of men," he said.

"Oh, ah, with ladies, perhaps," assented Bartley Bradstone, grudgingly, "but he can't sit and take his glass of wine like other fellows," and he filled his glass again.

"He doesn't drink much," said the squire, absently, and he sighed.

"You seem a cup too low to-night, squire," said Bartley Bradstone, with affected carelessness. "Anything wrong?"

The squire hesitated a moment, then took the letter from his pocket.

"I did not mean to trouble you with it, though Olivia asked me to do so," he said. "But perhaps it is my duty to tell you," and he leaned his head on his hand.

Bradstone read the note slowly, then emitted a low whistle.

"Mowle, Mowle. I seem to have heard the name before," he said, as if trying to recall it. "I've an idea he is a kind of money-lender. Do you know him?"

The squire shook his head, the fingers of his thin, right hand beating a mournful tune on the tablecloth.

"No. I've no doubt you are right. It doesn't signify who or what he is; his claim is a lawful one, and I must meet it. I thought you ought to know."

"Yes, if it's the man I think it is, you will have to meet it," said Bradstone. "These fellows will have their bond; and you can't blame them. Business is business."

"I do not blame him," said the poor squire, simply. "What troubles me is the fact that I do not know how to arrange for his claim."

Bartley Bradstone looked at the letter again.

"What is the amount?" he said.

The squire, after a few minutes' reflection, told him, and he whistled again. It was not a loud whistle, but it jarred upon the squire's nerves.

"Look here," said Bradstone, after an artistic pause. "If you will leave this to me I will try and arrange it for you— —"

The squire looked up, and his face flushed.

"I—I could not permit you to pay it," he said, gravely.

"No, no; but I can arrange it. I can get time, and time is everything in these matters. Things are going to improve presently, and the property will be worth a great deal more money than this. Leave it to me, will you?"

"You are very kind," said the squire in a low voice.

"Not at all. I'm doing it for Olivia, don't you know! But I say, I must ask you to keep it quiet."

The squire looked up inquiringly.

"I mean, don't mention it to any one—not to Faradeane, for instance."

"It is not the kind of thing one talks about," said the squire, slowly. "I should certainly not mention it to Faradeane or any one else."

Bradstone nodded with an air of satisfaction.

"All right; I'll do the best I can, depend on it; and don't you worry about it. Mr. Rowle, Mowle, or whatever his name is, will find he has a business man to deal with, and alter his tune, no doubt."

The squire sighed.

"If one could only wipe out one's past!" he said.

"Oh, there's no use in crying over spilt milk," responded Bartley Bradstone. "Shall we go in to the ladies now?"

"You go," said the squire. "I will take a turn on the terrace with Faradeane."

Bartley Bradstone's face darkened.

"Oh, very well," he said, with a curt nod, and left the room.

Olivia looked up from the book she was supposed to be reading as he entered the drawing-room.

"Where are papa and Mr. Faradeane?" she said.

"On the terrace," he replied, speaking in a low tone, so as not to awaken Miss Amelia, who was sleeping the sleep of the just in an armchair. "He is rather out of sorts to-night."

She looked at him apprehensively.

"He is in trouble. Has he told you?" she asked, below her breath.

He drew a chair near hers, and sat down, bending close over her, his eyes resting on her lovely face with a hungry and cunning regard.

"Well, yes, he has. Do you know what it is?"

She shook her head.

"No. Will you tell me?"

"A man has come down upon him for a large sum of money," he said. "A man named Mowle."

She drew a sharp breath, and her face grew pale. Then she looked at him quickly.

"But—but I thought——"

His face did not change, and he shrugged his shoulders.

"I know. You mean that I told you I had got all the debts. Well, I thought I had, but I must have missed these somehow. At any rate, this fellow has got them, and he wants them paid, and the squire can't see his way——"

"Oh, poor papa, poor papa!" she breathed.

He ventured to take her hand.

"Don't be cut up about it," he said in a low voice. "I have promised to see the man and arrange with him."

She raised her eyes to his, and her face grew crimson.

"That—that is good of you," she said.

"No, no. Of course I'd do anything. It will keep the man off for a time; but——"

He stopped.

"But?" she said, anxiously.

"The money must be paid before long, you know," he went on, "and—and——See here, Olivia, it rests with you."

"With me?" faintly.

He nodded, keeping his eyes upon the carpet.

"Yes. You—you know our agreement. The day we are married it shall be in your power to take all this trouble off your father's shoulders. I've said what I'll do, and I'll do it. The morning of the marriage I shall pay into the Wainford Bank the sum of fifty thousand pounds in your name. You can do what you like with it. Pitch it in the gutter, buy diamonds, or clear the squire——"

Her head drooped lower and lower, then she raised it slowly, and waited for him to continue, for she felt that more was coming.

"Why should we wait?" he continued, insidiously. "I hate long engagements; and the sooner we are married the sooner will the squire be rid of this trouble of his. Will you marry me in a fortnight, Olivia?"

She started, and every drop of blood seemed to leave her face.

She could hear her father's and Faradeane's footsteps outside, could catch a word or two spoken by the latter, and his musical, true voice seemed to strike in with that of the man at her side and caused it to sound falser.

"In a fortnight?" she breathed, and her voice sounded strained and harsh.

"Why not?" he insisted. "You can get everything ready by that time. But you are not the one to think of clothes and all that sort of thing when your father's happiness is at stake."

"No," she said in a hard, mechanical voice. "But— —" and her hands locked together. "Give me another week!"

"Very well," he said, and his eyes shone with satisfaction, for he had expected her to plead for a month at least. "Say three weeks, then. Three weeks!" his face flushed and he smiled, "that will give me time to do up The Maples and make it fit for its mistress, its queen. Ah, how happy we will be, dearest! Where shall we go? Italy, Switzerland, the lakes?" and he clasped her hand, which seemed to grow colder each moment. "There is nothing in the world you may want that you shan't have, I promise you—nothing! I'm rich, as you know, and I'm prepared to spend any amount you like; you shall see."

She looked at him. It seemed to her marvelous that he should so little understand her.

"I want nothing—nothing but to see papa happy!" she said.

"Very well," he assented, "and you will do so, and have the satisfaction of feeling that it's all your doing! It isn't every girl who could pull her father out of the mud as you will do."

She winced; every word he uttered jarred upon her as it did upon the squire.

"I—I think I will go upstairs," she said. "I have a headache to-night."

"Oh," he said in a tone of disappointment; then he added, with a cunning glance, "Don't forget you promised to sing that duet with Faradeane."

Her lips quivered, and she turned her head aside.

"I had forgotten," she said, simply.

He got up to hide the evil look which crossed his face.

"Yes, you'll stop to please him, my lady," he muttered. "But wait a while, wait a while!"

Faradeane and the squire came in, and the former went up to her.

"Will you sing?" he said, "or are you too tired?" he added, quick to notice her pallor and weariness.

"No," she said, and went to the piano, and he found one of the modern ballads set duet fashion, and they began.

Their voices harmonized perfectly, and the squire settled himself in a chair to listen with something like peace in his eyes.

"If you had loved me years ago,
When Time was young and Fate was free
What happiness we now should know!
Love came too late for you and me."

the refrain of the song ran; but at the last line of the second verse Olivia's clear voice faltered and broke, and the music ceased.

The squire rose apprehensively, and Bartley Bradstone glowered across the room suspiciously, but, with a quick, yet apparently natural motion of his hand, Faradeane caused the music to slide from the stand.

"I beg your pardon," he said. "It was my clumsiness."

She looked up at him gratefully, the moment or two giving her time to recover herself.

"Let me try it again," she said in a low voice; but he shook his head.

"No; you are tired, I can see, and I am out of voice."

"I am tired," she said, with a smile that cut him to the heart. "And I think I'll say good-night."

He went and opened the door for her, and, after bidding the rest "Good-night," she passed him with bent head, and without giving him her hand.

When she had gained her own room she flung herself down beside the bed, and hid her face in her hands.

"Three weeks! Three weeks!" she moaned. Then she rose with a desperate laugh, and sang softly, with the delight in self-torture which a woman alone can feel:

"If you had loved me years ago,
When Time was young and Fate was free,
What happiness we now should know!
Love came too late for you and me."

Olivia Or, It was for her sake | 179

CHAPTER XX
AN APPALLING APPARITION

The announcement of Olivia's approaching marriage caused almost as much excitement as the news of her engagement.

She had insisted upon the ceremony being as quiet a one as possible, and, for a wonder, Bartley Bradstone assented.

At least a score of young ladies were desirous of acting as bridesmaids upon so famous an occasion, but Olivia desired to limit the number to two, and chose Annie and Mary, much to their delight and Aunt Amelia's chagrin.

"My dear Olivia," she remonstrated in her most dignified manner. "Only two bridesmaids! Why, the veriest pauper has three or four! Let me beg of you to remember your position, and what is due to it! I've nothing to say against Annie and Mary, but I cannot forget that there are others who have a claim upon us. For instance, there are those six dear girls of the duchess'. Now, why—I ask, why—cannot you choose them?"

But Olivia remained as firm over this point as she did upon the question of her trousseau. Aunt Amelia had looked forward to a visit to town, resulting in an extensive outfit, in which costly lace, and still more costly furs and tailor-made dresses should figure largely, and was proportionately disgusted when Olivia announced that she intended buying her things at Wainford, and evidently meant to confine her purchases to very narrow limits.

"Really, my dear Olivia," said Aunt Amelia, "one would think your father hadn't a penny to bless himself with! I call it ridiculous. If you have no proper pride in your own appearance you might at least show some regard for him."

And Olivia, with an aching heart, had to meet the old lady's reproaches with a smile.

On one thing at least she was resolved—that she would not spend one single sovereign more than was absolutely necessary of the money which she knew her father could so ill spare; and perhaps the sharpest pang she endured was felt by her on the morning when he called her into the study and gave her a handsome set of pearls.

"This is my present, dear," he said, his eyes dwelling on her with tender love and pride. "Your mother's jewels are yours by right, and I shall give them to you on the morning of your marriage; but this is my present. It is not"—he faltered for a moment—"it is not so rich as I should like, but——"

She stopped him by putting her arms round his neck and drawing his worn face to hers.

"Why did you buy me anything, dear?" she murmured. "I only want what I have got—your love!" and she strained him to her with an almost protecting embrace. But though the squire's eyes filled with tears as he bent over her, hers were dry and hot, and wore a restless, feverish expression.

Restless would indeed best describe her state of mind since the day had been fixed for the wedding.

As Aunt Amelia said, reproachfully, it seemed as if she could not remain in one place for five minutes together, or settle to any one occupation. She wandered about the house and grounds during the day, and paced her room at night, her eyes fixed with a restless unquiet upon vacancy. But she wore the mask before the world so well that not even Faradeane could read the anguish and misery which tortured her; and if at times the ordeal through which she must pass seemed too terrible to be endured, the thought of her father and the peace she would purchase for him nerved her for the sacrifice.

Meanwhile, Bartley Bradstone had filled The Maples with an army of upholsterers, and new and luxurious as the place was already, it was to be made still more gorgeous for the reception of his bride.

Two days before the wedding, which was to take place on the Wednesday, it suddenly occurred to him that he had not yet got a best man; and, promoted by a malicious desire to make the most of his triumph, he proposed that Faradeane should occupy that position.

They were sitting at lunch, and Faradeane had walked across to the Grange, and allowed himself to be persuaded to stay.

"I want you to be my best man on Wednesday, Faradeane," said Bradstone in an offhand way, and with a sidelong glance at Olivia. She kept her eyes fixed upon her plate, and did not see the swift change which came over Faradeane's face. For a moment he was silent, and Bartley Bradstone, taking it for consent, went on, airily, "It isn't a difficult part, I believe; anyway, I'm sure you'd play it capitally—wouldn't he, squire?"

The squire looked at the grave face, which had grown paler even than usual, but was perfectly calm and self-possessed.

"Will you, Faradeane?" he said in his quiet way.

Faradeane, carefully avoiding looking in Olivia's direction, shook his head.

"I feel honored by Bradstone's request, sir, but I am sorry to say that I am engaged on Wednesday."

"What!" exclaimed Bartley Bradstone. "You don't mean to say that you are not coming to the wedding? Why, I should fancy you will be the only man in the county who won't be there—won't he, Olivia?"

She made a slight gesture which might mean anything, but did not raise her eyes.

"Then my room will be more acceptable than my company," said Faradeane, with a smile. "You will have no difficulty in getting some one to fill so honorable a post, Bradstone. I am sorry I cannot."

"Oh, but you must manage to come to the wedding and the breakfast—or whatever they call it now; it can't very well be breakfast at half-past three o'clock in the afternoon. You must come, Faradeane—mustn't he, Olivia?"

She looked up for a moment, and past Faradeane, avoiding his eyes.

"Mr. Faradeane says he is engaged," she said, quietly.

"Oh, but——" began Bradstone; but Faradeane stopped him with a certain compression of the lips which Bartley Bradstone remembered seeing on his face when he seized him by the arm outside the terrace.

"It is impossible," he said, almost curtly.

Bartley Bradstone shrugged his shoulders.

"I counted upon you," he said. "But if you can't, you can't, and there's an end of it. I'm awfully disappointed, and so's Olivia, I'm sure."

Olivia said nothing, but, directly lunch was over, rose to leave the room. As she did so Faradeane took a morocco case from his pocket.

"You must be quite tired of presents, Miss Vanley," he said, "but I have ventured to bore you with one, if you will accept it," and he placed the case in her hand, and turned aside to speak to Bradstone.

"Eh?" said the squire, "let us see what it is, my dear," and he put up his eyeglasses.

She opened the case, her hands trembling and her color coming and going, and revealed a superb necklet of gems in an antique setting.

It was no "wedding present" of the commonplace type, but evidently a rare and costly, perhaps priceless, specimen of ancient jewelry.

The squire uttered an exclamation.

"Why, Faradeane, this is—isn't this rather too big a present for my little girl?" he said, with a smile, but a grateful and affectionate light in his eyes. "If she had been a princess, instead of the daughter of a country squire, you could not have been more generous."

"Miss Olivia is a princess to all of us, sir," he said in the half-sad and melodious voice which rendered even his commonplaces significant. "It is an old relic I have had by me for some time, and I thought that Miss Vanley would forgive its old-fashionedness."

"Which I expect increases its value; and that must be great, apart from the antiquity of the thing. These stones are very large and very lustrous. Look at this, Bradstone!"

"Yes?" said Faradeane, carelessly. "I am no judge of gems. None could be too pure for Miss Vanley."

"Yes, very jolly," said Bartley Bradstone. "Put it on and let Faradeane see how you look in it." She did not offer to comply, but stood with the necklet in her hands; and he took it from her and put it round her neck, and struck an attitude. "What do you think of it, Faradeane?" he exclaimed.

Faradeane looked at her for a moment and smiled.

"The old gems were never so honored before," he said; and, though he tried to speak lightly, there was a perceptible quiver in his voice.

"They are very beautiful," said the squire. "Take care of them, my dear. I am sure they are extremely valuable, although Mr. Faradeane treats them so cavalierly."

Olivia put up her hands to unfasten the necklet, but could not do so.

"Let me try," said Bradstone. "They like you so well that they don't care about parting from you. I can't do it! Where's the spring, Faradeane, do you know? Just come and see, will you?"

Faradeane came slowly forward, and as he did so Olivia put up her hands again.

"I—I think I can do it," she said, with a strange tremor in her voice.

"Don't you try," said Bradstone, with a malicious enjoyment of her embarrassment. "Let Faradeane do it; he knows the trick of the fastening, I dare say."

"It is very simple," said Faradeane; "will you allow me?" and he forced his voice into a tone of ordinary politeness.

She bent her head, and he touched the hidden spring lightly; but, as the necklet parted, his fingers touched her, and her face and neck grew crimson as she raised her eyes to his face.

Then she took the necklet from his hand, and without waiting to put it in its case, left the room.

Bartley Bradstone thrust his hands into his pockets, and looked after her, and then at Faradeane's pale, set face.

"What ingratitude!" he said, half-mockingly and with a loud laugh. "She didn't even say 'Thank you!'"

Olivia went up to her own room, her heart beating, her neck still burning where Faradeane's fingers had touched, and as she opened the door she started and uttered an exclamation. But it was only Bessie who rose to meet her.

"Bessie!" she exclaimed. "How you startled me!" and she sank into a chair, panting.

Bessie looked at her gravely, and brought her a bottle of *sal volatile* from the dressing-table; but Olivia put it away with a faint laugh.

"No, no; I am not so badly frightened as that," she said; "but I did not expect to see any one, and"—with a piteous little smile—"I have grown nervous lately, Bessie."

"I am so sorry, miss," said Bessie, meekly. "They told me to come upstairs and wait as usual——"

"Yes, yes; quite right," said Olivia, quickly, "and I am very glad to see you. Take your things off and let us have some tea. Have you come to say 'good-by' to me, Bessie?" and she smiled again.

"No, not good-by, miss," replied Bessie; "I've come to ask you to take me with you."

"To take you with me! Why——"

"Yes, miss," she went on, with downcast eyes, "I am going out into service, and I've come to ask you if you'll engage me for your maid."

"Why, Bessie!" exclaimed Olivia, catching at her arm and drawing her toward her. "You are going out to service! I thought your father could not spare you?"

"Yes, he can now, miss," she said, as if she were repeating a well-rehearsed speech. "He has got my cousin Polly to keep house for him, and he wishes me to go out."

"It is wonderful!" said Olivia, more brightly than she had spoken for weeks. "And you came to me, of course! How good of you! Of course I will take you—and how gladly! Fancy you being my maid! Why, it is too good to be true! I nearly engaged a girl from Wainford yesterday—my old one went to-day. How glad I am I didn't do so quite! And you only just made up your mind to go into service! How fortunate I am!"

"It is me that's fortunate, miss."

"And when will you come?" asked Olivia, eagerly.

"Now, miss," said Bessie, quietly. "I presumed so far as to bring my box, for he said I was to stay if you'd let me."

"You dear, thoughtful girl!" exclaimed Olivia, pressing her arm. "But who is 'he'—your father? How kind——" She stopped short, noticing that Bessie's face had suddenly grown crimson. "What is the matter? Who is 'he'?" she repeated, fixing her lovely eyes on the girl's downcast face. "Answer me, Bessie! Of whom do you speak?"

"Must I tell?" whispered Bessie.

"Certainly you must," replied Olivia. "I don't understand——"

"It was Mr. Faradeane, miss," said Bessie, in a low voice.

Olivia drew her hand from the girl's arm, and sank back in the chair.

"Mr. Faradeane!" she said, almost inaudibly.

Bessie dropped down beside her.

"Yes, miss. It was he who brought me to think of it. He said he'd heard that your maid was going, and he said to me how nice it would be for you to have some one—he said some friend—with you in that big, new house of Mr. Bradstone's, and he put it in my head to come and ask you. He knows how I love you, Miss Olivia! Nothing escapes him—he thinks of everything! Are you angry, miss?" she half-whimpered.

Olivia put her hand from her forehead, and turned her face—it was very pale—to the girl.

"Angry? No, Bessie. And so it was Mr. Faradeane who sent you? Yes, it was very thoughtful."

"Yes, miss," said Bessie, with a sigh of relief. "He said that you might feel lonely when you were away on your travels abroad and when you get back to The Maples, and that you'd like to have some one you knew and loved, he said, to be near you, and—and I came at once. We all do whatever Mr. Faradeane says," she added, with a little, suppressed sigh.

"Yes, it was very thoughtful, and I am very much—obliged—to him," said Olivia in a low voice. "And now go and get some tea; bring it up here, and—and keep near me. Yes, it was like him to think of it!"

And long after Bessie had left the room, her mistress sat with her hands tightly clasped, her eyes fixed on the necklet in her lap.

The following day was one of bustle and excitement. Some of the wedding guests, connections of the Vanleys, were coming from a distance, and had been asked to sleep at the Grange; Annie and Mary, who were also to stay the night, arrived soon after breakfast, and at once plunged into the business in hand with infinite gusto and enjoyment. The wedding feast was preparing in the kitchen, and upstairs the dressmaker was working frantically at the finishing of the wedding garments.

In the afternoon the bishop—Aunt Amelia had insisted upon a bishop—arrived, and he and the squire wandered about the place in the aimless, shiftless manner peculiar to males on these occasions.

"I'm sure I don't know whether you'll get any dinner to-night, my lord," said the squire, "the whole place is in such confusion."

"I dare say we shall have something to eat," said his lordship, with bland conviction. "You must remember that I am used to this kind of thing. Let me see! the last time I saw Miss Vanley she was in short frocks. She was very pretty then, she is beautiful now. I think this Mr.—Mr.—What's-his-name?—Bradstone, thanks—is a very lucky young man. He is very rich, is he not?"

"Yes," said the squire.

"Well," said the courtly bishop, "he will not have in all his treasure-house a more precious gem than your sweet child. By the way, I think I have seen him before."

"Indeed!" said the squire.

"Yes; I met him as I was driving in, I think. He was riding a remarkably good horse; a tall and exceedingly handsome young man, with a rather grave and pale face. The kind of man that attracts one's attention. It was a dark chestnut horse."

"No, that was not Bradstone," said the squire; "that was a very great friend of mine—Mr. Faradeane."

The good bishop looked puzzled.

"Dear me! A tall man with a mustache, and a—er—certain distinguished bearing?" he said.

"Yes, that was Mr. Faradeane," said the squire. "Do you think you have seen him before?"

His lordship stopped and knit his brows.

"I could have been certain of it, if you had not mentioned his name; but I suppose I must be mistaken, for I do not remember it. And it was not your future son-in-law?"

"No, no," said the squire. "You will see him this evening; I have asked him to dine with us."

"Yes, yes, delighted," purred the worthy bishop. "Strange mistake of mine, and yet I felt quite sure I had seen this Mr. — —"

"Faradeane," supplied the squire.

"Thanks, yes. I don't remember the name in the least, and, as you may be aware, I pride myself on never forgetting a name. Who and what is this Mr. Faradeane? One of the local magnates?"

"No," replied the squire. "He has purchased a small house here — there it is, you can see the chimneys — and settled among us. I like him extremely."

"I should like to meet him," said the bishop, amiably. "I very seldom forget a face, and his seems familiar to me."

"If you'll come with me to his cottage, I'll ask him to dine with us tonight. He is a most charming companion," said the squire, eagerly.

The bishop inclined his head, and the two men walked toward The Dell. As they did so they saw Faradeane in the garden, pacing up and down the gravel walk, and the squire stopped at the gate, and called to him.

Faradeane walked toward them, but at sight of the bishop stopped suddenly. It was only for a moment, however, and he came and unlocked the gate.

"Good-afternoon," said the squire. "Let me introduce you to the Bishop of Latham, Faradeane."

Faradeane raised his hat, and the bishop followed suit, and smiled.

"We have met before, Mr. Faradeane, have we not?" he said, pleasantly.

Faradeane looked him straight in the face.

"Your lordship mistakes me for a better man, I hope," he said, with a smile.

The bishop bowed with ready courtesy and self-possession.

"It is not so, then. Pray forgive me."

"Dine with us to-night, will you, Faradeane?" said the squire, with affectionate familiarity.

Faradeane hesitated a moment, then shook his head.

"Not to-night," he said.

The squire knew him too well to dream of pressing him; and the bishop, having exchanged a few words with him, he and the squire turned homeward.

Half-an-hour later Bartley Bradstone left The Maples to walk to the Grange. Most men are nervous and restless on the day before their marriage, but Mr. Bartley Bradstone was nervous and restless to a remarkable degree. He had wandered about his huge house all day, bullying the workmen and the servants, and it was not until his brougham had been brought to the door that he had suddenly decided that it would do him good to walk instead of ride to the Grange.

He had got himself dressed in his evening suit with even more than his usual care, as his badgered valet, driven almost to distraction, could testify, and he lit up a cigar at starting to steady his nerves. He had also drunk a full glass of brandy-and-water for the same reason.

There was a short-cut through the wood—the same wood in which Faradeane had pleaded for Bertie—and, the moon lighting up every inch of the way, Mr. Bartley Bradstone decided to go through the wood.

Many another man would have been struck by the beauty of the scene, the soft light throwing the shadow of every leaf upon the ground in a delicate tracery, and silvering every branch of the grand old oaks which had been the pride of generations of Vanleys; but Mr. Bartley Bradstone was too fully occupied with thoughts of to-morrow to bestow any attention upon scenery.

"Only a few hours more," he muttered, "only a few hours! I'm a plucky devil, and I deserve to win; and I will, too! She's plucky, too. Lord! it's wonderful what a girl will do to save her father. How beautiful she is, and how proud! But I'll cure her of that, I rather think. I'll let her know who's master, once I've got her safe and tight. I'll have no more of that fellow Faradeane, for one thing. She thinks a great deal too much of him—a great deal. If he fancies he is going to hang about her skirts after she's my wife, as he's been doing lately, he'll find his mistake out. That Faradeane's a beast, and I hate him!"

He repeated this charming sentiment twice, and with such energy that he let his cigar go out.

Flinging it away, he took out his case, and, after selecting another, lit a match. As he did so he heard a rustling among the undergrowth, but, thinking it was a chance rabbit, took very little notice; but suddenly, as the match was falling from his fingers, the figure of a woman slipped out from among the shadows and stood right in his path.

He stepped back with a start of surprise, and stared at her; and she, with a quick movement, flung the shawl she was wearing from before her face and laughed.

It was only a woman's laugh, but it made Bartley Bradstone shrink back trembling and shaking like a leaf; the cigar fell from his fingers, and he stood—or, rather, leaned—against a tree like a man who is suddenly confronted with a ghost.

The woman, planting her feet firmly on the path, stared at him for a moment in silence, then burst into another loud, mirthless laugh.

"Why, it's you!" she exclaimed, and her laugh rang through the wood. "You! Well, this beats anything! You of all men!" and she struck her hands on her hips and laughed again.

Bartley Bradstone's tongue seemed to cling to the roof of his mouth, and his face, ashen pale, was distorted like a man's in mortal agony.

"Bella!" he said at last.

"Yes, that's me," retorted the woman. "Oh, I'm no ghost, though you look as if you thought I was! Great goodness, fancy meeting you—and here! Well, wonders will never cease. You! Why, I thought you were thousands of miles away, and you ain't. By Heaven, I'm in luck! Come, man, pull yourself together; I'm not a ghost, I tell you, not me! Don't pretend you forget Bella. How are you, Mr. Bradstone?" and with a mocking smile she held out her hand.

CHAPTER XXI
THE AVENGER

Great drops of cold sweat stood upon Bartley Bradstone's forehead as he looked at the handsome, devil-may-care face of the woman who, with her arms akimbo, stood regarding him with a mixture of amusement and contempt, combined with an enjoyment of his discomfiture which was almost tigerish.

At last he managed to find his voice, a very weak and feeble one.

"This—this is a surprise, Bella," he said, forcing a sickly smile.

"Yes, I suppose it is," she retorted. "A pleasant surprise, of course. What's become of the elegant manners you used to sport so freely? Any one would think I was an ogre instead of 'handsome Bella!' You see I haven't forgotten some of your compliments. Yes, it is a surprise for both of us. I thought you were across the sea. That was a clever idea of yours, sending the money every quarter from France. It took me in, it did, indeed! I suppose you thought I should run after you, didn't you? Run after you!" and she laughed with scorn. "What are you doing down here? Give an account of yourself, Bartley? Have you got such a thing as a cigarette about you? The smell of that cigar has set me off longing for a puff."

He handed her his silver cigar case, and she smiled as she saw how his hand shook.

"Here, light it," she said, with a nonchalant air of command.

He lit the cigarette, and handed it to her.

"Now, then," she said, blowing the smoke through her handsome nostrils. "Let's have a true and particular account of yourself."

"I'm—I'm staying here for a time," he said, trying to speak in a careless, matter-of-fact tone. "I—I haven't been quite the thing—France didn't suit me—and I ran down here for a change. I'm going back almost directly."

She looked at him with charming incredulity.

"I don't believe a word of it," she said, flicking the ash from her cigarette, and leaning against a tree in an easy attitude, as if she were leaning against the ropes of her trapeze. "I don't believe you've been out of England at all; and what's more, I don't care. You may go where you like, and do what you like, for what I care, Bartley."

He drew a breath of relief, and the color came slowly back to his face.

"Then—then you didn't come down here after me?" he said, with a pitiful attempt at a laugh.

"I certainly did not," she retorted, with unaffected scorn. "I came down here"—and her eyes twinkled—"because the air of London didn't agree with me, and I thought I'd take a change. Come down after you! Why, man, what do I want with you while you pay me my allowance regularly?"

"I thought——" he began.

"You flattered yourself too much," she broke in. "And you don't ask what I've been doing?" with a smile.

"I—I hope you've been enjoying yourself," he said, conciliatingly.

"A lot you care! As it happens, I have been enjoying myself. I've made a hit, and I'm one of the great London favorites, Bartley. What do you think of that, eh? Did you ever hear of Bella-Bella?"

He shook his head.

"Not you! You've been away from England so long, don't you know!" and she laughed sarcastically. "Well, I'm Bella-Bella, the Flying Swallow. There isn't one to touch me on the trapeze, they say; and I believe they're right. I'm making quite a pile, I am; but I'll take my allowance all the same, thank you, Mr. Bradstone! Lord, how frightened you look still!" and she stared and laughed at him. "I dare say you wish I was dead."

He started, and glanced at her under his brows.

"I'm sure I've wished the same many and many a time. But I'm alive still, you see, and kicking," and she folded her legs and stuck out her ankles. "Very much alive. I fancy I shall outlive you, my dear, though I do risk my neck every night. Drop in at the Palace of Amusement when you're in London next, and have a look at me."

"I—I will," he said.

"And so you're staying in this dead-and-alive hole, are you?" she said, eying him curiously. "I wonder what you're up to; some sly game or other, I'll be bound. You always were up to a lay of some kind, weren't you? What is it now, eh?"

"I don't understand you," he said, with affected carelessness. "I'm just staying on here——"

"Do you know many of the people of the place?" she asked, interrupting him contemptuously.

"A few, yes," he replied.

"Tell me their names—the swells, I mean."

"What do you want to know for?" he asked.

She stared at him.

"What's that to you?"

He bit his lip.

"You are no more civil than you used to be, Bella," he said, meekly.

She laughed.

"No; I was never very civil to you, was I? I knew how to treat you, don't you know. You're the sort that must be beaten like a spaniel—you are, Mr. Bradstone. But answer my question, will you? Who are the swells in this forsaken hole?"

He pretended to consider for a moment.

"There is Lord Carfield, and a baronet named Penstone, and Lord Granville——"

"The Cherub; I've heard of him, and seen him," and she nodded. "He's almost too good to be a swell. Well, who else?"

"There's the squire here—Mr. Vanley—and that's all."

"That's all, is it?" she added, reflecting. "Oh!" She was silent for a moment, as if pondering over the names, then she looked up. "And I suppose you are a swell, too, eh? You're cutting a dash down here with your money, ain't you? It's like you. You always liked to be thought a gentleman, didn't you?" and she laughed.

The color flushed his face, then left it pale again.

"I wonder what your game is," she said, after a moment or two. "But I don't care. I shan't interfere. Where are you staying? At the inn where I've put up? You may as well come and have some supper with me. We can have a chat over old times," and she showed her white teeth in a grin.

"I'm—I'm staying with a friend here," he said, "and I'm going there now."

He pulled out his watch.

She stretched out her hand and took it as calmly as if it had belonged to her.

"Handsome ticker—jeweled back. You always were fond of that kind of thing. I've lost mine." She slipped the watch into her waistband and smiled, and Mr. Bartley Bradstone bore the appropriation of his property without a protest.

"So you won't come," she said. "Very well. But you haven't done with me yet; don't flatter yourself I'm going to let you off so easy! Let me see; I'm going to stay here till to-morrow night, just for change of air," and she laughed. "Meet me here at four o'clock to-morrow afternoon."

He started, and his face reddened.

"That's impossible, Bella," he said, quickly. "I've got an—an important engagement."

"Oh! you've—got—an—important—engagement, have you?" she said, with slow contempt; "then you'll have to put your important engagement off for one more important still."

The sweat started out on his forehead, and he wiped it away covertly.

"Don't be absurd, Bella," he said, with a sickly smile. "I tell you I can't meet you to-morrow—not at that time. I'll meet you at night, or the next day."

"No you won't; to-morrow night I shall be gone. Four o'clock in the afternoon, please; and you may as well bring a few notes with you—say for a hundred. I'm rather short just now."

He affected consternation.

"A hundred pounds! You must think I'm made of money! Well, you shall have it, for—for the sake of old times. But you needn't trouble to come for it, Bella. I'll send it to you here——"

She smiled.

"No, you won't. I've a fancy for making you bring it—just for the sake of old times! You seem very disinclined to meet me to-morrow; what's your reason, I wonder?" and she eyed him suspiciously.

The lids of his downcast eyes quivered.

"There can't be much pleasure in our meetings now," he said. "I don't care to be reminded of the past; you must feel that. Look here, you shall have the money. I'll make it a hundred and fifty, though I can't very well spare it, but only on condition that you let me send it to you."

She shook her head, and, with a laugh, caught at a branch of the tree with one hand and drew herself up, hanging for a moment gracefully motionless, then dropped like a feather to the ground, and kissed her hand to him.

"No, I'll have my way. Bring it here to-morrow at four o'clock, or—I'll go with you now! I'm not exactly in evening dress; but you can explain—you're good at explaining, you know."

His face paled, and his breath came fast for a moment, as he thought of this woman with her cigarette in her mouth, her stage smile, and loud, defiant voice, accompanying him into the pure presence of Olivia; then he nodded.

"Very well," he said, sullenly. "I'll come. And now I must be going."

He put out his hand for his watch, and she laughed mockingly.

"I'll tell you the time," she said. "No; I can't see. Off with you. Remember, four o'clock, and you can make it the extra fifty. Here! wait! give me the rest of those cigarettes."

He held out the silver case, and she was about to pick out the cigarettes, then looked up at him exasperatingly, and put the case in her pocket.

"Perhaps I'll give it back to you to-morrow, perhaps I won't. Good-night," and with a nod she motioned him to go on.

She stood looking after him for a few minutes, puffing at the cigarette, and thinking with half-closed eyes, very much like a lithe, graceful cat.

"I wonder what your little game is down here, Master Bartley," she muttered. "No good, I'll bet. You never did anything but mischief wherever you went. Well, it doesn't matter to me. So long as you keep up my allowance and yourself quiet you may do what you please."

Then she pinned her shawl round her, and, walking quickly out of the wood, went down the lane, and stepped in front of The Dell.

"This ought to be the place," she said. "Yes, it's like him to choose a place like this. I should die of the doldrums in a week. But he——"

She stopped a moment or two, standing before the gate as if she were collecting her courage or her mind, then put her hand on the gate.

"Locked!" she said, with a smile. "I don't think that will keep me out!" and, resting her strong hand on the side post, she sprang over the low gate as easily as a boy of fifteen could have done.

As she did so, the dog came bounding down the path with a threatening growl.

She drew herself together, tightening every muscle, just as she did before one of her dangerous feats on the trapeze, and waited for him, her teeth set, her fist closed. The dog came up to her, and sniffed at her, then wagged his tail.

She laughed softly.

"You're a fraud, my friend," she said, stooping down and patting him; then suddenly she gave him a kick, exclaiming: "I'll make you afraid of me before many hours are passed, bow-wow!"

The dog retreated with a yell, and she walked up to the door and knocked.

The servant, in his gamekeeper suit, opened it.

"Is Mr. Faradeane at home?" she asked.

The man held a small lamp above his head, and surveyed her, then looked beyond her at the gate with not unreasonable surprise.

"No, he isn't," he said. "What do you want?"

"I want to see him," she returned, firmly.

"My master is not at home," he said. "What name shall I say, ma'am?"

She thought a moment, her dark eyes flashing past him into the small hall.

"It's of no consequence, my name; if he's at home" —and she raised her voice—"he'd see me, I know."

"But he is not at home," said the man, in a matter-of-fact voice.

"I'll come in and wait, then," she said, and she made a forward movement.

He quickly filled up the doorway.

"You can't do that," he said.

"Why, what are you afraid of, you and your master?" she demanded, scornfully, a spot of red burning on each cheek. "Do you think I want to steal something?"

"I don't think and I don't care," he retorted, much less respectfully; "I know what my orders are, and I'm carrying them out. If you want to see my master leave your name, ma'am, and when he comes back I'll tell him. You can't come in, that's certain."

Her white, even teeth clicked viciously.

"Oh!" she said, with a sneer. "Perhaps you'll tell me where he's gone."

"I don't know," said the man, phlegmatically, "and I shouldn't tell you if I did."

"You insolent— —" she began, furiously; then she pulled up short, and, eying him closely, put her hand in her pocket and held something out to him.

The man shook his head.

"No, thank you, ma'am. I'm acting under orders, and I can't break them."

"You'll be sorry for this, my fine fellow," she said, between her teeth; "when your master comes home and finds who it is you've been treating like a dog, you'll sing a different tune."

The man looked at her grimly.

"What am I to do?" he said; "I'm only obeying my orders, I tell you. I don't know who you are, or what right you have to come in; I only know I can't let you. If you'll take my advice, you'll leave your name and come again."

She thought a moment or two.

"Tell your master——No, I'll wait for him outside if I can't wait in," and she leaned against the door-post, and folded her arms in sullen defiance.

The man looked perplexed and nonplused.

"Well, I can't help it," he said at last, and he leaned against the other door-post, with his hands thrust in his pockets.

She remained in her attitude of stubborn patience for some minutes, then she walked down the path.

The man followed her.

"That's right, ma'am," he said, soothingly; "you'd better go. I'll open the gate——Why, dash it all, it's locked! How did you come in?"

She vouchsafed no answer, but turned and walked up the path again. He stepped past her and guarded the door as before; and she, with an angry snarl, went down the garden and leaned on the gate. There she remained till the darkness wrapped the lonely lane.

The man spoke to her two or three times urging her to go, but she made no reply, and took no notice of him whatever. The weary hours rolled along, then suddenly a firm step was heard in the lane, the man hurried to the gate and held up the lamp, and its light fell upon Faradeane.

It shone, too, upon the woman's face, defiant still, but now pale with some new emotion, as the black eyes flashed up at the handsome face of the man for whom she had been waiting.

He did not start, but into his grave, weary eyes came a strange look, as if the long-expected had come to pass at last.

"So I've found you," she breathed. "Do you know," she panted, "that this fellow has kept me out here—that he has treated me like a dog?"

"I beg your pardon, sir," the man broke in. "I told the lady she mustn't come in—she wanted to. I asked her to leave her name."

Faradeane unlocked the gate, took the lamp from the man, and signed to him to go in; then he turned to the woman and regarded her with a dead calmness.

"Yes, you have found me," he said, not defiantly, but in a still, steady voice. "What is it you mean to do—what is it you want?"

Her black eyes flashed up at him, and her lithe, strong hands clinched at her side.

"You talk as if I was nobody—nothing!" she said, hoarsely.

"You are as nothing to me," he responded, with no trace of scorn, but with something in his tone that cut her more deeply than any outspoken contempt.

"Oh, I am, am I?" she retorted. "I'll show you differently presently. Do you think I'm afraid of you? You'd like to kill me—you wish me dead—I know that! I can see it in your face. But I'm not dead, worse luck for you."

He turned his head slightly. Some one was passing in the lane. The footsteps stopped as if the passerby had heard the words and had paused to listen.

Faradeane raised the lamp. "Good-night, Alford," he said.

Alford—for it was he—glanced from Faradeane to the dimly-seen figure of the woman with an air of surprise; then, touching his hat, returned the "good-night" with deep respect, and walked on.

"Do you think I'm afraid of you?" she repeated. "You're mistaken if you do! You've got more cause to fear me. You know the secret between us. Drive me too hard with your cursed coldness and I'll shout it out here and now!" and she raised her clinched fist and shook it at him.

He looked down at her in silence, with an impassive face, but with a strange expression in his eyes; a mixture of loathing and something like pity—the expression a man might wear who looks upon a wild, furious animal.

The look seemed to madden her.

"Why don't you speak?" she demanded. "Are you going to keep me standing out here any longer. Do you know how long I have been kept waiting by that brute of yours?"

"Say what you have to say here," he said, quietly.

"And suppose I refuse? Suppose I use the power I've got over you and insist upon going in? I've got my rights."

"No," he said; "you forfeited them long ago. Why have you come here? What benefit can you gain by tracking me down?"

"Tracked you down! Yes, you're right. That's just what I have done!" she retorted, with a laugh of triumph. "And now I've found you, I don't mean to leave you! You can't force me to, either."

"No," he said, as quietly as before, with an accent of weariness, "you are quite right; I cannot force you to leave me, but I can leave you. You demand, by the right of the secret between us, to enter that cottage; do so if you will, but I shall never cross the threshold again. You know that."

"You—you hard devil!" she panted, with impotent fury.

"Am I so hard? Think!" he said, sternly. "Do I treat you hardly or unjustly? I have yielded to all your demands—all of them. All I asked of you in return was that you should leave me in peace to live out the life you have degraded and ruined. Can you not do this? Are you not satisfied?"

She bit at her underlip till it showed a livid scar, and tore with one restless hand at the edge of her shawl.

"Suppose I'm not satisfied?" she said.

"Not satisfied!" he repeated. "Even you should be contented with your work, Bella!" and he smiled grimly. "Remember what I was when my evil fate threw me across your path, and think what I am now!"

She glanced up at him with a malicious sneer.

"Oh, you're sorry enough, I dare say," she said.

"Yes, I am sorry enough," he assented, sadly. "Sorry for us both. And now what will you do? Wait"—for she had been about to answer furiously—"if you demand the rights our secret gives you, you know my reply, the course I shall adopt. It will cost me a great deal in shame and further suffering; but I shall not shrink from the cost; and you—what will you gain? Are you dead to all sense of shame? Yes, I suppose so. But there is something dear to you that you will lose—the money I give you to squander."

"Curse your money!" she hissed. "I can earn enough for myself. No; I want my revenge, and I'll have it. I want my rights, I want all the world to know what you are."

He inclined his head.

"I see," he said, with grim resignation. "Go into the house and tell my man all that you care to tell him. To-morrow you can make the whole story public," and he pointed to the open door.

She stood and looked at his calm face, still gnawing her lip.

"And you, what are you going to do? Do you mean to try and give me the slip?"

"No," he replied; "I will leave you in possession, and go down to the village. You will find me there in the morning."

She did not even pretend to disbelieve him, but she hesitated and pondered, beating her foot on the gravel path with restless fury.

"And you've made up your mind? You'd better think it over," she said, threateningly.

He looked at her.

"I have thought it over, and my mind has been made up months, years ago," he said. "I always knew that you would not be satisfied until you had brought yourself and me to further shame; that the time would come when you would find me, track me down, and adopt the course you are taking, and I am, therefore, prepared."

"You'd best think it over," she said, huskily. "I—I don't want to drive you too hard. Look here, I'll give you till to-morrow night; if you come to your senses by that time and decide that—that"—the color came and went in her face—"we are to be friends, we needn't stay in England. I don't care where we go." Her voice faltered, and her dark eyes dropped under his calm, steady gaze. "If you'll be sensible, things might be all right between us even now."

He smiled grimly.

"Yes, they might. Anyhow, I'll give you till to-morrow night. I'll be here at"—she paused a moment—"at six o'clock."

"My answer will still be the same," he said, quietly. "But take the time, and reflect yourself; reflect well and wisely. I am immovable. But you know that."

"You'll sing a different tune to-morrow," she said, threateningly; and she walked toward the gate.

He held the lamp to light her and opened the gate courteously.

"Wait," he said. "Do you want money?"

She glanced at him, then kicked at a stone sulkily.

"I always want money," she retorted.

He put his hand in his pocket and took out a leather *portemonnaie.*

"Take this," he said. "Do not look upon it as a bribe, please."

She snatched it from his hand with an oath, and her black eyes glittered with mingled covetousness and anger.

"I could have every penny you possess, if I liked," she exclaimed, "and I will if—but wait till to-morrow," and, with a threatening gesture, she swept past him.

CHAPTER XXII
AT THE ALTAR

The morning broke as brightly as even the most superstitious of brides could desire. Annie and Mary knocked softly at Olivia's door as the first bell rang, and Olivia opened the door herself, fully dressed in her plain morning-frock.

"Why, dear," they exclaimed, "up already, and dressed, too! We were afraid we should wake you."

"I have been up some time," said Olivia. She did not add that she had lain awake all night listening to the hours as they chimed, and thinking how hideously unlike wedding bells they sounded.

"Isn't it a lovely morning!" said Annie. "I am so glad, you can't tell, dear. I should have hated it to be wet. Don't you look rather pale this morning, or is it my fancy, Olly, dear?"

"Am I pale?" said Olivia, glancing at her white face in the glass. "But it is quite correct, is it not? Brides should be pale, shouldn't they?" and she smiled.

The two light-hearted girls looked at her with a slightly puzzled stare. The change that had come over the subject of their worship bewildered and troubled them; but they were as far from understanding it as they could well be.

"Everybody is up early to-day," said Mary. "The whole house is on the move. Oh, dear, I begin to feel quite nervous. Is there anything we can do, dearest? Perhaps you would like to try your dress on again," coaxingly.

Olivia shook her head with another forced smile.

"I think not, Mary, dear. I'm afraid we are all rather tired of trying on the wedding garment."

"Oh, no, indeed we're not!" they exclaimed in chorus. "We like it. You can't tell how lovely you look in it, Olivia. I should like all the world to see you," said Annie, with a pensive sigh. "I wish I were a man and Mr. Bradstone."

"I wish you were!" said Olivia, absently.

The girls laughed.

"What a strange speech for a bride-elect, Olly. But, oh, I wanted to ask you," said Mary, "is it true that Mr. Faradeane is not coming to the wedding? We only heard it from Aunt Amelia last night. She came into our room to look at our dresses."

Olivia was arranging some flowers which Bessie had brought up in her hand when she came to prepare the bath, and the two girls could not see her face or the swift and sudden quiver of her lips.

"No, he is not coming. He is engaged to-day," she said.

"How vexing!" exclaimed Mary. "I should have particularly liked him to have seen you. It's very disagreeable of him not to have put off his engagement; and it's not like him to be disagreeable, is it, dear— —"

"No," said Olivia, in a dry voice.

"Perhaps if you asked him— —" began Mary, thoughtfully.

Olivia turned upon her with a flash in her lovely eyes, and the look of one tortured beyond endurance.

"How can you suggest such a thing!" she began; then, at the sight of the dismay on their faces, her voice softened and she forced a laugh. "You silly girls, you think everybody must think your goose is a swan, as you do! What does Mr. Faradeane care about weddings? All men hate them, and very sensibly, too."

"Oh, Olly! And he is such a great friend of yours!" said Mary, meekly.

"Is he?" said Olivia, with a laugh that sounded strangely in the girls' ears. "Well, all the more reason that we should spare him the infliction." She drew a long breath and turned to the window. "Let us go downstairs into the garden; it seems hot and stifling this morning," and she pushed the hair from her forehead with an impatient, weary gesture.

They went downstairs, the two girls feeling somehow chilled and perplexed, and found the house, as Mary had said, all alive. His lordship the bishop was in the garden discoursing on roses to the squire, who looked grave and preoccupied, for he was thinking that in a few hours his choicest rose would be taken from him. Aunt Amelia, in a morning-robe of brilliant hue and Parisian fashion, was hopping about among the flower-beds, bestowing simpers and smiles upon all and sundry; and the stir and bustle of an unusual excitement seemed to pervade the air.

Olivia went up to her father, and kissed him with the tenderness which seemed to have deepened since her sacrifice, and, with his arm round her waist, they were leading the way to breakfast, when a footman in the Bradstone livery rode up, and, touching his hat, delivered a box to Olivia.

Mary and Annie uttered an exclamation.

"Oh, do open it! It is only tied with string."

"Allow me," said the bishop, benignly, and, removing the lid, he disclosed three bouquets.

One, the largest, was composed of rare, white blossoms, and had a gold bracelet round the stem, with "Olivia" inlaid in pearls. There were similar bracelets for the two girls, who fell to exclaiming, rapturously:

"Oh, they are too lovely, aren't they, dear? How kind of Mr. Bradstone! And all alike, too!" and they ran from one to the other to show their treasures.

"Extremely handsome," said the bishop, smiling. "Really, so generous a bridegroom deserves to be happy!"

Olivia said nothing for a moment; then, as if suddenly remembering, said:

"I am glad you like them," and as Bessie passed near she called her, and was giving the bouquet and bracelet to her, when Mary exclaimed:

"Oh, Olly, dear! How can you part with it, even for a moment! I mean to keep mine beside my plate and stare at it all breakfast-time."

And Olivia, with a faint smile of resignation, retained the bouquet and walked toward the house.

His lordship the bishop would have been rather surprised if he could have seen the bridegroom at that moment, for Mr. Bartley Bradstone looked anything but happy.

He, too, had lain awake and listened perforce to the record of the slowly moving hours, and all night he had seen the defiant, mocking face of the woman called Bella, and heard the scornful tones of her voice.

He had promised to meet her at four o'clock, and he lay there and cursed himself and her, for he knew that he dared not break the promise. Four o'clock! and the wedding was to take place at two. How should he manage to get away from the party and keep this appointment? For hours he tossed to and fro, scheming and planning, the mocking face of the woman dancing before him. He must slip away somehow, if only for half an hour.

Now and again a shudder of terror ran through him, and he sat up and shook as if with some horrible fear. Then he would fling himself down again, wiping the perspiration from his forehead and muttering: "No, I'll go through with it. It's too late to draw back now."

When his valet came to him at nine, he found his master looking, as he expressed it afterward, "like a man who had been drinking all night," and Bartley Bradstone bore out the resemblance by ordering a soda-and-brandy, which he took with a hot and shaking hand.

Then he went downstairs and drank a cup of coffee, and made a pretense of eating some breakfast; but the face of the woman hovered between him and the dish the butler handed to him, and his throat seemed dry and parched.

After breakfast he went into the library, and unlocking the safe which he had so delicately pointed out to his tool—Mr. Mowle—he got out a cash-box, and, counting out two hundred pounds in notes, placed them in his pocketbook. As he was putting the cash-box back he pushed some small, heavy article from a shelf, and, picking it up, saw that it was a revolver.

It was one of the silver-plated toys which nearly every man possesses, but, for all its smallness, it was deadly and dangerous.

He held it in his hot hand, looking down at it absently for a minute or two; then he tossed it back into the safe with a suddenness and force that made the iron side ring again, and shut the door with a clang.

Then he packed and sent off the bouquets, and, taking up his hat, walked into the garden and stood watching the groom as he rode down the road toward the Grange.

He stood a long time looking in the direction of the village with a half-fearful, dreading gaze, then turned and paced about the grounds, but always returned toward the gate and his nervous watchfulness of the road; and the face of the woman still danced mockingly before his eyes.

One o'clock struck, and with a start he went back to the house. Luncheon was laid. He made no pretense of eating this time, but tossed off a glass of brandy-and-water, and, going upstairs, sent for his valet.

The man appeared with the wedding garments, and dressed his master in the regulation blue frock-coat and lilac trousers.

For once Bartley Bradstone seemed quite indifferent to the effect produced by his clothes, and stared at the glass with lack-lustre eyes.

He scarcely spoke, took the handkerchief and his various rings and jewelry from the man without a word, and when he had left the room, sank into a chair and let his head droop on his breast, his eyes fixed with a strange expression upon the carpet.

A quarter of an hour afterward the valet came in again.

"The carriage is at the door, sir!" he said.

Bartley Bradstone looked up with a start, and the valet, who hated him—as all the servants did—glanced at his white face curiously.

"Shall I get you something before you start, sir?" he said.

"No—yes," was the response. "Get me a glass of champagne. Bring it here. And"—he hesitated a moment—"and ask the butler if any one has been here this morning. Any man—or woman—to see me," he added, with assumed carelessness.

The man came back with the champagne.

"No one has been, sir."

Bartley Bradstone drank the wine and drew a long breath.

"It's fearfully hot," he said; "and I had a bad night. If—if any one should come, tell her—I mean him—that I will see him later in the day."

"Yes, sir," said the man; "any name?"

Bartley Bradstone interrupted him with a curse.

"Just do as I tell you, will you?" he said, angrily. "That's enough for you to do!"

Then, pushing past him, he went downstairs.

As his foot was on the step of the brougham he paused, stood for a moment or two looking at the ground, then turned, and, re-entering the house, went into the library.

He came out again almost immediately, and, getting into the carriage, was driven to the church.

A crowd had collected round the ivy-covered porch, and lined the path to the church door. All the villagers were in their Sunday best, and some of the young men had spent the early morning in decking the road with flags and banners.

As the brougham pulled up there was a stir of excitement, and when Bartley Bradstone got out a cheer rose, but it was forced and faint, and his appearance did not increase the enthusiasm.

"D—n me, if he don't look as if he was going to be hanged instead of wed," said one man, in an almost audible whisper.

He looked around him with a sickly smile, and with the restless suspicion more marked than ever in his glance, and, just raising his hat, went into the church. The clergyman and the clerk were in the vestry, and the latter greeted him with the stereotyped remarks:

"The bridegroom first! Quite right, Mr. Bradstone. Ah! here they are! The bells are just starting. What a lovely morning! 'Happy is the bride,' etc.," and he laughed.

Bartley Bradstone went to the door, stood a moment till the first carriage came dashing up, then returned to the vestry and paced up and down.

Other carriages followed, the little room began to fill, and guests were taking their places in the pews near the altar.

Bartley Bradstone shook hands with one and another, and a faint flush began to rise on his face; but it still looked haggard and anxious, and several times the remark which the man in the crowd had made was echoed by the young fellows who envied him.

Presently a cheer, loud and hearty, burst from the crowd outside, and the bishop, with a bland smile, said:

"The bride."

A moment afterward, amidst still more cheering and cries of "God bless you, Miss Olivia!" the squire entered, with the bride on his arm.

There was an instantaneous movement toward them, and amidst the excited whispering they entered the vestry. She carried in her hand the bouquet he had sent; but the snow-like flowers were not whiter than her face, and she clung to her father's arm with a clasp which seemed as if it could never be loosened.

With downcast eyes she stood for a moment, scarcely seeming to breathe, more like a lovely statue than a living woman; then Bartley Bradstone, who had been standing in the center of a group, came toward her.

"Have you got what I sent you?" he said in a low voice.

She raised her eyes and looked at him as if she scarcely heard him.

"Do you mean this?" she said, raising the bouquet.

"Yes, and inside it," he said.

She looked at him as if she did not yet understand, and, taking the flowers from her hand, he parted them and showed her an envelope lying half hidden in their midst.

"You did not examine it very closely," he whispered, with an attempt at a smile. "Open it; come this way."

Slowly, reluctantly, she drew her arm from her father's and followed him. Those near delicately drew back and moved away, leaving the two alone. She opened the envelope and looked at the paper it had inclosed.

It was a formal acknowledgment of fifty thousand pounds having been paid into the Wainford Bank in her name.

For a second, a second only, the deep pallor of her face changed, and her lips quivered, and with a look—not at him, but at her father—she thrust the paper in the bosom of her dress.

"Are you satisfied?" he whispered, bending over her as if to look at the bouquet.

Her lips opened, but no sound came; and, with the same vacant expression in the lovely eyes, she got away from him to the protection of her father's arm again.

"Are we all—er—ready?" asked the smooth voice of the bishop.

"Quite ready," said Bartley Bradstone, his voice sounding harsh and dry.

The bishop inclined his head, and the procession started for the altar.

White to the lips, with the look in her eyes of one from whom all that life holds of good or bad had passed forever, Olivia stood and uttered her marriage vows.

Only once throughout the ceremony did she show any sign of feeling or of life itself, and that was at the moment when Bartley Bradstone's hand took hers. Then, unseen by any one but himself, a shudder ran through her, causing the hand he held to shake as if with palsy. It was only for a moment; the next she was the statue again, and she walked with firm, unfaltering steps down the church to the vestry.

There was the usual crowd round the register, every one being anxious to sign, but the business was accomplished at last, and, with her arm in her husband's, Olivia passed out of the church.

They stood for a second at the door. The sun blazed down upon them and the cheering crowd, and Bartley Bradstone put up his hand to screen his eyes, and looked round upon the excited people. As he did so his restless, suspicious glance fell upon what he expected: there in the second rank of the living lane stood the woman whose face had haunted him all the past night and all the morning, and even as he stood beside his bride at the altar.

With her hands on her hips, her black eyes all aglow with mocking derision, she stood and stared at him. As his eyes met hers she broke into a laugh that seemed to him to ring above the din of the cheers, and, pushing herself into the front rank, stooped and snatched up some flowers which had been thrown on the path.

"Here's wishing you and your bride every happiness, Mr. Bradstone!" she shouted, and flung the flowers in his face. Then, with a laugh, she slipped back again, and was lost in the crowd.

CHAPTER XXIII
THE ASSASSIN

The words and action of the woman were unnoticed in the excitement, and she slipped back behind the crowd and was instantly swallowed up.

Mr. Bartley Bradstone's face could not have looked whiter than it had done, and after the first start of alarm as the flowers struck him in the face, and the woman's mocking voice rang in his ears, he collected himself sufficiently to force a smile, which he bestowed upon the lines of people.

As the carriages dashed off to the Grange the crowd of spectators closed up behind them and followed in the same direction, for the squire had invited every man and woman and child to a good, old roast-beef-and-beer banquet, which was to be served in a huge *marquee* on the lawn.

In a whirl of excitement the guests thronged into the drawing-room. There is an old-fashioned custom which ordains that the bride shall hold a kind of *levee* in the interval between the ceremony and the breakfast, and Olivia took her place in the drawing-room to receive the usual homage.

She was still pale, and the absent, preoccupied expression was just as marked as it had been in the church, and her voice as she spoke to one and another seemed like that of one who was repeating some well-learned lesson.

The ordeal—for it is an ordeal to even the ordinary commonplace bride, with happiness to help her through it—passed, and the party went into the dining-room.

Most wedding breakfasts or lunches are alike, and there was the usual amount of chatter and laughter among the young people, mingled with the clatter of knives and forks, and the popping of champagne corks. Bartley Bradstone sat beside Olivia, making a pretense of eating, and trying to talk and look at his ease; but the bridegroom is not much noticed on these occasions—so utterly disregarded, in fact, that it would seem almost possible to give the play of "Marriage" with the part of the bridegroom left out. But all eyes wandered to the bride, the loveliest and most charming girl in the county; and many a young fellow who had, perhaps for years, cherished somewhere in the bottom of his soul a vague hope that he might win her for himself, felt his heart throb and ache as he looked at her in her pure loveliness and realized that she was lost to him forever.

The servants did their spiriting nimbly, and before very long the bishop, who had been carrying on a dual flirtation of a mild order with Annie and Mary, laughed softly, looked round with a blandly benedictory air, and rose to propose the bride and bridegroom.

No man could do this kind of thing better than his grace, and eyes grew moist and the lace handkerchiefs fluttered, as, in melting tones, he wished the dear and well-beloved child of a beloved and honored parent all happiness in this and the next world.

Bartley Bradstone fidgeted with his wineglass, which he had permitted the butler to fill pretty frequently; but Olivia sat white and impassive as a statue.

Then, after the well-bred cheering had subsided, all eyes were turned upon the bridegroom. His face flushed and went pale by turns as he rose, and for a moment it seemed as if he would sit down without saying a word; but he seized his full glass and drank off the wine it contained, and started, nervously at first, but presently fell into his usual bombastic, self-satisfied tone, and declared his intention of making his wife happy if he spent every shilling in the attempt.

People exchanged glances, the men of cold, critical contempt, the women with a little shudder; but they applauded him as in duty bound, and as he sat down Lord Carfield rose to propose the remaining toast—the health of the squire.

In few, well-chosen words, which in themselves and in the manner of their delivery presented a striking contrast to the last speaker, he spoke of his deep regard and affection for his old neighbor, who was not only the lord of their manor, but of their hearts, and declared that, speaking for himself, he felt that he, too, had lost, like the squire, a well-beloved daughter.

And now for the first time, as the squire just rose and bowed—too moved to speak, his aristocratic, high-bred face working visibly in his attempt to suppress his emotion—for the first time a change came over Olivia's white face. It seemed to melt as did the Snow Maiden's, but not into a smile. Her lips quivered and trembled, and as she raised her eyes to the old man's face, a tear rolled down her cheek. Then Aunt Amelia made a signal to the rest of the ladies, Bartley Bradstone looked at his watch—a silver one, by the way—and said to Olivia:

"There's just—just an hour and five minutes; don't hurry—I mean I'll keep the carriage a few minutes for you."

"Very well," she said, without looking at him, and she followed her aunt out of the room. Annie and Mary seized her at the door and hurried her upstairs. Bessie was waiting for her with her traveling dress laid out on the bed, and everything that required packing ready to start.

She glanced at her beloved mistress with an inquiring look, and her eyes grew moist as she saw that the cold, stony look which had been upon her white face still dwelt there.

"Are you tired, Miss Ol—ma'am?" she said, coloring at her mistake.

Olivia started and stared at her; then, seeming to realize all that had happened to her in the loss of the maiden prefix, she made a gesture of assent, and sank into the old chair in which she had spent so many hours of late, dreaming of the past and dreading the future.

Bessie bent over her.

"Wouldn't you like to rest, miss? There is plenty of time; I can dress you in half an hour."

Olivia raised her eyes to the face of the devoted girl.

"Oh, if I could!" she breathed.

Bessie turned to the others instantly, and said, firmly, but respectfully:

"Miss Olivia—my mistress would like to rest a little while, ma'am, if you wouldn't mind leaving her."

"To rest, my dear Olivia!" exclaimed Aunt Amelia; but Annie and Mary, after a glance at the white, weary face of the bride, took the old lady gently by the arm and drew her out of the room.

Then Bessie tenderly, but quickly, took off the wedding finery, and, wrapping Olivia in a soft dressing-gown, put a pillow under her head, and drew the curtains over the window.

"Try and sleep, ma'am," she said, in the loving voice of a sister rather than a servant. "I will wake you——"

"Sleep!" said Olivia, in a voice of despair, but she turned her head from the light and closed her eyes.

Meanwhile the guests of the gentler sex were drinking tea in the drawing-room or flirting with some of the young fellows upon the terrace. Bartley Bradstone moved from one group to the other restlessly, for a few minutes, then, after glancing at his watch for the third or fourth time in a quarter of an hour, he went up to the squire.

"I'll just run over to The Maples," he said, with eyes that carefully avoided the squire's. "I—I—there are one or two things I have forgotten. It will not take me long."

"Let me send for them," said the squire, going toward the bell. "It is a pity you should trouble."

"No, no," he replied quickly. "I—shall have to go. You—you need not tell Olivia. I shall be back long before she is down."

"Very well," said the squire. "Take any carriage you can find."

"Take mine, pray," Lord Carfield called after him.

The squire sighed as, with a hurried step, his son-in-law left the room.

"It has been a trying day for Bradstone," he said.

"Yes, it is always so, when the bridegroom is really in love with the bride," said Lord Carfield.

The squire pressed his hand.

"Thank you for that, Carfield," he murmured, and his voice trembled with emotion. "Yes, I know that he loves her, and that—and that is everything."

"Is everything," echoed the earl, encouragingly.

Bartley Bradstone almost ran down the terrace steps, and stopped before one of the long line of carriages which stood in the drive; then, as if he had changed his mind, he glanced at his watch and hurried down the avenue.

After going a hundred yards or so he pulled up and looked round. Not a soul was in sight; almost the whole village was feasting in the *marquee*, from which shouts and laughter floated toward him, and, climbing the low park railing, he, running now, made his way into the wood.

The clock struck the hour; three minutes afterward he emerged from among the trees into the open space where he had arranged to meet Bella. She was not there. While yet breathless he flung himself on to the trunk of the tree, and, taking off his hat, mopped his wet forehead.

Five, ten minutes passed; he got up and paced to and fro with his watch in his hand, cursing and chafing.

Then he heard a laugh, the laugh that had made him writhe yesterday, and she stood before him. For a minute she stood and looked at him with a mocking smile that scarcely harmonized with a certain angry light in her black eyes, and a hard tightening of her lips.

"Well," she said, eying him up and down. "So you were too afraid to stop away, were you? By Heaven! you were right. Do you know what I would have done if you hadn't come?"

"Well, I'm here, am I not?" he exclaimed, timidly. "What are you going to do, Bella? Don't—don't be too hard upon me——" and he moistened his lips.

"Hard upon you!" she echoed. "As if anybody could be too hard upon you. You! Do you know what I meant to do if you hadn't turned up? I'll tell you." She came a step nearer. "I meant to go up to the house—what's it called, your father-in-law's grand place?" (no words would convey an idea of the diabolical mockery of her tone)—"your father-in-law's place, and ask for you. I don't think they'd have refused me, when I'd told them who and what I was to you."

"For God's sake, don't go on like this, Bella," he said, nervously, his eyes half-raised imploringly. "I'm—I'm at your mercy, I know. If—if you had turned up before yesterday, if it had only been the day before, I wouldn't have done this; but—but it was too late then. I—I couldn't break it off."

"You're a nice villain, ain't you?" she sneered. "I wonder what they'd do to you if I up and told them all, eh?"

"God knows," he said, hoarsely. "But you won't do that, for your own sake."

"For my own sake," she repeated, advancing upon him threateningly. "Why should I care? I wouldn't mind. Don't you dare me! If you only knew what a little would make me do it, how I'm simply dying for the fun that it would make, you wouldn't talk like that, you scoundrel!"

"Hush, hush," he said, looking round nervously. "You'll—you'll have somebody hear you. The place is full of people; some one may come this way any moment——"

"And find Mr. Bartley Bradstone has left his newly-made bride to meet a strange young woman in his father-in-law's park." She leaned against the tree and laughed with malicious enjoyment. "What a row there'd be! What a prime, glorious row! Lord! I'd like to be in it. As for you"—her tone changed—"you deserve anything. Nothing's too bad for you. You to go and make a victim of that girl! What harm had she done you, I should like to know?"

"Hush!"

"And what did she marry you for?" she went on, unheeding his remonstrance. "You don't mean to tell me she cares for you, because if you do I'd tell you that you lied. She care for you! Why, you ain't fit to wipe the dust off her boots! And—you've—married her!"

"Bella, listen to me," he said, hoarsely. "I've—I've met you as you insisted, you know at what risk, and I've brought you what you wanted and fifty pounds more. Now, what are you going to do? Be sensible, for Heaven's sake, be sensible. It—it can't matter to you what I've done."

"You're right. So far as you are concerned," she put in with unmitigated contempt, "you might marry twenty times a month for what I cared."

"I know that; don't I say so?" he went on hurriedly, "and—and so—as it's a matter of indifference to you—you said so, you know—why—why, you can keep your tongue quiet. There's—there's no reason why—why anybody should know anything about. If—if we meet at any time, you—you—can pass me by— —"

She stopped him with a laugh.

"Do you think I'm a child?" she said, scornfully. "I know what you want, and I'll do it—for a price."

"That's right," he said, with a gasp of relief. "That's talking sensibly. I knew you'd say so, Bell."

"Yes, you knew I'd sell myself, didn't you?" she retorted, with a dangerous flash of her black eyes. "Well, we'll see. Give me hold of that money first."

He took out his pocketbook, and with a hot, trembling hand extracted the notes and held them out to her.

She took them carelessly, but counted them.

"Right," she said. "And now about the future. You think I'm a fool— —"

"Bella— —"

"No; I suppose we lived long enough together for you to think different to that; it wasn't long, was it?" with a grin.

"It wasn't my fault we didn't get on," he stammered.

She laughed scornfully.

"Yours? No, I'd had enough of you pretty quickly. I don't like your kind, Mr. Bradstone. I like a gentleman or a rough; you're a half-and-half, and a thorough cad! Poor girl! how I pity her!" and she laughed.

He winced and his face went livid.

"Never mind her——" he said, hoarsely.

"Oh," she cut in, "I'm not good enough to mention her, ain't I? What's her name?"

"Olivia," he said, reluctantly.

"O—livia. And she's a swell, of course? Oh, I've heard all about her, excepting how you managed to get her in your clutches. And I'll know that soon. I'll get her to tell me."

He started, and let his shifty eyes fix themselves on her face.

"You'll get her to tell you?" he breathed.

"Yes," she said, defiantly, with a grin. "I'm going to make you open your eyes, Mr. Bradstone. I'm going to be a great lady myself. Oh, you may stare! And I mean to know your wife. I've took a fancy to her; she's the swellest thing I've ever seen, even among the swells, and I mean to get as close as wax with her."

"You——"

He put his hand to his forehead and looked at her in amazement.

She laughed.

"Yes, and you can't prevent me, Mr. Bradstone. No, I think not! Oh, I know your game; but it won't do. Just whisper a word against me to your pretty wife, and I'll up and tell her the whole story."

His hand dropped, and he stood as if turned to stone, his small eyes fixed upon her mocking face.

"I—I don't understand. By God, you're enough to drive a man mad." His teeth clinched. "If this is a joke, get it over and come to business. How much do you want to hold your tongue? Out with it and have done with it."

She advanced toward him, threateningly.

"Drop that," she said. "Don't use that kind of tone to me. I'm not going to be bullied, Mr. Bradstone. You'd better come down a peg or two, or I'll——" She looked round. "I suppose I could collect a reg'lar crowd in a couple of minutes," and she opened her lips.

He seized her arm, his face working.

"Hush!" he said. "I—I was only in fun. What is it you do mean? How can you be a great lady, as you call it? How can you—you know my wife?"

"Your wife!" she laughed, scornfully, and he winced. "Never you mind; you're too curious, you are. Don't ask me any questions, and I'll tell you no lies. Anyhow, you can tell your wife that I mean what I say. Your wife—

your wife!—and me is going to be great friends. I shouldn't be surprised if she asked me to stay with her. That will be fun!" and she threw her head back and laughed with malicious enjoyment of the vision her words called up. "Only fancy, Bella-Bella chumming with a great swell's daughter! Oh, Lor'!"

He stood and looked at her, and a new expression was coming into his eyes, an expression of watchful cunning.

"Well," he said, "funnier things have happened. It's—it's a strange world——"

"I should think it is after the wedding I've seen this morning!" she retorted.

"And—I've nothing to say against it," he went on, trying to speak carelessly; "only I should like to have a warning. But I'll make a bargain with you, Bella. Give up the idea—I don't see anything in it to your advantage—and I'll give you——"

"How much?" she said, with a sneer. "But don't trouble yourself, I shan't want it. I shall be as rich as you, I expect; and if it wasn't that I love bleeding you, you skinflint, I'd fling these notes back in your face. But I'm going to keep 'em for the present. Perhaps I'll buy a weddin' gift for your pretty, young wife, Mr. Bradstone," and her laugh rang out again.

He took out his watch—the silver one; and she, with a smile of derision, pulled out his watch—the gold one.

"Gettin' late, I suppose. You want to be off for the honeymoon. Well, I'll come with you—just as far as the drive. Perhaps we shall meet the young lady, and you can introduce me, here and now. Ah——" she broke off, for with a snarl he snatched something from his breast-pocket. There was a flash, a sharp twang, a little puff of smoke, and the next instant the magnificent form of Bella-Bella, the Queen of the Air, was lying full length on the mossy ground.

She had scarcely uttered a cry louder than the fear-breathing "Ah!" and yet it seemed to the trembling wretch who stood with the smoking revolver in his hand that the wood echoed with fiendish yells. The great trees waved and danced before him, the earth seemed to rock under his feet, and he quaked like one of the rustling leaves, which all had tongues to cry "Murder!"

So he stood, and so she lay, breathing short, but speechless, while one could count twenty. Then the assassin's first instinct, flight, smote upon him, and he turned and fled. But no farther than the edge of the drive. There a horrid remembrance flashed upon him. On that prostrate figure which he had left for dead, were the notes, which could be traced, his watch, his silver cigar case, which a hundred people would recognize as his.

There was a direct path to the scaffold before him. With a low cry, he turned back, and, bending over her, forced the notes from her hand, keeping his eyes away from the white face, and above all—ah, above all—the thin stream of red which trickled from her side.

The notes were his. With a shudder he thrust them into his pocket, and bent over her again, when suddenly he uttered a cry, a smothered yell of hysterical fear, and looked up. Above him stood Harold Faradeane!

CHAPTER XXIV
THE MAN AND THE COWARD

The miserable wretch shrank back, putting out his hands as if to ward off the stern, accusing eyes, and groaned. Faradeane flung himself down on one knee beside the prostrate form, and raising her head, looked into her face. As he recognized her, he gave a start of surprise, but instantly placed his hand over her heart. Then he turned his eyes upon the cowering Bradstone.

"You have killed her!" he said, in a low, hoarse voice.

"No, no!" groaned Bartley Bradstone. "She—she is not dead. For God's sake, don't say that!"

"You have killed her!" repeated Faradeane, grimly. "Why did you do it? What was she to you——"

He stopped, for Bartley Bradstone had crawled to his knees.

"Faradeane, have mercy on me, have pity," he whined, almost speechless with terror. "I—I didn't mean to—to—kill her, only to stun her—to—to—I'll tell you all, so help me Heaven, if you'll let me go——"

Faradeane, with Bella's head upon his knee, held up one hand.

"They will hang you," he said, grimly. "You are mad! What have I to do with saving you? You are beyond help, and you must know it."

Bartley Bradstone uttered a whine.

"Oh, my Heaven! What shall I do? Faradeane! Faradeane! save me!"

Faradeane scarcely heeded him; his brain was whirling as he loosened the woman's collar, and tried to pour some brandy past her paling lips.

"Save me, save me, Faradeane!" cried Bartley Bradstone, in a kind of suppressed shriek. "I can explain everything. I'll do anything! I'll—I'll—oh, God! if you won't do it for me, do it for her! Remember whom I married this morning!"

A quick shudder ran through Faradeane's veins, and the blood left his face. In the horror and excitement of the moment he had forgotten—forgotten that this blood-stained wretch, who crawled at his feet and begged like a cur for his life, was the husband of Olivia Vanley! The husband!

He looked up speechless for a moment.

"Great God! I had forgotten!" dropped from his white lips. "You—you fiend!"

"Don't—don't!" whined Bartley. "I—I know all you can say; but—but if you'd seen how she drove me! She had no mercy! She drove me till I was mad! Yes, that's what I am!" he gasped, hoarsely. "I'm mad! Tell them I'm mad! They can't hang me! They can't! You said so yourself. Oh, Faradeane, have pity on me! Think how young I am! I—I am no older than you! Have pity on me!"

"Silence!" said Faradeane, and his voice rose like that of a stern, relentless judge. "I am thinking. But not of you! I am thinking of her—of the girl whose life you have wrecked and ruined, whose heart you have broken! Don't speak!" He held up his hand. "Every word you utter tempts me to call for some one to drag you away. You, the husband of——For your own sake, don't speak to me."

Bartley Bradstone crouched on the ground, his hands clutching at the grass, his face hidden.

A minute or two passed, as Faradeane bent over the pallid face upon his knee, his own almost as white, his heart racked by the awful torture of the position. All his thought was of the sweet, innocent, pure-hearted girl, for whom he would have gladly laid down his life, and whom this blood-stained wretch had linked to his own shameful name.

Then, as he looked down upon the woman, scarcely seeing her, he was recalled to the fact of her presence by a slight movement of her eyelids.

They opened. For a moment there was nothing but a dense shadow over them; then she recognized him.

"You!" she breathed, with a faint flicker of surprise in her face.

He bent down.

"It is I," he said. "My poor Bella!"

The shadow of a smile swept over her face.

"Poor Bella, eh?" she gasped, so low that he could just hear her, and no more. "You—you didn't speak like that last night, Cly! No! But—but why am I lying here—what's this pain in my side? Ah!" a shudder ran through her; "I—I remember! Cly, he—he shot me! The coward! the coward! He didn't give me time! If he had——" She tried to raise her arm. "Cly," and a spasm quivered on her lips, "am I—am I—going to die? Tell me the—truth? You always did that."

"My poor girl!" dropped from his lips again.

She closed her eyes, and for a second or two remained silent; then she opened them with a lurid light in them. "Cly, listen to me. Take—take down what I—I tell you. The man who shot me—was—was Bartley Bradstone! You know—him?"

He made a faint gesture of assent.

"He—he is a scoundrel; the worst, the meanest; he's—he's married an innocent—girl—this morning, and—and—he wanted to put me out of the way."

She gasped for breath.

A strange change flashed into Faradeane's face. Was it a sudden hope—a sudden, almost overwhelming relief?

"Bella!" he whispered, hoarsely, "what was there between you? Was he your husband?"

She understood the significance of his tone, the hope that shone so vividly in his dark eyes, and she managed to shake her head.

"No! Yes—we were married, but—he is not my husband. You——"

Her breath failed her; the hope died out of his eyes, but he raised her into a more comfortable position. Both had forgotten the miserable wretch who crouched near them, listening as well as the tolling of the death bell in his ears would let him. After a pause—during which she struggled for breath—she panted, her voice almost inaudible:

"Don't—don't spare him, Cly! He—he isn't—worth it! Ah—I—I can't tell you! And there's so—so much! so much! If I could, you'd—you'd forgive me! Yes, you would! Hold me higher, Cly! Have pity on me, and—and forgive me! I'm not so—so bad as you—think! Oh, if I—could tell you! Cly—there's—there's a mistake! I——" a low cry of terror and dread, a piteous cry rang from her lips, and her eyes dwelt upon his face with a terrible entreaty. "Forgive me, Cly, it's—it's not so bad—you are——Forgive——"

She stopped. Death, who had been hovering over with outstretched hand, let his iron fingers fall and grasp her. A slight tremor passed over her face, and then——

Will it be remembered when the final account is settled that the last words on her lips were a prayer for forgiveness?

The silence of the grave reigned in the dreadful spot for a moment or two; then Bartley Bradstone raised himself, and, crawling nearer, peered at her. He fell back with a moaning whine.

"She's—she's dead!" he gasped.

"Yes," said Faradeane, in a strangely subdued tone, "she is dead. Your work is finished."

He laid the body down gently, reverently, and looked at his watch.

Bartley Bradstone rose to his knees.

"What are you going to do?" he demanded, hoarsely. "Are you—are you going to betray me?"

Faradeane stood looking down at the still form, scarcely seeming to hear him.

"Are you? Are you?" persisted the wretch. "Think, for Heaven's sake, think! It isn't for me! It isn't for me! I don't care what becomes of me! No, I don't. They—they may hang me when they like! But it's her—Olivia——"

Faradeane started, and turned his eyes upon him.

"It's of her I'm thinking; and you'd—you'd better remember her, too. If—if I'm taken it will kill her with—with shame. You know that! Oh, be quick, for God's sake! I—I can get away if—if you'll help me. There's—there's time even now," he panted, in a frenzied tone. "Nobody knows she was here, nobody heard the—the shot! She won't be missed till I'm clear away! For her sake—for Olivia's, Faradeane. I know you love her."

"Silence!" broke from Faradeane's white lips. He turned his back upon him, as if the sight of him was more than he could endure.

The leaves rustled overhead, the noise of the villagers over on the lawn came faintly on the breeze, mingling with the joyous music of the bells— Olivia's wedding bells!

Suddenly he turned as if he had made his decision, and Bradstone, who had been watching him, caught a shred of hope from something in his face.

"Ah!" he gasped.

Faradeane held up his hand.

"I will save you," he said, and his voice sounded grim and solemn. "Do not speak, but listen. Every moment is one of life or death—to you.

You speak of flying. It would be useless. You cannot get away; if you did, suspicion would turn upon you at once. You understand, you realize that? Get up!"

Bradstone obeyed with the prompt obedience of a dog, and stood shuddering and shivering, wiping his face and lips. Faradeane thought for a moment.

"Go to The Maples and change your clothes, and stay there."

Bartley Bradstone looked at him.

"And stay there," said Faradeane, slowly and sternly. "On one condition only will I attempt to save you. You can guess what it is."

The red of shame, perhaps of remorse, flickered on his pallid lips.

"You—you mean that—that I'm not to go near her!"

Faradeane made a gesture of assent.

"You know it is that," he said, in a low voice. "Attempt to claim her as your wife"—he seemed scarcely able to go on—"and I denounce you! That is my condition; do you accept it? Quick!"

"I accept, I accept," panted Bradstone. "I agree to anything. I swear"—he uttered a frightful oath—"I'll do anything, everything you tell me," he whined.

Faradeane averted his face with disgust and loathing.

"Your life depends upon it," he said. "Go now, and say nothing to any one. Did any one see you on your way here?"

"No, no!"

"Answer no questions; keep silence. Now go," and he pointed toward the drive.

Bartley Bradstone took a step, then with a shudder he looked at the still form at Faradeane's feet.

"There—there's something of mine there," he said, hoarsely. "If—if it's found I'm—I'm lost."

"Take it," responded Faradeane, grimly.

He bent down, then shrank back, shuddering.

"I—I can't!" he gasped. "I can't touch her! It's—it's a watch and my cigar case——"

Faradeane bent down and reverently took the things from the dead woman's pocket, and dropped them at Bradstone's feet.

"Go, quick!" he said.

Bradstone snatched at the things, and turned; then he stopped and looked over his shoulder.

"What—what are you going to do?" he asked, hoarsely. "I—I haven't thanked you; but by Heaven——"

"What I am going to do rests with me," came the stern response. "Let it be what it may, it is not for your sake, but for her sake!"

He raised his hand again, and Bartley Bradstone, with one last parting glance at the woman he had murdered, staggered from the glade.

Faradeane leaned against a tree, and hid his face in his hands, and thought. And, incredible as it may seem, it was not of the woman who had ruined his life, and who now lay dead at his feet, not of the awful peril in which he had placed himself in shielding the murderer, not of Bartley Bradstone; it was upon Olivia his mind was fixed.

Surely never was a woman placed in a more awful, a more heartrending position. The wife of a scoundrel who had stained his hands with blood upon her wedding day!

"Oh, my darling, my darling!" broke from his lips in a despairing moan. Then he let his hands fall and looked up at the bright sky which shone through the thick branches of the trees. "Something I can save you from, something of the shame, the misery; but yet how little, how little! Oh, my darling! my poor, poor darling!" and in his burning eyes the hot tears gathered—tears wrung from his heart by the thought of the anguish which awaited her. "Yes, something I can save you and I will! I can save you from him even now! Thank God, thank God it is not too late!"

The thought restored him somewhat, and struggling for self-command, he looked around him. A small, shining object lying on the moss caught his eyes. It was the revolver which had dropped from Bradstone's nerveless hand.

Faradeane took it up and looked at it absently. He thought a moment. Then he took out his penknife and scratched some initials on the glittering surface of the weapon.

He glanced down at his clothes as he did so, and a shudder ran through him. Two or three red spots stared up at him from his white wristband; there were similar spots on his coat and waistcoat.

He dropped on the trunk of the fallen tree, and with clasped hands and set face—waited!

And the sun streamed through the trees brightly, the birds flitted over the accursed spot with joyous trills, and, but for the music of their song, the echo of the villagers' voices, and the ringing of the wedding bells, all was silent.

Olivia started awake with a low cry of fear, as Bessie's gentle hand and loving voice aroused her.

"It's time, miss," she said, regretfully. "I'm sorry; I waited till the last moment——"

"I'm ready," said Olivia, rising pale and wearily. "Have I been asleep long, Bessie?"

She tried to smile, but her strength of will, great as it was, failed her, and the smile was a look of agony.

Bessie turned away and caught up the traveling dress.

"Oh, try, try and keep up, miss!" she said, in a low, imploring voice. "Let me get you something—a little wine?"

Olivia shook her head.

"No, no; I do not want it. Don't be afraid," and she laid her hand on Bessie's. "If I have kept up till now, I can——"

Bessie trembled at the stony, icelike touch, and went on with her work.

"I—I shall go down with you, miss," she whispered.

"Yes, keep with me, dear," said Olivia, calmly now. "Don't"—her lips quivered—"don't leave me alone with my father."

Bessie understood the prayer. Her beloved mistress might endure all else on this day, but not a scene with the father she loved so passionately and was leaving.

"Yes, miss, I understand," she murmured.

"Shall we go down?" said Olivia, as Bessie put on her hat. "I am ready!" and she raised her eyes to the glass mechanically.

The sight of her white, deathlike face startled her.

"I—I look as if I were going to die," she said, dully. "Oh, if it were but true! If I could die now—now!" and a spasm convulsed her face.

"Hush, hush, dear, dear mistress!" implored Bessie. "Wait; there's a little time left still. Wait till they send for us."

She flung on her own jacket and hat, and then, going on her knees beside Olivia, put her arm round her.

"Forgive me, miss," she whispered, "but I love you, and my heart bleeds— —"

For answer, Olivia laid her cold face against the girl's faithful one and let it rest there.

The time was up; the guests had gathered in the hall with the customary slippers and handfuls of rice. The bride and bridegroom's carriage was at the door.

Pacing to and fro in the study was the old man who was now to lose his darling, only child, the pride, the joy, the solace of his life.

He, too, had borne up well throughout the trying day; but he was feeling that his strength to command himself was growing weaker; and he waited, longing, dreading, for the moment of farewell.

The best man hurried to and fro, glancing at his watch anxiously.

"Time's up," he said to Lord Carfield. "They'll lose the train if they don't mind. Where the deuce has the fellow got to?"

Lord Carfield looked up at the great hall clock.

"He went home to fetch something he had forgotten. That was—oh, an hour since; he should have returned long ago. Perhaps he is with the squire, or somewhere about the place."

The young fellow went to the study door and opened it, then closed it softly and reverently.

"No," he said, anxiously. "The squire is there—alone. Bradstone may be in the house; but I don't see how he could get in without our seeing him. But I'll look."

He was gone four or five minutes; then he came back looking still more worried and anxious.

"He's not in the place, confound him!" he said. "I don't know what to do."

Aunt Amelia came fluttering out of the drawing-room with one elaborately embroidered slipper—which would have fitted a child of four, but which she fondly hoped would be mistaken for her own.

"Where's dear Olivia? Where's Bartley?" she simpered, with an hysterical little giggle. "Isn't it time they started? Why, what is the matter?" she demanded, looking from one to the other of the now silent and curious groups.

"Hang it all," said young Vernon, the best man, "I must do something or I shall get mad. Look here, I'll dash off to The Maples. If I find him there, I'll bring him; if I don't—I mean if he passes me on the way—tell him I've gone on to the station to take the tickets. Every moment will be of consequence. Don't be upset, Miss Vanley," he added to Aunt Amelia, who was already exhibiting signs of hysterics; "it's all right! I'll bet ten to one Mr. Bradstone will be here before I'm back," and he dashed off.

The study door opened and the squire looked out.

"Olivia," he said, "isn't—isn't the time up?"

Lord Carfield went to him, and putting his arm through his, drew him into the study again.

"There's a little delay, squire," he said. "There is plenty of time."

Five, ten, fifteen minutes passed, and then there came upon the air the sound of rapidly approaching wheels, a carriage stopped at the door, a groom sprang to the heads of the steaming horses, and Vernon jumped out. Then he turned, and the crowd watching from the hall saw him help Bradstone out.

He was pale, but for two spots that burned like blood upon his cheeks, and his eyes glittered unnaturally.

"Hurrah! here they are!" said some one. "Look sharp, Bradstone!"

The two men came up the steps into the hall, Vernon with Bradstone's arm in his.

"I'm—I'm late, I'm afraid," stammered Bradstone; "the fact is I was kept by a most important letter involving thousands!"

As he spoke, those nearest him noticed that his lips were dry, and that he smelled strongly of brandy. Vernon left him and ran to the study, and Lord Carfield, hearing the shout, came out and seized him by the arm.

"I've got him," whispered Vernon, "but—but—confound it, I have to say it! but—but I think the fellow is more than half drunk!"

"Impossible!" said Lord Carfield, in a low tone of horror.

"But—but I'm afraid it's true, my lord," said Vernon. "I've given him soda water, and made him bathe his head. Oh, Lord! it's too awful to think of! That sweet young creature!" and the young fellow uttered an oath which will probably be forgiven him.

Lord Carfield held the study door in his hand.

"Keep him out of the squire's sight," he said, in a troubled voice. "I suppose she must go now with him. What can have come to him?"

"Oh, she must go," assented Vernon, despairingly. "Here"—to the footman—"tell Miss—confound it! I mean Mrs. Bradstone's maid—that the carriage is waiting. Be sharp."

The footman was hurrying across the hall, when, forcing his way through the crowd of guests, a man whom everybody recognized as the head keeper, caught him by the arm.

"The squire!" he said, breathlessly. "The squire! Where is he? At once! I must see him!"

"S—sh!" warned the footman, "don't make that noise, Browne. You can't see him now!"

"I must—or Lord Carfield."

The earl came forward.

"What is it, Browne? Why are you so excited? What's the matter?"

"Beg pardon, my lord," said the man, agitatedly. "It's murder; that's what's the matter!"

CHAPTER XXV
FOR ANOTHER'S SAKE

"Murder!" It is an awful word. No wonder that a shudder ran through the gayly dressed guests. Even Aunt Amelia may be excused for falling into hysterics, which, of course, she did instantly.

Lord Carfield stepped forward and held up his hand to the keeper, warningly; but the warning gesture came too late. Miss Amelia's shrieks were ringing through the vaulted hall, and at the head of the stairs, looking down upon the scene of confusion and consternation, stood Olivia. Bessie was by her side with her traveling wrap over her arm, and instinctively she stretched out her hand and grasped her mistress'. So the two girls stood and waited.

"Now, my man," said Lord Carfield, sternly, "if you haven't taken leave of your senses, tell me what has happened."

The keeper looked round, confused in his excitement by the crowd of anxious faces, and still more by the sight of the squire, who came forward and stood beside the earl.

"Shall we go in the library?" whispered Lord Carfield.

The squire shook his head and glanced round.

"It is too late now," he replied, in as low a tone. "He may as well speak out before them now. Go on, Browne."

The keeper touched his front lock.

"I beg your pardon, squire, but I'm skeard-like. It—it come so sudden. I was passing through the wood to the big tent, when I see it lying on the ground just by the felled oak there— —"

"Saw what?" said the earl.

"The woman, my lord," replied Browne, with a shudder. "I—I thought, seein' as she was a stranger, that—beggin' your pardon, my lord—she might have had too much drink in the tent—some of 'em has, you see—and was just lyin' asleep; but when I stooped down to wake her, I saw that she was—dead."

A thrill of horror ran through the group of silent listeners. Death is a grim visitor at all seasons; but at a marriage feast!

"Dead!" echoed the earl.

"Yes, my lord; quite dead. There weren't no difficulty in telling how, for there was the wound in her side plain enough. She'd been shot, squire; shot."

Bessie's hand closed more tightly on Olivia's.

"I called out for help, squire, and then— —"

He stopped and hesitated, like a man reluctant to go farther.

"Go on," said the earl, gravely.

"Well, my lord, a gentleman came up. I—I think he was waiting near. I—I—don't know; but he came up at once. He—he—says to me"—he stopped again and looked troubled—"'Go for the constable, Browne. You'll find him at the entrance to the lawn. I'll wait and watch here.' I—I ran off at once, and I found the p'liceman and sent him to the wood, and—and then I came on here."

There was a moment's silence, then Lord Carfield said, solemnly:

"Who was this gentleman, Browne?"

The keeper opened his lips, and, glancing round, hesitated.

"Am I to say, squire?" he asked.

Before the squire could reply, a roar as of an approaching crowd reached the hall. It came nearer and nearer, until it seemed as if it were just outside; then, as the footman opened the door, the wedding guests saw an immense throng of people gathered outside. The policeman, with another man beside him, separated themselves from the mass, and walked into the hall.

A thrill of surprise ran through the spectators, for the man beside whom the policeman stood so closely and watchfully was Harold Faradeane.

His ordinarily pale face was graver even than usual, but it was perfectly calm, and he looked round and met the curious gaze of those about him with a calm steadfastness. For a moment only, as he saw Olivia on the staircase, his eyes wavered and his lips trembled; then he seemed to recover himself, and stood silent and self-possessed.

"Faradeane!" exclaimed the squire. "What is this?" and he went toward him agitatedly.

If Faradeane intended responding, the constable prevented him. Almost stepping in between him and the squire, he said, respectfully enough, but firmly:

"Beg pardon, squire; but I caution Mr. Faradeane. I've done so already, as he'll bear witness. I've told him that anything he says may be used against him."

There was a movement of suppressed excitement. Faradeane stood perfectly silent and calm.

"You have cautioned Mr. Faradeane!" said Lord Carfield. "Do you mean to say——"

He stopped, unable to form the question.

The constable nodded grimly.

"Yes, my lord. I'm very sorry to have to do it, but it's my duty to charge Mr. Faradeane with willful murder."

The crowd of guests exchanged murmurs and glances of amazement, and in the midst of the excitement Olivia glided down the stairs and stood beside her father. She clung to his arm, but did not remove her eyes from the face of the accused.

The last person who was expected to speak broke the silence. It was Mr. Bartley Bradstone. In moments of great peril, sometimes, your thorough-paced coward is stung into something that has, at any rate, the appearance of courage.

With flushed face and a forced laugh, he stepped forward.

"What nonsense is this?" he said, and he looked round with an air of impatience. "Mr. Faradeane charged with——It's perfectly ridiculous!" and he laughed the forced laugh again. "Of course Mr. Faradeane can explain this—this absurd mistake. Better do it at once, and let the constable look for the right man, Faradeane."

Faradeane just glanced at him; it looked a mere casual glance, but Bartley Bradstone read it as one of warning, and changed color slightly.

"Let—let us go into the library," faltered Lord Carfield.

But the poor squire shook his head.

"There is no need for that," he said, confidently. "As—as Mr. Bradstone says, Mr. Faradeane can explain this mistake at once, and in a few words," and he looked at him with anxious appeal.

The constable waited a second. Every one seemed to wait while the clock ticked a full minute; then, as Faradeane remained silent, the constable, after a glance round, said:

"This is the case, squire; I was at the end of the lane when Browne ran up and told me to come with him into the wood—something had happened. I went, and I found the body of a young woman. She was quite dead—been shot. Close beside her stood Mr. Faradeane. I asked him what he knew about it, and he——" He paused a moment. "Well, squire, he refused to say anything!"

"Well!" said the squire, sharply. "That is not sufficient reason for charging Mr. Faradeane with—with——"

"No, squire," assented the man, respectfully. "But while I was trying to persuade him to answer my questions and tell me what he knew, I saw something lying on the ground. It was this," and he took the revolver from his pocket and handed it to the squire.

He took it and looked at it, and then at Faradeane. Every eye was fastened on the tiny toy.

"Well? What has this to do with Mr. Faradeane?" demanded Lord Carfield.

"Yes, what has it to do——" echoed Bartley Bradstone, indignantly.

The constable glanced at him.

"If the squire will please to look at the pistol, he'll see why I arrested the gentleman," he said, stubbornly.

The squire held the revolver to the light, looked at it, and let it drop. It fell upon the tiled hall with an ominous clang, and Lord Carfield stooped and picked it up.

"That revolver has got Mr. Faradeane's name engraved on it," said the constable. "I asked him to explain—he'll bear me out, squire—how it came there, just close to the body, and he wouldn't tell me. There wasn't nothing for it but for me to do my duty, and I did it. I told Mr. Faradeane he'd better come with me to you and my lord, the magistrates, and I advised him to clear the matter up, squire. Perhaps he'll explain what he was doing there, and how his revolver happened to be lying beside the woman as was shot, my lord."

Lord Carfield nodded.

"You did quite right," he said. "Mr. Faradeane will explain, of course," and he looked at him.

Every eye was fixed on him, every ear strained for his response to this appeal.

Slowly and distinctly came the accused man's reply:

"I have nothing to say."

A thrill ran through the listening and watching crowd. Charged with a cruel murder, and—nothing to say! A half-articulate groan burst from the squire's lips.

"Faradeane!" he made a movement toward him. "You—you have nothing to say! No answer! Impossible!"

Faradeane's grave, sad eyes met his anxious ones steadily.

"What the constable says is true," he said, slowly. "I have nothing to add to it—nothing to explain."

Insensibly—but how significantly!—the constable drew closer to him.

"That's what he said over and over again, squire. I couldn't persuade him into anything else. It's my duty to ask for a warrant——"

"No! no! Impossible!" said the squire, hoarsely.

"A warrant on the charge of willful murder," said the constable, firmly, but respectfully.

As the words rang in the ears of the horrified group, Olivia left her father's side, and approached Faradeane.

For a moment she stood speechless, her dilated eyes fixed on his face, her lips moving, her hand pressed to her heart.

He did not flinch; but there was no assurance of his innocence in his eyes, nothing but a sad impassiveness.

"Why—why do you not tell them?" broke from her, at last. "Why do you not tell them that you are—innocent?" and she caught his arm and clung to it. "You are innocent! Tell them so! Tell them so!"

It was an awful moment. It was an ordeal compared with which the torture of the rack is as nothing. Bartley Bradstone's face blanched, and he made a slight movement; then, as Faradeane raised his eyes, he fell back, for he read in them the assurance that his substitute would remain firm.

"I have nothing to say," said the calm, sad voice; "I am quite ready," and he turned his face away from her.

Her hand lingered on his arm in an imploring clasp for a moment, then, without a cry, she swayed slightly and fell to the ground.

Faradeane bent down to raise her, but Bradstone and the squire—half a dozen of the horrified crowd, indeed—sprang forward, and he drew back with a sigh.

"For God's sake take me away!" he said to the constable, hoarsely. "I—I cannot bear much more!"

Lord Carfield signed to the constable to go into the library, and Faradeane followed, stopping for a second to glance back as they carried Olivia up the stairs, with a yearning and agonized expression in his eyes.

Bartley Bradstone pushed his way into the library.

He was very white, but calmer and more self-possessed than he had been all day notwithstanding that his bride had been carried from him lifeless.

"This—this is all nonsense, of course," he said, addressing no one in particular. "Faradeane can explain it, if he likes, I'm sure. I don't know why on earth he don't. But, anyway, I'll be bail for him, Lord Carfield."

There was a murmur of approval, for not one of the spectators who looked in the face of the accused believed in the possibility of his guilt.

"Bail is not granted in cases of—in cases of this kind," said Lord Carfield, in a low voice, and he sat down and wrote out the warrant. "If—if you choose to confine Mr. Faradeane in his own house——"

The constable shook his head.

"I couldn't take that responsibility, my lord," he said, respectfully. "The gentleman will have to go to the lockup."

"I am quite ready," said Faradeane, again. "Do not make any exception in my favor."

"Once more, Faradeane," said Lord Carfield, rising and stretching out his hands, "will you not explain?"

He shook his head.

"I have nothing to explain, my lord. Ah"—and his voice almost broke—"don't think me ungrateful for your consideration! If you knew——"

He stopped and turned aside.

Lord Carfield sank into the chair, and covered his eyes with his hands, and the constable retired with his prisoner.

At sight of them the crowd, which had been impatiently waiting at the front, set up a roar; but as Faradeane looked down at them, something in his face silenced them, and a man's voice cried out:

"Shame on ye! What! will ye judge a man guilty 'fore he's tried?"

It was Alford, and he forced himself to the front, and made a lane through the mob by the simple expedient of swinging his huge arm. "Don't be cast down, sir. We knows you're innocent, right enough; but most of us have had too much liquor. Now, make way there!"

"Thank you, Alford," said Faradeane, simply, and the three passed through the crowd, which closed up behind them, and followed them to the end of the drive.

The constable had taken the precaution to order a carriage to await them at this point, and he and Faradeane got in, and were driven sharply away.

Faradeane sank back with a sigh, and closed his eyes, and remained silent for a few minutes; then he said, quietly:

"Where are you taking me?"

"To Wainford, sir," replied the constable. "You'll be more comfortable in the regular prison there than in the Hawkwood lockup."

"Thank you," said Faradeane. "That is thoughtful of you."

The man eyed him with a strange expression.

"Come, sir," he said, bending forward. "You know, and I know, that you didn't do this. Why not up and out with the truth? If you didn't like to do it before all these people, why not tell me? I know it's not quite regular, but I'll be hanged if I uses a word against you!"

Faradeane shook his head.

"You mean well," he said, wearily. "I appreciate and understand your kindness, my good fellow; but you cannot help me. You must do your duty."

"Yes, I must do that," said the man, gravely. "But every minute you let this charge hang over you, settles it more firmly down, and—there's danger in it, sir."

"Yes, I know that," assented Faradeane, calmly.

They reached Wainford, and found the prison officials prepared for them by telegraph.

The governor, as he read the warrant, glanced once or twice at the pale face.

"All right and regular, Wilcox, I suppose?" he said. "No mistake, eh?"

"No, sir," said the constable, and he rapidly recounted the facts, and showed the revolver.

The governor nodded.

"Anything to say?" he asked of the prisoner, courteously.

"Nothing," replied Faradeane, gravely.

The governor signed to a turnkey, and Faradeane was conducted to his cell.

As the lock sprang into its place with an ominous click, and he found himself alone, he started, and looked round like a man awaking from some hideous dream, and made a step toward the iron door; then he stopped, and, with a sigh, sank on to the prison bed.

"God give me strength to go through with it!" he murmured. "Let me remember it is for her sake! Oh, my darling, for your sake!"

CHAPTER XXVI
"WILLFUL MURDER"

The shades of evening fell upon the wedding day; the guests had gone, with one theme upon their lips; the village was all astir with excitement; the Grange was thronged with a hustling crowd, all talking of the tragic event which had fallen like a thunderbolt upon the marriage festivities.

Olivia lay still unconscious. The Wainford doctor was in close attendance, and had issued a strict command for profound quiet. A hush deep as that which waits on death prevailed throughout the great house, which a few hours ago had been brimming over with talk and laughter.

Beside the bed, his white head buried in his hands, sat the squire, and, kneeling with her beloved mistress' hand in hers, was Bessie. She was almost as white as the face that lay so calm and still on the pillow, but every now and then her lips twitched, and a spasm of agony passed across her face.

Downstairs in the library Bartley Bradstone paced to and fro. He had got a decanter of brandy from the dining-room cellaret, and every now and then he filled a glass with unsteady hand.

Now and again he stole to the door and, opening it cautiously, listened intently. Then, as no sound reached him from the room upstairs, he went back to his brandy and his restless, fearful pacing.

For hours, far into the night, Olivia lay wrapped in the deep unconsciousness which is so nearly akin to the great sleep; then suddenly the doctor held up his hand and bent over her.

"Do not speak to her!" he whispered to the squire, who rose tremblingly.

She opened her eyes, and looked round dully and vacantly, then she murmured, faintly:

"Where am I?"

Bessie drew herself up and put her arm across her.

"Here, Miss Olivia, here in your own room, at home, at the Grange. I am with you—Bessie—and the squire."

A look of relief crossed the lovely face.

"Thank God!" she breathed. "I—I thought—I dreamed—ah!" and she made an effort to rise. "Where is he?"

"Hush, hush, my darling!" said the poor squire. "He is downstairs in the library."

She sank back, and her lips quivered.

"In the library. Here, and—and safe! Ah, what a dreadful dream!"

"Bartley is safe, quite safe, of course, dear," he said, soothingly.

She started, and her eyes dilated, as they fixed themselves on his face.

"Bartley Bradstone! Is he here? Father!" and her voice rang with an awful dread. "You will not let him take me away, you will not——"

"No, no, no, dear!" said Bessie, quick to divine her fear. "No one shall take you!"

She sank back again, but tossed her head from one side to the other, her eyes glittering feverishly.

"I—I am trying to think; I can't remember! What has happened? Something dreadful—dreadful! Tell me, Bessie—tell me, or I shall go mad!"

The squire bent over her; but the doctor held up his hand.

"Let the girl speak to her," he whispered.

With the tears filling her eyes, Bessie drew the hot, restless head upon her bosom.

"Is it this mistake about Mr. Faradeane, miss?" she said, with forced carelessness.

"Yes, yes!" panted Olivia, her eyes seeming to glow upon Bessie's face. "Tell me!"

"It's all a mistake," said Bessie, calmly, setting her teeth almost defiantly, "a stupid, senseless mistake that people will be sorry for——" and unconsciously her voice rose.

The doctor raised a warning finger.

"Don't excite her," he said.

Bessie's voice sank again.

"Don't think anything of it, dear Miss Olivia. It will all come right. You and I—everybody knows he didn't do it—couldn't do it."

"Couldn't? Ah!" Her hand clutched Bessie's arm, and she stared at her wildly. "They say he had committed murder! I heard them! I heard them! They have taken him away, Bessie. Bessie, I must go. No"—and she moaned—"I cannot. But you must go and tell him that I know—do you hear?—I know he is innocent. That if any harm comes to him I—shall die!"

She sank back breathless and exhausted. The squire's face went white, and he turned his head away.

"She is wandering, poor girl," said the doctor, with prompt presence of mind. "The shock of—of this terrible business coming so closely upon the excitement of the day has prostrated her. There has been a strain upon her mind for some time past. Don't attach any value to her wild words, sir."

The squire drew back into the shadow and groaned:

"My poor girl!"

The doctor went round and, taking his arm, led him outside into the corridor.

"Come, squire," he said, gently but firmly, "you mustn't give way; our only chance is to keep her free from excitement. If I can only keep her quiet she will be safe. If not—the first thing to do is to get rid of Mr. Bradstone."

"Get rid of him?" groaned the squire.

"Yes," he said; "his presence here in the house affects her; there is no accounting for the fancies of fever. Tell him how ill she is, and persuade him to go home, so that I may tell her he has gone. Leave the rest to me. I can manage very well with Bessie for nurse; and no one else must enter the room. You understand?"

The squire grasped his hand and wrung it.

"Yes, I understand," he said, sorrowfully. "I will do as you say—if he will go."

"Tell him her life depends on it," said the doctor, sternly.

The squire went downstairs into the library, and Bartley Bradstone turned and faced him. His eyes were bloodshot, his lips hot and dry, and his hands plucked nervously at the edge of his coat.

"Is—is she better?" he demanded, huskily.

The squire shook his head.

"My poor child is very ill, Bartley," he said. "I fear there is—danger! You must go home!"

"Go home?" repeated Bartley Bradstone, dully.

"Yes," said the squire; "the fact of your being here in the house agitates her—her mind is wandering. You will go home, will you not? I will send to you every hour."

To his surprise, Bartley Bradstone made no remonstrance.

"I'll go if you—if she wishes it," he said, staring at the carpet like a man in a dream. "Yes, of course."

"I'll tell them to get a carriage—and yet the noise. Will you walk?"

"Yes," he said; then he looked up with a sudden start of fear, and shuddered. "Yes, I'll walk; but—but I'd like to have some one—one of the servants with me. I'm—I'm upset, you see," he stammered, wiping the cold sweat from his brow.

The squire looked at him and the decanter; but his gentle nature found some excuse for him.

"My poor fellow!" he said. "But this will not help you," and he pointed to the brandy.

"No, I know; but—I'm upset, I'm dreadfully upset. This—this murder business——"

The squire sighed deeply.

"My brain is in a whirl. It was the sudden shock that struck my poor girl down. There is some hideous mistake, some dreadful mystery! It is impossible that he can be guilty!"

"He—he didn't deny it," said Bartley Bradstone, sullenly.

The squire looked at him with sad surprise.

"You do not think him guilty?" he said.

"I? Oh, no; certainly not," was the quick response. "But—but—of course it's a mystery. I—I wish it had happened at some other time. Curse it! It will never be found out."

"Yes, it will be found out," said the squire, solemnly.

He took two or three turns across the room, his hand to his brow; then he stopped suddenly.

"Why, I remember! It must have occurred while you were on your way to The Maples. Did you hear nothing? The glade is not far from the drive."

Bartley Bradstone was putting on his overcoat, and stopped with one arm in the sleeve.

"Who, I?" he exclaimed, indignantly. "What do you mean? What do I know about it?" Then, recalled to himself by the squire's look of sad astonishment at his tone, he continued, more quietly, "For Heaven's sake, don't get me mixed up in the business; that—that would make it bad for Olivia, you know. I don't know anything about it. I—I cut across the park in the other direction."

"With the carriage?" exclaimed the squire.

"No, no, I didn't take a carriage; didn't I tell you? I thought I should save time by running across the park, and—and I wasn't anywhere near the spot, I'm glad to say. They can't force me to attend the inquest and all that, can they?" he asked, averting his face.

The squire shook his head.

"No, as you know nothing about it," he said.

Bartley Bradstone drew a breath of relief.

"That's all right!" he said. "Olivia would be awfully cut up if I got mixed up in this wretched business. It would make her worse than she is."

"She can scarcely be worse," said the poor squire, sorrowfully.

"She'll get over it," said Bartley Bradstone, putting on his hat. "It's—it's the shock, and all that. I'll go now, I think. Give her my love, and tell her I'll come and see her directly they'll let me. We'll get away the moment she's strong enough; the—the change will do her good. If it hadn't been for their dragging that fellow Faradeane here we should have been miles away by this time, confound it!"

He passed into the hall and beckoned to a footman who was passing.

"Let him come with me, will you, squire? It's—it's dark, and I'm upset and nervous. It's enough to drive a fellow out of his mind."

The squire motioned an assent to the servant, who brought his hat and a lantern.

At the hall door Bartley Bradstone paused, and came back to where the squire stood, looking vacantly and sadly out at the silent night.

"Don't—don't tell anybody I walked over to The Maples unless you're obliged," he said, with forced carelessness. "These police fellows are always too ready to get a gentleman mixed up in the business, and they'd make a mountain of a molehill, and want me to appear at the trial, and all that. Good-night. Give my love to—to—my wife."

He held out his hand, with his restless, bloodshot eyes fixed on the squire's boots, and as the old man took it, he noticed, in a dull way, how cold and clammy it felt.

The door closed on Mr. Bartley Bradstone and his protector, and the squire went upstairs again.

As he approached the door, he could hear his darling's voice talking wildly and incoherently, and the doctor met him with a grave face.

"She is delirious," he said, gravely. "Has Mr. Bradstone gone?"

They entered the room. Olivia was lying in Bessie's arms, her eyes open and staring, a torrent of words streaming from her feverish lips.

"Bessie! Bessie! Save him! He is not guilty! My love commit—murder! Ha, ha!" and her wild laughter rang through the room. "He's so good and gentle! They are mad, mad, mad! Take me to him, father! Take me to him! It is my place! I tell you that if all the world pronounced him guilty, I would love—love—love him! He is innocent! Father, don't let him take me away! No! Let me stay! Hide me from him! I hate him! I hate him!"

"What does it mean?" moaned the squire, piteously.

"It means just nothing," replied the doctor, who had watched beside many a delirious patient, and was as discreet and silent as the grave. "Pay no attention. Who's that?"

It was Aunt Amelia's voice at the door, begging to be admitted.

"Miss Amelia can do no good. Keep her away, please," he said, quietly; and the squire persuaded her, weeping bitterly—for Aunt Amelia's heart was sound, though her head was flighty—to go back to her own room.

All through the night—and how long it seemed!—the three watched beside the fever-stricken girl, listening to her delirious cries; but toward morning they grew less wild, and as the dawn broke they ceased altogether and she lapsed into a deep sleep.

The doctor's grave face cleared.

"Thank God!" he said, with a long breath of relief. "Go and lie down, squire; the worst has passed. We shall only have to fight against the weakness and exhaustion now. But mind," he added, as he gently forced the squire out of the room, "keep Mr. Bradstone out of the way, and don't mention his name before her. There must be no excitement."

The squire asked if he should send to Wainford for a skilled nurse; but the doctor shook his head.

"No," he said, decisively. "You could not get a better than this girl Bessie, and—nurses talk," he added, under his breath.

The morning came and the long day passed. The hushed household moved about on tiptoe and spoke in whispers. Almost every hour, as he had promised, the squire sent word to Bartley Bradstone; Olivia was lying in the sleep of unconsciousness.

About six o'clock in the evening Bartley Bradstone entered the library, where the squire sat, his head resting in his hands.

"I—I couldn't stop away any longer," he said, sinking into a chair. "How is she now?"

"Just the same," replied the squire, looking at his white face, pityingly. "She lies now like one dead, indeed——"

Bartley Bradstone groaned and wiped his forehead.

"I've spent a wretched night," he said; "wretched. I suppose you've heard the news?" he asked, suddenly.

The squire shook his head.

"They've held the inquest and brought in a verdict of willful murder against Faradeane."

The squire sprang to his feet, then dropped down again.

"They must be mad!" he exclaimed, tremulously.

"I don't know anything more than I've heard," said Bartley Bradstone. "My man was there and—and told me what passed. They had Faradeane up, and he—he just behaved as he did here. Wouldn't say anything, or give any explanation. What were they to do, under the circumstances?"

The squire let his hand fall upon the table.

"I would stake my life upon his innocence!" he said, solemnly.

Bartley Bradstone eyed him with sullen displeasure.

"That wouldn't save him," he said. "Things look black against him."

"I care not how black they look," responded the squire. "I know that Faradeane is incapable of such a crime."

As he spoke the door opened.

"A gentleman wishes to see you, sir," said the butler; and as the squire made a motion of assent, a short, commonplace-looking man, dressed like a well-to-do farmer, entered.

"Good-evening, sir," he said, quietly and respectfully. "My name is McAndrew, detective, from Scotland Yard. I've got charge of this case."

The squire waved him to a seat and leaned back wearily.

"Why do you wish to see me?" he asked.

"Yes, we know nothing about it," said Bartley Bradstone.

The detective looked at him as if he had not noticed the presence of a third person, and bowed.

"Certainly not, sir; but I called to pay my respects and to ask a few questions. You've heard how the verdict of the coroner's inquest has gone, sir?" addressing the squire.

"Yes."

"Well, sir, I don't attach too much weight to coroners' verdicts, but this seems reasonable enough. There's the fact of the prisoner's presence on the scene, and the revolver with his name engraved on it being found near the body."

"That's very bad," remarked Bartley Bradstone.

"Yes, sir, very bad, as you say," assented Mr. McAndrew; "but I'm not quite satisfied yet. I've seen the prisoner, and watched him through the inquest. And—I've had a good deal of experience, Mr. Vanley—he doesn't look guilty."

"He is not guilty!" said the squire, earnestly.

Mr. McAndrew nodded respectfully.

"He's a friend of yours, sir?"

"He is," assented the squire; "a very dear friend."

Bartley Bradstone shot a glance of jealousy at the sad, worn face.

"Just so, sir; then you can tell me something about him—who he is and so on."

The squire passed his hand across his brow.

"I—I'm afraid I cannot," he replied. "I know nothing about Mr. Faradeane, excepting that he came here, to a cottage called The Dell, a few months ago— —"

"When, sir?"

"In May; and that he is distinctly a gentleman, and incapable of the crime laid to his charge."

"That's it, sir," exclaimed the detective; "Mr. Faradeane is a gentleman, as you say, and I've never in all my experience known a real, genuine gentleman commit a crime of this kind. In the heat of the moment—in a sudden fit of jealousy, for instance—a gentleman might do it. But this was premeditated."

"How do you know that?" said Bartley Bradstone, sharply.

The detective looked at him calmly and thoughtfully.

"Because the man who shot this woman went to meet her fully intending to shoot her," he said, quietly. "What I want to get at is this gentleman's, Mr. Faradeane's, motive for getting rid of the woman. That's what I want to find out."

"Do you know the woman? Have you identified her?"

It was Bartley Bradstone who asked the question, and he did so with affected indifference, as if he were merely asking from curiosity.

The detective shook his head.

"Not had time yet, sir; but I shall know all about her directly."

At this tone of confidence Bartley Bradstone shifted in his seat.

"What does Mr. Faradeane say?" he asked.

"Surely he has explained his presence on the spot, and the revolver?" said the squire.

Mr. McAndrew shook his head.

"That's the queer part of it, sir," he said. "I've seen Mr. Faradeane before and after the inquest, and he declines to say a word. Now, if he had been the man he'd have been full of explanations; do you follow me, sir?"

"Perfectly," responded the squire, with a sigh.

"They always are. They can account for everything; but Mr. Faradeane doesn't seem to take the trouble to explain. That strikes me as being peculiar."

"Perhaps he can't explain," said Bartley Bradstone, his eyes fixed on the carpet.

The detective looked from him to the squire, and then out of the window, abstractedly.

"If he can't, then——"

He stopped.

"Well?" demanded the squire.

"Then he's a lost man," replied the detective.

CHAPTER XXVII
A LOST MAN

Not within the memory of the oldest inhabitant had there been so much excitement in the county.

That a murder should have been committed within a quarter of a mile of the Grange, on Olivia Vanley's wedding day, was bad enough; but that the suspected man should be the mysterious Mr. Faradeane of The Dell, raised popular curiosity and interest to fever heat. Then came the news that the bride had been stricken down with fever, and was lying dangerously ill at her father's house.

Scarcely any other topic was discussed, and persons eagerly asked one another whether any new phase of what was already called "the Hawkwood tragedy" had appeared. The only man who seemed to have retained his calmness in the midst of the excitement was the prisoner himself. While everybody else was eagerly debating the probability of his guilt or innocence, and endeavoring to ascribe the motive for his crime, if indeed he committed it, Harold Faradeane uttered no word which could tend toward a solution of the mystery.

Some thought that it was impossible for him to be innocent; and when the coroner's jury had returned a verdict of willful murder, people shook their heads, and pursed their lips significantly.

Then came the examination before the magistrates. Long before the hour appointed for the sitting, the small court at Wainford was crammed. Men who had met and taken a sudden liking to the grave, handsome stranger, and ladies who had admired and wondered about him, filled all the available seats. On the bench sat Lord Carfield, the chairman, and two of his brother magistrates, but, as was expected, the Squire of Hawkwood was absent; though it was remarked that a groom from the Grange was on his horse outside the court, ready to carry home the result of the examination.

A look of grave and painful earnestness sat upon the old earl's face, and he leaned his head upon his hand, and bent his eyes upon his desk. He, like the squire, had taken a great liking to the man accused of this terrible crime, and, but that it was a principle of his life never to shirk a duty, however painful, he too would have been absent from the bench. In the well of the court, near the clerk, sat the commonplace-looking London detective, keenly noting every face and every voice around him, though to all appearance wrapped in stolid reflection.

Presently, in the midst of the hum and buzz, the clerk called "Harold Faradeane," and a policeman opened the door of the dock, and the prisoner entered.

He was very pale, and those who knew him felt a thrill of pity as they saw how haggard and drawn his face had grown during the days of his imprisonment. But with the feeling of pity was mingled one of puzzled surprise. It seemed impossible to connect a vulgar crime with the grave, patrician face and bearing, which remained calm and dignified under the battery of eyes, and seemed to give a direct denial to the charge which the clerk read out. As he would not be required to plead guilty or not guilty until the trial—if the magistrates should decide to send him for trial— Harold Faradeane remained silent.

"I propose to produce sufficient evidence to warrant my demanding that the prisoner should be sent for trial, my lord," said the superintendent of police, and he called the constable and Browne, the keeper.

They told the now-familiar story of the finding of the body, and Faradeane in close proximity, waiting, as it almost seemed, for detection, and the picking up of the revolver near to his feet.

The spectators listened breathlessly; some of them had heard the story in the Grange hall on Olivia's wedding day; but they listened as intently now as if it were all new to them.

Faradeane stood with one hand resting on the rail in front of the dock, his eyes fixed on the ground, his whole bearing that of a man completely resigned to whatever might happen; not indifferent, but simply resigned.

The earl looked up and at him as the evidence was concluded.

"Have you any questions to ask, Mr. Faradeane?" he said in a grave voice, and the crowded court remarked that he addressed the accused by his name instead of as "prisoner."

"No, my lord," came the quiet reply.

Lord Carfield's brows came together.

"Surely you must have some explanation to offer," he said, just as he had said on the day of the murder. "Is it possible that you should fail to recognize the serious position in which you are placed?"

Faradeane raised his sad eyes, in which, sad as they were, there was nothing of craven fear or imploration.

"I fully appreciate my position, my lord," he said, "and I regret that I have no explanation to offer."

Lord Carfield pushed his notes aside with a grave impatience.

"Was there no one near the body excepting Mr. Faradeane?" he asked Browne.

"No, my lord."

"You met no one? Think, and answer carefully. There was a large number of persons present at the Grange on that day; did you meet no one in the drive or in the wood?"

"No, my lord. The folks were all on the lawn listening to the singing and speech-making in the tent. I met no one, till I fetched the constable."

Lord Carfield asked the same question of the constable, and received the same answer. No one had been seen in the wood or coming from it but the dead woman and the man Harold Faradeane, who stood so patiently and calmly waiting.

"Has the murdered woman been identified?" asked Lord Carfield. "Is anything known about her? There should be some evidence of motive."

"The woman has been identified, my lord," said the superintendent, entering the box. "Her name is Bella Lee, but she was known as Bella-Bella. She was a professional acrobat, and quite famous in London, my lord."

"And in what way do you connect Mr. Faradeane—the prisoner—with her? I cannot see——"

He stopped. It was apparent that he was endeavoring to find any loophole for escape or explanation.

The superintendent hesitated; then, catching the placid eye of Mr. McAndrew, replied:

"Some information is in our possession, my lord; but we do not propose to produce it at this stage. We depend upon the evidence of the gamekeeper and constable."

"Our duty is clear," said Lord Carfield, but with a reluctance which was distinctly palpable. "We must commit the prisoner for trial. Have you anything to say?" he asked.

At this moment there was a slight disturbance among the closely-packed persons near the door, and Mr. Bartley Bradstone entered. He looked round him with the air of a man determined not to show nervousness, and then up at the face of the prisoner. Had he anything to say?

Harold Faradeane glanced ever so slightly at Bartley Bradstone, then met Lord Carfield's grave and troubled regard.

"Nothing, my lord," came the reply.

"Remove the prisoner," said Lord Carfield in a low voice, and Faradeane followed the policemen from the dock.

A murmur of pent-up excitement rose from the crowded court, and several ladies who had grown pale and somewhat hysterical during the examination drew long and audible breaths of relief.

"That man is not guilty," said one of them. "I am as certain of it as I am that I am sitting here. No man capable of shooting a defenceless woman could stand up and look as he did. If he were a bad man he would brazen it out, and he would show himself to be a hardened criminal; and if, on the other hand, he were only a weak man, who had yielded to a sudden temptation, he would, this morning, have been utterly cast down and overwhelmed with grief and remorse. Instead of presenting either appearance, he looks round like a man who—who is too noble to have committed the vulgar crime, and still too noble to despise us for suspecting him."

Now, Mr. McAndrew was standing just beneath the lady who had delivered her opinion, by no means in a whisper, and he looked up at her, and smiled behind the hand which he passed over his mouth. And he was still smiling as, shouldering his way out of the court, he came upon Mr. Bartley Bradstone, who in a purposeless kind of fashion was standing and being generally pushed about, as he stared with a species of fascination at the dock in which Faradeane had just stood.

Mr. McAndrew touched his hat.

"Good-morning, sir; quite a crowd."

"Y—es, yes," replied Bartley Bradstone.

At that moment there came the tramp of drilled footsteps in the corridor in which they were standing, and a cry of "Make way there! Stand back!"

It was the prisoner being escorted to the closed fly which was to take him back to the prison.

Bartley Bradstone started, and took half a step forward, his eyes fixed on Faradeane's face.

"How is Mrs. Bradstone this morning, sir?" asked Mr. McAndrew, standing right in the way of the policemen and their charge.

"Very ill, dangerously ill still," said Bartley Bradstone, still with his eyes on Faradeane.

Faradeane started and stopped. He had caught the reply. His face went white, and seemed to quiver, as if with some sudden fury.

"Ill! Dangerously ill!" he said in a hollow voice.

There was still a crowd in the corridor, and all eyes were turned upon him.

"Move on, please, sir," said the policeman, not roughly but firmly.

"One moment," said Faradeane, with a kind of gasp. "Give me one moment. Is—is she in danger, do you say?"

"You must move on, sir; you cannot be permitted to talk," said the sergeant.

Faradeane sighed and inclined his head, and was passing on, when Mr. McAndrew, who had never taken his eyes from his face, said:

"If Mr. Faradeane desires it, I can give him all the news; but I can only see him at his desire now."

"Yes, yes!" said Faradeane, quickly and anxiously, looking back over his shoulder. "Come at once, please."

The crowd closed up after him, and the shouting and cheering and groaning announced the departure of the fly.

Bartley Bradstone stood in the corridor biting his lip, and looking after the prisoner in a dull, vacant fashion, and had quite forgotten Mr. McAndrew until that gentleman's voice sounded at his elbow.

"Carrying it with a high hand, isn't he, Mr. Bradstone?"

Bartley Bradstone started.

"Eh? Y—es, yes! You think that—that there isn't any chance for him? You think he's guilty still?"

The detective looked at him with a sudden and utterly expressionless stare.

"I never give an opinion myself, sir," he said. "Never. It's unprofessional. But I think the jury, when he goes for trial, will think him guilty."

A strange expression, it almost seemed like relief, shot across Bartley Bradstone's face, but it was gone in an instant, and, with a shake of his head, he said:

"They'll be a parcel of fools, then. He's no more guilty than I am."

"Just so, sir," remarked Mr. McAndrew. "But it's strange he doesn't say so, isn't it? And Mrs. Bradstone is still in danger, sir?" he broke off, respectfully.

"Yes, yes," assented Bartley Bradstone, with a heavy sigh and an anxious, troubled look, and he moved down the corridor to the door where a closed carriage and pair stood waiting. "Oh, stop!" he said, with his hand on the door and looking back at the detective. "I—I forgot. Mr. Vanley asked me to say that if there was anything that could be done for the—the prisoner, he should like to do it. I suppose there will be lawyers and—a counsel. Just see to it, will you?"

Mr. McAndrew regarded him with the same stolid stare.

"I'm afraid I can't interfere, sir," he said, thoughtfully. "You see, I'm for the prosecution; at least, I'm for the truth!"

Bartley Bradstone shot a glance at him; but the man's face was so wooden that it robbed the words of any significance.

"But I'll put Mr. Faradeane in the way he should go—I can do that without going beyond my duty, though whether he'll pay any attention to my advice is quite another thing."

Bartley Bradstone got into the carriage, and, as the footman in the gorgeous Maples livery closed the door, Bradstone leaned forward.

"Anything discovered about the woman—what's her name?—Bella?" he asked.

Mr. McAndrew shrugged his shoulders.

"Nothing of any consequence, sir," he replied.

Bartley Bradstone sank back out of sight, and, being out of sight, wiped the perspiration from his forehead.

Mr. McAndrew looked after the carriage for a moment or two, passing his hand over his mouth in the manner peculiar to him; then turned and made his way to the jail.

The governor of her Majesty's prison at Wainford was a certain Colonel Summerford; a gentleman, and a man of sound common sense. He had been governor for nearly twenty years, but during all that long experience he had never had so strange and puzzling an inmate as Harold Faradeane. Colonel Summerford knew the ordinary jail-bird by heart, and understood every song that bird could sing; but this man, charged with the murder of a woman in Hawkwood woods, scattered all the good colonel's experiential theories and ideas, like chaff before the wind. In the first place, the colonel saw that his "new man" was a gentleman; and, secondly, that he was no fool, as some gentlemen—too many, alas!—often are. He felt greatly interested in him, and did his best to make him as comfortable as a prisoner committed for trial on a capital offence can be made. He gave him the largest and airiest cell, and, in fact, treated him as a man who, though accused, has not yet been found guilty.

Mr. McAndrew arrived at the prison about half an hour after Faradeane's return, and found the colonel walking up and down his office in deep thought.

"Good-morning, colonel," said the detective, putting his head in at the door and touching his hat with his forefinger in farmer fashion.

"Ah! is that you, Mr. McAndrew? Come in," responded the governor. "You have just come from court, I suppose? You have got a more interesting case than country ones usually are, eh?"

"Yes," assented Mr. McAndrew; "it is rather interesting."

"Confound the man!" exclaimed the colonel. "I wish they hadn't brought him here," and he tugged at his mustache.

"Gives you a lot of trouble?"

"Not a bit. That's just it. Look here, McAndrew, I can't make him out."

"No, colonel?"

"No; and I'm an old hand at 'em, too. I didn't think there could be a case that would puzzle me—I mean so far as the man goes. I'm used to reading them right off the reel; but this man Faradeane baffles me."

"Ah," commented the detective, thoughtfully; "doesn't behave like the usual run, then, colonel?"

"Not a bit," said the governor, testily. "Some of them are sullen, others are hysterical, and others again dogged and taciturn; while I've seen some half-mad. Now, this man just takes the whole thing as quietly as if there was nothing extraordinary in it. If the evidence was not so black I should be ready to swear that he is innocent. It is black, isn't it?"

McAndrew nodded.

"About as black as it could be," he said in a matter-of-fact voice.

"And you can make nothing of it—of him?" asked the colonel. "It isn't my way to be overcurious about my prisoners," he added, half-apologetically, "but I will own to feeling a deep interest in this Mr. Faradeane."

McAndrew nodded.

"A good many other people do that," he said. "I do, for one. I don't know yet whether he's guilty or not; but I should like to know, if he is guilty, why he did it. By the way, colonel, I want to see him."

The governor pulled up short and frowned.

"Come, you know, McAndrew," he said, "you are engaged against him. I can scarcely give you admittance to him— —"

"You can trust me, colonel," said the detective, quietly. "If he told me straight out that he did it I shouldn't use the information against him. So far as that goes, he hasn't once denied it. But you can trust me, colonel. I shan't do your friend any harm by seeing him. Besides, it is at his request."

Strangely enough, the colonel, upright and honorable gentleman that he was, did not resent the prisoner being described as his friend, but rang the bell for a turnkey, and Mr. McAndrew was conducted to the prisoner's cell.

Some articles of furniture, a table, a chair, and writing materials had been provided by the kind-hearted colonel; and the bed, though plain, was not so uncomfortable as it might have been. Faradeane was sitting on it, with his head resting in his hands; but he rose as the key clicked in the lock and the turnkey opened the door—rose to receive his visitor with the courtesy he would have displayed if it had been his own parlor at The Dell.

Mr. McAndrew waited until the door had clanged upon the turnkey.

"I hope you are as comfortable as you can be under the circumstances, sir," he began.

"Yes, yes," said Faradeane, "thanks to Colonel Summerford; he has done everything, has been very kind. I am obliged to you for coming to me so soon," he went on, his voice sounding sad and anxious, yet strangely calm. "I overheard your inquiry concerning Miss Vanley—I mean Mrs. Bradstone," he corrected himself with a slight catch in his voice, "and Mr. Bradstone's reply. Will you tell me what has happened? I have heard nothing since my arrest. Mrs. Bradstone fell at my feet"—he paused a moment—"but I hope that it was nothing more than a fainting fit caused by the shock. Is it true that she is dangerously ill?"

With all his effort to keep calm, his hand, which rested on the plain deal table, quivered, and Mr. McAndrew's keen eyes noted it.

"She is very ill and in danger," replied the detective, watching him, and yet apparently doing nothing of the kind.

Faradeane went to the barred window, and looked out upon the prison yard in silence for a moment.

"It is my fault," he said, huskily. "When they told me that they would take me to the Grange on my arrest I thought they would do so quietly, that she should not know—it is all my fault. Miss Vanley is a close and very dear friend of mine," he added, as if to explain the emotion he suppressed with such difficulty.

"I understand," said McAndrew, slowly. "It was the shock of seeing you in trouble and the story of the murder coming on the excitement of the wedding. You see, she wasn't to know that you were innocent," he added, easily and smoothly.

"No; she believed it, she believed it!" said Faradeane, unwarily, with a deep sigh.

The detective's eyes twinkled, but only for a second.

"You see, things looked black against you. She wasn't to know—no one was to know—that it would all come right at the trial."

Faradeane turned and looked at him gravely, and with quick self-possession.

"Why do you say that?" he asked, calmly.

Mr. McAndrew shrugged his shoulders.

"Oh, I suppose you'll explain everything then, sir?" he said. "What surprises me and everybody else is that you don't do it now. But I dare say you have your reasons."

"I have nothing to explain. I am almost tired of repeating it," said Faradeane, and he turned to the window with a weary gesture.

The detective watched him closely.

"Well, yes, you've said it often enough; but how much longer do you mean to stick to it?" and he leaned forward with sudden earnestness.

Faradeane remained silent.

"Look here, sir," continued McAndrew, quietly but impressively. "I've no business sitting here talking to you. I've got the case in hand, and it's my duty to prove you guilty, if you are guilty. But I'm not so sure that you are. It's right out of the ordinary track, this business, and I come to you, knowing you to be a gentleman, and I say, 'Here's a hard-working man trying to earn his living honestly; will you help him?' That sounds strange to you, I dare say, sir, but it's my fancy to lay all my cards on the table, and I'll tell you"—he spread his palms out as if they really held cards—"I tell you, sir, that I've got enough evidence already to——"

He did not utter the dreadful word, but the pause supplied it.

Faradeane looked down at him with pale, calm face.

"Now, most men would be satisfied with that," continued Mr. McAndrew, "but I'm not. I don't want you to give me any information that shall go further toward convicting you. No, I could get that for myself, but I want you to tell me," he rose and stretched out one forefinger, "*who did this murder?*"

It was a strange and startling speech, and another man would have been thrown off his guard and committed himself; but Faradeane had steeled himself for all ordeals.

"Be content," he said, gravely, almost solemnly. "You have your evidence; act upon it, and do your duty, sir!"

Mr. McAndrew reached for his hat at once.

"Very good, sir!" he said, as if he accepted Faradeane's response to his appeal as final. "I shall do my duty. Is there anything I can do for you—any message? You will communicate with your lawyers at once, of course?"

Faradeane was silent for a moment, then he said:

"I shall not need a lawyer."

The detective looked at him fixedly.

"No lawyer! No counsel!" he said.

"What lawyer, clever though he might be, could disprove the evidence?" said Faradeane, wearily. "You yourself have said it is conclusive."

Mr. McAndrew turned his hat round in his hands, still watching him.

"Very good, sir; and there is nothing I can do—no message?"

Faradeane went to the window, and his lips twitched.

"If you should see Mr. Vanley—the squire," he began, "will you tell him, please——" He stopped, then shook his head. "No, I can send no message even to him. Things must take their course."

"And no message to—Mrs. Bradstone, sir?" inquired Mr. McAndrew, softly, and with the deepest respect.

For a moment Faradeane's face changed color, then he said, almost haughtily:

"What message should I have to send to that lady?"

Mr. McAndrew inclined his head.

"Very good, sir," he said. "I wish you good-day." He tapped at the door, and as the warder opened it for him he looked over his shoulder. "I forgot to say that Mr. Bradstone asked me if there was anything he could do for you, Mr. Faradeane."

Faradeane's face did not move a muscle.

"Thank him; no," he replied, firmly.

Mr. McAndrew paused outside the closed door, with his hand to his mouth, looking hard at the stone floor; then he went out. As he was passing the office the governor tapped at the window.

"Well?" he said, with an affectation of carelessness.

"It isn't well; it's bad, colonel," replied Mr. McAndrew, grimly, and with just a shade of annoyance and disappointment. "Your friend—Mr. Faradeane, the prisoner—is resolved upon giving himself away, as the Americans say, and I'm afraid he'll be sorry when it's too late."

With these oracular words Mr. McAndrew left the governor, and went to the hotel for his lunch. Several times during the consumption of a modest chop he paused with a morsel on his fork, and stared thoughtfully before him, as if he were struggling with some knotty problem; and after his lunch was finished and paid for, he lit a cigar and sauntered to Hawkwood Woods. He stood in the glade where the murder had been committed and Faradeane arrested, for several minutes, carefully noting the fallen tree, and indeed every inch of ground; then he walked back to the Grange, and back from the Grange to The Maples. Having surveyed that huge pile of red brick for some minutes, he made his way to the railway station and disappeared.

CHAPTER XXVIII
A PRISONER AND HIS VISITOR

For more than a fortnight Olivia wandered in the valley of the shadow of death; then the crisis came and passed, and life still counted her among its subjects. But her recovery was so slow that another fortnight elapsed before, thin and pale, a bruised and broken lily, she was carried from her bedroom to her boudoir.

During all the time of almost unendurable anxiety and suspense Bessie had scarcely left her. No nurse could have shown more devotion, no sister more tender and self-sacrificing love.

Almost as thin and pale as Olivia, she watched beside her night and day, fully repaid if Olivia's hand closed upon hers with a feeble pressure, or if she murmured gratefully her name.

Quite a thrill of relief ran through the county at the news of her convalescence, and attention, which had been mainly devoted to her, concentrated itself upon the man who lay in prison awaiting his trial, and upon Mr. Bartley Bradstone.

He had never been popular; but those who liked him least—and no one liked him overmuch—felt constrained to pity him. He seldom left The Maples, excepting to walk up to the Grange to inquire after his bride, and those few persons who chanced to meet him were struck by the change in his appearance. He had been rather ruddy and robust, but he was now thin and emaciated, and looked ten years older than he had done on the day of his wedding. There was not only a look of age, but an expression of anxious unrest, which struck every one who saw him; and, strange to say, the wan and haggard expression on his face did not leave it when Olivia was pronounced out of danger.

"That poor devil Bradstone has been completely bowled over," one man said. "Looks as if he had all the care of the world on his shoulders," and that very exactly described Bartley Bradstone's appearance.

He haunted the Grange daily; but he had not seen Olivia since the wedding day.

"Keep him away from her, if you wish her recovery to continue," the doctor had said, and the poor squire repeated his words.

"Oh, I won't worry her," said Bartley Bradstone, in the dull, apathetic manner which had settled upon him. "Sick people take all sorts of fancies; she'll see me when she's better, and—and we'll get away."

"Yes, yes," said the squire, with a heavy sigh. "When all this trouble is over. It is this terrible murder which hangs like a dark cloud over us all."

"Does—does she speak of it at all?" asked Bartley Bradstone, looking down at the carpet, as if he were suddenly interested in the pattern.

The squire shook his head.

"Not to me; not to Bessie, I think. She has seen no one else, excepting the doctor."

"That's right," said Bartley Bradstone. "Don't let anybody talk to her about it; she'll forget it before long."

It almost seemed as if Olivia had already forgotten it, for day after day passed and she made no mention of the terrible incident which had stricken her down. She lay on the sofa, her thin and now fragile form carefully enwrapped, her hands folded lightly in her lap; her lovely eyes, strained with hidden pain, fixed on the elms which showed through the window. Bessie, who even now scarcely ever left her, would sit silent for hours, sometimes with a book, sometimes at needlework. It was only when the squire entered that Olivia's pale face warmed with a smile. But one morning, after a long silence, she said, so quietly but suddenly that Bessie started and let the work fall from her hands:

"Bessie, tell me all; tell me the truth."

"About Mr. Faradeane, miss?" faltered Bessie, who had not yet learned to call her mistress by her wedded title.

"Yes," said Olivia, turning her eyes upon her with solemn entreaty and insistence. "Don't be afraid; I am strong enough. Tell me all. What have they done with him?"

Bessie's lips quivered and her eyes filled.

"They have sent him for trial, miss," she replied in a low voice.

Olivia looked at her steadily, and her breath came in quick little pants.

"Sent him for trial? They think he is guilty?" she said. "He, who would not hurt a dog, shoot a helpless woman! Why should he do it? Who was she?"

Bessie shook her head.

"No one knows, miss. Mr. Faradeane will not say anything, and—and that is why they say he did it. If he would only speak and explain, then people would believe him."

Olivia remained silent for a few moments, thinking deeply, her hands tightly clasped.

"And he will say nothing?" she inquired in a low voice.

"Nothing, miss; not a word!" said Bessie, the tears rolling down her cheeks; "and they all say—the servants in the hall—that the detective from London"—Olivia started and looked at her—"says that if he will not explain he—he will——"

She stopped with a choking little sob.

There were no tears in Olivia's eyes. Hot and brilliant, they looked out at the window, the lines graven deep in her white forehead.

"There is some mystery," she said in a low voice. "I know that he did not do it."

"Who did, miss?" sobbed Bessie. "Some one did it—some one they can't find; and everybody knowing Mr. Faradeane was in the wood, and that the pistol was his, will believe him guilty. Why, oh, why doesn't he speak out?"

Olivia was silent for a moment, then she raised herself on her elbow.

"Where is he?" she asked.

"In Wainford jail, miss," replied Bessie, piteously. "He has been there ever since—ever since the day of the wedding——"

"And the murder!" breathed Olivia. "He is shut up there with no friend to help him, while the guilty man is free!" Her eyes flashed, and she drew a long breath of repressed and passionate indignation. "Is there no one to help him—no one trying to save him?"

Bessie shook her head.

"I don't know, miss. They say that no one can help him, unless he will help himself."

Olivia thought for a moment, then she sat up with a strange expression of resolution in her eyes.

"Bessie, I must see him."

Bessie started and stared at her.

"You, miss! Oh, how can you! They will not let him come out to you!"

"No, I must go to him," said Olivia, quietly.

"To him—to the prison!" exclaimed Bessie. "Oh, miss, you cannot! The squire—Mr. Bradstone—would not permit it!"

Olivia's lips twitched at the sound of her husband's name.

"They must not know," she said, slowly and thoughtfully, as if she were earnestly considering the question; "they must not know. Stop, Bessie"—for Bessie, aghast at the proposal, was about to remonstrate—"I have made up my mind. If all the world said I should not see him, I would contrive to do so. In Wainford jail?" She put her hand to her brow. "That is Colonel Summerford's. He would do anything for me; he will not refuse to let me see him."

Her hands began to move restlessly, and she glanced at the clock with wistful impatience.

"Oh, no, no; not to-day, miss," pleaded Bessie. "You are not strong enough; you will be ill again, and—oh, not to-day, dear, dear Miss Olivia!"

"I am quite strong," said Olivia, rising and stretching out her hands. "How do I know that to-morrow may not be too late? We will go this afternoon—yes, this afternoon."

"But what can you do, miss?" gasped Bessie, who knew that when her mistress had made up her mind any further remonstrance would be useless.

Olivia sighed heavily.

"I do not know," she said, looking from side to side with a troubled expression in her eyes. "I cannot tell—till I see him. I shall know then!"

"Oh, dear!" breathed Bessie. "I am so afraid; you are so weak still."

"I am strong enough to walk to Wainford and back to help—him," came the low but quick response. "But there is no need for that. Go down and order the brougham; say that I wish to go out for a drive—that I will have no one but you with me. No one need know where we are going. Afterward, I do not care who knows."

Then, as Bessie still stood hesitating and trembling, she turned upon her almost fiercely.

"Did he stop to think of the consequences when you were in danger? Have you forgotten that?"

Bessie's face went crimson, and she flung up her hands before it; then, her face quite pale again, she looked at Olivia with a strange, intense reproachfulness, and left the room.

At three o'clock Olivia, leaning on Bessie's arm, went down the stairs. Notwithstanding her assertions, she felt very weak, and her limbs seemed to quiver and tremble. The brougham was at the door, and the squire stood ready to help her in, with a couple of thick wraps on his arm.

"Are you sure you are strong enough, dear?" he asked, anxiously. "And will you not let me come with you?"

She put her arm round his neck and kissed him.

"No, dear; Bessie and I are going alone. Don't be anxious; I am getting quite strong again now. Tell James to drive round the park."

The squire wrapped the shawls round her tenderly, and the brougham drove off.

Olivia leaned back with her eyes closed for some minutes, but when the lodge had been left behind she sat up with a new life and eagerness in her eyes.

"Tell him now to drive to the jail," she said.

Bessie gave the order, and the coachman, after a moment or two of inert astonishment, turned the horses' heads.

The brougham pulled up at the prison, and Olivia made ready to get out.

"Shan't I ask the colonel to come to you, miss?" asked Bessie, who was white with anxiety.

Olivia shook her head.

"No," she said. "It would be easier for him to refuse while I am sitting here; it will be more difficult—oh, I will make it impossible for him to do so, once I am inside his office," and her voice seemed suddenly to have got back something of its old ring and firmness.

They got out, and, without knocking, Olivia opened the office door.

The colonel looked up from the desk at which he was writing, and stared speechlessly for a moment at the vision of fragile loveliness. Then he sprang to his feet and came round to her.

"Great Heaven, Miss Olivia! I beg pardon—Mrs. Bradstone. You here! What is the matter? Where is the squire?" and as he held her hand he tried to lead her gently to a chair; but Olivia stood firm, and with her thin fingers twining round his, looked at him steadily, though her heart was beating wildly, and the color coming and going in her face.

"Nothing has happened, dear Colonel Summerford, and my father is not here. I am alone, excepting for my maid. I have come to ask a great favor of you. You will not refuse me?"

"A favor?" echoed the colonel; "my dear young lady! Come out of the draught, for Heaven's sake!" he broke off, for she looked so wan and slight that it seemed to him as if a breath of air would waft her away. "I did not know you were well enough to be out. Are you? And to come here! What is it you want me to do? Of course I will not refuse you; you know that."

"Yes, I know that," she murmured, in the sweet voice which had never failed yet to reach men's hearts. "I want you to let me see Mr. Faradeane."

The colonel literally gasped for breath.

"To—to see the prisoner—Mr. Faradeane!" he exclaimed under his breath. "My dear, dear girl, you cannot be serious."

She forced a smile.

"Do not be alarmed, Colonel Summerford. I am quite sensible now, and not delirious. And I do want to see Mr. Faradeane."

"To see Mr. Faradeane!" he repeated, as if he could not quite realize it even yet. "But what for, in the name of Heaven?"

"Must I tell you that?" she asked, still looking at him steadily, though her lips quivered. "I want to tell him that I know he did not commit this—that he is charged with, and that— —"

She stopped.

"It's quite impossible!" he said, gravely. "Quite—quite! Don't ask me, I beg of you!"

"But I do ask you," she murmured, her eyes melting with entreaty. "Why is it impossible? You are governor, and can do what you like"—the colonel was too much troubled to smile—"and you said you would not refuse me."

"But," he retorted, soothingly, with a look of relief, "fortunately, it isn't for me to grant or refuse. It is for Mr. Faradeane, and he has informed me that he will see no one."

"I do not care for that," she said, in the tone which only a woman knows how to use. "He will see me, because I shall not wait to ask him!"

The poor colonel tugged at his mustache.

"But—good Heaven, my dear girl, does your father know?—surely he doesn't know that you have come on this—forgive me—mad errand?"

"No, he doesn't know," said Olivia, steadily. "But if he had known, he would have let me. Colonel Summerford, you know I have been very ill?" she purred, bending toward him with a piteous entreaty in her lovely eyes. "You don't want to send me away to be as bad again?"

"God forbid!" responded the colonel, anxiously.

"Well, then, do as I ask you. Ah, you and I are such old friends—you won't refuse me what I have so set my heart on."

"Well, well, well!" he exclaimed, pacing up and down, and tugging at his mustache furiously. "I— —Confound it, how can I refuse you? You would coax the heart out of a stone dog. But I'm doing the maddest, wickedest thing, and I'll have to answer for it to the squire, and Lord knows whom else! There—don't cry!"

"I am not crying!" she said, biting her lip.

"I'll send up and ask him— —"

"No!" she said, quickly, and she put her hand on his arm. "You must not do that; you must take me to him unannounced; you must not give him time or the chance to refuse to see me. Take me to him now!"

Colonel Summerford pursed his lips.

"I don't know who could resist you; I can't!" he said in despair, and he held out his arm. "Mind, you are to stay a few minutes only, and the warder— —"

"There must be no one with us," she said, firmly. "No one. I must be alone."

The colonel groaned.

"In for a penny, in for a pound! My dear, if I am sacked for this, you will have to keep me in my old age."

And he tried to smile. He led her along the corridor, and, dismissing the warder with a nod, himself opened the cell door.

"A visitor for you, Mr. Faradeane," he said.

Olivia drew her arm from his, paused a moment to draw a long breath, then entered the cell.

Faradeane was lying on the hard pallet, his face resting on his arm. He raised his head, and opened his lips as if about to speak; then he rose and stared, his eyes dilating, his arms stretched out. He had not been asleep, but had been dreaming awake, and it is possible that he thought her a vision conjured up by his infinite longing and despair.

"Olivia!" he murmured, unconsciously. "Olivia!"

She glided across the narrow cell, and held out both her hands.

"Yes, it is I!" she said, and at the sound of her voice he trembled, and his pale, worn face grew crimson.

"You here!" he said, almost inaudibly. "Why have you come? This is no place for you—a prison!"

"It is no place for you!" she retorted, and as she spoke her lovely eyes flashed into his, and her fingers closed tightly on his thin hands.

CHAPTER XXIX
A TERRIBLE SELF-SACRIFICE

He looked at her for a moment, then turned away slightly, as if he could not meet the direct gaze of her lovely eyes, which said so plainly: "Let others think what they may, I know you are innocent!"

He did not offer to draw forward the only chair, but stood in silence while one could count twenty. By this time he had recovered his usual self-possession, and could speak to her without a quiver in his voice.

"You have been ill," he said, gently. "You are ill and weak still, too unwell to—to come here. Why did you come?"

She sank into the chair, and looked up at him, leaning her arms on the table and clasping her hands. There was entreaty, and yet a touch of firmness and resolution in her attitude and her face.

"Yes, I have been ill," she said. "I think I have been very near death. I tell you this that you may know why I have not sent a message to you, why I have not come."

He fought hard against the thrill of joy which ran through him, and, keeping his eyes closely guarded, as it were, responded:

"Why should you send to me? I—I have no claim upon you."

"Have you not?" she said at once, her eyes fixed on his with the light of a woman's truth and devotion shining in their depths. "Are you not in trouble?"

"Yes," he assented, "in great trouble, God knows!"

"And did you not offer me your friendship, did you not insist upon my accepting it—for Bertie's sake?"

"For Bertie's sake, yes," he said in a low voice. "It was a promise I made him, and I would have kept it; but I am no longer capable of keeping it. No one's friendship could be more valueless—or dangerous—than mine."

"Because you are in trouble," she said, and her eyes glowed upon him with tender indignation. "Because you cannot help me, you think that I do not care for your friendship. It was to be all one-sided. Is that it? I was to use you when I wanted you, to come to you for help and advice as to a true and firm friend; and then—when you were in trouble I was to desert and turn my back on you!"

He hung his head, and sighed.

"Mr. Faradeane, your experience of women must have been unfortunate!"

He looked up, as if her words had cut deeper than she had intended.

"You are right, Miss Vanley," he said, so gravely and sadly that she uttered a little cry of dismay and remorse.

"Ah, what have I said?" she murmured.

"Nothing, nothing!" he replied, quickly, soothingly. "Nothing you could say would wound me. But—forgive me!—I know the kindness of heart which prompted you to pay me this visit; but was it wise? Your father——"

"He does not know that I have come. But I should not care if he did." She spoke calmly and resolutely. "I am not ashamed of standing by a friend when all the world is against him."

He shook his head as he looked down at her tenderly, reverentially.

"It is like you; yes, I might have known!" he said, almost to himself. "But you have not counted the cost. Already the story of Miss Vanley's visit to Harold Faradeane, the mur——"—he stopped in time, warned by her sudden pallor—"the prisoner, is on its round. Why should you make yourself a victim to scandalous tongues? Tell me why you came, and—forgive me once more—but you must not stay here another minute. Why have you come?"

"I have come because I want you to tell me who did this thing!"

He turned away from her, and looked through the barred window again, a wistful, anxious expression in his eyes.

"I cannot do that," he said. "You—you ask too much. You have heard the evidence——"

She uttered an exclamation of impatience.

"Yes; oh, yes! But what is all that to me who knows that you are innocent?"

He sighed, and glanced at her sadly.

"You cannot know that," he said, gravely.

"But I do know it!" she said. "Do you think if I had doubted your innocence——"

"That you would have come to see me," he finished.

Her face flushed, and her eyes glowed.

"No, that was not what I was going to say," she retorted at once. "If I had thought you were guilty I should still have come; yes, if they had had to carry me here!"

He uttered a low cry, and held out his arms to her, then restrained himself and sank upon the pallet.

"Ah, yes!" he murmured. "I might have known! I might have known!"

"Yes," she assented. "You might have known. You should have judged me by yourself. Would you not have come to me if I had been accused of a crime—yes, even if you had thought me guilty?"

He looked at her; it was sufficient answer.

The look seemed to sink into her heart, and for the first time her eyes faltered in their steady gaze.

"And now you will tell me who did this, will you not?"

He remained silent, shading his face with his thin and already wasted hand.

"You will tell me," she persisted, and her voice floated across to him like the sweetest, softest music. She saw his hand tremble. "You will tell me, me alone, if you like. Have I not proved that I can be stanch? I can be secret. Tell me, and I will promise that I will never repeat it until you give me permission!"

By leaning forward she could almost touch him, and he felt rather than saw her white hand near him.

He dropped his hand from his eyes with a cry that was like a smothered groan.

"I cannot!" he said, simply.

She fell back a little. She was still weak, and the excitement was telling upon her.

"Ah, how hard you are with me! How distrustful!" and she gave a piteous little sigh. "I thought that I had only to come to you, only to ask you, and that you would have told me—me!"

He leaned his head upon his hands, and sat like one tried almost beyond endurance.

"If," she went on in a low, soft voice, every note of which rang in his heart—"if I had been in your place, and you had come to me and asked me to confide in you, as I now ask you, do you think I would have refused? No! I could not have done so! See," she pleaded, touching him timidly, tenderly, "see how little it is I ask! I do not want you to tell me why you have refused any explanation to the world at large; no, I don't do that! I only ask you to tell me the name of the man for whom you are enduring all this, whose burden of crime you are bearing—will you not do that? Can you refuse me?" She glided nearer to him imperceptibly. Before he knew it she was on her knees at his side, her hand, soft and quivering as a bird, upon his arm. "Ah, tell me! Tell me!" she murmured.

He took her hand and held it in both his, his white face working like a man's in a mortal agony, his eyes gazing into hers with intense entreaty.

"Oh, don't ask me! don't, don't!" he said, hoarsely. "I cannot tell you! It is impossible! Will you believe that? If you knew what it costs me to refuse you! If you knew how I dread that you should come to think me guilty——"

He stopped and compressed his lips as her face flushed and her hand closed on his arm.

"Go on!" she breathed, "go on!"

He turned his head aside.

"No, I can say no more! Not one word. There is danger——" He stopped. "Miss Vanley——" He started, and put his hand to his brow with a sudden gesture of despair and sorrow. "Ah, I forgot! Forgive me. Does he—your husband—know?"

Her face paled, and her lips twitched.

"No, he does not know. I—I have not seen him since the wedding."

He was silent a moment; and she, glancing up at him, saw a strange look of trouble and anxiety in his face, and she knew that he was thinking of her.

"I—I have a message for him," he said, slowly, as if he were guarding every word. "It—it is a matter of business, which I had intended telling him before they arrested me. Will you ask him if he will be so good as to come and see me? No! do not!" he said, suddenly; "I will write. If—if it be possible, do not let him know that you have been here. Tell me who knows it already."

"There is Bessie—she came with me; and the coachman and the colonel," she replied, listlessly and indifferently.

"Good, faithful Bessie," he said, thoughtfully. "You—you will keep her near you. She loves you with all her heart and soul."

"Yes, I will keep her; you sent her."

He looked at her gratefully.

"And those are all who know? It may be kept from the scandal-mongers, even now. You must go." He rose quickly, and she stood looking at him. "They need not know that you have seen me—that you have come in contact with the contamination of a prison cell. You may have come to see Colonel Summerford!"

She shook her head.

"I care nothing for all this," she said; "all the world may know."

"No," he said, "but I care. To know that your name was being lightly dealt with, would increase my unhappiness tenfold. Go now. I have not thanked you for coming. If I were to try and tell you, I could not. My heart is too full of the sense of your goodness and sweetness——" He stopped. "Let happen what may, the remembrance of your presence in this cell, your gentle, pitying voice will be with me—yes, even to the end. Oh, hush! Forgive me!" for she had uttered a little cry, and wavered as if he had struck her. "No, I cannot tell you; but some day, perhaps——" He stopped, his voice breaking. "Go now," and he took her hand and gently drew her to the door.

"And you?" she said, faintly; "are you going to keep silent? Are you going to let them do what they will with you? You spoke of the—end! What is that? Do you mean to let them—kill you?"

Her voice died away into a sob, and she gazed up into his face with dry, anguished eyes.

"God knows!" he said, reverently. "We are all in His hands. If you knew all—and you will never know, thank God!—you would understand; yes, and you would say that if you had been in my place you would have done the same."

"You say that?" she asked, with an inscrutable expression in her eyes—"that I should do as you are doing; that I should take another person's crime upon my shoulders and suffer for him?"

"Yes," he said, and he met her gaze steadily, "I do say that; and you know that I would not speak untruthfully, even to persuade you to do what I want you to do."

"What is it?" she said, with a little pant.

"I want you to forget that such a person as Harold Faradeane ever existed; to erase from your life all memory of him, and—his misfortunes. Don't let me have to reproach myself with the thought that I have cast a shadow over the life of the only woman I ever——"

He stopped.

Her lips quivered, and her gaze fell for a moment, then she raised her eyes again.

"You ask me to do this?" she said.

"I do, with all my heart and soul," he responded.

"Then I tell you that if I were capable of such baseness, I should be as vile—as vile as the man who committed the murder—the man you are screening! No! You ask too much. The rest of the world may take your silence for guilt, but I will not accept it! I will not rest until I have discovered the truth you are concealing."

He uttered a cry of alarm, of dread.

"Olivia!"

"Yes!" she repeated, her eyes flashing, her lips trembling. "I am only a woman, but I will do what you would have done in my place—save my friend even in spite of himself!"

He grasped her arm, his face white and set, his eyes full of a terrible fear.

"If any words of mine, if any entreaty can stop you in this course—— Believe me—believe me—it would be useless. The evidence is conclusive. No jury in England could fail to find me guilty. No one can stretch out a hand to save me——"

"Excepting yourself!" she said.

He turned away, and laid his hand upon the door.

"And you will not?"

"And I—cannot!" he responded. "Go now—every moment——"

He put out his hand to her, and she took it in hers and held it for a moment, her tearless eyes fixed on his, as if she hoped even against hope, at that last moment, to see some signs of yielding; but his eyes met hers with the sad firmness and resignation they had worn all through.

"Good-by—God bless you—the best and sweetest and truest——" His voice broke; the warder opened the door, and Faradeane, seeing Bessie standing in the corridor, beckoned to her. "Bessie!" and he held out his hand with a faint smile. "Take care of her! She looks so ill—and weak. Take care of her—and never let her come here again! Good-by—don't cry, Bessie."

"Now, ladies, please!" said the warder, respectfully, but firmly.

As the door closed with a heavy clang, Olivia started and turned with a little cry of agony and despair toward the cell.

Then Bessie drew her aside. The colonel put them in the brougham, and Olivia sank back, white and exhausted; but there were no tears in her eyes, though Bessie cried bitterly.

When they got home Olivia made her way upstairs, and, throwing herself down on her knees beside the bed, hid her face in her hands, one thought taking possession of her to the exclusion of all else. She forgot that she was married to Bartley Bradstone, forgot that in the bosom of her wedding-dress was the sum for which she had sold herself, forgot even her father and his great need. All she remembered was that Harold Faradeane lay in prison charged with the awful crime of murder; and that, unless some hand was stretched forth to save him, his days were numbered.

CHAPTER XXX
"QUITS"

That afternoon a policeman walked up to The Maples and inquired for Mr. Bradstone. That gentleman was standing at the window, his hands thrust in his pockets, his head sunk on his breast, and the sight of the constable sent the blood rushing through his head, and made him clutch at the window-sill with a gasp of dread.

"A letter, sir, from the prisoner," said the man.

"Eh? Oh, yes, certainly," stammered Bartley Bradstone; and he took the note to the other end of the room.

It was only one line.

I wish to see you.—F.

Bartley Bradstone stared at it, and bit at his lips nervously.

"Just say all right, will you?" he said to the policeman. "You—you can get something to drink in the servants' hall. Er—er—by the way, is Mr. McAndrew back yet?"

"No, sir," replied the man. "Not yet, sir. Rather strange his keeping away so long; but I suppose he's getting evidence in London. There's never any knowing what these big detectives are after."

When the policeman had gone, Bartley Bradstone dropped into a chair and bit his nails, glancing now and again at the peremptory summons.

"He—he orders me about like a dog," he muttered, with an oath. "Just like a dog! But I've got to go. Yes, though I'd rather give a thousand pounds than face him, I've got to go. He's got me, curse him! Got me tight! If there was any way out of it, any chance——"

He got up with a groan, and went to the sideboard for the familiar brandy, then put on his hat, and with as calm a countenance as he could command, walked down to the prison.

Faradeane was pacing to and fro with a steady, thoughtful stride; and, as he faced his visitor, Bartley Bradstone started at the change which the close confinement—and the ordeal of Olivia's visit, though Bartley did not know that—had worked in the handsome face and stalwart figure.

"You—you sent for me," he said, unsteadily, and carefully avoiding Faradeane's stern, searching eyes.

"Yes; you were wise to come."

"Of course I should come," mumbled Bradstone. "If there is anything I can do—God knows I'm wretched and miserable enough," he broke off with a whine. "I feel as if I could shoot myself."

"I dare say," said Faradeane, not contemptuously, but with simple assent more biting than the most polished scorn. "But you cannot do that; it would reveal the truth, and cover her with the shame from which I—and you—have resolved to shield her at all cost. At all cost, do you hear me?"

"I hear," said Bartley Bradstone, leaning against the table and looking round the cell with a shudder. "I'll do anything. I said I would when—when——"

"I agreed to take your crime upon my hands and suffer for you," said Faradeane, grimly. "I have sent for you to tell you what you must do."

He looked up almost eagerly.

"What is it?"

"You must leave England," said Faradeane, slowly and deliberately, as if he were propounding a carefully considered scheme.

Bartley Bradstone's eagerness increased.

"I'll do it," he said. "I—I've thought all along it would be better for me to get away. There's no knowing what may turn up. This detective fellow from London, I don't like the look of him," and he covertly wiped the perspiration from his pallid forehead. "He might find out——"

"What can he find out?" asked Faradeane, sternly, and with a searching look. "What had this woman done to you that you should shoot her?"

"I didn't mean to! I swear it!" exclaimed Bradstone, with a terrible oath. "I—I only meant to frighten her, and—and the cursed thing went off, and——"

He dashed his hands before his eyes and shuddered.

Faradeane turned away with a spasm of disgust.

"What hold had she on you?" he demanded.

Bartley Bradstone shot a suspicious, cunning glance at him.

"She—she wanted me to marry her," he said, in a low voice.

Faradeane sighed.

"You—you cur!" he said, not angrily, but with infinite scorn.

"When—when she found I was married already she threatened to—to go then and there to the Grange and blare out a scandal before—before Olivia."

Faradeane winced as the beloved name left the man's lips.

"And I—I couldn't stand it! It drove me mad! That's it! I was mad—mad! But I didn't mean to shoot her, only to frighten her."

Faradeane got as far from him as the small cell would permit, and, looking down at him, said, slowly and sternly:

"Take that paper, and write as I tell you."

Bartley Bradstone looked up fearfully.

"What are you going to get me to do?" he whined. "Don't—don't be hard on me for—for her sake."

Faradeane pointed to the paper.

"Let there be as few words as possible between us, if you please. Write as I tell you. Refuse, and I give you up here and now."

Trembling and shaking, the wretched man clutched the paper.

> I, Bartley Bradstone, shot the woman called Bella-Bella in Harkwood Spinney.

"Sign it."

Bradstone lifted his ashen face.

"Good God! You—you seem to mean to hang me, after all," he gasped. "After all your fine talk of saving her from trouble——"

"Silence!" said Faradeane, sternly. "Do as I bid you. There is no time for hesitation; the warder will be here in a very few minutes. If that is not written and you have not solemnly pledged yourself to carry out my scheme for your safety—for your safety, do you hear?—-I send for Colonel Summerford and denounce you."

With a groan, Bartley Bradstone wrote the short confession. It was so feeble a scrawl, so twisted and broken as to be almost illegible.

Faradeane took it—and as he did so the real criminal noticed that he touched it as one touches some noxious thing—then folded it and put it in an envelope.

"Address it to Miss Van—to your wife," he said, grimly.

Bartley Bradstone started and clutched at the table.

"To Olivia! To her!" he gasped. "Is that your game? You—you know what she'd do. You know she'd hang me twice over, with joy, to save you."

Faradeane raised his hand, but let it fall to his side.

"Do not try me too hard," he said, hoarsely. "Address it."

With another groan, Bartley Bradstone obeyed. Faradeane took a sheet of paper from his breast-pocket and placed it before him.

Bartley Bradstone read it and uttered an exclamation, and staggered to his feet; then sank down again, as if too weak to stand. This is what Faradeane had written:

> Your husband has left England forever. If, at any time, under any pretence, he should break the vow he has made to me, and attempt to claim you, open the enclosed envelope. While he refrains from troubling you, keep it sacred and inviolate, and if he should die, leaving you unmolested, burn it. You have spoken of our friendship: in the name of that friendship, with all the earnestness of a man over whom hangs the shadow of death, I leave you this charge. My honor is in your hands.
>
> Harold Faradeane.

He took the paper from Bartley Bradstone's trembling hands, and, inclosing it, together with the confession, in an envelope, addressed it in firm, steady writing to Olivia.

Bartley Bradstone sat staring at the floor like a man dazed.

Faradeane waited in silence for a moment or two, then he said:

"You will leave England to-night."

"To-night?" repeated Bartley Bradstone, dully.

"Yes, there is no time to lose. Strange as it may seem to you, there may be some who will not believe me guilty."

"She—for one," muttered Bradstone between his teeth.

"Let suspicion be once aroused, and the truth may be discovered. You are a business man; give business as an excuse for your sudden departure. Go on the Continent; there are still some remote spots where you will be safe from the English law. Find one—and stay there. Remember," he spoke slowly and distinctly, "if you are in any rash moment tempted to break your word to me, and claim as your wife the woman upon whom you have fastened your name, that she holds your life in her hands! That is all I have to say to you," he added, significantly.

Bartley Bradstone passed his hand across his lips.

"Well, I—I must do it. You're right; I—I don't feel safe. I'm better out of the way. As for Olivia; she—she never cared for me, and since this—this affair I've—I've wished I hadn't married her. When are you going to give her that letter?" he asked, with a suspicious glance at it.

"Now," said Faradeane. "Did you think it was a trap I had laid for you? Call the warder."

Bartley Bradstone got up, but sank down again.

"I'm all to pieces," he groaned.

Faradeane went to the door and knocked.

"Mr. Bradstone wishes this letter sent to Mrs. Bradstone," he said.

"Very good, sir," said the warder; and he took it.

Bradstone listened to his heavy step as it clanged along the stone corridor. Then he got up and shook himself like a man trying to recover from a bad dream.

"I'll go now," he said. "There'll be just time to catch the up-train. Is—is there anything I can do for you?" he added, lifting his bloodshot, wavering eyes shamefacedly.

"Nothing, except keep your promise," replied Faradeane, slowly and wearily. "As you say, there is no time to lose. Good-day, and remember."

Bartley Bradstone, with lowered head, went to the door and knocked at it feebly.

It was opened after a moment or two by another warder, and Bartley Bradstone passed out. He went slowly down the corridor into the stone hall, trying to drive away the hangdog expression which he knew was eloquent in every feature, and was passing the colonel's room with as firm a step as he could manage when his heart leaped within his bosom, for Colonel Summerford called him.

He turned and entered the office, and the blood rushed like a torrent through his veins, for there in the colonel's hand was the letter!

"Oh, Mr. Bradstone," he said, "sorry to stop you; but this letter——"

"Yes," said Bartley Bradstone, trying to speak and look indifferently, though there was the sound of singing in his ears, and he could scarcely keep his eyes from the letter.

"This letter for Mrs. Bradstone," continued the colonel. "I was just sending some one with it; I don't know whether you would like to take it."

Danger makes a man, especially if he be a Bartley Bradstone, sharp. He was just on the point of holding out his hand for the letter, when there flashed upon him the thought that Faradeane would probably ask if it had been delivered, and, hearing that it had been consigned to Bradstone's care, would make him account for it.

"I—I am going straight to The Maples, and from there on to London on important business, connected with my unfortunate friend, Mr. Faradeane," he said, with a happy inspiration. "If you could kindly send it on by one of your men."

"Certainly, certainly," responded the colonel. "It was from no reluctance to do Mr. Faradeane a service, but in the desire to save time. I trust that you may be able to do some good for him, Mr. Bradstone. I don't mind admitting that I'm deeply interested in the case, and more especially in him, prisoner as he is."

"We all are, we all are," said Bartley Bradstone, with a deep sigh. "My wife especially——"

"Yes, I judged that by her visit here this morning," said the colonel.

Bartley Bradstone started, and his face went pale, one might almost say green.

"She—she was here this morning!" he exclaimed. "Oh, yes," he added, hastily, as the colonel colored and looked as if he could have bitten his tongue out. "Yes, I'd forgotten for the moment. Oh, yes, we are all doing what we can. Of course, he is innocent, poor fellow!"

The colonel shook his head gravely.

"I hope you will be able to convince a jury of that," he said; "but——"

Bartley Bradstone sighed again.

"We shall leave no stone unturned, not one," he said. "And you will send the letter? Thank you."

He walked out of the office briskly, and down the street in the direction any one going straight with the letter must take. He turned a corner sharply, then pulled up, and, with a wildly beating heart, waited. Two, three minutes passed, then a policeman came round the road.

Bartley Bradstone waited until the man had reached the corner, then hurriedly ran against him.

"Hallo!" he said. "I beg your pardon. I was going back to Colonel Summerford to tell him that I should have to go to the Grange, and that I would take Mrs. Bradstone's letter myself."

The man produced it instantly; he had overheard the conversation between the colonel and Bradstone.

Bradstone took the note, with a casual glance at it, gave the man a shilling, and walked on.

All the way to The Maples the letter—the words in his own handwriting which could, if they were allowed to escape from that envelope, hang him—seemed to be burning through his clothes and eating a fiery way into his heart.

"Curse him, curse him!" he muttered, as he dragged himself heavily and feverishly through the great gates and up the drive to the house which he had prepared for the woman he had entrapped. "Curse him! he'd separate us forever! He'd send me into a kind of transportation for life! I'd—I'd almost rather be hanged——" He shuddered. "No, no; anything's better than that. But to lose Olivia; to lose her forever, forever! After all I've done, all I've spent, all I've risked!"

He drew a long breath, and, unlocking the door of the library, dropped, exhausted by his walk and the excitement, on to a sofa.

"If there was only some way out of it, some way of quieting him!"

The words rang in his brain until he found himself repeating them in a dull, mechanical fashion. Suddenly his face crimsoned.

"Why, he'll be quiet enough presently!" he exclaimed, as a swift hope rushed into his craven heart. "If—if I can only wait, keep out of the way and wait, he'll think the letter's delivered, and I mean to keep my promise! It's not for long. The trial will be here directly, and—and he'll plead guilty——"

He stopped, and sprang to his feet, white and trembling.

An idea had struck him, one of those ideas which come to unscrupulous men in desperate straits.

"I'll do it! By God, I'll do it!" he exclaimed. And, going to the writing-table, he wrote:

> Dearest Olivia—I leave England to-night. I have been ill. I am still ill, with a terrible anxiety. I have seen F—— this afternoon, and he agrees with me that it will be better that I should leave England at once. I cannot tell you how my heart yearns for one word from you whom I have not seen since the day you became my wife. Think of me, my dearest, dearest Olivia.
>
> Your loving husband,
Bartley Bradstone.
>
> P.S.—Inclosed is my address.

But, in addition to the Hotel Meurice, which he wrote on the inclosed slip, were these lines:

> Faradeane does not know what has been driving me almost mad, what I have kept, but cannot keep from you longer, dearest. I was in the wood, and saw that poor woman meet her death by his hand. A word from me, one word, would be fatal to him! I cannot—cannot risk the chance of being called at the trial! Poor, poor fellow! I fear there is no hope for him! Burn this at once.

It was a piece of diabolical cunning. He knew that Olivia would rather die than repeat what he had written, that it would account to her for his absence, and that it must—for he knew her, all unworthy of her as he was—estrange her heart from Faradeane.

"Now I think we're quits, my friend!" he said, gloating over the two letters—Faradeane's and the one he had himself written. "I've burned my boats behind me now. If she should tell them that I was there, and saw him do it—well"—he drew a long breath and shuddered—"I'll go into the box and swear to it! Yes, Mr. Faradeane, you've put your head into the noose too far to draw back, I'm thinking! Too far, by a long way. Steady, Bartley, my boy; go steady, and play your game carefully, and you'll pull through this."

A drink of brandy increased his confidence still further, and he rang the bell for a servant, that he might send the note; then, with a sudden return of caution, called for his overcoat and hat, and went out.

"I'll take it up to the Grange myself," he said, "and I'll give it to nobody but Olivia herself, or the girl Bessie. Perhaps she'll see me—confound her, she was well enough to go to the prison! Well enough for that! But not well enough to see her husband! Wait, oh, only wait!" and he half-stopped and shook his fist in the air.

He was so absorbed in his reflections that he entered the Grange avenue without noticing it, and, suddenly looking up, he found himself by the rail over which he had leaped when he went to meet Bella-Bella. He stopped for a moment, and glared fearfully toward the shadows of the wood, then, with a shudder and a shake, as if a chill had fallen on him, hurried on.

The squire was out, the butler said, and Miss Olivia—he begged pardon, Mrs. Bradstone—was lying down, and not well enough to see any one. Would he come in and wait for the squire?

Bartley Bradstone shook his head, and turned aside that the man might not see the evil look that crossed his face. At that moment Bessie crossed the hall, and he called her.

"Here!" he said. "Just give this to Mrs. Bradstone, and tell her that I am so glad to hear she was able to go out to-day."

In taking out the letter, he also pulled out Faradeane's, which he thrust back again hurriedly into his breast-pocket. Then he went down the steps. At the bottom he paused and looked round, thinking he would go home by a road that avoided the awful spot; but he set his hat firmly on his head, and clinched his teeth, muttering:

"No, no; no use giving way like that! I shall have to pass the cursed place half-a-dozen times a day in the future."

He walked down the avenue, but, though he had nerved himself to the utmost, as he approached the particular railing his heart began to thud and his cheeks to whiten. And suddenly, as he neared in the direction of the glade, his heart seemed to stop beating and his brain to whirl, for there, there on the very spot, was something, something in the shape and hue of a woman's dress coming toward him. Was it a living woman or— —

With a low cry of horror he staggered, and clutched at the railing with both hands to keep himself from falling, for his knees bent under him, still staring at the dimly-seen figure.

A second or two, that seemed like years, passed in that awful suspense; then the figure—living or dead—disappeared among the trees.

With a moan of terror he managed to stand upright, and, mopping his livid face with his handkerchief, struggled for courage to call out.

His voice came at last, and huskily and feebly he called: "Who's there?"

No answer came. He waited for a minute, until the use of his legs came back to him, then set off, as fast as his trembling limbs would permit, down the avenue.

Almost before he had reached the lodge, the figure came out from among the trees, and, gliding from the shelter of one trunk to another, made for the railing and looked after him.

Then, if Bartley Bradstone could have summoned up courage to look back, he would have seen that what he had taken for the wraith of the woman he had shot was Seth the gypsy, clad in an ordinary carter's frock and wearing a slouch hat that nearly concealed his face.

Seth got over the fence and stood looking up and down the avenue warily. The smock was torn with brambles, Seth's face looked grimy and drink-worn, and there was a furtive, sinister gleam in his black, cunning eyes.

"Give you a fright, did I, Master Bradstone!" he muttered, huskily. "I'll give you one or two more afore I've done with you."

Then he was about to leap over the railing back into the wood again, when something white lying on the ground where Bartley Bradstone had been standing, caught his eye.

He pounced upon it as only a lurcher or a gypsy can, and turned it over with eager curiosity.

It was the letter containing Bartley Bradstone's confession, which he had pulled out from his pocket with his handkerchief.

Seth shrugged his shoulders. "Only a letter. 'Tain't no use to me; if it 'ud been his hankercher, now!" With a contemptuous grimace he tore it in half, and was about to fling it away, when he stopped his hand. "I dunno," he muttered, "perhaps I'd better keep it; he might give me something for it. I'll offer it him anyhow." And he thrust it carelessly into his trousers-pocket.

CHAPTER XXXI
"WE SHALL SAVE HIM YET"

Bessie took the note up to Olivia's room, and found her still kneeling beside the bed, her arms stretched out upon the white coverlid in utter exhaustion; and yet the hands were moving to and fro restlessly, as if the brain were racked by anxious thought.

Bessie bent over her and softly drew the long hair from her face, which was burning hot.

"Ah, miss, you will be ill again!" she said, reproachfully. "And he said I was to take care of you."

"Yes! It is always of me or some one else he is thinking!" Olivia moaned, impatiently. "Always of some one else—never of himself. Oh, Bessie, what shall I do to save him? What shall I do? Every hour, every minute, that slips by so stealthily and swiftly, adds to the danger. I can't think; I can't even pray. What shall I do?" and she wrung her hands.

"Hush, hush, miss!" murmured Bessie, soothingly. "Something will be done; the truth must come to light."

But though she tried to speak confidently, her voice trembled, and she had to turn her face away.

"Yes, the truth will come to light when it is too late and they have—killed him. Oh, if there was only some one I could go to, some one to help me! If I were only a man instead of a weak, feeble woman! What is that?" she broke off sharply, as she caught sight of the note in Bessie's hand.

Bessie held it out reluctantly.

"From him!" panted Olivia.

"No, from—Mr. Bradstone, miss," replied Bessie, pronouncing the name as if with an effort.

Olivia drew the hand back as if the envelope had power to sting her; then she took it slowly and read it.

With a cry she let the letter fall from her hands, and flung them before her face as if to shut out some fearful sight. Bessie flew to her with an exclamation; but suddenly Olivia's emotion seemed to change, and, darting upon the letter, took it to the window and read it again with dilating eyes. Then she turned and grasped Bessie's arm.

"Bessie," she whispered, hoarsely, a strange thrill in her voice, a strange light seeming to shine upon her face, "did you ever doubt his innocence? Did you? Did you?" she demanded, feverishly.

Bessie looked at her indignantly.

"No; nor I! But if I had, if even for a moment such a doubt had entered my heart, I should doubt no longer! Do you know why?" and her grasp tightened upon Bessie's arm and terrified her. "I will tell you! Because Mr. Bradstone says that he saw him do it!"

Bessie shrank back with a low cry of horror.

"Says— —Oh, no, no, miss!"

"Yes! Listen! No, I will not sully my lips with the lie—for it is a lie! If it had been true he would not have waited until now! Ah, no!" She stopped and looked before her into vacancy, her dark brows drawn straight. "No, he would not have waited; he would have been only too glad to tell it. Then"— her voice dropped still lower—"why does he say it now? Why? why? Help me, Bessie," and her hands worked convulsively. "There is some reason. Ah!" she started and shrank, and her face went white. "I see!"

Panting and trembling, Bessie clung to her.

"Oh, what is it, miss? What is it you think you have found out?"

"I have found out this: I am sure that Mr. Bradstone knows who committed the murder!" replied Olivia, almost inaudibly.

Bessie's brain reeled, and it was she who clung to Olivia for support— Olivia, who every moment seemed to be gaining greater physical and mental strength.

"He—he knows, and he says it was Mr. Fara— —Oh, Miss Olivia!" and she began to cry.

"Hush, hush! Let us think!" said Olivia, almost sternly. "Why does he accuse him? Why does Bartley Bradstone screen the real criminal? Is it some friend—some one he knows? Ah, I cannot see; it is all dark! If there were only some one to help me! But there is no one, no one. If Bertie— —" She stopped with a cry. "But I sent him away! I have brought trouble, nothing but trouble to all who—who loved me!" and she hung her head and sighed. "He will not speak, he will keep silent, but Bartley Bradstone will not be silent. He will tell this lie in open court, and— —" She stopped, and a shudder shook her from head to foot. Then she was silent for a moment, still thinking deeply. Suddenly she looked up. "Bertie may be in England; no one can tell. If he were—he loves him, I know. Bessie, you must go to London——"

"Me! To London!" said Bessie, with a start; then almost instantly she added, quietly, "Yes, miss, I can be ready in a quarter of an hour," and she drew herself up and stood with flashing eyes expectantly.

Olivia drew her toward her and kissed her.

"Now listen to me," she said, in a low voice, that was firm and steady for the first time since the awful day of the wedding—and the murder. "First, Bessie, go to Lord Carfield's—I will give you a note." She darted to her desk and wrote rapidly. "It is asking him to tell me Lord Bertie's address. If he says he does not know it, go to London to the detective—Mr. McAndrew, of whom you have told me—and tell him to find out if Lord Bertie is in England or within reach. If he is, Mr. McAndrew is to give him this message: 'Olivia Vanley——'" She stopped, and her face grew red and then white. "No, 'Olivia,' only Olivia, 'wants you to come to her on a matter of life or death.' That is all. He will ask you for money, very likely." She flew to her jewel-case, which Bessie had arranged, and snatched the first thing that came to hand.

It was Faradeane's present. Her lips quivered and her eyes filled with tears as she looked at it, and she was putting it back in the case, when, she stayed her hand and exclaimed, suddenly:

"Yes, this! How better could I use it than in his service? Take this and give it to Mr. McAndrew. You will find him at Scotland Yard; see, I have written down the address. Telegraph to me, or come back to me with the news; and, oh, Bessie, remember that you and I, two helpless women, are trying to save the life of the man who saved yours, and who is risking his life now to screen some one else!"

Bessie gave a great sob, then set her teeth hard, and hurried from the room.

In half an hour she had reached Carfield Towers and delivered the note. Lord Carfield came out to her, as she was waiting in the brougham.

"Tell your dear mistress, my girl," he said, sadly, "that I am as ignorant as she is of my son's whereabouts. Of course, it is on account of Mr. Faradeane and this terrible mystery that she wants him?"

"Yes, my lord," said Bessie, firmly, "and I will find him and bring him to her, if he is to be found."

She caught the evening up-train, and though she had never been in London before, she faced its strangeness and its vastness without quailing; it seemed as if Olivia had infused something of her own desperate courage and energy into the timid country girl.

She drove to Scotland Yard, and after five minutes' waiting, during which, by the way, Mr. McAndrew had been calmly and keenly scrutinizing her from behind a curtain, he entered.

Bessie delivered Olivia's message, word for word.

He looked at her with the simple smile which made his face so innocent and commonplace, then nodded.

"So your mistress wants to see Lord Bertie, does she?" he said, in a kindly fashion. "Hem! so do I; and perhaps we shall both see him presently. What's this?" he asked, as Bessie put the necklace-case in his hand.

"My—my mistress said you would want money, and sent this," faltered Bessie.

The great man smiled softly and opened the case, then suddenly his face changed, and his eyes, as they scanned the magnificent gems closely, grew sharp and keen. But it was only for an instant; the next moment his expression was that of the simple, commonplace individual.

"Where did you get this from—your mistress, I mean?" he asked.

"It was her wedding present from Mr. Faradeane," replied Bessie, in a faltering voice.

"Oh," he said, slowly, "from Mr. Faradeane. Hem!" He snapped-to the case and put it in his pocket. "Yes, we detectives always want money, and you can tell your mistress I'll take care of this. Oh, yes, she can rest easy. I'll take care of it." He stood looking at her in silence for a moment, then he said: "And so your mistress saw Mr. Faradeane in prison this morning, eh?"

Bessie started and crimsoned, and he laughed.

"Now you can go back; you don't mind traveling all night, do you? Because your mistress will be anxious, you know."

"Oh, yes, yes," assented Bessie, eagerly, "and if I can only take her some good news!" and she clasped her hands.

Mr. McAndrew looked down at her thoughtfully, then he smiled and offered her his arm. "I'll take you to the station," he said. He got her some refreshment, put her in a first-class carriage, and, but not until the train was upon the point of starting, said, "How is Mr. Bartley Bradstone?"

Indeed, the engine shrieked and was off with its burden before Bessie could reply.

It was not until she had traveled some distance on her return journey that she realized, what a great many other persons before her had realized, that, she had not got anything very definite out of Mr. McAndrew. She had seemed, indeed, to have had no will of her own while in his presence, and to have done exactly as he told her.

She reached Wainford very tired and very dissatisfied, and found a carriage waiting for her.

"Why, how did you know I was coming?" she asked the coachman, who was an old friend of hers.

"The mistress had a telegram from London," he said. "Leastways a telegram came for her this morning."

Bessie stared at him with her eyes widely opened.

"I didn't telegraph," she said. "I meant to take a fly home."

"Well," he laughed, "here we are, you see, and you'd better get in, anyhow."

Puzzled and bewildered, she was about to follow his sensible recommendation, when a woman, with a child in her arms, came up quickly, and, pulling at her jacket, said, with a mixture of timidity and earnestness:

"Stop, stop, for God's sake, miss. I—I must speak to you! I've been waiting and watching——"

Bessie turned affrightedly, and, as the light fell upon her face, the woman shrank back with a cry of disappointment.

"Oh!" she cried, "I thought it was the young lady—leastways Mrs. Bradstone."

"No, I am her maid," said Bessie. "What is it? Are you ill?" for the woman looked worn and pale, and there were deep lines of anxiety and trouble on her thin face.

"Ill? Yes, miss. I'm ill enough, but it isn't that. I'm no account. It was——" She looked round fearfully. "Come out of hearing, miss!" she whispered, imploringly. "It may be too late—but it's not my fault. I've waited and watched, but I'm watched, too. It's about the—murder, miss!"

Bessie's courage and self-possession came back in an instant.

"Wait a moment, James," she said to the coachman, and she followed the woman into the shadow of the station wall.

"I thought it was the young lady," she said, speaking timidly, and with palpable agitation, and hushing the child she carried under her shawl. "I tried to speak to her before, by the lodge gate, where you lived."

"I remember," said Bessie. "You are the gypsy woman."

"Yes, I'm Liz Lee," assented the woman, "and I want to tell her something that I'm a'most afraid to whisper. I'm doing it at the risk of my life, miss, I am, indeed!" and she looked up with a piteous terror into Bessie's eager eyes. "He's promised to do for me, if I dare open my lips! And he'll keep his promise!"

"He? Who?" asked Bessie.

"My husband," came the reply. "He thinks I'm safe at the camp; but I slipped out—and followed the carriage; I thought I was going to meet the young lady." She struggled for the breath which her agitation and alarm seemed to deprive her of; then, looking round fearfully, went on: "Is it true, miss, that he'll be hung?"

Bessie's face paled.

"Do you mean Mr. Faradeane?"

The woman nodded, with a sob.

"Yes, yes. Oh, miss, if they only knew! Him commit a murder! Why, he wouldn't kick a dog as bit 'im, leave alone shoot a helpless woman!"

Bessie could have fallen upon the poor creature's neck.

"Go on, go on!" she said, trembling. "You know something! You will not let him come to harm?"

"No, miss—if I could help it. Look here!" She drew her shawl aside, and revealed the face of a little child sleeping peacefully in her arms. "If it hadn't have been for him she'd have been underground by this time! He saved her life; yes, he did! He spoke to me as nobody ever spoke before, and I can't—I can't—let him come to harm!"

"Go on! go on!" implored Bessie.

The woman drew closer to her.

"I know who did the murder, miss!" she whispered, huskily.

Bessie caught her arm.

"Tell me! tell me!" she panted.

The woman trembled under the grasp.

"Promise me, swear to me, miss, that you won't tell who told you—that you won't give my name up."

"I promise," said Bessie, solemnly; "whatever happens, you shall come to no hurt. I promise for him, as well as for myself."

"Ah, no; he wouldn't see me hurt!" said Liz Lee. "Well, then——"

She stopped suddenly and uttered a cry.

A carriage had dashed up to the station at a tremendous rate; the whistle of the up-train was heard in the distance.

"Quick! quick!" exclaimed Bessie.

But the woman seemed to have lost all power of speech, and was staring at the carriage from which a gentleman had alighted.

Bessie looked over her shoulder. It was Mr. Bartley Bradstone.

"You know him!" she said, instantly. "Does he know anything of the murder; does he——"

The woman shuddered as she watched him go up the stairs.

"No, it's a fate!" she gasped. "Oh, I'm afraid to tell, afraid, afraid!" and she seemed unable to remove her eyes from his receding figure.

Bessie almost shook her in her agony of suspense.

"You must!" she said. "You have gone too far."

"If I must!" panted the woman. "Yes, he does know. Don't let him go! Do you hear? Stop him! Follow him——"

In her uncertainty and excitement, Bessie took half-a-dozen steps toward the station platform.

Then she turned, and, with a start, found a man standing between her and the woman, who was cowering against the wall, as if she had just received a blow.

"What, you, Liz!" he said, addressing the woman, but keeping his eyes on Bessie. "You're drunk again, are yer? What plant have you been a-puttin' on this young lady? You ought to be ashamed of yourself. What's she been a-sayin', miss?" And he turned to Bessie with a half-threatening, half-whining air. "Something about this yer murder, wasn't it? Blessed if this yer murder haven't gone and turned my missis' head. Don't pay any attention to her, miss! I 'umbly begs pardon for her. She ought to know better than to stop a lady with her rubbidge!" and, seizing the woman's arm, he hurried her to the steps.

"Stop!" said Bessie, "stop! She is not drunk, and you know it! She shall speak!"

The man glanced hurriedly up at the platform, at which the up-train was just arriving, and, tightening his hold on the woman's arm, swung her round. She was crying covertly.

"Now, then, you fool, just tell the lady you was only a-playin' it low down on her, on the chance o' gettin' a copper or two," he said. "Yah! I'm ashamed of you! Come on, speak up. There ain't no time."

"Time! time, Seth?" the woman sobbed.

"Yes!" he snarled. "You know we're a-goin' by the train, as well as I do."

She shrank back, but he pulled her forward.

"Now, then, tell the lady."

She turned her eyes upon Bessie, then let them drop.

"It—it wasn't true, miss, as I was going to tell you," she said.

"There you are!" exclaimed Seth, triumphantly. "Now come along!" and he hurried the woman up the steps.

Poor Bessie sprang after them in such haste that she trod upon her dress and fell. As she got up and raced up the steps, she heard the slamming of the carriage doors, and found the station gate locked. There was only one porter, and he did not hear her until the train had started; and she leaned against the gate, trembling and almost fainting, as the train bore Bartley Bradstone and the two gypsies toward London.

She got back to the carriage, and was driven to the Grange, and flew to Olivia's room.

Olivia met her at the door. "Well!" she exclaimed, seizing her by the hand and drawing her in, and Bessie told her all that had happened.

Olivia paced up and down.

"Oh, Bessie! Bessie! Fate is working against us. That he should have come up at that moment! Oh, if I had but listened to her that night by the lodge! What does it all mean? But we will find them." She snatched up her hat. "Help me! No, you poor thing, you are tired and worn out. Stay there and rest."

"Where are you going, miss?" exclaimed Bessie; but Olivia was out of the room before she could stop her.

She came back in a little over an hour, pale, but with a resolute look in her eyes.

"What have you done, miss?" she asked, tremulously.

"I have telegraphed to the London terminus to stop the gypsy and the woman!" she said. "I" —her color rose for an instant— "I let them think they had robbed me."

Bessie uttered a cry of satisfaction.

"Oh, Miss Olivia, we shall have them, we will make that woman speak out, and we shall save him yet."

And the two girls, mistress and maid, cried together.

Alas! It did not occur to them that Seth the gypsy would, being as cunning as a gypsy, give them full credit for the telegraphing idea, and get out at some intermediate station.

CHAPTER XXXII
THE TRIAL

The days wore on. To Olivia they appeared sometimes to drag with leaden weight, at others to fly by on wings. No news had reached her of Bertie, no tidings of Bartley Bradstone, or Seth the gypsy, and Liz Lee. It seemed as if, indeed, Fate were fighting against her, and that the mystery which surrounded the murder in the woods grew deeper and darker as the hour of the trial drew near.

And it was very near now. For on the twenty-ninth, Harold Faradeane was to be tried, and it was now the night of the twenty-eighth.

Since she had sent the telegram to stop Seth, Olivia had not left the house; and though she had regained her strength, there was a look on her face, an expression of indefinable suspense and terror and sadness which almost drove the poor squire distracted.

But in his mind, as in others, the thoughts of all that the morrow night might mean to Harold Faradeane blotted out all else, even the remembrance of his darling's situation: married to a man to whom she had not spoken since her wedding day, and who had gone off, left the country on "important business," as he had written, with no intimation of his return.

But the finishing stroke to his anxiety was dealt him by Olivia herself, when, on the eve of the eventful day, she announced her intention of being present at the trial.

"You!" exclaimed the poor squire, aghast.

"My—dear—Olivia!" gasped Aunt Amelia.

But Olivia glided round to where her father sat, and stole her arms round his neck.

"Papa, you will not try and prevent me?" she said, in a strange voice, at once pleading and resolute.

"But—but you have been so ill, are still weak and unfit for the slightest excitement. How will you bear to see that poor fellow standing there, and being tried for his life? My dear, my dear, think!" and he stroked her hair with a trembling hand.

"I have thought, dear," she said, quietly, laying her pale face against his. "I must go! I should die if I stayed at home to wait, wait, wait! Besides"— and her eyes flashed—"will not all his enemies be there—people who believe that he committed this wicked crime—and are only his friends to be absent?"

The squire kissed her and sighed.

"Have your own way, my dear. But I wish—I wish that Bartley were here!" he added, with a troubled frown. "I have heard nothing from him."

She drew away from him suddenly, and without a word left the room.

All that night she lay awake, looking at the silent stars with hot, tearless eyes, thinking of Harold Faradeane in his narrow cell, waiting the verdict of life or death; and going over and over all the points of the strange mystery, which grew darker and more impenetrable the more she struggled to pierce it.

The morning broke with all the mature splendor of late summer; and as Bessie dressed her, she still thought of the man awaiting his fate, the man whose faith and honor she would have answered for with her life.

The trial was to begin at ten; but long before that time the court was crowded and all the avenues were blocked with eager and curious people, who were excitedly discussing the incidents of the murder and the chances of the prisoner. Not a few of them had been present at the entertainment, and heard him recite the tragic poem of "Eugene Aram," and the sensation he had produced was recalled, and put in evidence against him.

No wonder he had made them all shudder and tremble: he who was capable of committing a murder himself, they said.

The story of his mysterious purchase of The Dell and the strangely secluded life he had led, of the man who was always on the watch to keep people from seeing his master, and the dog kept to attack all visitors; what could it mean, but that there was some dark mystery connected with him, of which this crime in the woods was the logical outcome?

At ten o'clock the streets were crowded, and the buzz of excitement grew into something like a roar as the Grange carriage was seen to pull up at the townhall, and the squire, with Olivia and Bessie, alighted. The curiosity to see the beautiful girl who had been stricken down on her wedding day, and had not seen her husband since, overmastered the respect they felt for her, and there was a rush toward the door; but half-a-dozen policemen drove the crowd back and made a lane, and the three passed through it to the hall.

Olivia wore a veil, and her arm trembled for a moment as it rested upon her father's, but it was only for a moment, and she walked, and compelled him to walk, slowly.

They entered the court, and the crowd made way for them. The judge was making his way to the bench at the moment, and, as he looked round with his calm, serene eyes, he saw the worn, pale face of the squire, and stopped to shake hands with him, and motioned him to seats just below him.

Olivia sat with clinched hands, trying to still the throbbing of her heart; then she looked round. The well of the court was filled with barristers, and among them the great London counsel, Mr. Sewell, the man whose acuteness and eloquence had sent many a man to the scaffold. Beside him she saw—and her heart throbbed again—the terrible London solicitor whose proud boast it was that no malefactor upon whom his legal claws had fixed had ever slipped through them! She looked for Mr. McAndrew, but he was nowhere to be seen. Then she looked toward the dock, and, as she did so, there was a stir and a murmur of excitement, and Harold Faradeane entered.

Pale and haggard, worn thin by the confinement of his cell and his sleepless nights though he was, there was still the look in his dark eyes which, when she had first seen it, had drawn her heart irresistibly toward him: and it drew her now.

He raised his eyes and looked round at the judge and the jury and the counsel, and then he saw her. She, if no one else, saw the light that flashed for a moment in his grave eyes, and the color that passed swiftly over his face.

Obeying an impulse she did not try to resist, she raised her veil, and, looking at him steadily, bowed her head with the deep respect which only a woman can convey in a bow.

Every eye in court saw it, and a thrill ran through the crowd.

Faradeane's lips quivered, and his hand grasped the front of the dock; but he did not acknowledge her salutation in any other way.

"By Heaven, she'll believe in him if they bring him in guilty twice over!" muttered Colonel Summerford to the solicitor.

That gentleman merely shrugged his shoulders.

Then the usher cried, "Silence!" A deep hush fell upon the court, and the clerk rose to read the indictment. "Prisoner at the bar, do you plead 'guilty,' or 'not guilty'?" he demanded.

One could have heard a pin drop, so intense was the silence, as all breathlessly awaited the answer. It came:

"Guilty."

A murmur arose, a dull sound of amazement.

"Silence!"

The judge leaned forward, and regarded the calm, set face with grave attention.

"Do you plead guilty, prisoner?" he asked, in the slow, judicial tone, impartial, almost insentient. "Where is the counsel for the defense?"

"I desire no counsel, my lord," said Faradeane, in a voice that, though low, was distinct enough to reach the remotest corner of the court.

The judge looked at him thoughtfully for the space of a moment.

"Do you say that you are undefended?"

"I have no defense, my lord," came the response, almost apathetic in its calm weariness.

Olivia's heart seemed to stand still. She clutched her father's arm.

"Father! father!"

"Hush!" he said, and looked toward the judge.

"Prisoner, are you sensible of the awful position in which you stand? I fear not. But it is my duty to see that you have a fair trial, without fear or favor. With the sense of my responsibility upon me, I take upon myself to advise you to withdraw that plea and to permit a counsel to defend you. Mr. Edgar"—and he leaned forward and addressed a young barrister—"will you defend the prisoner?"

˜ The young counsel sprang to his feet at once, and bowed to the judge.

"I will, my lord."

He made his way to the front of the dock, and looked up at Faradeane.

"You are mad!" he said, in too low a voice for those around to hear. "We plead 'Not guilty,' my lord," he added, firmly.

Faradeane made a slight gesture of weary resignation; and Mr. Sewell, the famous London counsel, rose, hitched his robe on to his shoulder, and commenced his address. The judge leaned back; the deep hush once more settled upon the court.

"My lord and gentlemen of the jury: I shall not have to detain you long with the recital of this tragic story. I shall, in the fewest and plainest words consistent with my painful duty, recount so much of the history of this case as can be sworn to by trustworthy witnesses, who, if they did not actually see the crime committed—and how seldom are there any witnesses present at the precise moment the blow is struck, the shot fired!—who, if they were not actually present at the fatal moment, arrived almost before the breath had left the body of the victim."

Then, in well-balanced sentences, and in a grave, solemn voice, he told the story of the finding of the dead woman, and the prisoner's presence near the body, together with the discovery of the revolver bearing his name.

The judge glanced now and again at the pale, composed face of the prisoner, and the crowd marked that, though he kept his eyes fixed on the ground, his face showed no sign of fear or emotion.

"I shall call witnesses who will prove these facts, as I submit, irrefutably. And now, my lord, I come to the point which doubtless you and the gentlemen of the jury have been waiting for—the question of motive. Why should the prisoner, a man of evident refinement, a gentleman on behalf of whose character my learned friend, his counsel, will no doubt bring a cloud of witnesses, commit this awful crime? Why should he shoot this woman? My answer is: Because she was his wife——"

A thrill ran through the court; and as the crowd seemed to stir and sway with astonished excitement, a faint cry rose from Olivia's lips.

Faradeane heard it, and for a moment he raised his eyes and looked at her—a look that pleaded for forgiveness, for mercy. White as a ghost, she clung to her father's hand.

"It—it—is not true!" she breathed.

"His wife; the woman who, in a moment of passion, as unreasoning as that in which he slew her, he had secretly married. It does not become any man to speak ill of the dead; but, gentlemen of the jury, it will be my painful duty to produce evidence to prove that the tie which the prisoner had in a rash moment contracted with the deceased was of so galling, so unendurable a nature, that he was compelled to fly from her. Most men would have severed the bond. The prisoner could have sought and obtained a release in the Divorce Court, for she had given him cause; but there were reasons why such a step should be unacceptable to him. My lord, gentlemen, up to the present, we see in the prisoner only an ordinary, private gentleman, living in a quiet, country spot secluded from the eyes of the world. But such was not always his position. The prisoner has not always borne the name of Harold Faradeane; and it is my painful task to ask you to recognize in him the person of the Earl of Clydesfold!"

A murmur quite audible, and not to be suppressed, rose from the crowd. The barristers put their heads together, the judge leaned forward and looked at the prisoner.

"The Earl of Clydesfold!" went from lip to lip.

Olivia uttered no cry, but sat white and statuesque.

"His wife! His wife!" rang in her ears.

She understood that scene in the wood, when he had held her in his arms and called her his love, and then drawn back, like a man stepping from the edge of a precipice. His wife!

"The Earl of Clydesfold!" continued the counsel. "Witnesses will be called who will tell you the story of his unfortunate, his ill-fated marriage; will show you how a man, gifted by nature, favored by fortune, of ancient and noble birth, possessed of enormous wealth, was induced by a mad passion to forget all that was due to his rank, to the honor of an ancient name, and to marry a young gypsy girl whom, blinded by that passion, he believed to be all that was innocent and pure; but who, before the honeymoon had passed, proved herself utterly unworthy to bear the name of any honest man!"

He paused and arranged his papers.

"Consider his position. Consider the nature of the prisoner. He had, all unwittingly, married this woman; was it possible for him, having discovered her true character, to drag the story of his shame, to drag the honor of his name through the mud of a divorce case? As many a man in his position had done before, he elected to hide his misery and his dishonor from the eyes of the world, in which he had held so lofty a place. He put aside the name rendered famous by a long line of distinguished ancestors, and, leaving the woman who had ruined his life, he came and hid himself in this retired spot. For a time he succeeded in concealing himself. The woman—his wife—was free to live in riotous splendor upon his money, and he may have laid the flattering unction to his soul that she would be content to leave him in peace. But, gentlemen, the consequences of such a folly as the prisoner committed are not to be avoided or escaped. The woman to whom he had given his name, in an evil and ill-fated moment, resolved that she would compel him to own her before the world or lay bare the story of his shame. She succeeded in tracking him to the place of his concealment. She had an interview with him on the night before her death. The incidents—some of the words that passed at that interview—I shall place before you. An appointment was made for the morrow. On that morrow she was found lying dead at his feet, the weapon by which she was slain beside her, bearing his name. Such evidence, so conclusive, so convincing, so damning, cannot, I fear, but lead you to the painful decision that the deceased came by her death at the hands of the prisoner."

The spectators drew a long breath, as he concluded, and all eyes turned to the prisoner.

He had scarcely moved; but the weary expression on his face had deepened, and he looked as if the crowded court had slipped from his consciousness, and he was going back, mentally, to the terrible folly of his life.

A thrill of pity stirred the hearts of the crowd, and one or two women put their handkerchiefs to their eyes and sobbed audibly.

The excitement was intense. Mr. Sewell conferred for a moment with the solicitor for the prosecution, and the counsel called:

"Viscount Bortoun."

A young man, the son of a well-known statesman, stepped into the box, and with a sad look at Faradeane, repeated the words of the oath.

"Do you know the prisoner?"

"Yes, indeed, I do," was the low and mournful reply. "He is the Earl of Clydesfold," and he looked at Faradeane as if imploring his pardon for appearing against him. "I came here because I was obliged," he faltered.

"That will do, my lord; we can understand how painful it must be for you," said Mr. Sewell, gently; and the viscount stepped from the box.

"I shall now call witnesses to the marriage."

Mr. Edgar sprang to his feet.

"But I submit, my lord, that my learned friend has not sufficiently proved my client's"—he did not use the word "prisoner," it was noticed—"identity. The motive—the motive for this crime is all-important. One witness is not sufficient!"

The judge nodded.

Mr. Sewell bent down and whispered to the solicitor; he shrugged his shoulders. There was a pause. Then a strange coincidence happened. There was a movement in the crowd. It parted, and a young man forced his way to the dock, and with a cry of "Clydesfold!" seized the prisoner's hand!

The spectators shouted, the usher yelled "Order!" the judge leaned forward and first looked amazed, then frowned.

"Bertie!" sprang from Olivia's white lips.

He turned, still holding Faradeane's hand, and looked at her. Ah, such a look! No pen can describe it; no poet, no painter could convey it.

"Order!" cried the usher, sternly.

McAndrew tugged Sewell's arm, and "I call Viscount Granville," he said, instantly.

Faradeane smiled down at him sadly, and drew his hand away; and, with a wild, angry look on his handsome face, Bertie was led by the arm to the box.

"You are Lord Granville?"

"I am," he answered, in a low voice.

"You know the prisoner at the bar?"

"I know Lord Clydesfold," he responded. "He honors me with his friendship!"

The court thrilled.

"Yes, honors me!" he repeated, looking at Faradeane with mingled affection and indignation. "And I say that to accuse him— —"

"You may stand down, my lord," said Sewell.

"One moment," interposed the judge's grave voice. "You have only just arrived in court, Lord Granville?"

"I have, my lord," said Bertie, eagerly. "I have been abroad"—he looked at Faradeane—"and reached England yesterday, midday. I heard of this— this ridiculous charge against my friend only this morning, a few minutes ago. I know that he is as utterly incapable of committing a crime as— —"

He stopped, almost breaking down.

The judge bore with him in patient sympathy and silence for a moment, then he said:

"Do you know anything of the prisoner's marriage?"

"I know nothing of it, and I do not believe it," replied Bertie, instantly.

A buzz of applause rose, and was instantly quelled by the usher.

"When did you see the prisoner last?" asked Mr. Sewell.

"I—I can't give you the date—the day I left England. Here at The Dell."

"Did you ask him—did he tell you— —"

"Oh, my lord!" said Mr. Edgar. "Hearsay evidence! Really!"

But Bertie rushed on:

"No, I do not know why he was living under an assumed name. He would not tell me. I wish he had; but he refused."

He stopped, feeling all eyes upon him. He had spoiled the effect his affectionate greeting and indignant assertion of the prisoner's innocence had produced.

"You may stand down, my lord," said Mr. Sewell.

He went and stood beside Olivia, and took her hand.

Then Mr. Sewell called the landlord of the George Inn, where Bella-Bella had stopped; Faradeane's man, who had prevented her entering The Dell—the case looked blacker—and then he called William Alford.

It was Bessie's turn to shrink and cry now.

"You were passing The Dell, the prisoner's cottage, the night of the visit of the deceased. Tell us the conversation you heard between her and the prisoner."

Alford, with a piteous look at Bessie and Faradeane, hesitated.

"I—I don't remember. I couldn't hear distinctly."

Mr. Sewell looked at him sternly.

"Come, sir; were these the words?" and he repeated Bella's speech, which in a tipsy moment poor Alford had blurted out one night at the George. "You heard her say that she knew the prisoner wished she was dead, that he would like to kill her? Answer, sir!"

"I——Oh, Mr. Faradeane, what am I to do, sir?"

"Answer," said Faradeane, in a grave, compassionate voice.

"Silence!"

"Well," with a groan, "I did!"

CHAPTER XXXIII
A GYPSY'S EVIDENCE

We must leave the court—now adjourned for luncheon—and follow Bartley Bradstone.

He reached home more dead than alive after his fright in the woods, and as he recovered his scattered senses, there flashed upon his remembrance the note inclosing the confession. He would destroy that the first thing, then he would pack his portmanteau, and, obeying Faradeane's instructions, run over to the Continent.

He thrust one hand into his coat pocket, and drew a candle toward him with the other. Then he fell back, white to the lips, and with an inarticulate cry. The packet had—gone!

He felt in every pocket, though he knew well that he had put it in his overcoat breast-pocket as he stood on the steps of the Grange—shook his coat, unfolded and shook his handkerchief, and examined the room. With quaking limbs he put on his hat, and, scrutinizing every inch of the way, retraced his steps through the house and down the drive, along the road and up the Grange avenue, almost as far as the railings where he had seen the apparition, but not quite so far. Even to recover the fatal letter he could not bring himself to face that awful spot again.

But the letter was nowhere to be seen. Worn out with anxiety, he went back to The Maples and flung himself into a chair. To leave the place with that damning confession of his guilt he knew not where, he felt was an impossibility. A dull kind of despair seized upon him, and held him in complete thrall. He crawled up to bed at last, but not to sleep. All night he tortured himself by imagining the discovery of the confession by some one who would either carry it to the police station or to Olivia. If the person who found it followed the former course, then all was over with him, and flight would be useless. Before he could reach London—now—the telegraph would be in operation, and detectives would be waiting for him at every station. If, on the other hand, it should be carried to Olivia—well, she would, she must send for him, and he would have to face a new phase of the danger.

He went downstairs the next morning casting restless, suspicious glances over the balustrade, expecting to see a policeman in the hall; but as the day passed and no one came—no detective, and no message from Olivia—his spirits rose somewhat.

"I may have dropped it as I stood leaning against the railing; it must have come out with my handkerchief when I saw— —" He stopped with a shudder. "Perhaps luck is going to stand by me still, and the cursed thing has been blown into the wood and is hidden under the bracken. If so"—he got up with renewed energy—"if so, let it lie there until after the trial, after I come back. He will be put out of the way then!"

This view of the case was so encouraging that he dwelt on it, repeating it over and over again, and then went upstairs and secretly began to make preparations for his departure. He prepared the way by reading one of his letters, while the butler was in the room, and uttering exclamations of impatience and annoyance.

"Tut, tut! I shall have to go to town, I'm afraid," he said.

"Yes, sir," said the butler, as he removed the untouched breakfast.

"Yes. But I'm not certain. Let me see, what are the trains?"

"There's the one at midday—you have just lost the morning one, sir—and the evening train."

Bartley Bradstone thought rapidly. It was just possible that even now, or later in the morning, some one might pick up the letter and take it to Olivia, and he might hear from her. He would wait until the evening train.

He passed the day going over his papers and letters, destroying some and placing the others in the safe. He had not opened it since the wedding day, on which he had taken out the revolver, and he stood before it, looking into its depths with a dull apathy. It was difficult to realize that he—Bartley Bradstone—was—a murderer; that but for the noble heroism and self-sacrifice of the man he hated most in the world, he would at that moment be in the cell, instead of Faradeane, awaiting his trial!

He had been a cunning, an unscrupulous man, an adventurer who had never hesitated at any mean or base action, so long as it was just within the law; who had never hesitated to secure or push an unfair advantage, at whatever cost to others. But murder! With a shudder he shut the safe to, as if he would shut out all remembrance of his crime.

Having secured and destroyed his papers, he finished his packing. He had always been lavish in decking his person with jewelry, and the trinkets and odds and ends of gold and gems which he possessed represented a large sum of money. He thought of packing them and taking them with him, but ultimately decided to leave them behind, and locked them in his safe.

Then he forced himself to eat a little of the early dinner which had been provided for him, and at last got into the carriage and was driven to the station. He noticed the Grange carriage standing at the steps, but he saw that it was empty, and concluded that it had been sent to bring the squire, who may have been traveling up the line on some business.

He did not see Bessie, who was standing in the shadow; and, more important still, he did not see Seth and the woman who entered the train just as it was starting.

Coiled in a corner of a first-class compartment, he tried to sleep, but every jolt and rattle of the train seemed to voice that sudden shriek which rose from the lips of Bella-Bella as the bullet struck her, and he tossed and turned in that hideous, acute wakefulness which is a signpost on the road to madness.

Then it suddenly occurred to him that possibly the note had been found and the police were already searching for him! If so, to alight at the London terminus would be to step into the arms of his captors. His ready brain met this new difficulty and danger. He resolved to get out at one of the stations on the line this side of London, and, after some consideration, fixed upon Basingstoke.

When the train pulled up at the station, he called a porter to take his portmanteau, and stepped quickly, but not hurriedly, from the train and passed into the refreshment room.

As he did so, a window in a third-class compartment was gently let down, and Seth looked out in time to see Bartley Bradstone's back, as it disappeared. Seth turned to Liz, who was crouched in the corner.

"I'm going to get out here," he said. "You go on to London to the old shop, and don't you stir hand or foot till I come to you—if it's days or weeks, d'ye hear?—or I'll——"

She looked at him; then, with a sigh, flung her shawl over her face.

He got out, and with an affectation of indifference, sauntered along the platform, and hiding himself behind the projecting side of the book stall, took out a paper and held it up before his face as if he were reading, but every now and then glanced round it toward the door of the refreshment room.

Presently the man he waited for came out and walked up the platform. He stopped at the book stall and bought a London paper and some magazines. A porter came up, and Bartley Bradstone beckoned to him.

"There is a branch line from here to Paddington, the Great Western station, isn't there?"

"Yes; but it's rather a roundabout way, sir," answered the porter.

"I know," said Bartley Bradstone, as if he had expected to meet the remark. "But I'm in no particular hurry to reach London. I want to sleep."

"All right, sir," said the porter. "Train is due in ten minutes."

Bartley Bradstone gave him some coppers, then went and took a ticket. The station was comparatively empty by this time, and Seth was too cunning to emerge from his hiding-place, in which he waited, still studying his newspaper, until the train came up.

Then he watched Bartley Bradstone enter a carriage, and, carefully screening himself behind the passers-by, Seth stole gently into a third-class compartment, and, covering his face with his handkerchief, began to snore. The ticket collector came and shook him; but Seth seemed only capable of muttering "London," and eventually the collector gave it up, remarking:

"Well, you'll have to pay at the other end, my friend."

The murky haze of an early autumn morning hung over London, as the train steamed into the terminus. Bartley Bradstone woke—he had fallen into the deep sleep of exhaustion—and got out.

During the journey he had come to a decision as to his movements. He had remembered reading somewhere, in connection with the case of a criminal who had succeeded in evading the most rigorous police search, that there was no place in which a man could conceal himself as in a great city.

Why should he go to the Continent, where he could be so easily traced, if anybody wished to track him? Why should he not hide himself in London, where he could inform himself, through the newspapers, of every detail of the trial at Wainford? Then, if all went well—that is, if Faradeane were found guilty and—and——Even mentally he could not conclude the sentence. But if "all went well," then he could go back and claim Olivia; then he could leave England with her—with her!—forever!

In some of the quiet streets leading off the Strand there are several private hotels, as quiet as the streets in which they stand. The patrons of these hotels are colonial and provincial folk, who come and go, appearing on the scene once only, perhaps, and then disappearing, unquestioned and unnoticed—caught up, as it were, on the wheel of the great city, and lost like a drop in the ocean.

He called a cab and told the man to drive to Barlow's Hotel, Denmark street. A minute or so of delay occurred in the hoisting of his portmanteau on to the roof, and in that space of time Seth, with the unobtrusive movements of a gypsy, had got into another cab.

"Just follow my master, will you?" he said.

The two cabs sped on their way; but suddenly the first came to a stop.

Bartley Bradstone, in sheer absence of mind, had opened his newspaper, which he had put in his pocket unglanced at when he bought it, and the first words that met his eyes were:

"Disaster in the City. Failure of the South Indian Bank!"

For a moment the line of large type conveyed no special significance to his mind; then suddenly it flashed upon him that the bank was one of the schemes in which he had taken a part, and a large part.

He put his hand to his aching brow and tried to remember what he had lately done in the matter. It seemed to him that he recollected sending his tool, Ezekiel Mowle, instructions to sell out his shares and close his connection with the affair; but his brain would not act with its usual readiness in the direction of his ordinary business; it was all too absorbed in the more important matter of life and death.

Had he or had he not given the proper instructions to Mowle? He tried to put the question, the whole business out of his head; but the instincts of the money-spinner overreached the cunning caution of the criminal, and with a muttered oath, he put up the trapdoor in the cab and told the man to drive him to Ethelred Chambers in the city.

Cabmen are accustomed to these sudden re-directions, and without a word, the man turned his horse in the direction of the city.

"Your guv'nor didn't seem to know his own mind," growled Seth's cabman, through the hole in the roof.

"Follow him!" said Seth, whose blood was beginning to stir within his veins, as the lurcher's or the sleuthhound's will when hot upon the trail.

Bartley Bradstone's cab pulled up at Ethelred Chambers, and, telling the cabman to wait, he went up the stairs, and, without knocking, opened the door of a dingy office and walked in.

Ezekiel Mowle was seated at a table, his huge mouth open, his lantern jaws working eagerly, as he sprawled over a desk, writing apparently for dear life. The office, the furniture of which would not have realized five-and-thirty shillings, was in extreme disorder, and a Gladstone bag was lying half open on the floor, as if it had been hurriedly thrown there.

Mr. Mowle looked up with a start, and, uttering an exclamation, covered the paper before him with his huge, bony hand. If his employer had been a ghost—and, indeed, Bartley Bradstone looked not unlike one—Mr. Mowle could not have been more startled.

"Mr. Bradstone, sir! This is a surprise. How do you do, sir? I am afraid you're not looking well. Take a chair, Mr. Bradstone," and he drew the chair out and stood with his head thrust forward, rubbing his hands and eying Bartley Bradstone with a wary and still startled watchfulness.

Bartley Bradstone took off his hat and wiped his brow.

"I am not very well, Mowle," he said. "I have come up on important business. What the devil is the office in such a state for? Where are you going?"

Mr. Mowle changed color, but stood rubbing his hands and working his long neck.

"The fact is, Mr. Bradstone, I was just thinking of coming down to you."

"Coming down to me!" said Bartley Bradstone, with a frown.

"Why——Well, sir, I wanted to place one or two matters before you. The fact is, things have not been very bright in the city of late, and I have not had the advantage of your advice quite so much, and perhaps you have heard the news."

"What news?" asked Bartley Bradstone.

"I allude to the South Indian Bank, Mr. Bradstone," said Mr. Mowle, passing his hand over his mouth and eying Bartley Bradstone with the same watchful and deprecatory manner.

"Well, what about it?" said Bartley Bradstone; "I wrote and gave you instructions to sell those South Indian Bank shares a week ago."

Mr. Mowle gave a little start, and shook his head apologetically.

"I—I beg your pardon, sir; I think a slight misunderstanding," as if he were trying to gain time to collect himself.

"Misunderstanding! What do you mean? Do you mean to say I didn't write?"

"I did not say you did not write, Mr. Bradstone; but I certainly did not receive the letter."

Bartley Bradstone rose and clutched the back of his chair, and for a moment seemed incapable of speech, and then he said:

"Do you mean to tell me that the shares of the South Indian still stand in my name?"

Mr. Mowle put out one hand.

"No, no, no, Mr. Bradstone, I don't say that," he said, with a sudden change of face; "I said I did not receive your letter. Pray take a seat. Pray sit down again, sir, and compose yourself. Fortunately, I have had my eye upon the bank for some time past, and when the critical moment came, I sold out."

Bartley Bradstone sank into a chair and drew a breath of relief.

"That is well, Mowle," he said. "You gave me a turn. If you had not unloaded those shares for me, things would have looked bad. Now I want you to realize these things."

He took a list from his pocket and handed it to Mr. Mowle.

Mr. Mowle went back to the table and examined the list with respectful anxiousness, and as he did so, he put up his hand before his face, which underwent some peculiar changes of expression.

"I think I had better see to some of these things at once, sir," he said.

"Do," said Bartley Bradstone, curtly.

"Will you wait, sir? Or will you come in again? I shan't be more than half an hour or so. I hope things are all well down at The Maples, Mr. Bradstone? What a lovely place it is, to be sure; quite a palace. And Mrs. Bradstone, sir—I do trust she is better. What a painful, mysterious affair that murder is, sir!"

"Yes, yes," said Bartley Bradstone. "Yes, Mrs. Bradstone is better, and a man's being tried for the murder. I think I'll go down to the bank, while you sell that stock. Why the devil don't you open the window in this room? It smells like a charcoal house," and he wiped his burning forehead.

"Yes, yes, it is, sir," said Mr. Mowle; "it is rather close," and he shuffled to the window and made a vain attempt to open it.

Bartley Bradstone put on his hat and walked out of the room, telling the cabman to wait while he walked toward the bank. There he changed a check.

The cashier did not, as usual, scoop out the money with a respectful smile, but took the check, apparently, into the manager's room. He came out after a minute or two and changed the check.

"We have not had your passbook for some weeks, sir," he said, as he passed the money over.

Bartley Bradstone scarcely noticed him, but went out into the street again. He turned into a refreshment bar and got a glass of sherry. Half an hour, perhaps, passed, then he made his way back to Ethelred Chambers. Just as he was within sight of them, a gentleman ran up against him, and was making the usual apology, when he broke off with:

"Hallo, Bradstone! is that you? I say, my dear fellow, what a deuce of a mess we're in!"

"What do you mean?" said Bradstone.

"Well! Good heavens, man, I mean this infernal bank."

"The South Indian?" said Bartley Bradstone, quite easily.

The gentleman stared at him.

"Well, you take it pretty coolly, Bradstone," he said. "But I suppose to a man with your pile a facer like this does not matter, though I had an impression that you were in it more deeply than any of us. Why, it was one of your pet schemes, was it not?" and he smiled and winked.

Bartley Bradstone nodded curtly.

"Yes, I was in it pretty deeply," he said. "But I sold out a week ago."

The other man stared at him.

"Why, man, your name is still in the list of shareholders published to-day. Look here," and he drew the city paper from his pocket, rapidly found the paragraph, and thrust it into Bradstone's hands.

Bartley Bradstone looked at it, then turned white.

"There is some mistake," he said. "I tell you I sold out a week ago— every share."

The man looked at him with something like pity.

"By the Lord!" he muttered, under his breath, "the blow has sent him off his head!" But pity is too expensive a commodity in the city. It requires too much time. With a "Well, good-by, old fellow," the gentleman hurried on and left Bartley Bradstone standing with the paper in his hand, looking like a man completely dazed.

The crowd of passers-by jostled him and pushed him all unheeded; but at last he seemed to awake, and hurrying onward, ran up the steps and into Mr. Mowle's office.

Mr. Mowle was not there. He had gone, and so had the Gladstone bag! The office, too, was in greater disorder than before; and Bartley Bradstone, sinking into the chair before the table, saw a letter addressed to him lying on the desk. He tore it open with shaking fingers.

Am detained. Shall be back in an hour.

Suspicious and bewildered, Bartley Bradstone paced up and down the office, then he went to a safe which stood in the corner of the room. Unlocking it, he began to examine its contents. Then he uttered a cry of mingled rage and despair.

Like a flash of lightning the truth burst upon him. Ezekiel Mowle, the tool whom he had held under his thumb—the worm upon whom he had trodden so often—had turned at last. Scrip, securities, mortgages had all gone. The South Indian Bank shares had not been sold.

He remembered now the cashier's manner when he presented the check, and he knew, as well as if Mowle had confessed, that he had embezzled every penny of the vast sum which Bartley Bradstone had, with contemptuous confidence, left at his disposal.

Quite faint, sick, feeling more driven and helpless than he had ever felt before, he struggled to the table and drank a glass of water. What should he do? Throughout all the terrible time of peril he felt that at least he had one thing to help him—his immense wealth. Now that that had gone, what should he do?

He leaned his head upon his hand, and forced himself to think.

With the exception of the sum which he had obtained at the bank, he had no ready money whatever.

Mr. Mowle could not make away with The Maples, and probably only that remained. That could not be realized without time. Then he remembered his jewelry. At all costs he must get that. It would sell for something—would bring enough, perhaps, to enable him to leave England. He must go back to Hawkwood.

Pulling himself together, he went downstairs. On the way, the desire to punish the man who had betrayed him took full possession of him; but he knew that the longing for vengeance could not be satisfied. Any attempt to punish Mowle would reveal to the whole world the connection between them, and would brand him with infamy and disgrace. He got into the cab, and told the man to drive to Waterloo.

Seth, in his cab, followed at a discreet distance.

Luck favored Bartley Bradstone. The West of England train was leaving in a few minutes. Weary, tortured by anxiety, he threw himself into the corner of a carriage and closed his eyes.

It was nearly midnight when the train reached Wainford station, and a true Devonshire drizzle had set in. With the exception of a solitary porter, there was no life about the station.

Exhausted as he was, he must walk to The Maples. Perhaps it was as well; he could secure his jewels, and, by good luck, leave the house without being seen.

Slowly he dragged himself along the muddy roads, reached the lodge, and had got his key in a side door which he sometimes used, when he heard a voice close behind him.

With a hoarse cry he turned and staggered back. The night was dark, and he could distinguish nothing for a moment or two. Then he saw a man standing at the bottom of the steps, with his hands thrust in his pockets, and an expression of sullen impatience on his face.

"Who are you, and what do you want?" demanded Bartley Bradstone.

Seth came up the steps and looked at him.

"I want to know how much longer this is a-goin' on, Mister Bradstone," he said. "This 'ere game's a-gettin' too thin. If you ain't tired, I am. I suppose you thought you could give me the slip, but you reckoned without your man, Mister Bradstone."

Bartley Bradstone leaned against the door and stared at him breathlessly.

"I do not know you," he said. "You've made some mistake. You know my name. What do you want with me?"

Seth laughed shortly.

"Let's go inside," he said.

Bartley Bradstone took the key out of the door and put it in his pocket.

"Say what you have to say here," he said. "I never saw you before. I do not know what you want with me; if you have come to extort money on any pretext, you've come to the wrong man."

"Oh, no, I haven't," sneered Seth. "I've come to the right man. You don't know me; but I know you and I knew Bella Lee."

Bartley Bradstone drew a short breath and put his hand to his heart.

"You knew Bella Lee?" he said. "What has that to do with me?"

Seth laughed unpleasantly.

"A good deal, I should think, seein' as you was 'er 'usband."

Bartley Bradstone's face went livid, and he looked from side to side, like the hunted man he was.

"How do you know that?" he demanded. "Who told you?"

"I saw you married," replied Seth, coolly. "Come, Mister Bradstone, don't put my back up. I'm rather tired of this game o' chevyin' you up to London and back again, and I want to come to business. I know more about you and Bella than you think for."

"Go on," said Bartley Bradstone. "Tell me what you know or think you know."

"I will," said Seth. "I know more than the judge and jury as 'ull try Mr. Faradeane, and, by God, I'll tell 'em, if you don't make it worth my while to hold my tongue."

Bartley Bradstone stood with his eyes upon the ground, his lips tightly compressed. He seemed to feel the meshes of a huge, wide-spreading net closing round him. Whichever way he turned, he was met by some obstacle to his escape.

And this man who had, unseen, tracked him step by step throughout the day, what did he know? And how much? At all costs he must learn this.

He opened the door. "Come inside," he said; and leading the way to the library and turning up the gas, looked keenly at Seth's dark face and slouching figure. "You say, my man, that you know something about this murder. Do you know who did it?"

"I do," said Seth, seating himself on a corner of the costly inlaid table and kicking his leg to and fro in an insolent fashion.

"You do!" said Bartley Bradstone, with a long breath. "I was just going to offer a hundred pounds reward for such information as would lead to the discovery of the man who committed the crime. I will give you that hundred pounds now if you will tell me what you know."

Seth stared at him, then smacked his leg and laughed.

"A hundred pounds! I should think so! If you was to ask me, I should consider it cheap at a thousand, and that's the figure I mean to ask for it. And if yer takes my advice, the advice of a man as don't wish you no particular harm, you'll hand over that thousand pounds, and say no more about it. You can rely on me. I can keep my mouth shut. I'm sick o' England, and I'm ready to go wherever you like and keep there."

Bartley Bradstone remained silent for a moment or two, then he said, huskily:

"Supposing your information were worth the money, my man, I could not give it you."

Seth stared and laughed incredulously.

Bartley Bradstone bit his lip.

"What I tell you is true. I can no more give you a thousand pounds than you can give it to me."

"Now, guv'nor, come, no gammon," said Seth, impatiently. "If you've got any sense, any gratitood, you'd fork out the money and say 'thank you.' What's a thousand pounds when a man's life's at stake!"

Bartley Bradstone shuddered and sank into a chair.

"I tell you, I can't do it," he said.

Seth looked round at the handsomely furnished room, at the costly hangings, the rows on rows of elegantly bound books and silver knick-knacks on the tables, the carved oak and beveled mirrors, and laughed again.

"It won't do, guv'nor," he said. "Look 'ee here," and he leaned forward and shook his fist in Bartley Bradstone's face, "I'm not to be trifled with. Give the money I asks yer for, or I go and give the police the information I have offered you. They'll pay for it, and be only too glad."

Bartley Bradstone rose and nerved himself for the struggle.

"What information can you give them? You say you know something of this murder. How much?"

"Everything," retorted Seth. "Why, guv'nor——"

He bent forward and whispered a few words in Bartley Bradstone's ear.

Bartley Bradstone shrank back, and great beads of perspiration stood out upon his forehead; but then, bracing himself together, he laughed.

"Oh! that is it, is it?" he said. "My friend, you know too much. You threaten me! You seem to have forgotten that a man who knows so much, very probably knows more than is safe for himself."

Seth looked at him with knitted brows.

"What d'yer mean?" he said.

Bartley Bradstone thrust his hands into his pockets.

"It seems to me," he said, "that if you carried this story to the police they'd probably be inclined to ask how it happens that you haven't spoken before. They'll want to know what was your connection with the dead woman, and what has become of the property which she had on her person when she was shot; and I should think it not unlikely that the police would make it unpleasant for a gentleman of your appearance, and with your past history. In fact, if you ask me my opinion, I should say that before an hour had passed you yourself would be charged with the murder of the woman of whom you know so much. What's to prevent my telling them what you've now said against me? In fact, my friend, why should I not turn the tables? Now, come; you look like a sensible man. Take the money I have offered you to leave the country."

Seth, with white face and flaming eyes, glared at him for a moment in breathless silence. Then he said, hoarsely:

"By Heaven, you are a cool hand, Mister Bradstone, and I admire yer; but it won't do. I mean to have that thousand pounds if I dog yer day and night. I don't want to blab on yer; it 'ud be awkward for me to come forward as a public character. I admits as much, so I'll come to terms with yer. Hand up the money, and save yer cleverness for the time you'll want it—and from what I knows of such men as you, that time won't be long a-comin'."

Bartley Bradstone buttoned his coat.

"You may do your worst," he said. "The hundred pounds is still yours, if you like to take it, but not one penny more."

Seth laughed.

"Will you take my offer?"

"No," said Seth, with an oath.

"Very well," said Bradstone, and he put on his hat and walked toward the door.

"Where are you a-goin'?" demanded Seth.

Bartley Bradstone made no reply; he unlocked the side door and opened it. It was still raining, and dark as pitch. He went down the steps, Seth following close upon his heels, down the drive, out of the lodge and into the muddy lane; and, like a shadow, Seth still followed.

From the lane Bartley Bradstone turned to the left, into a path that led toward the wood. He could scarcely have told, had he been asked his object in taking this path. His one idea was to get away from The Maples, where Seth could give the alarm. In the confusion of his mind, in the deadly agony of his fear, he almost lost consciousness of the spy who still hung on to him.

Suddenly Seth reminded him of his presence. Stepping up beside him, he put his hand upon his arm. "'Ere, guv'nor," he said, "I'm sick o' this. I think I'll be able to show you that you'd better come to terms. I was only playing with you, up there at the house. I've got evidence that'll put you out o' the way without an ounce o' trouble."

"Evidence?" said Bartley Bradstone, with a sneer; "evidence of a gypsy pickpocket against the word of a well-known gentleman."

"Yah!" snarled Seth. "Look 'ee 'ere!" and he took from his pocket an envelope torn in two. "Look 'ee 'ere; do yer know that?" and he flourished it in Bartley Bradstone's face.

Dark as it was, Bartley Bradstone saw the piece of paper and knew that it was the confession which he had dropped in the Grange avenue. With a cry he sprang forward, but desperation even could not lend him the activity which is the gypsy's birthright.

With an answering cry of triumph, Seth whipped the letter behind him and caught Bartley Bradstone by the throat. For a moment or two the men struggled in that deadly silence. Despair and excitement lent Bartley Bradstone fictitious strength, and as he locked his arms round the gypsy's lithe form, he exerted every muscle and succeeded in getting him down upon his knee; but as he did so, Seth slipped, as if he had fallen, and, turning like a greyhound, again caught Bartley Bradstone by the throat and laid him full length upon the ground.

Panting as much with rage as want of breath, the gypsy glowered down upon him.

"You're a pretty customer to deal with," he said. "Get up! Put your hand on me again and I'll—I'll kill you. Now, what do you mean to do? You ain't got to deal with a helpless woman, Mr. Bradstone, but with a man. Will yer give me the thousand pounds now, or shall I take this letter to the police?"

Bartley Bradstone got up and leaned against a tree.

"I'll give it you," he said.

"Walk in front, then," said Seth, motioning to him suddenly.

Breathing hard, he obeyed. Thus they went slowly to The Maples. Bartley Bradstone unlocked the door and went into the library. Seth looked round.

"Give me something to drink," he said, hoarsely.

Bartley Bradstone, without a word, as if he were completely cowed, went to the sideboard and got out the brandy. Seth instantly took the decanter from his hand and helped himself.

"Now," he said, "look sharp—the money—the money!"

Bartley Bradstone drew a checkbook from a drawer. Seth watched him suspiciously.

"What's that?" he said.

"A check."

"What's the good of that to me?" said Seth. "I want money—gold, notes."

Bartley Bradstone forced a smile.

"Do you think I keep a thousand pounds in the house in gold or notes?" he said. "You're not so ignorant as you pretend; you have only to take this check to the bank to get it turned into money—gold or notes."

Seth looked at him with half-closed eyes.

"And suppose you stop it?" he said.

Bartley Bradstone smiled again.

"Is that likely?" he said. "Do you think that I am likely to run any more risk? Give me the letter. Take the check and leave me in peace."

Seth took the torn note from his pocket and looked from it to Bartley Bradstone's white face, doubtfully and suspiciously.

"What hold have I got on yer," he said, "if I give yer this note and find the check ain't honored?"

Bartley Bradstone raised his eyebrows.

"You'll have to trust me," he said. "You shall have the check on no other terms. I'm a desperate man to-night; I feel so sick, so driven, that I'd as leave balk you of your money and tell the truth myself. I give you two minutes to decide. Take the check, give me the note, and be off, or go and do your worst."

Seth slouched round the table, still holding the note, and looking fiercely into Bradstone's eyes.

"By God!" he said; "if I thought you were playin' me false—but I don't think you'd dare. Give me over the check; there's the note."

Bartley Bradstone clutched the two halves of the envelope and pointed to the door. Seth, still looking at him, poured out a glass of brandy.

"All right, guv'nor, I'm off. And now, if a cove as knows what's what may offer a word of advice, I'd say, make yersel' scarce as soon as possible. This is an awkward business. This 'ere Mr. Faradeane has got friends, and they won't let him be scragged if they can help it. Why, even now they may be on the right scent. When I was a-follerin' you in the city, there was a gent with a smooth face as came across you twice, and looked at you in a way as I knows pretty well by this time; and I see him at the station agen when you was comin' back. It might mean nothin', but a nod's as good as a wink to a blind hoss. Hook it, guv'nor, sharp," and with a nod he turned up the collar of his coat, pulled his cap well over his face, and went out.

CHAPTER XXXIV
THE SUMMING UP

Faradeane was led to the cell in which he was to wait during the adjournment. Five minutes afterward the warder announced Mr. Edgar.

Mr. Edgar waited until the door closed, and then held out his hand.

Faradeane took it with the faintest gesture of surprise.

"I suppose you don't remember me, my lord!" said Mr. Edgar. "I was a guest at a river party you gave some years ago."

Faradeane passed his hand across his brow.

"I beg your pardon," he said, "I had forgotten. I am sorry that we should meet again under such circumstances."

"Yes, my lord," said Mr. Edgar, "and yet I cannot help feeling glad that the judge should have trusted your case to me. We have so short a time in which to confer, that I am sure you will forgive me if I proceed at once to discuss the matter. I need not say, my lord, that I myself, speaking as a counsel, am quite convinced of your innocence. It is not for me to ask you why you have seen fit to plead guilty to a crime for which I, for one, am perfectly sure you were utterly incapable. But I wish most earnestly, in fact, it is my duty, to point out to you that unless some evidence can be produced to rebut that which the prosecution have already produced, and that which I believe they have still in hand, you stand in the most terrible peril. I will ask you only one question bearing directly on the death of this unfortunate woman. Will you tell me, my lord, as man to man—as prisoner to his counsel—did she commit suicide?"

Faradeane turned his head away, and was silent for a moment; then he said, "No."

An expression of surprise crossed Mr. Edgar's face, and he looked down and bit his lip as if puzzled.

"She did not commit suicide?" he said. "Then how am I to account for the presence of the revolver bearing your name? If she had committed suicide, I could have accounted for the revolver being in her possession, as part of the property which may have fallen into her hands as your wife. How am I to account for this?"

"Mr. Edgar," said Faradeane, gravely, "I can understand your desire to do your duty, and to assist me; and, believe me, it costs me a great deal not to be able to tell all that I should like to tell you; but I have reasons for remaining silent. That these reasons are all-powerful with me you may well believe, when I am content to plead guilty to a crime the penalty for which is the scaffold. I can render you no assistance. It was not by my wish that you were appointed my counsel. I cannot close your lips. I cannot, in the face of the court, decline the aid which it has appointed; but I can say nothing to help you in this matter."

Mr. Edgar took one or two paces up and down the narrow cell.

"Every word you have said, my lord," he said, "goes further and further to convince me that you are not guilty. Oh! I do beg of you—with all the earnestness of which I am capable—consider the position in which you stand. Such a name as that which you bear, surely you owe something to that. If you have no thought for your own life, think of that name which has been handed down to you honored and stainless——"

Faradeane put up his hand.

"Stainless no longer," he said. "The story of my shame, and my wife's, is by this time all over England. In a word, Mr. Edgar, I am utterly weary of the life which you would endeavor to save. I repeat, I can tell you nothing; my lips are closed, let the end be what it may."

The young counsel's face paled, and he bit his lips.

"So be it, my lord," he said; "but give me leave to tell you that though you will render me no assistance, will give me no information, I shall still do my duty. Forgive me if I tell you that there are no reasons grave enough to warrant a man sacrificing his life, and I shall still do my very utmost to prove that the plea of guilt which you set up this morning is an utterly false one."

Faradeane inclined his head.

"I am sure you will do that, Mr. Edgar," he said, "and I am sorry I cannot wish you success."

Mr. Edgar bowed, and was leaving the cell, when Faradeane put out his hand with a gesture to arrest him.

"One moment," he said. "You can do something for me."

Mr. Edgar stopped, and looked at him with a sudden hope.

"There is a lady in court," said Faradeane, in a very low voice, "Mr. Vanley's daughter—Mrs. Bradstone. Will you do me a favor?"

"I will do anything you ask me, except believe you guilty of this murder, my lord."

"You will go to her and ask her—beg her to leave the court. I ask it as the last favor I shall ever demand of her; I beg of her, in the name of the friendship which existed between us, to leave the court and go home."

Mr. Edgar inclined his head.

"I will do as you wish, my lord," he said; and he left the cell.

If that were possible, the excitement had increased during the luncheon hour, and the crush in and about the court was greater than it had been when the trial commenced.

Olivia, the squire, and Bessie had not left their seats.

Mr. Edgar, when he entered the court, made his way toward them.

"Mr. Vanley, I believe?" he said.

The squire nodded.

"I ask your permission to speak a few words to Mrs. Bradstone," he said.

Olivia rose, inwardly trembling, but outwardly calm.

"I have just seen Lord Clydesfold, madam," he said, "and he has asked me to be the bearer of a message to you."

Olivia's lips moved.

"He has asked me to beg you to leave the court and avoid this, which must be a most painful scene."

"He asked you that?" said Olivia. "He wishes me to go?"

"Yes, madam; he does most earnestly."

"Will you tell him," said Olivia, "that I will do anything he asks me but that? I cannot go."

Mr. Edgar bowed respectfully and went toward his place, an expression of keen, earnest thought on his face.

There was a buzz of the most profound interest and curiosity when, pale and haggard, but still calm, and with a kind of weary indifference, the prisoner was led into the dock.

As the judge took his seat upon the bench, Mr. Edgar rose.

"My lord," he said, "I have had an interview with the prisoner, and upon the result of that interview I have to ask your lordship to adjourn the trial until next sessions."

A murmur of astonishment ran through the court.

The judge looked grave.

"This is a very unusual application, Mr. Edgar, at such a period. I do not know that I should be warranted in adjourning the trial, unless you can assure me that you have evidence directly bearing upon the alleged murder, evidence which has only just come into your possession."

An older man might have made the assertion with brazen confidence, but Mr. Edgar labored under the disadvantage of being a young and honest man.

"As to evidence, my lord," he began, with a slight hesitation.

But Mr. Sewell rose.

"My lord," he said, "it is my duty to oppose the application of my learned friend. If, as your lordship said, he had come into possession of material evidence, I, as representing the Crown, should certainly not oppose his application. But I would point out to your lordship that, as we think, our chain of evidence for the prosecution is complete and unbroken, and I submit that the adjournment would be both unusual and uncalled for."

"I am afraid I must agree with Mr. Sewell," said the judge, gravely. "The trial must proceed; we must go on."

The spectators drew a long breath. It would have been a terrible disappointment to have been robbed of so exciting a drama at the conclusion of only the first act.

Mr. Sewell proceeded to call his witnesses.

The first was Browne, who had found the body, and Faradeane standing beside it. The revolver was produced and handed to the jury.

Mr. Edgar asked: "Do you identify this?"

There was a moment's pause.

"It bears the prisoner's initials," said Mr. Sewell.

Mr. Edgar examined the revolver closely. Then he said:

"Has any one a magnifying glass?"

A buzz went round, and a gentleman—a doctor—handed his pocket glass to him.

He took it and examined the initials closely, long and closely, while every eye was fixed upon him.

"I call your attention, gentlemen of the jury, to the fact," he said, slowly and impressively, "that these initials have been recently made. Now, Browne, I ask you—and be careful how you answer—were those initials upon this revolver when you picked it up?"

Every soul in the court waited for the answer.

"They were, sir," said Browne.

Mr. Edgar drew a penknife from his pocket and handed it with the revolver to the jury.

"I ask you, gentlemen, to compare the engraving upon that pocketknife and the initials scratched upon the revolver. Further than that I cannot go, unless his lordship permits me to go into the dock and swear that the initials on that knife were engraved nine months ago."

Mr. Sewell rose.

"My learned friend cannot be witness and counsel at the same time."

"I am aware of that," said Mr. Edgar, boldly. "I simply place the knife beside the revolver for the jury's inspection."

While this little scene had been enacting, Olivia had leaned forward with parted lips and dilating eyes, her heart throbbing with a faint hope. Then she sank back, her hands tightly clasped in her lap.

Inch by inch, with terrible sequence, Mr. Sewell unfolded his case, and minute by minute the case for the prosecution looked darker and more unanswerable.

Faradeane stood apparently unmoved, his hand resting without a tremor upon the front of the dock, his eyes fixed upon the ground.

At last Mr. Sewell said: "This is our case, my lord."

Mr. Edgar rose, and squaring his shoulders as a man does who is facing a more than ordinarily difficult task, said:

"My lord and gentlemen of the jury: I know that I have no need to ask your indulgence. I know that I need not point out to you how terrible is the responsibility which rests upon my shoulders. With you lies the verdict, but with me lies the awful responsibility of so pleading for the life of the prisoner at the bar that no chance, however slight, shall escape my notice. I am aware that expressions of belief in the innocence or guilt of a client made by a counsel can have but little weight; but, gentlemen, I feel that I must tell you that if there should be any shortcomings in my pleading on this man's behalf, such shortcomings will not arise from any doubt of his innocence.

"I stand here to fight for his life, and if I needed any spur beyond that of a sense of duty, I should find it in the thorough belief which I entertain of his innocence, and that notwithstanding that he has, for reasons of which I am not afraid to state I am ignorant, seen fit in the first instance to plead guilty.

"Gentlemen of the jury, you have heard from the eloquent lips of the counsel for the prosecution the story of my client's life. You have heard how, in a moment of unreasoning passion, he, the bearer of a high and noble name, married an ignorant and low-born gypsy girl.

"Now, mark, gentlemen of the jury, this man who is accused of this crime. He did not—as, alas! too many men of his position have done—take advantage of the lowliness of this girl, use her as a toy, and as a toy tired of, throw her away; but, remembering his noble name and all that belonged to it, he married her.

"Is that consistent with the story, gentlemen, of the prosecution? But let me proceed. Having soon after this marriage discovered the character of the woman he had made his wife; having found to his cost that he had committed a folly which must mar his life, what does he do?

"Most men, as my learned friend truly said, would have rid themselves of what had become an unbearable burden But Lord Clydesfold, the prisoner, does not do this. Rather than drag the honored name of his forefathers in the mud, he elects to leave this woman, to drop the name which he had given her, and, providing for her every want—ay, and luxury—he separates from her, bargaining only that she shall leave him in peace.

"I ask you, gentlemen, is this consistent with the guilt which the prosecution lays to his charge? Under this assumed name my client seeks refuge in this secluded spot. He does not dash into a life of dissipation, he does not seek forgetfulness in a reckless course of living, but he comes here, and for months leads the life of a student and of a gentleman.

"The only notice that is bestowed upon him by his neighbors is that which is attracted by deeds of charity. It is impossible that such a man as my client should live, however much he might desire it, a life of seclusion. And though he shrank from making friends, friendships are, so to speak, thrust upon him. He is the honored guest of the highest and the best known of the inhabitants.

"I think I shall not go too far when I say that I shall call witnesses who will speak of this man, not only with respect most deep and profound, but with affection. And this man you are asked to sentence to death for a crime of the most vulgar and sordid description.

"What is the story? That this unfortunate woman came to Lord Clydesfold's cottage on the night before her death, and demanded to see him. I shall not attempt to disprove the evidence of the servant or of Alford, who heard the deceased declare that her husband wished her death.

"But, gentlemen, I call upon you to draw a distinction between such words used by her, and such words used by him. All through this interview his manner to her was one of patient forbearance, while hers was one of furious taunting. Had Lord Clydesfold intended murdering her he would have committed the crime that night, and not have waited until she had time to go back to the village and spread the story of her marriage."

There was a buzz of excitement. Olivia's hands clasped each other more tightly.

"He goes to meet her in the Hawkwood Spinney at four o'clock the following day. He knows that on that day the marriage of a well-known and well-beloved young lady takes place at Hawkwood itself; that there will be an excitement attending such a marriage; that the whole of the village will be congregated in those very grounds; that persons will be roaming all over the place.

"And yet the prosecution ask you to believe that this man, who throughout has shown so much patient resignation, a man possessed of no ordinary intelligence—that this man, my client, whose demeanor you have an opportunity of witnessing at this moment——"

Here he raised his hand and pointed with a really splendid gesture to Faradeane's calm and dignified face.

"That this man was mad enough, fool enough, to go and meet this woman with the intention of murdering her, surrounded by a crowd, and murdering her not in a silent manner, but by shooting her. Do you think any man in his senses would have conceived so wildly and ridiculously foolish a plan?

"Gentlemen, I have not to establish the innocence of the prisoner at the bar. It is sufficient for him if I convince you that his guilt is not certain. If I can show you that there is a doubt—a doubt of the faintest or slightest shadow—his lordship will tell you that I have the right to demand a verdict of 'not guilty,' and I say that such a doubt cannot but exist.

"It is not incumbent upon me to show how this woman met with her death. She may in a moment of passion and disappointment have committed suicide. She may have attempted to take the life of the husband who had put her from him, and, in the struggle which took place, the weapon may have been pointed toward her, and she may thus have received her death.

"These hypotheses are for your consideration. No one saw that woman die. No man can come forward and say that Lord Clydesfold's hand committed the deed. Therefore, no one on my behalf can come forward to say that she did not meet with her death in either of the ways I suggested. Gentlemen, there is a doubt, and that doubt, I venture to assert, will grow into certainty when you have heard the testimony of this man's character, which I shall now produce."

CHAPTER XXXV
OLIVIA'S TESTIMONY

It was an extraordinary trial, and the interest and excitement increased as it progressed. Of course, the judge and all the lawyers saw plainly that Mr. Edgar knew nothing of the true facts, and that he was fighting in the dark. And Olivia knew also—felt, rather than knew—that Faradeane had refused to tell the story of the murder to the counsel, as he had refused to tell it to every one else.

Mr. Edgar looked round.

"I call Lord Granville," he said; and Bertie, who had been standing as near the box as he could possibly get, stepped again into the witness-box.

"Now, my lord," said Mr. Edgar, boldly, "please tell us all you know of Lord Clydesfold. I ask you to reserve nothing. I have no fear of the truth."

Then Lord Bertie, with an earnestness which went to the hearts of all who heard him, spoke of his long knowledge of Faradeane; how they had been at Eton together—he the younger and the weaker, Faradeane (or Lord Clydesfold) the stronger and the protector; how, all through their lives, Faradeane had proved himself the truest of friends and the most upright, honorable, and lofty-minded of men. "Such a man as my friend Lord Clydesfold is simply incapable of murder!" he wound up, and there was a buzz of applause.

"You knew nothing of this secret marriage with the gypsy?" asked Edgar.

"Nothing," replied Lord Bertie.

"Have you ever seen this revolver in Lord Clydesfold's possession?"

Bertie took it in his hand.

"Never. I do not believe it to be his. I feel sure that it is not his. It is quite unlike him to carry, or even possess a revolver. Why, you know, Cly," he said, turning quickly and reproachfully to the prisoner, "you know you have always ridiculed the practice of carrying a revolver——"

"Silence!" cried the usher. "Do not address the prisoner."

Bertie crimsoned, and a faint, sad smile passed over Faradeane's face, as if he should say:

"It is all of no use, Bertie; give it up."

Olivia clutched her father's arm.

"You hear! The revolver is not his."

The squire shook his head silently.

"Look at the revolver again. You see those initials? Is it usual for Lord Clydesfold to cut his initials—the initials of his assumed name—on articles belonging to him?"

"No. I never knew him to do such a thing before."

"Do you consider that those initials have been recently cut, Lord Granville?"

"Really, my lord," said Mr. Sewell, "this is not evidence."

"I shall not interfere," said the judge, almost grimly.

"They are recently cut," said Bertie. "It never belonged to Lord Clydesfold. He wouldn't have bought a revolver of this description; a trumpery, a silver-plated thing!" and he put it from him with a gesture of contempt which made the crowd exchange glances.

"You left England suddenly, Lord Granville," said Mr. Edgar; "you saw your friend Lord Clydesfold before you left?"

"I did; a few hours before. I have cause to remember it."

Mr. Edgar pricked up his ears.

"May I ask you what you mean?" he said. "Will you tell us why you left England?"

Bertie glanced for one half-second toward the pale, lovely face which to him was like a star in the eager, crowded court.

"Must I answer that?" he said.

"You must."

"I—I left in consequence of a great disappointment," said poor Bertie, his face downcast.

"A love disappointment?" asked Mr. Edgar, who would have spared no one in his endeavor to save the client who would not stretch out a finger to save himself. "Did Lord Clydesfold know of this?"

"He did," said Bertie in a low voice. "He had been, as he has always been, the truest, stanchest friend through—this trouble. It was he who advised me to go abroad, who gave me the sympathy and counsel of a brother. I owe it to him that I did not give way and go to the bad——"

He stopped and raised his eyes—they were moist—to the spot where Olivia sat.

Mr. Edgar saw the glance, and his own eyes grew keen.

"I am sorry to have to ask you the question, but I must do it. Was the lady with whom you were in love, Miss Vanley?"

Bertie flushed, then he raised his head, and said in a low, grave voice:

"It was Miss Vanley."

"Now Mrs. Bradstone?" said Mr. Edgar.

Olivia covered her face with her hands, feeling that every eye was fixed upon her. Then she withdrew her hands and looked full at Bertie with an expression of sisterly love and pity.

"And Lord Clydesfold knew of your devotion? Now, Lord Granville, I am going to ask you a question which may give you and others pain; but I am fighting for my client's, your friend's, life, and I charge you answer it! Have you reason to believe that Lord Clydesfold also loved that young lady?"

Bertie started, and his face went pale, then he said:

"I did not think so, but——"

"Go on."

"I think so now!"

The crowded court swayed to and fro in its intense excitement, and looked from the pale face of the prisoner to Bertie, and then to Olivia as she sat white as a statue, her eyes fixed on vacancy, and yet seeing the dark, sad ones of the prisoner.

Mr. Edgar's brain went to work. He was still in the dark, and yet he began to feel as if a glimmer of light were penetrating the mystery.

"Knowing that he was already married, he would not admit this to you?" he asked.

"No, a thousand times no!" said Bertie. "I have already said my friend is the soul of honor," and he half-turned to the dock.

Mr. Edgar bowed to him.

"Thank you, Lord Granville. I call now Mr. Vanley."

The poor squire went into the box, Bertie taking his hand and pressing it as he passed.

"How pale and worried the poor squire do look!" murmured a man, and an echo of sympathy ran around.

"Tell us what you know of Lord Clydesfold, if you please, sir," said Mr. Edgar, with all a young man's respect for age.

The squire, in a low yet distinct voice, told the story the reader knows so well.

"Do you think him capable of committing a murder?"

"Quite—quite incapable," said the squire, and he was about to leave the box, when Mr. Edgar stopped him with a question.

"This murder was discovered some few hours after the marriage of Miss Vanley to Mr. Bradstone?"

"It was," said the squire, gravely.

"He was a friend of Lord Clydesfold's. I will call him next. He is in court, I suppose?" and he looked around.

"He is not in court. He is abroad," said the squire.

Mr. Edgar's eyes glittered.

"Abroad," he said, as if carelessly. "Why has he gone abroad?"

"He was called by business."

"When did he leave, sir?" asked Mr. Edgar.

"Two nights ago," said the squire.

"Really, my lord, I must submit that this appears to me quite irrelevant and calculated to cause unnecessary pain to others," said Mr. Sewell.

"I see no reason to interfere," said the judge again.

"When did you see him last?"

The squire thought a moment before answering.

"When did Mrs. Bradstone see him last?" asked Mr. Edgar again.

The squire paused a second.

"On the wedding day."

Mr. Edgar began to fidget with his brief; his keen eyes veiled by their lids.

"The tidings of the murder were brought into the hall while the wedding party was waiting, and—and my daughter fell in a swoon. She has been ill for some time since—is ill now," and the poor squire's voice quavered.

Mr. Edgar inclined his head.

"Be assured, sir," he said, "that you have my sympathy, and that of all well-intentioned men. But it is my painful duty to ask you more questions. She has not seen Mr. Bradstone since the wedding day?"

"You cannot ask him that; how can he answer it with any certainty?" said Mr. Sewell, as if really his patience at these irregular questions had become exhausted.

"Good," said Mr. Edgar, promptly. "I call Mrs. Bradstone."

A thrill ran through the court; and suddenly Faradeane leaned forward and laid his hand on Mr. Edgar's shoulder.

"No!" he said, sternly.

Mr. Edgar looked up at him with respectful firmness.

"Pardon me, my lord," he said. "Mrs. Bradstone, please!"

Olivia rose trembling, and now, for the moment, her pale face was crimson. Bertie sprang forward and gave her his arm, and she walked into the box. And now, for the first time, the calm demeanor which the prisoner had maintained with apparently no effort, broke down. He was seen to tremble, and his hands clasped and unclasped each other on the edge of the dock.

As she passed, she raised her eyes to his, and looked at him with such a steadfast gaze of pity and trust and devotion, that his own gaze faltered, and, with an almost audible groan for the suffering she was about to endure, he turned his head away.

She grasped the front of the box tightly; Bertie stood close beside her, her father just below her. Mr. Edgar arranged his notes to give her a few moments to prepare herself, then he said:

"Mrs. Bradstone, I deeply regret having to call you, and believe me I will cause you as little pain as possible, and will detain you not one moment longer than I am obliged. You know Lord Clydesfold—that is, Mr. Faradeane?"

"Yes," came from her pale lips.

"He is as close a friend of yours as he is of your father's?"

"Yes."

"Did you know that he was married?"

"No," and a spasm of pain passed over her lovely face.

"You did not, until this morning, here in court?"

"No."

"I ask you—I am sorry to have to do so—has Lord Clydesfold ever expressed his love for you?"

It was an awful moment.

She raised her eyes bravely.

"Yes."

"When?"

"He spoke—in an unguarded moment—a few words; that was all."

"And recalled them instantly, I imagine?"

"He did; ah, yes, he did!" she said.

"Did he know that you were engaged to Mr. Bradstone; did you tell him?"

"I did."

"So that," said Mr. Edgar, with one eye on the jury, "he knew there would be no hope of winning you, even if he were free?"

"No," she answered, faintly.

"And you still continued friends?"

"Yes."

"Such friends that you would have gone to him in any trouble?"

"Ah, yes!" she breathed.

"Then you married Mr. Bradstone, with whom you were in love?" he went on, his keen eyes, made pitiless by his desire to win the unequal battle, fixed searchingly on her.

"I married him, yes," was the almost inaudible reply.

"With whom you were in love?"

"I submit, my lord——" began Mr. Sewell; but the judge held up his hand. With the rest he was hanging upon these questions in breathless silence.

"Answer me, please. Wait! I shall ask you, I must ask you: Did you love, had you given your heart to my client, Lord Clydesfold?"

She covered her face with her hands and seemed as if she were praying for strength; then she let her hands fall, and said in a whisper that, low as it was, reached the farthest corner of the court:

"Yes, I loved him."

Faradeane's face worked, and he sank down in the chair that had been provided for him, and leaned his head upon his hand.

The crowd drew a long breath. Surely there had never been so enjoyable a sensation as this!

Mr. Edgar, still groping for light, went on:

"Again my duty compels me to ask you why, if you loved Lord Clydesfold, and knew nothing of his marriage, did you marry Mr. Bradstone?"

Intense silence.

Her face went white, almost deathlike; then Mr. Edgar pointed to the Testament on which she had sworn.

"The whole truth; you have sworn!" he said.

"Because" — her voice faltered — "because he promised to give me the money to save my father — —"

A cry rose from beneath her, and the squire sprang forward.

"Silence! Silence!" shouted the usher.

The judge leaned forward, the crowd murmured their astonishment.

But the effect upon Faradeane was more marked than upon others.

He sprang to his feet and regarded Olivia with a horrified gaze.

"To save your father — Mr. Vanley? He was in debt? Mr. Bradstone offered to assist him?"

"Yes," came the reply, dropping like an icicle from the pale, set lips. "He gave me the money."

The squire moaned.

"I — I — before God I knew, I guessed nothing of this!" he exclaimed in accents of misery.

"Silence!"

"My father knew nothing," said Olivia, and she reached down, and put out her hand to him over the box.

"Have you that money still?"

Olivia started.

"Yes," she said. "But I shall not have it an hour longer."

As she spoke she glanced at Bessie.

For a moment Bessie looked as if she were trying to understand the glance; then a light broke over her face, and she rose and made her way out of the court.

Olivia watched her until she disappeared, then drew a breath of relief.

"Now tell me," said Mr. Edgar, when the excitement had subsided. "When did you see Mr. Bradstone last?"

"On the day of the wedding," she replied, and she gave the answer coldly. The worst had passed; there could be no keener shame for her to endure than that which she had already borne.

"At what time?"

"Nearly four o'clock."

"You have not seen or exchanged a word with him since?"

"No."

The crowd pressed as close as they could to the witness-box, that they might not lose a word of this never-to-be-forgotten evidence.

"Do you know where he is?" asked Mr. Edgar, still with deep respect.

Olivia shook her head.

"I do not."

Mr. Edgar paused a moment; the faint light which he thought he had descried seemed fading, and leading him nowhere.

"Did you ever hear Mr. Bradstone allude to Bella-Bella, the deceased?" he asked, in the vague hope that the question might lead to something, some new thread or clew to the mystery. For he was more than ever convinced that Faradeane was not guilty, and that if he—Mr. Edgar—could gain time, he could succeed in proving his client's innocence.

"Never," said Olivia.

"Have you received any communication from Mr. Bradstone in reference to this murder?" he asked.

All eyes were fixed upon her, and all saw her wince and shrink.

"You have?" said Mr. Edgar, prompt to mark every change of expression in her eloquent face. "Answer, please. Remember your oath, remember that a man's life—Lord Clydesfold's life—is hanging by a thread."

She cast a piteous glance at Faradeane, who had risen and stood looking at her in a silent agony of sympathy. He had risked his life, would lose it in all probability, to save her husband from the hangman's hands, the convict's shame, and yet she had come to this!

"You have?" said Mr. Edgar. "Tell me, please. I must, unfortunately, press for an answer."

"I have!" she replied, almost voicelessly.

"What was it? Have you the letter here?"

She uttered a piteous little cry, and drew Bartley Bradstone's letter from her pocket.

Mr. Edgar took it calmly, though his heart beat. He read it, and his face fell slightly, master of it though he was.

Mr. Sewell was on his legs in a moment.

"I must see that letter," he said, firmly.

"It is——" began Mr. Edgar, but the solemn voice of the judge broke in:

"You must put in the letter, Mr. Edgar; the prosecution, the jury, all of us must see it, please."

"As your lordship pleases," said Mr. Edgar, resignedly, and he held out the letter.

Mr. Sewell's face cleared.

"My lord," he said, "the letter is evidence, such as it is, on the side of the prosecution," and he read it.

"Where is this Mr. Bradstone?" inquired the judge, sternly.

"One moment!" put in Mr. Edgar. "Do you know if Mr. Bradstone was aware of Lord Clydesfold's affection for you?"

Olivia's face flushed, then grew white again.

"He may have known."

"Had Lord Clydesfold and Mr. Bradstone ever quarreled?"

"Yes," she faltered, clutching the front of the witness-box.

"So that I should not be far wrong if I said that Mr. Bradstone bore Lord Clydesfold a grudge?"

"No," dropped almost inaudibly from her white lips.

Mr. Edgar bowed with deep respect.

"Thank you, madam."

As she left the box Bertie and the squire took her hands.

"You will leave the court now?" whispered Bertie.

She shook her head.

"I cannot! I cannot!" and they took her back to her old seat.

Mr. Sewell rose, and in a few words seemed to scatter Mr. Edgar's defense to the winds. The evidence for the prosecution was complete, unanswerable. If there had ever been any doubt in the minds of the jury on the score of motive, Mr. Edgar had supplied it. Lord Clydesfold was in love with Miss Vanley, and married to this gypsy, and he, driven desperate, had rid himself of his lawful wife. He called upon the jury to find the prisoner guilty.

Then, amid a solemn silence, the judge arranged his notes and summed up.

It was evident to all that he put forward every iota in favor of the prisoner; but the awful evidence of his presence by the body, his connection with the deceased, the revolver, and his blood-stained clothes, the judge was compelled to give; and it was evidence which Mr. Edgar had not been able to overweigh by rebutting testimony.

The crowd grew pale in the intensity of their excitement and suspense, and the jury were rising to leave the box, when a loud noise was heard at the entrance of the court, and a smooth-faced, commonplace-looking man was seen to push his way through the throng, followed by a dark, sinister-looking man, who, as he advanced, looked from right to left in a furtive, half-suspicious, half-frightened way.

"McAndrew!" muttered Mr. Sewell; "where on earth has he been, and what is he doing? We have got a conviction!"

McAndrew—for it was he—went straight for Mr. Sewell, and whispered to him, and an eager dispute followed between them.

"Eh?" then said Mr. Sewell. "Oh, if you like, I don't care!"

Then he looked up to the bench.

"My lord, the only desire of the Crown is that the truth of this matter should be made apparent. I call Seth Lee!"

The judge looked and frowned, and held up his hand.

"You may call him," he said.

CHAPTER XXXVI
A FORGERY

Seth glided into the box, and stood with his eyes fixed upon Mr. McAndrew, as if he looked to him for guidance and protection. McAndrew, close to Mr. Sewell's elbow, whispered his instructions, and that eminent counsel, evidently struggling against an overwhelming astonishment not unmingled with a certain professional indignation, addressing the judge, said:

"My lord, I have received—I am indeed only now receiving—intelligence bearing upon this trial, of the most extraordinary nature. I am sure I shall have the indulgence of your lordship and the jury, and that they will credit me with my sincere desire to obtain the truth. Mr. Edgar, I think this witness should belong to you, but as I am in possession of the information, I will examine him."

Mr. Edgar bowed, scarcely taking his eyes from Seth's cunning face.

"I reserve all my rights, my lord," he said.

"Your name is Seth Lee?"

"It is," said Seth, clearly enough, and as readily, his gaze still fixed on Mr. McAndrew.

"What do you know of this murder?"

"Everything," came the response.

The crowded court was so still that the ticking of the clock in the corridor could be heard distinctly.

"Do you know the prisoner at the bar?"

"I do. He's Lord Clydesfold."

"Did you know the deceased?"

"I did. She was a gypsy, one of my tribe, a Lee."

"When did you see the prisoner—Lord Clydesfold—last?"

"In Harkwood Spinney, the day of the murder."

A rustle in the crowded court as people turned and looked at one another.

"At what time did you see him?"

"A little after four," said Seth. "Say twenty minutes, half-an-hour."

"Who was with him? The deceased?"

"She was."

"Alive?"

"Alive."

"Then you saw her killed? Be careful."

"I'm careful," replied Seth, doggedly. "I saw her killed; yes, shot."

"Now, on your oath; who fired the shot?"

"Bartley Bradstone!" was the grim reply.

No pen can describe the sensation which for the moment seemed to paralyze the court. The judge raised his head, the jury craned forward; a murmur that was almost a cry ran round.

Faradeane drew a deep sigh, and looked toward Olivia. For a second it seemed as if she were about to fall; but she caught her father's arm, and hid her face on his shoulder; then she turned and looked at Faradeane.

"Bartley Bradstone," said Seth. "I see it all. I knew he was to meet her. I watched 'em from under the bracken; I could have touched 'em a'most."

And in rapid but perfectly distinct words he told the story of the crime.

Amazement sat upon every face. Mr. Sewell, himself pale and disturbed, held up his hand as McAndrew whispered in his ear.

"More slowly, please; every word is of importance."

"Do you know the relationship between the deceased and Bartley Bradstone? You know that they were married?"

"They were," said Seth.

"Before or after her marriage with Lord Clydesfold?"

"Before," replied Seth.

Olivia sank into a seat, and hid her face.

"Come away, my poor darling," murmured the squire.

But she made a gesture of refusal.

"Then she was his wife?" asked Mr. Sewell.

"No," said Seth, grimly, "she was neither his nor his lordship's here. She was mine. We was married years ago, quite boy and girl like. She was a reckless one, was Bella. I allus told her that she'd get into trouble with her desperate ways, but she took no heed of anybody. She'd have married twenty times over, to get money. She was my wife, true and fast enough."

Faradeane made a strange and involuntary movement; it was the gesture of a man who had suddenly been relieved from an intolerable, galling burden—a burden weighing down the soul, instead of the body.

"What followed when Lord Clydesfold came up?" inquired Mr. Sewell. He used the word "prisoner" no longer.

Seth told them, and the recital of Faradeane's great sacrifice of self, of honor, of life, for the woman he loved, so thrilled the crowded court that it was in vain the usher shouted "Silence!"

"It was for her, the lady, Miss Olivia, he did it," said Seth. "He'd have hung rather than let her be pointed at as the wife of a murderer."

The judge held up his hand to still the murmur of excitement.

"Silence!" he said. "The court shall be cleared if these demonstrations are repeated. Why did you not appear before, and tell us what you have now told us?" he demanded of Seth, sternly.

Seth hung his head, then looked furtively this way and that.

"I'm a poor man," he whined, "and he said he'd give me a thousand pounds. Curse him!" he snarled, with a sudden change of voice and manner. "A thousand pounds! And he did! Yes! And when I takes it to the bank, they laughs at me. He'd drawed all the money, every penny," and he shook the check in the air.

Mr. Edgar deftly seized it, glanced at it, and handed it to the judge.

"Then when I come outside, vowing as I'll go for him and settle him, this gentleman collared me, and brought me down," and he pointed to McAndrew.

The judge passed the check to the jury without a word. There were some among them who had often seen Bartley Bradstone's writing, and they recognized it instantly.

"When did you see Mr. Bartley Bradstone last?" asked Mr. Edgar, springing to his feet.

"At his own house, the night afore last!" said Seth.

Amazement again.

"At his own house!" said Mr. Edgar. "My lord"—and he turned quickly to the judge—"I ask for a warrant, for the arrest of Bartley Bradstone."

Mr. McAndrew looked up gravely.

"That's been done already," he said.

"Have you any other evidence?" said the judge. "Can you call some one, produce something confirmatory of this man's testimony?"

Before he could reply a commotion arose in the corridor, and, with much shouting and talking and pushing to and fro, a policeman entered, followed closely by Bessie.

He went up to Mr. McAndrew, and said something, amid a dead silence; then Mr. Sewell very gravely and solemnly said:

"I have one piece of evidence more to produce, my lord. It is a letter written by Mr. Bartley Bradstone. It is addressed to Mrs. Olivia Bradstone, and is a distinct and clear confession that he was the murderer of Bella Lee."

"Read it," said the judge.

Mr. Sewell read it slowly and solemnly, then handed it to the judge, who passed it to the jury.

Mr. Sewell then motioned the policeman to the box.

"How did you obtain this letter?" he said.

"One piece of it from the hand of Mr. Bartley Bradstone," he replied, evidently with suppressed emotion; "the other was on the table just beside him, sir, and near the burnt-out candle."

Intense silence.

"Then Mr. Bartley Bradstone—where is he?" asked the judge.

"At his own house, The Maples, sir. When I went with the warrant Mr. McAndrew had brought this morning from London, I met this young woman—Miss Bessie. She'd got a letter from her mistress to give to Mr. Bradstone, or to leave at the house if he was away. And she and me went into the hall together. The servants said Mr. Bradstone was out—had gone to London some days since. Then I told them that I'd information that he'd been back. They all said they hadn't seen him. But they owned that he might be in the library, which they weren't allowed to enter lately. I went to the door and found it locked, my lord, and me and the butler forced it. The room was quite dark, with the blinds down; but when we'd pulled 'em up, we found Mr. Bartley Bradstone lying face downward across the table with the half of the letter clutched in his hands. He was quite dead and stiff. There wasn't no mark nor speck upon him, and the doctor as we fetched says that he died all in a minute of heart disease."

They let him go on with his tragic story uninterruptedly, and, when he had finished, the judge said, solemnly, amid profound silence:

"Gentlemen, this case has been tried by a higher court than this. It still remains for us to humbly put on record man's verdict as made plain by Him who sees all things and weighs all hearts. Do you find the prisoner guilty, or not guilty?"

"Not guilty!" came the quick, sharp response.

A roar burst forth from the hot, parched throats of the excited crowd. Two or three men standing near the dock made a rush for it; in an instant they were followed by a hundred others, and before the police could interfere, Faradeane was torn out of the box and carried through the corridor and into the streets—a free man!

A scene of the wildest confusion followed. Men—ay, and women, too—shouted and danced, as if they had suddenly gone mad. It was in vain for the police to attempt to clear the streets, in which the crowd seemed to grow thicker every moment. Amid the intense excitement, the Grange carriage was seen to be making its way slowly through the throng, and the mob instantly surrounded it, and cheered for the squire and Olivia.

At last they set Faradeane down on the steps of the marketplace, and permitted him to speak.

At first he seemed unable to speak, and stood looking at the crowd with his grave eyes moist with emotion; then he said:

"I thank you—I thank you with all my heart for your kindness. I think that many of you believed in my innocence——"

"All of us! All of us!" some one shouted. "You're a nobleman all round, that's what you are, my lord!"

"What I have done, any man placed as I was would have done—yes, every man worthy the name of man. And now will you go home quietly, my friends, remembering how dark and heavy a trouble hangs over those both you and I—love?"

"That we will; we'll do anything you ask us, my lord," shouted the same man, and the crowd began slowly and reluctantly to melt away.

Colonel Summerford sprang up the steps, and held out his hand.

"Thank God, thank God, my lord!" he said, and his strong voice trembled. "I can never be too grateful that I believed in you all through."

"And I," said Mr. McAndrew, quietly. "I'm afraid your lordship thinks I was rough on you in letting the case go so far. But what was I to do?"

"You did your duty—I am sure," said Lord Clydesfold, holding out his hand.

Mr. McAndrew took it respectfully.

"You see, my lord, I had my doubts from the first. The very first time I saw Bradstone in the squire's library I felt—well, we detectives have our presentiments like other people. But what could I do? I knew you would stand firm and bear the brunt to the last, and I could only wait and hunt up evidence; and it was difficult work. It was all so strong against you; and Bradstone was clever and cunning. If it hadn't been for the gypsy Seth tracking him down and getting the check I should have been driven hard. If it hadn't been for the confession, indeed, I wouldn't have answered for the case even now!"

"And he is dead?" said Lord Clydesfold in a low voice.

Mr. McAndrew nodded gravely.

"Yes; they found him as the constable said. He must have fallen across the table almost the moment Seth left the room with the check. Heart disease. The strain that man must have endured—without food, and drinking continually—must have been a perfect hell. And to think that he committed the murder without any real reason. Ah, she was a wonderful woman, and deceived you both. If Bradstone can know what is going on, and is conscious that she was not his wife after all, and that he might have been living still——" He stopped and shrugged his shoulders. "Well, I could almost pity him. Not that he deserves it, my lord, for he was a bad lot. He fairly trapped that poor young lady; got his net round her father, unbeknown to him, and fairly drove her to marry him. When I tell you all we've discovered you'll be surprised, my lord."

"He is dead now," said Lord Clydesfold, solemnly.

Mr. McAndrew nodded.

"I've a message from Lord Carfield," said Colonel Summerford. "He wishes me to tell you that Lord Bertie has gone home with the squire—poor fellow! and that he—Lord Carfield—doesn't wish to intrude upon you; but that he will feel honored—I repeat his words, Lord Clydesfold—if you will go straight to him and stay with him."

Lord Clydesfold inclined his head, deeply moved.

"Thank him for me, Summerford," he said; "but I will go to my own place. I—I must have time to think. Bertie has gone with the squire?" and he breathed a sigh of satisfaction. "That is like his thoughtfulness!"

"Yes; he said he knew you would rather he went and took care of him and Miss Vanley than come to you. And now, if there is anything I can do, my lord, I shall be only too happy."

Lord Clydesfold thought for a moment or two.

"This unhappy man who lies dead," he said; "we must not forget that she bore his name, though for only a few days, Summerford."

"I understand, my lord," said the colonel, gravely. "Everything shall be done as quietly as possible. Leave it all to me and McAndrew here, who feels that he owes you something for his part—unwilling one as it was—in the terrible trial you have so nobly borne. And now, will you have my carriage?"

But Lord Clydesfold shook his head.

"I think I should like to walk," he said quietly, and, shaking hands with them, he set off, followed by the cheers of the people, who still lingered and watched him with eager but respectful interest.

An hour later Lord Clydesfold was seated in his little dining-room of The Dell. His man had rushed home and prepared a meal, and with affectionate anxiety had insisted upon his master's eating some of it; and Clydesfold sat thinking of the woman he loved, the woman for whose sake he would have given his life, and yet whom he dared not go near, when the door opened and the servant announced:

"Mr. Vanley."

Faradeane sprang to his feet, and took the trembling hands which the squire held out to him; and for a space the two men looked into each other's eyes in silence.

Then the old man found his voice.

"What can I say, my lord?" he faltered. "No words I could find would express a tenth part of all I feel—of my gratitude, my unspeakable gratitude to you! I have never read of a nobler act than yours. You would have given your life to shield my child's name from even the reflection of shame!"

"Yes," said the other in a low, grave voice, as he led the old man to a chair, "and would do it again to-morrow. Tell me how she is, sir. All concealment between us is destroyed forever. You know how it is with me, how it has been ever since we first met. I have loved her, sir— —"

He stopped.

"Dearer than your own life," said the squire, solemnly. "I do not know how she is. I expected to carry her home more dead than alive; but she has not broken down or given way. Bessie, who has been like a sister and as good as gold, says that my girl will not give way; that—that—I can scarcely speak of him"—and he shuddered—"that the sense of freedom, absolute freedom from that man, will sustain Olivia even through so terrible an ordeal as that through which she has passed; the sense of freedom and—and"—he pressed Clydesfold's hand—"the knowledge that you are safe."

Clydesfold turned his head to hide the expression of joy which lit up his face.

"I have come to you not only to try and thank you, but to ask you what I am to do. When Bessie left the court at an intimation—a mere word and look—from Olivia, the girl went to the Grange and got a letter of Bradstone's which he had given to Olivia on her wedding day." He shuddered again. "This letter contained the voucher for a large sum of money he had given her, the price"—he went on bitterly—"of her hand; the money to save me from the ruin which hung over me, and which will now crush me. I care nothing for that. But I do care most earnestly and deeply that you should know I was ignorant of this—this barter."

"I need no such assurance, sir," said Lord Clydesfold, laying his hand on the old man's shoulder tenderly.

"Thank you, thank you!" faltered the squire. "Will you take it and restore it? You see, I still come to you in my trouble."

"Will you always do so? Let me see it."

He opened the paper, and looked at it; then went to his desk and compared it with some letters and papers.

"It is a large sum. There may be near relations to inherit the unhappy wretch's ill-got gold— —"

"No man will be the richer for this," said Clydesfold, solemnly. "It is useless. It is—a forgery."

The squire started and looked at him with horror.

"A forgery!" repeated Lord Clydesfold. "I know the manager's writing quite well. See—there are his signatures to these papers. Compare them with this one on the voucher. It is a forgery." He took it from the squire's trembling hand and tore it in pieces, which he threw on the fire. "Do not tell her this," he said, after a moment's reflection. "It is better that she should not know it. From this moment do not permit her to mention his name in anything connected with her"—he paused; he was going to say "marriage"—"with anything connected with him. Let the past die out—as it will, please God!" He pointed to the ashes of the paper as they fluttered on the hearth. "Let that be the last remembrance of Bartley Bradstone!"

CHAPTER XXXVII
CONCLUSION

He could not approach her. Though he longed to see her, to hear her voice, to touch her hand, ah! and to hold her in his arms as he had done for that one short moment in the woods, he felt that for the present it would be well for him to keep away from her.

She was bearing up wonderfully. He would waylay Bessie perhaps once a day, and get her to talk to him of her; and never was Bessie reluctant to talk of her beloved mistress, and Bessie told him how remarkably Olivia had escaped the dreaded return of her illness.

"If anything had happened, my lord," Bessie would say, and then Lord Clydesfold would silence her. He would not permit any one to speak of the past.

While the world was still talking and marveling over the romantic "Hawkwood Murder," and wondering why, now that he was free from the woman who had held him in thrall and free from the shadow of death, Lord Clydesfold did not return to the society which his rank and wealth would have so well adorned, the blow which he had been expecting fell upon the squire.

A distant cousin of Bartley Bradstone's rose up from the mists of obscurity and claimed what remained of his property; and, on examining his affairs, the mortgages on the Grange estate and the squire's bonds were discovered.

Then was the cousin jubilant; and, losing no time, swooped down like a bird of prey.

The squire was prepared. It is a question whether, in the joy of having his darling restored to him, he felt any very great sorrow.

"We must go, dear," he said to Olivia, from whom he now concealed nothing, and would never again conceal anything. "You will be brave, dear? It is a cruel business for you; but— —"

Olivia put her arms round his neck, and drew his troubled, careworn face to hers.

"Dear, if you knew how wickedly glad I feel!" she said. "Let them take everything so that they leave you and me—and auntie—in peace. Shall we take a cottage in Wales, or go abroad; one can live so cheaply abroad, can't one?"

"I—I don't quite know yet," said the squire, doubtfully. "I must ask Clydesfold."

Olivia's head dropped, and a faint color flew into her cheeks.

"Do you ask Lord Clydesfold's advice as to how many pieces of toast you should eat for breakfast, dear?" she whispered, with a little pout.

The old man rubbed his chin, and laughed absently.

"Well, I think I do, almost. I'll just go down to The Dell; I wish he'd come up here. But—but, I suppose——" and he looked at her.

"Yes, you suppose rightly," she said, hiding her face on his shoulder again. "Do you want me to die of shame, as I should do the moment I saw him?"

"No, I don't want you to die of anything," he said, tenderly stroking her hand.

"Why doesn't he go back to London, to his old friends, the lords and ladies, who used to be so fond of him?"

"I don't know. I told him that it was his duty to do so; and he remarked that he was rather tired of doing his duty."

A smile crept over Olivia's face, and her eyes grew dreamy.

"That is like one of his old speeches," she murmured. "And he looks better, and more as he used to do."

"Why, when did you see him?" asked the squire, with some surprise.

Olivia flushed crimson, and she covered her face with her hands as she whispered, "I—I saw him, with the fieldglass, from one of the windows!"

The squire could not suppress a smile, as he put her from him.

"And I always thought you were proud," he said.

"I'm—I'm the meanest creature in existence," she said, piteously, as she ran out of the room.

The squire walked down to The Dell, gravely thoughtful, but serene and resigned.

He found Clydesfold walking to and fro in the little front garden, smoking his pipe.

"It has come, Clydesfold," he said, putting the letter in his hand.

Clydesfold read it, then nodded.

"What will you do?" he asked. "What does she say?"

There was never any occasion for him to say Olivia; there was only one "she" in the world for him.

"She bears it wonderfully; one would almost think she welcomes it. She suggests a cottage in Wales or an exile on the Continent. I told her I should come to you."

Clydesfold nodded again.

"Better take her on the Continent," he said. "The change will work a miracle in her. This trouble of yours will lead her to forget her own, and all that has passed. Yes, take her to Paris," he concluded.

"Very well," assented the squire, as if he was a father taking a wise son's advice. "And what are you going to do? You will not live in this place any longer, Clydesfold?"

"No, not much longer. I shall leave it when you are gone."

"That is right," said the squire. "I am glad; but for your sake, and not for my own," and he sighed. "It will be hard to think of the old place having gone forever, and still harder to think of your having left it too. A double loss, Clydesfold. Where will you live? You have two or three places in England, have you not?"

"Yes; but I am going to live at Hawkwood Grange," he said, quietly.

The squire started and stared at him.

"At—at—the Grange?" he faltered.

Clydesfold nodded, and drew the old man's arm within his. "Yes; I have already written instructions to my solicitor to secure the place. And" — he added, slowly and distinctly, for the squire had begun to wince and draw his arm away as if he feared Clydesfold was going to offer to give it back to him — "and I am not going to part with it. I always liked it. I have learned to love and covet it. You don't mind my buying it, do you, sir? I shall treat it reverently, be sure."

"No, no, no!" said the squire, the tears starting to his eyes. "I would rather you had the old place than any man in the world. If you had been my son— —" He stopped. "We shan't keep you waiting long, Clydesfold," he said.

"Don't, please," said Lord Clydesfold, quite calmly. "The sooner you go the better I shall be pleased, for, you see, I want to do it up, and—and take her away at once, sir!" he broke off, rather inconsequently. "Come inside and let us talk over your plans. I wish"—the color rose to his face—"I wish I were going with you."

The squire returned to the Grange in about an hour.

"My dear, could you guess who has bought the old place?" he said.

"Yes; Lord Clydesfold," she replied, with her eyes flashing. "And—and—oh, papa, papa," and she burst into tears, "you would not take it from him?"

The squire soothed her.

"My dear, he hasn't offered it to me," he retorted, rather dryly. "He intends living here himself."

She stared and wiped her eyes.

"And when can we go?" she demanded, restlessly.

"Very soon," he said. "But not too soon for the new owner, it seems."

"Oh!"

"Yes, he wants us gone at once. Wants to do it up."

"Oh!"

"Yes; and we'll go to Paris, I think, dear."

"So he has sent us to Paris, has he?" she said. "One would think we were his bond slaves."

"We are—in gratitude," he said, gently.

She melted in a moment.

"I'll go and tell Bessie," she said, meekly.

In two days they started. All the preparations, those pertaining to business, had been made by Lord Clydesfold. He also saw to every little detail of their journey; engaged a special Pullman, took their Channel tickets, ordered rooms at one of the inexpensive hotels in Paris—but did not go near her.

The squire had bid him a good-by which was as affectionate as that of a father to his best-beloved son, and, as Clydesfold held the old man's hands, the squire said:

"I'm to say good-by to Olivia for you?"

"No," he said; "she will take my heart, my every thought with her; she has no need of a good-by. I have no message for her. I want her to forget; and the sight of me, a word from me, would cause her to remember."

"I understand. God bless you, my boy!" murmured the old man.

In a few days it was publicly known that the squire had been "sold up," and that Lord Clydesfold had bought house and lands, horses and cattle, every stick and stone.

Two days afterward, twenty or thirty men, carrying pickaxes and spades, were seen to tramp up the avenue, and, to the amazement of all, they were seen to set to work cutting a new road. But everybody understood Lord Clydesfold's intentions when it was observed that the new road diverged as far as possible from the old one, and his object was made still clearer when an army of men fell to work with Portland cement, and altered The Maples from red to white. And when they had finished, the villagers were startled by seeing, in neatly carved letters, "Hospital for Convalescent Children" along its front.

The Grange, too, was redecorated, and, though not altered in character, still very much brightened and lightened.

All this took time, and Lord Clydesfold never left the place for a day, but superintended the whole with as much—probably more—energy than if he had been a clerk of the works.

He and Bertie were constantly together, and Clydesfold almost lived at the Carfields'.

At last he had accomplished all he had planned, and one day he remarked quite casually at breakfast:

_"I think of running over to Paris to-morrow."

Bertie and Lord Carfield exchanged glances.

"Very well," said the latter. "Early train?"

"Thanks, yes; pass the marmalade, Bertie."

That was all; but as he got into the dogcart on the morrow, Bertie held his hand and pressed it.

"Good luck, dear old boy," he whispered; and Lord Clydesfold returned the pressure without a word.

He had received news of her almost daily, sometimes from the squire, sometimes from Bessie, and not seldom from the Paris society papers.

For, though they had striven to live in as much seclusion as is possible in the gay city, friends had hunted them up and had insisted upon Olivia going out a little. She withstood all entreaties for some time, but yielded at last; and the Parisians, who are always ready to acknowledge and welcome beauty and grace—even English, which are supposed to be non-existent!—made what Aunt Amelia called "a fuss" over her.

Before ten months had passed Olivia had received as many offers. One from a well-known nobleman, of so high a rank that he must be nameless in these pages, threw good Aunt Amelia into a flutter of excitement, which was turned into the agony of despair by Olivia's refusal.

"My dear," she exclaimed, with tearful indignation, "do you want to marry an emperor? Is that what you are waiting for?"

"I don't want to marry any one," returned Olivia; "and I am not waiting for any one."

"Well, I'm glad of it!" exclaimed Aunt Amelia, driven snappish by her disappointment. "Because if you are waiting for—for——"

"Well?" demanded Olivia, her eyes beginning to flash and her little foot to beat the carpet; by which sign the intelligent reader will understand how perfectly restored she was.

"Well, my dear, don't look as if you meant to eat me. All I meant to say was that he doesn't seem as if he were coming, or as if—if he meant to come."

"I—I don't know what you mean!" exclaimed Olivia.

Then she burst into tears, which seemed to indicate that after all she had some inkling whom Aunt Amelia intended by "he."

She dried her tears very quickly, and went to dress for a ball; quite "a quiet affair," with only about two hundred guests.

She had never looked more lovely than she looked that night, and had never shone more brilliantly. The romantic story, the more than rumored proposal of the prince, attracted all attention to her; and everybody of note—and there were some famous personages there—begged for an introduction to the beautiful, young English girl.

Suddenly she grew tired, and sent her rejected suitor—who could not tear himself away from her, notwithstanding his rejection—for her father.

"Take me home, papa," she said in a low voice.

"Yes, yes; certainly, my dear," he said; and he took her upon his arm down the great staircase.